By Aimee Friedman

Two Summers
Sea Change
The Year My Sister Got Lucky
South Beach
French Kiss
Hollywood Hills
Breaking Up: A Fashion High Graphic Novel
A Novel Idea

Short stories in:
21 Proms
Starry-Eyed: 16 Stories That Steal the Spotlight
Mistletoe: Four Holiday Stories

TWO SUMMERS

WITHDRAWN

AIMEE FRIEDMAN

Point

Library of Congress Cataloging-in-Publication Data available

ISBN 978-0-545-51807-9

10 9 8 7 6 5 4 3 2 1   16 17 18 19 20

Printed in the U.S.A.   23
First edition, May 2016
Book design by Ellen Duda

For my family—the best in any universe

In infinite space, even the most unlikely events must take place somewhere. . . . People with the same appearance, name and memories as you, who play out every possible permutation of your life choices.

Max Tegmark

I dwell in Possibility—

Emily Dickinson

Prologue

Monday, July 3, 7:37 p.m.

One, one thousand. Two, one thousand . . .

I stare down at the clock on my phone, silently counting the seconds until 7:37 p.m. becomes 7:38 p.m. My heartbeat seems to tick in equal rhythm.

Ten, one thousand. Eleven, one thousand . . .

"Summer, stop it," orders my best friend, Ruby Singh. I look over at her. Even though her dark-brown eyes are on the road, she can guess what I'm doing. "Obsessing over the time won't get us there any faster," she tells me.

"I know that," I protest, my cheeks hot. I shift in the passenger seat and transfer my phone from one clammy palm to the other.

Twenty-two, one thousand. Twenty-three, one thousand . . .

The thing is, I wish I could control time: slow it down, speed it up, bend it to my will. To me, minutes and hours are slippery, fickle things. For most of sophomore year (which ended just last week), I showed up to school late and breathless. But on those rare occasions I was invited to some Saturday-night party, I arrived dorkily early. I can't win.

On this sticky gray summer evening, I am losing the battle again. I chance another glance up from my phone—*thirty-five, one thousand; thirty-six, one thousand*—at the highway ahead, still clogged with traffic. Red taillights glow like fireflies.

"I'm going to miss my flight," I mutter, dread rising in my stomach.

I have no one to blame but myself. I was the one who repacked my suitcase twice, waffling over every item of clothing. And I was the one who got into a huge fight with my mother right before we left the house, which was why I had to call Ruby in tears and ask her to drive me to the airport . . .

"You won't," Ruby tells me firmly, changing lanes. Her stacks of woven bracelets slide up and down her wrists as she spins the steering wheel. "Not if I have anything to do with it. And seriously, put your phone away. Isn't your battery about to die?"

"It is," I concede with a sigh. I fiddle with my own woven bracelets—I always wear the two that Ruby made for me—and peek back down at my phone.

Fifty-eight, one thousand; fifty-nine, one thousand—

Before I can watch the minute switch over, I drop my phone into the bulging Whitney Museum tote bag at my feet. I shouldn't have even brought my cell along; I won't get service overseas. But I'm already missing it like a phantom limb. I wonder if Mom will text me to apologize—or is she waiting for me to text first?—and then I push the thought away.

The car lurches forward a fraction. I sneak a sad peek at Ruby's broken dashboard clock, which blinks an eternal, useless

12:00. To distract myself, I lean over and riffle through the rest of my tote bag, making sure I have all my essentials:

Chewing gum and magazines for the plane. The thick, shiny guidebook. A printout of the email from Dad with his address and phone numbers listed on it. My fancy new camera. My passport.

I pull out the navy-blue booklet, feeling a pang of excitement as I flip through its fresh, unstamped pages; I've never left the country before. When I reach the photo of myself, I frown. My dirty-blond hair falls in messy waves, my smile is crooked, and one gray-blue eye is *just* slightly larger than the other. At age seven, I saw my first Picasso painting—a woman with upside-down features—and I'd felt a sort of kinship. Ruby told me I was crazy when I'd shared that notion with her.

"Crazy!" Ruby says now, in mock disbelief. "I was actually right *again*?"

Blinking, I look up to see that we are moving swiftly. The exit sign out the window promises AIRPORT. Warm relief courses through me, and I squeal. I hardly ever squeal, but this occasion calls for it.

"You are never not right," I tell Ruby. My best friend shoots me a grin. As she heads onto the off-ramp, thunder booms overhead. We both jump a little.

A storm shouldn't be a surprise; all day, the air's been thick and humid—mosquito weather. I love summer, and not just because I was named for it. I love the feel of fresh-cut grass tickling my bare soles. Light cotton dresses. Freezer-burned Popsicles.

The smoky scent of barbecue as darkness falls. There's this magical sense of possibility that stretches like a bridge between June and August. A sense that anything can happen.

So far, this summer has promised even more magic—even more *possible*—than usual. But now, as swollen clouds amass above us, I feel a tremor of apprehension.

"What if it's a bad omen?" I ask Ruby, nervously twisting my hair up into a sloppy topknot.

The first runways come into view, and Ruby presses her platform sandal against the gas pedal. "You and your omens," she scoffs.

Another crackle of thunder makes me shudder. I know it's silly, my belief in signs and harbingers. But superstition can be helpful for indecisive people; it lets us off the hook. Takes the choice out of our hands.

Ruby pulls up to the bustling Delta terminal, and I don't feel the burst of anticipation I was expecting. I unbuckle my seat belt with uncertain fingers. Raindrops begin to hit the windshield.

"What if . . ." I start, my throat suddenly dry, my mind suddenly full of doubts.

"Those are your two favorite words," Ruby teases, lifting her now-watery iced latte from the cup holder. When I'd called her earlier, she'd been in the middle of her shift at the coffee shop. She'd had to invent some excuse for the manager so she could leave, but first she'd whipped up drinks for both of us. I'd sucked down my iced mocha between sniffles as we'd driven away from my house.

"What if," I continue, my stomach clenching, "the stuff my mom said is true?" I think back to how my mother and I faced off in the kitchen—the sharpness of Mom's words, her forehead etched with anger and worry. I squirm in my seat, listening to the roar of airplanes ascending and descending nearby. "Maybe this is a mistake . . ."

"Okay. No." Ruby shakes her head, her silky black hair swiping her tan shoulders. "This isn't a mistake. It's your *destiny*." Ruby widens her heavily lined eyes, giving me a look of such urgency that it almost feels like she's pushing me out of the car. "Don't think about your mom. You're going to have the best summer ever, Summer Everett." She giggles at this wordplay, and I can't help but smile, too, feeling myself relax. "You will find a gorgeous French boyfriend," she continues, arching her brows, "and Hugh Tyson will be a distant memory."

I laugh, a blush warming my neck. Leave it to Ruby to bring up my longtime, hopeless crush now. I think of Hugh—his gray-green eyes and light-brown skin. His probably-will-be-valedictorian level of brilliance. His unawareness of my existence.

"Being in a different country won't suddenly make me visible to the male population," I point out.

Ruby sighs. My best friend, with her abundant confidence and curvy figure, doesn't know the meaning of the word *unrequited*. She's already had three semi-boyfriends (it should be noted: three more than I've ever had), and she told me last week that she intends to "fall in love for real" this summer. I know better than to set such unrealistic goals for myself.

Still, I feel a tentative twinge of hope. It's enough to dissolve my Mom worries for the moment. I stuff my passport back into my tote and sling the bag over my shoulder.

"But thank you," I tell Ruby, meaning it fiercely. I lean over the gearshift and grab her in a big hug, choked up by the familiar smell of her flowery perfume. "Love you times two."

"Love you times two," Ruby echoes. We invented that phrase back in first grade, where we first met. I have a couple other good friends, but Ruby's the closest thing I've got to a sister. Suddenly, the thought of embarking on this adventure without her seems daunting. How can I survive on my own?

"Go," Ruby says, disentangling from me. She nods toward the terminal. "Text me when you—oh, you won't be able to from there."

"I'll call," I promise. "And email. And check Instagram. An unhealthy amount."

I hear Ruby laugh as I open the car door and step out into the curbside fray. Cars and taxis idle, their doors hanging open like mouths while people maneuver luggage and shout good-byes. Cold rain batters my legs and toes, and I regret having worn just shorts and flip-flops with my T-shirt and hoodie. I zip up the hoodie, race around to the trunk, and retrieve my suitcase, dragging it behind me to the terminal's sliding doors.

Then I pause, glancing back. I have the urge to reach for my camera and take a picture of Ruby's car in the rain. My last view before leaving. But then Ruby drives off, windshield wipers clacking. And even without a clock in front of me, I realize that time is hurtling forward. So I take a big breath, and enter the neon-bright airport.

Go, Ruby had said. My adrenaline surges and I navigate around crowds of travelers, the buzz of foreign languages filling the air. I manage to collect my boarding pass and check my suitcase, and I feel flushed and proud, surprised by my own competence. I've only flown alone once before, down to Florida to visit my grandparents one weekend. Every other trip has been with Mom.

Mom. My throat tightens and I trip over someone's luggage wheels.

Ruby told me not to think about Mom. But as I sprint toward security, Mom is all I can think about. I picture her back in our quiet house, adjusting her tortoiseshell glasses, watching the rain. Does she wish I weren't flying in such bad weather? Does she wish I hadn't left on such bad terms? Or that I hadn't left at all?

I recall how I'd bounded into the kitchen, bags in tow, running late and beaming. Ready. Mom had been leaning against the counter, her eyes down and her face pale. She didn't even have her shoes on. My belly dropped. I knew Mom didn't love the idea of this trip—she'd been acting weird about it ever since Dad had invited me. So I should have pretended not to notice this latest weirdness. I should have continued on out the door to our car. But it was like poking a wound; I asked her what was wrong.

"I'm . . ." She coughed. "Well, to tell the truth, Summer, I'm not sure you should go." I could feel the blood in my veins turn cold. "I'm not sure you're fully—prepared." Another cough. "I'm worried you'll be . . . let down. You know how *he* is."

My insides switched from icy to boiling hot. *He* was my dad: Mom's mortal enemy. Her annoyance at him annoyed me. Yes, they had divorced when I was eleven—a clean split, like a butcher cleaving meat. Dad had gone off to Europe while Mom and I stayed in our humdrum hometown of Hudsonville, New York. And yes, Dad had been a ghostlike presence since then, only sending the occasional email or making the rare Skype call. Once, he'd returned to Hudsonville to take me out for a quick, breezy lunch ("How's school? You're so big. I've got to run, sweetheart.") before flitting off again.

But I don't hold my father's flakiness against him; he's an artist after all. A famous artist. Not famous enough that he'd be recognized by the TSA agent currently waving me through the metal detector. But famous enough that his big, bright, beautiful paintings hang in museums and galleries. And famous enough to sometimes get mentioned in articles. I remember the pride I'd felt last year seeing his name, Ned Everett, in the *New York Times* Arts section, next to a photograph of him, handsome in his paint-spattered clothes.

Actually, the painting that made Dad artist-famous was a portrait he did of me when I was eleven: a fair-haired, big-eyed little girl standing in a field of poppies that he dreamed up. I've never seen that painting in person; it's displayed in a gallery in the South of France.

Which, as it happens, is where I'm headed this summer.

Excitement makes my heart cartwheel as I hurry away from security. *I am going to France!* Going not just to see "my painting," as I like to think of it, but to finally see and spend some real time with Dad. Jogging toward my gate, my tote bag bumping my hip, I remember the life-changing email he'd sent me back in April.

Sweetheart, it read, *I cannot believe you are turning sixteen this summer (where does the time go?). Come celebrate with me! As you know, I live most of the year in Paris, but I summer down in the South of France, in a beautiful region the French call* Provence. *I have a big vacation home on a cobblestone street, with artist friends always spilling in and out. You and I can eat croissants and catch up in the sunshine. What do you say?*

I'd stared at the screen, giddy and incredulous. But for once in my life, I hadn't felt hesitant. There'd been no second-guessing. I'd looked around my bedroom, at the stifling sameness of the posters and books, and out the window at the row of identical, squat ranch houses across the street. I could escape. I could experience summer—*my* season—in a place of cobblestones and croissants. My certainty dizzied me.

Mom, naturally, had been harder to convince. She'd flat-out said no at first, looking almost frightened by the prospect (I'd promptly burst into tears—I'm not a big crier, except, apparently, when it comes to this trip). Then came muffled phone calls between my parents—the first time, to my knowledge, they'd spoken in years—and I'd overheard Mom saying that I wasn't ready, which stung me. Other kids in school had already done teen tours across Europe and South America. Ruby had been to India with her family twice. Sure, I was shy, and sheltered by my placid suburban existence. But Mom couldn't keep me in a bubble forever, could she?

After a week of more whispered phone calls, and much nail biting on my part, Mom agreed to let me go—but only because Dad had agreed that I could work as his quasi-assistant. "If you don't have some sort of job there," Mom had explained, her tone ominous, "you'll be loafing around with too much time on your hands."

It was true that I'd worked every summer since I was thirteen, bandaging knees at the YMCA day camp, serving popcorn at the mall multiplex, and, last year, shelving paperbacks at the local bookstore, Between the Lines. Now I'd be organizing the sketches in Dad's studio and ordering new paintbrushes for him online. Which all sounded doable to me. As long as I wouldn't have to be artistic myself: I can't so much as draw a stick figure.

I reach my gate, sweaty and winded. My flight—Delta 022 nonstop to Marseille Provence Airport—is boarding all rows. Catching my breath, I glance out the long windows that face the runway. There is the plane, white and sleek and dotted with raindrops. Relief and exhilaration fizz up in me. *I made it!*

I join the snaking line, standing behind a mother and her little girl, who are conversing in French. I take Spanish in school (Mom's idea), but since April, I've been Googling French vocabulary online. The mother is saying something about the rain—*la pluie*—and the daughter is giggling. I swallow hard.

I'm an only child, so my mom and I are close in that way two-somes tend to be. Many evenings, we'll curl up on the couch with Netflix or sit out on our porch with a pint of ice cream, studying the stars. Mom likes to tell me about the theories she's teaching her philosophy students at Hudsonville College. Once, she told me that some philosophers and scientists believe that there *has* to be other life on other planets—there are so many galaxies that it seems inevitable. I'd had the thought that maybe, since there were no boys who liked me here on Earth, there was still hope that one from another galaxy, someday, would. Basically I was wishing for an alien boyfriend. Awesome.

My favorite of Mom's theories, though, is the one about parallel universes—the idea that somewhere out there, in space or time, endless versions of *ourselves* exist. And each version lives out every possible outcome of our different decisions. Kind of like a cosmic Choose Your Own Adventure. That idea haunts me: sends shivers down my spine and makes the night sky seem vaster.

This summer, I realize, Mom will be alone on the porch with just her theories and our grouchy cat, Ro, for company. True, my aunt—Mom's twin sister—might stop by to visit, but she's usually going off to some concert or play at night. So maybe Mom's reluctance about my trip had less to do with Dad or me, and more to do with the prospect of those lonely evenings.

Regret beats inside me like a second heart. As I step forward in the line, I rummage inside my tote bag for my cell phone. I'm still upset with Mom, but I should text or call her before I get on the plane. The memory of our last exchange, back in the kitchen, makes me cringe.

"You don't want me to be happy!" I'd shouted. "I *am* ready! I'm almost sixteen!" I may have stamped a childish foot. "Why do you even hate Dad so much? He's paying for me to go there. Can't you cut him some slack?" Hot tears had filled my eyes.

Mom hadn't comforted me. Her lips white, she'd snapped, "I know that your father has swooped in with this amazing opportunity. But you should be aware—" She'd coughed again. "It might not be what you're expecting. Not everything is as it seems."

Her vagueness had further frustrated me, like an itch in the middle of your back you can't reach. My tears had come loose, and I'd told her she was being unfair, and she'd told me she was only acting out of concern, which is an excuse parents love to trot out when they're being unfair. I'd stormed out of the kitchen, and when Ruby eventually came to pick me up, I'd left the house without telling Mom good-bye.

Now I take out my phone to see two missed calls and a text from Mom. I feel a mix of guilt and triumph; I guess she'd been the one to apologize first. However, all her text says is: *Let me know when you get to airport, okay?* Cool and clinical.

With my free hand, I twist the bracelets on my wrist. How should I respond? My battery bar is red and dwindling. I'm probably at two percent. I suppose I could simply write back, *Here, about to board*, matching her tone. Ruby would recommend that, I'm sure. Although what I really want to say is *I wish we hadn't fought, Mom, and please tell me it's fine that I'm going to France, because I'm actually a little scared. OK?*

Before I can write anything, I notice that the French mom and daughter have moved way ahead in the line, and I hurry forward to close the gap between us. In that moment, I see an enormous zigzag of lightning split the sky over the runway. I gasp, a dart of panic shooting through me. There are similar gasps around me. Thunder booms outside. *Omen, omen, omen,* I think.

Did you see that? I text Mom, fingers trembling.

No, she texts back instantly, making me wonder if she's had the phone in her hand all this time, waiting. *What?*

Hudsonville is a good ten miles from the airport, so it could be the storm hasn't reached there yet. Everyone at the gate is murmuring and peering out the window. There's a crackling sound over the loudspeaker, and the boarding agent calmly announces that all passengers should continue boarding, that weather conditions are safe to fly. My stomach twists and I grip my phone. I don't want to alarm Mom by telling her what I saw. And if conditions were truly dangerous, I assure myself, the airline would cancel the flight. Right?

What do I know? I'm not even sixteen.

I try to channel Ruby—unruffled, mature Ruby. I lift my chin and step forward. The line is moving quickly now.

Nothing, I write to Mom, fingers slightly more stable. *Here, about to board.*

Fly safe, Mom responds immediately. *Call me when you land.*

I study her words. Did she say *fly safe* because she knew about the lightning? Or am I reading into things, maybe grasping for a reason to—what? Not get on the plane? That's insane. Even without Mom's approval, even with my lingering doubts and nervousness, even with the storm, I want more than anything to go. I'm going to go.

The French mom steps forward, scooping her daughter up in her arms. I watch as the mom hands their boarding passes to the agent and walks through the open door that leads to the plane. The little girl eyes me cautiously over her mother's shoulder.

It's my turn.

I feel a jolt of excitement as I take a step forward, my boarding pass in one hand, my phone still in the other. No backing out now.

Then my phone buzzes with an incoming call.

I pause and look down. It must be Mom. Or Ruby.

But no. The words on the screen read UNKNOWN CALLER.

I hesitate.

Who could it be? A wrong number? Mom, calling from a different line?

Should I answer? Or ignore it?

A decision. I am terrible at making decisions.

Buzz, buzz. Buzz, buzz.

A portly man with a suitcase gives a loud huff and walks around me. He holds out his boarding pass to have it scanned, then heads through the open door. More and more people begin to stream past me. I remain motionless, like a pole planted in rushing water.

Buzz, buzz. Buzz, buzz.

"This is the final boarding call for flight 022!" The boarding agent speaks into the microphone at her desk, but her eyes are on me. She's wearing too much makeup, a trim navy-blue suit, and super-high heels. "I repeat, the final call."

My phone keeps buzzing. I should silence it. Ignore it. The battery is almost gone. There are only two minutes left until the scheduled takeoff time.

But . . .

What if? What if it's important? What if answering this call will swing the wheel of my life in a new direction?

The boarding agent looks at me with her eyebrows raised. My phone buzzes. My heart races. The thunder cracks outside.

And—

PART ONE

Cobblestones and Croissants

Monday, July 3, 9:43 p.m.

I don't answer the call.

I hit a button to silence the buzzing, and stuff my phone in the pocket of my hoodie. Then I stride forward, boarding pass extended. The agent smiles at me with her lips closed. As I step through the open door, I glance over my shoulder. The gate is empty; I'm the last passenger.

I break into a run down the carpeted corridor, my flip-flops thwacking. The walls are covered with advertisements for FedEx. THE WORLD ON TIME, they read, over and over.

I step from the corridor onto the plane, inhaling sharply. The cabin smells like stale coffee, and French and English conversations overlap. The flight attendants scowl at me, late, bedraggled girl that I am. Everyone is either seated or struggling to stash carry-ons in the overhead bins. I'm glad I have just my trusty tote bag, which I press close to my side as I head toward my row.

My stomach sinks. I'm in a middle seat, squished between the large man who'd walked around me earlier, and the French mom and daughter. I notice that the mom wears her hair in a neat brown bob, like my mother does. And the daughter's hair is dark blond like mine. Except the daughter is wearing two tidy, adorable braids, and *my* hair is spilling out gracelessly from its topknot.

I try to get comfortable in the seat, crossing my legs, unzipping my hoodie while the flight attendants begin their safety instructions. Then, from within my hoodie pocket comes the mournful spiraling noise that means my phone has died.

I pull out the phone and stare at the blank screen, feeling a drumbeat of curiosity. I wonder who was calling me before. Even if the mystery caller left a voice mail, I won't be able to listen to it until I get back to America in August.

The plane begins taxiing, slowly at first, then picking up speed. If I crane my neck, I can see out a window onto the runway. It seems the storm has passed; the night is calm, puddles reflecting the moonlight. Strange how quickly that shift happened.

"Flight attendants and crew," the captain announces. "Please prepare for takeoff."

I settle back in my seat. The large man beside me nudges my elbow, and the little French girl lets out a wail, a harbinger of things to come. But I don't care. The plane is zooming now. I am leaving it all behind—dull upstate New York, Mom's recent strangeness. My pointless pining for Hugh Tyson. My wistful watching when Ruby effortlessly flirts with boys. And most of all, my wanting to know Dad better.

The engines roar. The plane seems to move faster than time can measure. As we lift off the ground, my hopes rise. I remember what Ruby said in the car, and I smile with sudden sureness. This *is* my destiny—to have the best summer ever.

Tuesday, July 4, 11:32 a.m.

This is the worst.

I stand in the baggage claim of Marseille Provence Airport, my suitcase in hand, my tote bag digging into my shoulder. I am cotton-mouthed and crick-necked from the long, sleepless flight, and my spirits are falling by the second.

Dad is not here.

In our last email exchange, he said he'd pick me up at the airport. So as soon as I'd exited the plane, I'd been on the look-out for his ash-blond hair and tall frame. Maybe he'd even be playfully holding up a sign that read BONJOUR, SUMMER! and I'd hug him, laughing. But there'd been no such sign, and no sign of Dad.

All around me, people are shrieking with joy and rushing to embrace loved ones. I watch numbly as the French mother and daughter run over to a man who wraps them in his arms. I glance away, curling my fingers tight around my suitcase handle. Fear and annoyance tango in my stomach. Did Dad forget when my flight got in? Did he forget about me, period?

Don't think of what Mom said. Don't think of what Mom said.

But the crowd is thinning. Time is passing. Feeling desperate, I reach into my tote bag and push aside my useless cell phone. I snatch up the printout of Dad's email with his address and phone numbers. Should I call him? Are there payphones around here? How do payphones even work? I feel drained from already having done so much on my own, from being so bold and capable at the airport back home. I have reached Peak Maturity Level in this game and I am out of new lives.

Ruby, I think like a prayer, fighting the mounting urge to cry. I remember how, over winter break, she and I took the train to New York City, two hours south of Hudsonville. When we'd emerged from the station into the whirl of traffic and noise and fast-walking people, I'd wanted to curl up and hide. But Ruby had waved a gloved hand in the air, and a yellow taxi had slid to a stop for us, as if by magic.

I draw in a deep, shaky breath. Maybe I have one final ounce of capability left in me. Slowly, I walk toward the exit doors, dragging my suitcase behind me, along with my uncertainty. I'm not sure I'm doing remotely the right thing.

As I step out into the cool, blue-sky morning, I glance left and right, still searching for Dad. The curbside here looks eerily similar to the one back home, with its cabs and luggage carts and harried travelers. I tentatively wave my hand toward the oncoming traffic, half expecting Dad to materialize from somewhere and rescue me. Instead, a dented silver cab comes screeching to a stop. *I actually hailed a cab?*

The gray-haired driver, a cigarette dangling from his lips,

helps me cram my suitcase into the trunk. Then I climb disbelieving into the backseat, and we peel off.

"*Alors,*" the driver says, lighting his cigarette with one hand and steering with the other. "Where are you going, *mademoiselle?*"

I'm both surprised and relieved that he can tell I'm American. "Um," I reply, unfolding the email printout. "Thirteen Rue du Pain," I read out loud. My stomach squeezes. Talk about bad omens. *Street of Pain?*

The driver chuckles, swerving to avoid a guy on a moped. "It is pronounced *pehn,*" he tells me in his heavily accented English. "In French, *pain* means 'bread.'"

"Oh," I mumble, embarrassed. Of course. Like Au Bon Pain.

"But what is the town?" the driver demands, careening out onto a highway. "In Provence, we have many towns. Avignon, Aix-en-Provence, Cassis . . ."

"Right. Um. It's called . . . Les Deux Chemins," I read out loud again, certain that I am butchering the pronunciation. Again.

"*Très bien,*" the driver says, exhaling smoke. "*C'est une belle ville.* A beautiful town. You will see."

But all I see, as we continue at breakneck pace down the highway, are road signs and flat landscapes that could easily double as anywhere in America. I peer out at the passing cars as if I might catch sight of Dad on the opposite side of the highway, on his way to the airport to get me. Then I give up. It's warm in the cab, so I take off my hoodie and stuff it into my tote bag.

When I lift my gaze again, the scenery outside has changed. Dramatically.

Green-brown mountains rise up gently around us, and majestic trees—they look like dark emerald pines, but with wild, jagged edges—point toward the sky. *Cypress trees*, I think, remembering a famous Van Gogh painting. We drive past a field full of swaying golden sunflowers: another painting come to life.

For the first time since I landed, I smile. I can feel my stresses about Dad, and Mom, and everything, starting to ebb. What *is* this spectacular place? I roll down my window, and the fresh air floats inside. It smells sweet and earthy, like lemons. And olives. Maybe also lavender? Yes, lavender: I spot a hillside carpeted in purple.

I grab my new Nikon DSLR from my bag, and I carefully twist the black cap off the lens; I'm still figuring out how to use this professional-grade camera. My aunt, Lydia, who's a photographer, gave it to me last week, insisting—over Mom's protests—that she had plenty of extra cameras on hand, and that I should consider it an early birthday present. "I see you always taking pictures on your phone, kiddo," Aunt Lydia had said, reaching over to tug my ponytail, "which is all very well and good. But for your first trip abroad, I thought something a little more special might be in order."

Now I feel a rush of gratitude toward my aunt as I lift the lens to my eye. There is a pink stone cottage perched high above a vineyard. I manage to zoom in, and my heart jumps: I can make out the fat green grapes, shining in the sun. I snap the photo, even though it might come out blurry—the cab is going fast. Wind whips inside, undoing my topknot. My hair falls free and gets in my mouth and eyes. But I keep taking pictures—of thatched red rooftops, and rugged cliffs, and more fields that look like thick seas of lavender.

When I'd thought of France before, I'd imagined Paris: the Eiffel Tower, the romantic bridges. But Provence is clearly a whole other kind of enchanting. It seems impossible that this sun-drenched countryside occupies the same planet, the same *universe*, as Hudsonville, New York.

"*Et voilà*, we have arrived in Les Deux Chemins," the driver tells me, making a hairpin turn onto a wide avenue. I set down my camera and grab hold of the car door handle so I don't fall over. "This is the—*euh*, how do you Americans say it?" he continues. "The . . . main drag?"

"Yes, um, *oui*, the main drag," I reply with a laugh, righting myself again.

The driver nods, pleased. "It is called Boulevard du Temps."

The boulevard is lined with plane trees; their branches meet overhead to form a lush, leafy canopy. The plazas and streets are all cobblestone, and the low buildings, with their rounded corners, are all in shades of cream and ochre. We drive past a sidewalk café full of people sipping coffee from tiny white cups, and a shop with colorful dresses in the window. We pass an ornate stone cathedral, its bells chiming noon. Everywhere there are fountains spraying arcs of water. My breath catches. I'm not sure I grasped what the word *charming* meant until now.

Up ahead, next to a fountain carved with cupids, a boy and girl about my age are standing close together, kissing. They don't seem to care that everyone can see them. I blush, thinking of Hugh Tyson back home. Not that I've ever kissed Hugh. Or any boy, for that matter.

I'm still watching the couple out the back window as the driver turns off the avenue and onto a narrow street. Then he jolts to a stop.

We are in front of a rambling, peach-colored house with pretty green shutters. I squint, and see that the number 13 is carved above the wooden door. My pulse quickens. Somehow, improbably, I have arrived at Dad's house.

I fumble in my wallet for the euros Mom made me get from the bank last week, and I pay the driver. He helps me remove my suitcase from the trunk, I mumble *merci*, and he tears off, leaving me standing alone on the cobblestones.

There is a delicious scent in the air—fresh-baked bread. I turn to see a small, old-fashioned bakery across the street. The word BOULANGERIE is painted on its window, and browned loaves and long baguettes are on display. Aha. *Rue du Pain.* Street of Bread.

My stomach growls as I make my way toward Dad's front door. I could go for some *pain* right now. But really I'm too nervous to eat.

I push my hair out of my eyes, take a breath, and knock on the door.

Silence.

I gaze up at the house, at the curls of ivy climbing its sides. The windows look dark. Is no one here? Oh God. Where *is* Dad?

Don't think of what Mom said. Don't think of what—

There's a flash of movement. Up on the second floor, a lace curtain flutters aside, and a pale face peers down at me. After a split second, the curtain falls back into place.

I shiver. Who was that?

I remember that in Dad's first email, he'd said that there were "artist friends always spilling in and out" of the house. Great. I'm in no mood to meet new people now. That's not my favorite activity in general.

I'm debating whether or not to knock again when the door swings open.

A woman about my mom's age stands there, staring at me in confusion. She has reddish hair in a low ponytail and bright blue eyes, and she wears a striped shirt with cropped black pants. She holds a dry paintbrush in one hand. Definitely an artist friend.

"Um, hi," I squeak out. *"Bonjour."* I feel my reliable shyness creeping over me. "I'm, uh, Ned Everett's daughter? I'm—"

"Summer," the woman says. She studies me closely, her eyes widening. "You are Summer." Her French accent makes my name sound like *Some-air*.

I nod, relieved to be known. "Is my father here?" I ask, taking a tentative step forward. "He was supposed to meet me at the airport . . ."

The woman frowns and shuts her eyes, rubbing her temples with her fingertips. I wonder if she doesn't understand English that well.

"Pardon," she says after a long moment, looking at me again. "Your father, he did not reach you? He did not tell you?"

I freeze. "Tell me what?" I ask, dread twisting inside me.

The woman sighs and shakes her head. "I am afraid your father is in Berlin," she explains, still frowning. "He had to go there at late notice, for a museum opening."

Hold on. What? My mind reels. *Berlin?* Dad isn't even in this country? I'm here, in France, all alone? Something like panic rises in my chest, and my mouth goes dry.

"Do you—do you know when he'll be back?" I sputter. My voice sounds small and frightened to my ears.

"Perhaps next week?" The artist woman shrugs with her hands. "I am not sure," she adds, her tone apologetic.

I gaze at her numbly. Across the street, I hear the door to the bakery open with the ring of a bell. Why didn't Dad tell me he was going to be in Berlin? How could he put me in this position? What am I supposed to do now?

This time, there's no stopping Mom's words. They rush in and fill my head, playing on a loop. *I'm worried you'll be let down. You know how* he *is. I'm worried you'll be let down. You know . . .*

"Please, come inside," the artist woman is saying, and I blink. She is regarding me with concern; the shock and frustration must be plain on my face. "You are tired from your journey, *non?*" she adds, opening the door all the way. "And perhaps you would like to call your father?"

I don't know what I would like. Part of me would like to return to the airport, go back across the Atlantic, reverse everything. Another part of me would like to sag down in a heap on the ground, wailing like the little French girl on the plane.

I do neither. I remain glued to the doorstep, my thoughts whirling. I have to call Mom, too, of course, to tell her I arrived. But that means also telling her she was right.

"I can prepare you some *chocolat chaud*—hot chocolate," the woman adds, and I glance up at her. "Your father, he said you enjoy this, *n'est-ce pas?*"

I feel myself loosening. *That* is what I would like, I realize. Some hot chocolate to drink. The rest I can figure out later.

The fact that Dad remembered that I love hot cocoa, that he bothered to mention it to one of his artist friends, is enough to propel me forward, into the house. It's a relief to set down my heavy suitcase and tote bag in the dim entrance hall. A bunch of identical skeleton keys hang from a hook on the wall, and a bucket full of paintbrushes sits in the corner. I watch as the woman drops her paintbrush into the bucket. I realize that, even though she's a chic artist stranger, she's put me a bit at ease.

"Thank you, um . . . Madame . . . ?" I trail off, unsure of how to address her.

The woman smiles at me, revealing slightly crooked teeth. "I am Vivienne LaCour. Please, call me Vivienne."

"Okay." I fiddle with my bracelets. "It's nice to meet y—" I begin, but then Vivienne catches me off guard by stepping forward and kissing me once on each cheek.

Right. I remember reading in my guidebook that this is how French people greet each other, and say good-bye. As I stand there awkwardly, I decide I hate this custom.

Vivienne steps back and studies me once more, her expression a mixture of curiosity and sympathy. I wonder what she makes of me, if I'm not exactly how one might imagine the great Ned Everett's daughter to be. Then she claps her hands and turns around, leading me into a big, airy kitchen.

"*S'il te plaît*, have a seat," she tells me.

I sink into a chair at the old oak table. The kitchen is rustic, with brass pots and pans hanging from hooks, and windows facing a sprawling garden. From where I sit, I can see a red barn and a glimmering blue pool. My spirits lift. Dad's vacation home is even nicer than I expected. Maybe I can get by here for a week on my own. Maybe.

"Are you staying at the house?" I ask Vivienne as she places a saucepan on the stove. She nods, pouring milk into a pan. "Are there other people, too?" I add. I hope I'm not being impolite. I'm still foggy and disoriented, and I want to get my bearings as much as possible.

"Only my daughter, at the moment," Vivienne replies, stirring the milk.

"You have a daughter?" I blurt, surprised. Vivienne seems too hip, somehow, to be a mom.

"*Oui*," Vivienne says. She glances up, and raises her eyebrows at something behind me. "Ah. Here she is now."

I spin in my chair, rattled by the sight of a girl standing in the kitchen. How did she enter so noiselessly? She looks to be around my age, maybe slightly younger, and she's gorgeous, with long golden curls and sloping blue eyes. Her lacy white nightgown enhances her ethereal appearance. I am suddenly certain that hers was the face I spied in the second-story window.

Vivienne clears her throat. "Summer, this is Eloise. Eloise, this is Summer."

Eloise stares at me so hard I feel caught, like a bug under a cup. She does not blink or smile. In theory, I should be pleased that there is a peer here, someone whom I could potentially befriend. But I do not get a friendly vibe from Eloise. Not at all.

Finally, her icy blue gaze darts over to Vivienne, and rapid-fire French shoots out of her mouth.

"*Pourquoi est-elle ici? J'ai pensé que—*"

"*Pas maintenant.*" Vivienne's voice is stern. "*Sois polie. Dis bonjour.*"

I sit still, listening closely, wishing I understood anything besides *bonjour.*

Eloise crosses her arms over her chest, and looks down at me imperiously. "Hello," she says in the rote, resentful tone of a student forced to read her homework out loud. I'm pretty sure I won't have to worry about her kissing my cheeks anytime soon.

"Hey there," I mutter, my tongue feeling clumsy. I remember that, as a kid, I loved the book *Eloise*, about the lively little girl who lived in the Plaza, in Manhattan. Now all positive associations with the name are fading rapidly.

"You're really from New York?" this Eloise demands. Her English is impeccable, her accent barely noticeable. I catch her silently critiquing me, sizing up my messy, frizzy hair (I try surreptitiously to smooth it down) and the orange juice stain on my white T-shirt (turbulence on the plane; spillage).

"Not New York *City*," I clarify, resenting that my cheeks are flushing. "More, like, upstate." I fiddle with my bracelets. I'm sure that Eloise would wrinkle her pert nose at Hudsonville.

Actually, now that I'm thinking of Hudsonville, I realize who Eloise reminds me of: my classmate Skye Oliveira. The term *mean girl* would be too kind to assign to Skye. She and her pack of flawless friends prowl the school halls in their designer ankle boots, hunting for fresh prey. Apparently, Skye and her ilk translate to France.

Vivienne comes over to the table, handing me a huge mug—really, it's more like a soup bowl—filled to the brim with the thickest hot chocolate I've ever seen. *Yum.* I thank her and I take a sip, savoring the sweet, rich warmth.

"Wow," Eloise says snidely. "Royal treatment for you, Summer." I glance at her over the brim of my mug-bowl, wishing I had the guts to empty its contents on her head. Ruby would do something like that; my best friend is not cowed by the likes of Skye. "*Maman* never makes me *chocolat chaud*," Eloise adds, leaning against the doorjamb.

"I can prepare you some now, Eloise," Vivienne says, her tone tight. She is setting delicate floral plates on the table, along with a basket of golden croissants and jars of jam. I'm grateful; my hunger has returned full-force. "Come have a bite with us."

Please don't have a bite with us, please don't have a bite with us.

"No time, *Maman*," Eloise snaps, tossing her princess-like hair. I feel instant relief. "I have to get ready for class." She gives me a smug, pointed look, as if I'm supposed to feel jealous of this class. I ignore her, gulping down more cocoa.

"You should not have slept so late, then," Vivienne says, sitting down beside me with her own mug-bowl of cocoa. "Are you going out again tonight?"

"Probably, with Colette and everyone," Eloise replies lazily, studying her nails; they are short and painted pale pink with tiny black hearts in their centers.

This Colette must be delightful. I imagine a double of Eloise and repress a shudder, reaching for a plate.

"D'accord," Vivienne says, sipping her cocoa. "I am anyway having dinner out tonight with Monsieur Pascal." She is quiet for a moment, then takes a croissant and slices it down the middle with a bread knife. She glances at me, looking thoughtful, and then looks back at her daughter. I start to get a really bad feeling. "Ah. Eloise?" Vivienne adds, in a fake-casual tone.

No. No. Nooooo.

"Oui, Maman?" Eloise answers, her voice full of suspicion and hesitation. Rightfully so.

"Perhaps," Vivienne continues, very busy spreading jam onto one half of her croissant, "you would like to bring Summer out with you this evening?"

Bingo.

My stomach somersaults down into my flip-flops.

I understand that Vivienne is trying to be helpful, that I am stranded here with no father and no purpose. But the idea of spending time with Eloise and her evil minions is about as appealing as stabbing myself with the bread knife. I hazard a glance at Eloise and see that she is shooting daggers at her mother. At least we're on the same page.

"There's, um, there's no need," I speak up, too loudly. I grab a still-warm croissant from the basket. "I'm not really . . . the going-out type. And, um, I'm pretty beat. You know, from jet lag." As I say this, exhaustion does start to seep through me.

"Well, see how you feel later," Vivienne tells me, and then looks at Eloise again. "You go to Café des Roses on Boulevard du Temps, *non*? What time?" she asks her daughter. I remember that my cabdriver called Boulevard du Temps "the main drag," though I think it best not to pipe up with this factoid right now.

Eloise's face flushes. "Around. Nine," she says through her teeth, as if the act of speaking pains her. She shoots another glare at Vivienne, and then turns and stomps out of the kitchen. I'm reminded of how Mom and I fought in our kitchen, all those hours and an ocean ago.

"I must apologize for my daughter," Vivienne says quietly. She picks up her croissant half and takes a dainty bite. "She is having some . . . stress right now."

Stress? Like what? She ran out of conditioner? A boy didn't smile at her?

Instead of responding, I follow Vivienne's lead—I saw my croissant into (uneven) halves and slather strawberry jam on both sides. I take a big bite. The jam is sweet and tart, speckled with small seeds, and the croissant is the perfect blend of flaky and buttery. At least the culinary aspects of my day have proven successful.

"Eloise is taking an art class for *lycée—euh*, for high school students—this summer," Vivienne continues, stirring a spoon in her cocoa. I can't tell if this is an explanation for Eloise's "stress" or just a way to fill the silence.

I nod, chewing. I do feel a small prickle of jealousy; I've always wanted to attend some sort of cool summer program. Mom, though, ever practical, always encouraged me to get a job.

A job. "Oh," I say to Vivienne, swallowing. "I was supposed to—um, be my dad's sort-of summer assistant? Do you know where his studio is?"

Vivienne nods, looking distracted. She gets up and crosses over to the window. "That is the studio," she tells me, pointing to the red barn, her rings glinting in the sunlight. She takes out a pack of cigarettes from her back pocket and unlatches the window.

I want to go check out this barn studio, but my head feels heavy. It's all hitting me: the grueling trip, Dad's absence, my stunning but strange new surroundings. It's probably been twenty-four hours since I've slept—or has it been even longer? I can't calculate now.

I start to ask Vivienne where the house phone is so I can call Mom, and Dad, but my question is swallowed up by a big yawn.

"*Eh, bien,* you need to rest, *non?*" Vivienne says, turning to me with a cigarette between her fingers. "There is an empty guest room up on the second floor," she adds. "Next door to *la salle de bain*—the bathroom."

I wonder if Dad set aside a room especially for me. It doesn't matter, though. All I need is a bed I can collapse on. I stand and deposit my plate and mug in the sink, thanking Vivienne and hoping she'll help me carry my suitcase upstairs. But she seems lost in thought, gazing out the window and lighting her cigarette. It bothers me that everyone seems to smoke here. Mom would not be pleased by that.

Dazedly, I leave the kitchen and retrieve my bags from the front hall. Across from the kitchen there's a winding staircase and I climb it carefully, bumping my suitcase along behind me. The old, worn-in steps moan and groan, and I think of ghosts.

When I reach the landing, it's clear that the room immediately to my left is the bathroom; the door is shut and I hear the shower running. But over the water, I hear another sound: someone crying. A girl.

Eloise? Why is Eloise crying? I feel a mix of concern and intrigue, half wondering if there's more to the girl than what appears.

The door next to the bathroom is wide open, so I step through it, drop my bags, and frown. This must be the guest room. It's minuscule, with only a twin bed and rickety chest of drawers. The walls are bare except for a cracked mirror and a large painting of a grandfather clock that's floating in a blue sky. *Weird.*

At least there is a small window that overlooks the garden, letting in the dappled sunlight and the smell of blooming things.

There's also a ceiling fan; I tug its cord to turn it on, and the blades spin lazily, barely stirring the stale air.

I shut the door and flop onto the bed. The mattress is hard and unforgiving, the pillow flat. I think of my room back home, with its double bed and many pillows. I think of my air-conditioning turned up high, my stacks of books on the shelves, the colorful Renoir and Degas posters on the walls. I'd chafed against the familiarity before, but now I long for it. Miss it.

I roll over and peer down at my Whitney Museum tote bag. I wish I could take out my cell phone and scroll through Instagram. I wish I could text Ruby. I'd tell her about Eloise, and my best friend would give excellent advice. Maybe I'll call Ruby right after I call Mom. And Dad. Which I'll do soon. I'll just close my eyes for a little bit first.

As my eyes drift shut, I hear the faint ringing of a phone downstairs. It sounds like Vivienne answers it, and she begins speaking in agitated French. Or maybe I'm imagining it. Already, my thoughts are melding together in that slumber-like way.

The phone downstairs makes me think of my cell phone ringing before I got on the plane. I picture myself answering that call, but now I'm speaking in French, and lightning is flashing, and there are sunflower fields, and someone is crying, and softly, slowly, I switch over from the world of wakefulness into one of dreams.

Tuesday, July 4, 9:01 p.m.

The phone is still ringing. Loud. Insistent.

Didn't Vivienne answer it? I think, burying my head deeper into the thin pillow. *No*, I remind myself. *That was a dream.*

Why is no one answering it?

I open one eye, then the other, and then I sit up on the bed. My hair is mashed against my neck. The quality of light streaming in through the window has changed: before it was bright, golden. Now it's muted, rosy. The ceiling fan spins overhead. I get to my feet and stretch. I'm feeling groggy, but less cloudy than I was—when? A few minutes ago?

How long was I asleep?

Brrrring, brrrring, comes from downstairs. *Brrrring, brrrring.*

Rubbing my eyes, I open the guest room door. I expect to see Eloise emerging from the bathroom wearing a towel and a scowl. But the hallway is empty.

"Hello?" I call out, my voice croaky. I hear nothing but the shrill ringing.

Barefoot, I pad down the stairs and follow the ringing around a corner and into an elegant living room. There is a sea-blue sofa, a colorful painting on the wall, and a desk with a sleek computer—and the ringing phone—on it.

I'm hesitant as I lift the phone from its cradle.

"Uh, *bonjour*?" I venture.

"Summer!" Mom's voice explodes over the line, anxious and relieved all at once.

"Mom?" I blink and push a hand through my matted hair. Hearing my mother here is deeply disorienting. I stand by the desk and look out the window, which faces cobblestoned Rue du Pain. The bakery is closed.

I bite my lip. This is the first time Mom and I are speaking since our fight.

"Why didn't you call me?" Mom demands, and I feel a surge of guilt. "I checked your flight status first thing this morning and saw you landed, but it's been ten hours!"

"Wait," I say, turning in a circle, scanning the room for a clock. "Ten hours?"

"Yes." Mom sighs, impatient. "It's three in the afternoon over here. So it's, what, nine at night over there?"

Ohhh.

Now it makes sense: the shuttered bakery, the empty house, the rosy light. The summer sun must set even later here than it does at home. I picture myself asleep in the narrow bed upstairs while around me time was carrying on—Eloise and Vivienne going about their days, the sky over Les Deux Chemins turning from blue to dusty pink.

"I was taking an epic nap," I explain sheepishly, plopping down into the chair at the desk. "Sorry."

I wonder if this *sorry*, in some roundabout way, can serve as an apology for our argument. It's certainly easier than reopening that can of awkward right now. *Hey, Mom, remember how I freaked out when you said Dad might let me down? Well, turns out—you were onto something!*

"No, I'm sorry," Mom answers. I sit up straighter in the chair. Is that *her* version of a one-size-fits-all apology? "I didn't mean to wake you," she continues, sounding a bit calmer. "I wasn't planning to call the landline, but I tried your father's cell twice, and got no answer." She clears her throat. "How is he, anyway?" she asks gruffly.

I swallow hard, staring at the dark computer screen. So Mom doesn't know that Dad is in Berlin.

Maybe she doesn't have to know.

My heart starts to beat faster. I don't lie to Mom—thanks to my solid grades and subpar social life, I've never really had to. "Honesty's a two-way street," Mom likes to say, implying that if I'm forthright with her, she'll be forthright with me. At this moment, though, I wonder if I can take a little vacation from honesty.

Because if I tell Mom the truth, her *I told you so* will haunt me for the rest of my life. She will immediately make me come home, and there it will go—my destiny, up in smoke. Yes, it's upsetting and unsettling that Dad isn't here. But the scared, squirmy sensation I had when I first arrived has abated somewhat. I'm feeling braver.

"He's . . . fine," I finally say, my palms clammy. I haven't quite lied yet; Dad *is*, I guess, fine. Just, you know, in Berlin. "Busy," I add, which also seems valid, given what Vivienne said about museum openings or whatever.

"Isn't he always?" Mom snorts. Then she's silent. I hold my breath, praying she won't dig any deeper and hit upon a nugget of truth. "And—how are you?" she asks after a moment, her voice halting. "I mean, how is—you know, everything there?"

"It's really pretty here," I reply. "The food is good." All non-lies so far.

"Good," Mom echoes. She gives a small cough. "But is there any—" She pauses, as if cutting herself off. "I mean, have you m—"

The familiar roar of our blender drowns out the rest of Mom's words. Then I hear a familiar voice in the background saying something about blueberries.

"Aunt Lydia's over?" I ask Mom, eager to change the subject. "What are you guys doing?" My aunt, like my mom, is a professor at Hudsonville College, only she teaches photography, not philosophy. Actually, the two of them are both teaching courses on campus this summer. "Why aren't you at work?" I add. I fear that Mom canceled her class because she was so worried about me.

Mom lets out a sputtering sound. "Seriously? It's the Fourth of July."

I feel dizzy with the rush of realization. "Oh—that's right," I stammer. *Hello.* My brief time in a foreign country has apparently made me forget my favorite holiday. I peer out the window, half expecting to see kids running down the street waving sparklers and miniature American flags. But Rue du Pain is quiet, of course.

"We're making red, white, and blueberry smoothies," Mom says, talking loudly over the blender. "To drink later while we watch the fireworks."

I wonder if she is trying to make me wistful and nostalgic, because it's sort of working. There's a tightness in my chest, and in my throat. Suddenly, I want to spill everything to Mom: Dad not being at the airport; my learning his whereabouts from a random houseguest; the other, obnoxious houseguest; all the cigarette smoking . . . If I stay on the phone for one more second, I might not be able to dam up my confession.

"Um, I should go," I blurt. I push the chair back as if I'm really about to leave.

"Where are you going?" Mom asks, sounding suspicious.

"I—" I think fast, remembering Vivienne's suggestion from hours ago. "I made a friend here." And that, ladies and gentlemen, is a real lie. "I'm supposed to meet her, and, um, some of her friends at a café." *Thank you, Eloise.*

"A friend? That's nice," Mom says. But her voice is tensing up again, coiling like a snake. "How did you—I mean who—"

"Let Summer be!" I hear Aunt Lydia shout in the background. I wish there were a way to give a transatlantic hug.

"I'll talk to you later, Mom," I say hastily. "Say hi to Aunt Lydia. Happy Fourth!"

"Will you have your father call me, please?" Mom asks, but it's too late; I'm hanging up and returning the phone to its base.

I exhale and lean forward on the desk, shaky with uncertainty. My elbow bumps the computer mouse, and the screen lights up. In the upper right corner, where the time should be, are the numbers *21:14*. I don't know what those mean. I don't know anything.

No. That's not quite right. I do know that I need to get in touch with Dad, to tell him that Mom thinks that he's with me in Les Deux Chemins. That's why lies are complicated; they beget more lying.

Dad's number is buried in my tote bag upstairs, and I'm not sure I can endure another parental phone call anyway. So I position my fingers on the odd-looking keyboard—the letters are in a different order here—and log in to my email.

To my surprise, there's already an email from Dad waiting for me: a hasty message saying he called the house earlier but I was sleeping and he also tried to reach me before I left for France. He is so sorry to not be around, but I should make myself at home and he will be back in hopefully two weeks, and he loves me, and ciao, sweetheart.

Two weeks? I think, dejected. I'd thought it would be just one. And did Dad really try to reach me before I left? Something is ringing in my mind like a faint bell but I can't grasp it. Slowly, clumsily, I type my reply, filling Dad in on the Mom lie, and asking him if I should start organizing his barn studio.

I log off, then instantly wish I had emailed Ruby, too. I need her guidance on a whole *host* of issues now. I could call her; I know her number by heart. But first I'll see what she's up to on Instagram. That's our preferred method of being in touch, anyway, second to texting. We love leaving each other comments and private jokes under our respective photos.

I log in to my account. My page is all shots of Ruby and me making funny faces, or of my cat, Ro, dozing in weird positions. I consider posting the pictures I took from the cab today, though I'd need a phone to do that. Besides, I doubt any of them came out well.

I scroll through my feed, past various classmates' pictures of burgers on grills and pink watermelon slices on paper plates. Then I come to a picture that makes my stomach lurch.

It's Ruby's most recent photo, uploaded today. She and our friend Alice Johansen are grinning, their cheeks pressed together. Ruby's arm is extended to snap the picture, and Alice is applying lipstick. They're in Ruby's room; I recognize the purple lacquer dresser behind them, its surface cluttered with makeup and jewelry. But it's the caption that gets me: *Primping for party! #independencedayrealness #radwhiteandblue*

What party? Every Fourth of July, Ruby and I, and whichever satellite friends are in town, go watch the fireworks in Pine Park. We eat hot dogs and ice-cream cones, and it's perfect. I know that some other kids from school—like Skye Oliveira, the Eloise of

Hudsonville—host lavish barbecues. But Ruby and I never cared for such parties.

At least, I *thought* Ruby never cared. Sourness fills my mouth. Is she hosting a party? Going to someone else's? Why didn't she mention anything to me? She had plenty of time on our drive to the airport yesterday.

I study the picture. Ruby's eyes are sparkling with excitement. I'll admit it: I had kind of hoped that my best friend would be morose without me. That she'd go through the motions of her summer, counting the days until my return, while I was off having rich, juicy *experiences*. The evidence, though, is as clear as a picture: Ruby is still the one having *experiences*, and I'm here, slumped at a desk in an empty house.

A swell of jealousy rises in me. It seems that everyone in Hudsonville is moving forward in their lives, making smoothies and primping for parties, even though they are many hours behind me. Which almost feels like a betrayal.

Nice! I type furiously beneath Ruby's photo—after it takes me a few tries to hit the right letters, that is. *Arrived in France, and it's AMAZING.* All at once, I want her to believe I'm moving forward, too. *Heading out now to meet some new friends at a café! Love you times 2!*

Before I can overthink it, I post the comment and log out. Then I hurriedly stand up, as if to distance myself from all my lies.

I take a steadying breath. And I wonder: Does *this* lie even have to be a lie?

I shake my head. *What is wrong with me?* Am I truly entertaining the idea of going out to meet Eloise and her friends? *Don't be stupid, Summer.* Setting aside the guaranteed awfulness, I don't have a clue as to how I'd even find them.

Except . . .

Where did Vivienne say they'd be? I glance around the living room, the memory inching forward in my brain. A café . . .

My gaze lands on the painting on the wall. It depicts an elderly man standing between two rosebushes. It's beautiful and vivid. All at once, I recognize that Dad painted it: I can even make out his swooping signature on the bottom. I smile, feeling a burst of pride. Now more than ever, I'm longing to see Dad's painting of me in the gallery here. Dad is well known for painting people outside, in nature. In my portrait, I'm among poppies, and this old man is surrounded by roses . . .

That's it. That's the café. Café des Roses. Vivienne's words come back to me in one full string: *Café des Roses on Boulevard du Temps.*

So it turns out I do have a clue. Now I just need to decide if I have the courage.

Or the stupidity.

• • •

I head back upstairs, figuring I'll get ready to go out before making any firm choices. The bathroom proves to be a slight challenge; the toilet, weirdly, is tucked away behind a separate doorway. And the shower has no showerhead—only a handheld nozzle that keeps slipping from my soapy grasp.

It seems many things in France are puzzlingly different.

Back in my medieval chamber, I paw through my suitcase. I'd packed painstakingly, picking only outfits that I deemed sophisticated. But now, through new eyes, my skinny jeans and layered tank tops seem so ordinary. So . . . *Hudsonville-y*. I tell myself I shouldn't care if some snobby French girls sneer at my clothes. Still, I select what seems like a safe bet—a white linen sundress that's a hand-me-down from Ruby. It looked better on her, I realize as I comb out my wet, tangled hair in front of the cracked mirror. But it'll do. I slide on my flip-flops, grab my tote bag, and shut off the overhead light.

The door across from mine is ajar, and I peer inside the darkened room, feeling a bit like I'm trespassing. The floor is littered with lacy skirts, sandals, and thick fashion magazines, along with sketchbooks and charcoal pencils that spill out of a leather satchel. Eloise. She clearly dropped off her things after her art class and ransacked her fancy wardrobe before dashing off again. I wonder if she shares this guest room with Vivienne. How many other rooms are there in the house? I glance down the shadowy hallway and give a little shiver. I'll explore another time, when it's daylight out.

I flip-flop down the stairs, still split between staying and going. By the front door, I spot the hook on the wall; only one key hangs there now. My guess is that it's a spare that I can use to lock the door behind me when I leave. Or maybe not.

If the key doesn't work, I decide, it's a sign. A sign that my mission is foolhardy and I should stay put. If it works, then—well, Café des Roses it is.

Unfortunately, the key turns smoothly in the lock. So I draw in a big breath, square my shoulders, and step out into the warm, windy night.

Ruby's dress flutters around my knees as I walk past the other pastel-colored houses on Rue du Pain. Darkness is starting to settle, gently. While the air still smells of bread, there's also a sweet, flowery scent; I think it might be jasmine.

I'm pretty sure that when I round the corner, I'll be on Boulevard du Temps, right by the cupid fountain where I saw the guy and girl kissing earlier today. I have a decent sense of direction—surprising, considering how uncertain and turned-around I usually feel. "You inherited that talent from your father," Mom will say grudgingly, and it must be true, because Mom can get lost in our own house.

Sure enough, I find myself on Boulevard du Temps. The quaint, cobblestoned avenue I saw from the taxi has become a vibrant, sparkling swath swarming with people. Everyone is chattering and cheek-kissing, smoking and strolling, entering and exiting the brightly lit shops and restaurants. Overwhelmed, I pause by the cupid fountain, feeling its spray on my cheek. Then I urge myself onward.

A few steps from the fountain, there's a tiny store with a diamond-shaped red sign that reads TABAC; it seems to sell news-papers and cigarettes, candy and lottery tickets. Next door, a chic-looking boutique has its doors flung open, blasting French hip-hop onto the street. There's an aproned man standing at a cart on the corner, preparing fresh, hot crepes for a line of people.

Most of all, though, there are cafés. Nearly identical sidewalk cafés, all with round white-clothed tables and wicker chairs, all full of patrons leisurely eating and drinking. I read the names on the colorful awnings as I pass: *Café Cézanne, Café des Jumelles, Café de la Lavande* . . . Anticipation and dread mingle in me, and I wonder if it doesn't even exist, this—

Café des Roses.

There it is, spelled out in script on a red-and-white-striped awning.

I stop so abruptly that I almost crash into the family walking in front of me. I try to gather myself together, smoothing down the front of Ruby's dress, adjusting my tote bag on my shoulder. Meanwhile, my eyes anxiously scan the crowded tables.

Girls flirt with guys over paper cones of French fries. Women in silky scarves sit across from scruffy-bearded men, reading newspapers they probably bought at the *tabac*. Waiters in white shirts and black neckties whisk wine glasses and bottles of Perrier from table to table. I stiffen when I spot a group of giggling, well-groomed girls—but Eloise is not among them. Eloise does not appear to be here at all.

I turn around, gazing at the dolphin-shaped fountain across the street. I should be thrilled that I've missed Eloise and her friends. But at the same time, I don't feel quite ready to return to

Dad's house. Maybe it's the electric energy in the air, or the color of the pre-sunset sky: dark pink streaked with gold. I reach into my tote bag and remove my camera.

"*Bonsoir!*" I hear a male voice say behind me. A hand touches my shoulder, and my heart jumps. "*Pourquoi tu es ici si tard?*"

I spin around. In that millisecond, I process that the guy I'm facing is about my age, or a couple years older, and very good-looking, with dark-blue eyes, olive skin, tousled black hair, and sharp cheekbones. I also process that my camera, the precious Nikon DSLR, has fallen out of my hand.

The guy swiftly reaches down and catches the camera before it hits the ground.

I stare at him, confused.

"Um—thank you—*merci*," I finally manage to sputter. I feel my cheeks flame. What I really want to say is *Who are you and why were you talking to me?* but I don't know how to ask that in French.

"*Excusez-moi.*" The guy's bewildered expression must mirror mine. "I am sorry that I startled you," he tells me in charmingly accented English. "I thought that you were someone else."

"Well—I'm not," I reply, giving a short laugh. *Shut up, Summer. Stop now.* The breeze blows my hair across my eyes. For no discernible reason, I keep talking. "I'm . . . me. Just . . . Summer. That's my name."

Why do I allow myself to speak to boys?

"Hello, Just Summer," he says teasingly, his face breaking into a wolfish smile. "My name is Jacques Cassel. Here," he adds, handing me my camera. When I accept it from him, our fingertips brush and my blush deepens. Without warning, Ruby's prediction from yesterday pops in my head: *You will find a gorgeous French boyfriend* . . .

I slip my camera back into my bag, chastising myself for jumping to absurd conclusions. This random French guy becoming my boyfriend is as likely as my crush back home, Hugh Tyson, asking me out, which is basically the stuff of science fiction. And Hugh is quiet and kind of dorky, not smoothly confident like this . . . Jacques.

"*Alors,*" Jacques is saying. "You were waiting for a table?"

"A—what?" I glance up from my bag.

"A table," he repeats, gesturing back toward the café.

It is then that I take in the rest of him: He is wearing a white shirt, a black tie, and black pants, and, in the hand that didn't rescue my camera, he is holding a menu. He's a waiter. At Café des Roses. My brain slowly computes these facts. Cute. Waiter. Table.

Part of me thinks it would be wise to say *non* and bolt before I can make a further fool of myself. But a bigger part of me realizes that I'm hungry, and I'm here. And if my mouth is full, then chances are slimmer that I'll say something ridiculous.

"*Oui,*" I reply at last, attempting some dignity. "Table for one."

Jacques looks amused as he turns and leads me over to a small round table. I drop into the wicker chair in a daze. I've never eaten alone at a restaurant before. Jacques hands me the menu and disappears, returning a few moments later with a short glass of water. It comes with no straw, and no ice. Different from what I'm used to, again.

"You have decided?" he asks, taking a pen and pad of paper from his pocket.

Of course I haven't. I open the menu, skimming the items. *Poulet rôti. Bouillabaisse. Salade niçoise.* "It's . . . all in French," I say, sounding as lame as I feel.

I look up at Jacques and see that his lips are twitching. He has a dimple in his right cheek. "You are in France," he points out.

For a second, I grasp just *how* far away I am from Hudsonville, from my house, from Hugh Tyson. Everything here—the spicy scents wafting over from other diners' plates, Jacques with his French accent, the ice-less water, even the silver moon rising in the sky—is totally foreign to me. I feel anxiety flutter in my neck.

"Could I have a burger?" I finally ask. I want something that will taste like home, something Fourth of July–ish.

"*Non,*" Jacques tells me, his dark-blue eyes dancing.

"*Non?*" I glance back down at the menu, certain I saw *Hamburger* somewhere, unless it was an English-word mirage.

"You have just arrived in Provence, *n'est-ce pas?*" Jacques asks me, and I meet his mischievous gaze once more. I nod, frustrated that my own foreignness is so obvious. "That decides it," Jacques says, flipping his pad shut. "My parents—they own this café, you see—they would kill me if I served an American girl a burger for her first meal here. I will bring you something better. *Un moment.*"

Before I can explain to him that this isn't technically my first meal, and before I can ask him not to bring me any snails, which I know some French people like to eat, he's headed off. He strides past the tableful of pretty girls I spotted earlier, and they all look at him and nudge one another. Clearly, I'm not the only one who's noticed that he is the youngest and handsomest of all the waiters.

I watch the girls as they giggle and talk and clink their glasses of Perrier. I twist my woven bracelets around my wrist. I miss Ruby. Although if she were here, she'd order me to act like a normal person in front of Jacques. Or *she* would act normal in front of him, making me jealous. I take a sip of water, wondering what Ruby is doing right now. Are she and Alice at their party? I wish I had my phone on me. I'm not used to sitting alone without it.

"*Et voilà,*" Jacques says, reappearing. He apparently has a gift for sneaking up on me and causing my heart to flip over.

He sets down a bowl brimming with fragrant tomato broth, vegetables, and seafood. Two toasted slices of baguette sit crisscrossed artfully on top.

"*Bouillabaisse* for you," he explains. "A house specialty."

"Wow. *Merci,*" I say, debating whether I should take a photo or dig in. My hunger wins out, and I gulp down a spoonful of the stew. It's hot, and burns my tongue, but it's also wonderful, tasting of the sea and of fresh herbs, like rosemary and thyme.

I can feel Jacques watching me, which would be more embarrassing if I weren't so busy devouring the *bouillabaisse.* I dunk a baguette slice into the broth and take a bite.

"I am glad you are enjoying," he says, sounding pleased with himself. I expect him to turn then, and walk away. But he doesn't yet. "Your name is really Summer?" he asks me instead. Flustered, I nod, wondering why he cares. Jacques raises a dark eyebrow. "We do not have this name in France. Here, 'summer' is '*été.*'"

"*Été,*" I echo, the word as new on my tongue as the *bouillabaisse*. Despite my skittishness, I smile. "That would be a strange name, I guess."

"But maybe a cool one, *non*?" Jacques says, smiling in return. And then, to my surprise, he sits down in the wicker chair across from me.

I almost choke. "Why are—don't you have to work?" I stammer. I glance around at the other tables.

Jacques chuckles, loosening his tie. My heart flips over again. "It is almost the end of my shift," he tells me, leaning forward conspiratorially. "My parents, they will go easy on me if I take a little break."

"Are you from Les Deux Chemins?" I wonder out loud. This idyllic place seems like a vacation town, but, I remind myself, of course people live here, too.

Jacques nods. "I was born and raised. I have been helping my parents at their café for three years. Since I was, how you say, *quatorze ans*? Fourteen." His dark-blue eyes sparkle as he regards me from across the table. "And where are you from?" he asks.

I avert my gaze and swallow another spoonful of the *bouillabaisse*. "Hudsonville," I reply, remembering my earlier exchange with Eloise. Jacques, though, doesn't seem judgmental or snobbish.

"It's a town a couple hours north of New York City. Not a town like this," I clarify, motioning toward Boulevard du Temps. "Different. More, like, a suburb?" I bite my lip, not certain that Jacques understands me.

"*Oui*, a suburb," he says, smiling. "I know this word."

My hand trembles a little as I lift my water glass. "Your English is very good," I tell him truthfully. "I wish I spoke French."

The wind rustles the leaves on a lemon tree above us. I feel detached from the table, separate, watching myself having a conversation with this handsome French boy. *That can't be me,* I think hazily. *It's another Summer. One who isn't scared.* Over Jacques's shoulder, I notice the tableful of girls blatantly staring at us, their mouths half open. I totally understand their shock. I share it.

Jacques ducks his head, almost shyly. "I would like to be better at my English," he says. "We study it in school here, but I need more practice." He pauses, tracing a pattern on the tabletop with one finger. "Perhaps . . ."

"Jacques!" I hear someone snap.

I blink and look up to see a plump, beautiful woman standing by our table, hands on her hips. She's about my mom's age, and wears an apron over a green dress. She barks something at Jacques in French, and he shrugs, saying, *"Pardon, Maman,"* and I realize this is his mother. So much for his parents letting him take a little break. I get the sense, from her tone, that maybe this has happened before.

"I have to go," Jacques tells me unnecessarily, standing while his mother storms off. He shoots me a dimpled grin. "Would you like anything else? Something sweet?"

The blush that faded earlier now returns with a vengeance. My face must be scarlet as I shake my head and ask for the check. Lingering here, having dessert, would be pushing my luck, like trying to go back to a dream after you've already woken up.

The check, when it arrives, is delivered by an elderly, stooped waiter. I assume Jacques must have been banished to dishwashing or something as punishment. I feel my spirits sag—though, silly me, what was I expecting, anyway?—and I turn over the tissue-thin slip of paper, reaching into my tote bag for my wallet.

I freeze.

On the check, beneath the typed price of the *bouillabaisse*, is a string of numbers scrawled in boyish handwriting, along with the words:

For Summer: If you would ever like to practice your French, or help me practice my English. —J.

My heart begins beating double time. No. I don't get it. Are those numbers a phone number? Did a boy—not just any boy, but Cute Waiter Jacques—give me his *phone number*? This isn't real. I'm still sleeping, up in the guest room. Right?

But the evidence is in front of me. I stare down at the check in amazement before grabbing it with quivering fingers and stuffing it inside my tote bag. Then, my head floating somewhere above my body, I leave what is probably the wrong amount of euros on the table, get up, and go.

The sky is pitch-dark now, and the moon bathes Boulevard du Temps in a fuzzy glow. I missed the moment that night fell.

I drift along, my mind replaying my interaction with Jacques. His knowing smile. His words on the check, flirtatious and bold. There's no way he likes me, I tell myself. Boys don't like me. I probably misunderstood everything.

But what if? I wonder, my belly tingling. *What if I didn't misunderstand at all?*

What if Ruby was right?

I can't wait to tell her.

I laugh out loud, wondering if I look like a weirdo. I'm faintly aware that fewer people are out and about at this hour, and some shops and cafés are shuttering. I approach Café des Jumelles, which is still open, and crowded. As I pass by the outdoor tables, I catch sight of something in my peripheral vision that makes me stop and look twice.

A girl with golden curls, clad in a gauzy white sundress, sits at a table. My heart, previously buoyant, sinks. It's Eloise.

She is sipping from a coffee cup, talking animatedly with a guy and a girl. I do another double take—they're the couple I saw kissing in front of the cupid fountain earlier today. Strange. The boy is pale and sandy-haired, wearing a Daft Punk T-shirt. He has his arm around the girl, who is strikingly pretty, with dark-brown skin, brown hair in a short, fashionable pouf, and bright red lipstick. She is listening intently to Eloise. The vibe the three of them give off is less *popular clique* and more *artsy smart kids*. Also strange.

I'm hovering on the sidewalk, estimating how quickly I can flee, when it happens: Eloise turns her head. My blood runs cold. I see her see me. Her blue eyes widen and the color drains from her face. I think of that saying: *Like seeing a ghost*. I wonder if I should wave, or walk over, or pretend I haven't noticed her. But I can only stand still.

Eloise's face hardens, her eyes narrowing, the set of her mouth turning tight and cruel. She swivels her head and whispers something to the guy and girl. Then they turn their gazes toward me. The girl—Colette, maybe?—surveys me with curiosity in her dark eyes, but also a hint of hostility; obviously, she knows that I am an undesirable. The guy, though, looks sheepish, like he's been caught doing something wrong.

And then, I get it. I get what happened. Eloise and her friends purposefully avoided Café des Roses tonight, because Eloise knew *I* might go there. So here they are, at Café des Jumelles, dealing with the mild discomfort of seeing me anyway.

I fight down the lump in my throat. *Why does she hate me?* I think, meeting Eloise's frosty stare. *What did I ever do to her?* Then again, I did nothing to earn the disdain of Skye Oliveira and her crew back home, except maybe be bad at gym, or miss the memo with instructions on how to be a popular girl. Now, shifting from one foot to the other on the sidewalk, I feel suddenly self-conscious. Awkward. The opposite of how I felt seconds ago, all flushed and half hopeful.

In fact, Eloise's glare seems to undo whatever happened back in Café des Roses. *I am stupid*, I think. A babbling American girl with unkempt hair who wolfed down her *bouillabaisse* and blushed. Jacques just wanted some harmless fun. Or a good tip.

The lump in my throat isn't going anywhere, and worse, tears are starting to prick at my eyes. Swiftly, I look away from Eloise and her friends, lower my head, and keep walking, faster and faster, my flip-flops slapping the cobblestones. No doubt Eloise is laughing about me now, about how bizarre it was that I stared at them in silence.

The rest of the boulevard whips past me—the closed boutique, the *tabac* with its bright red sign, and finally, the cupid fountain. The stone cherubs seem to mock me with their bows and arrows. But I find myself walking right up to them and sitting down on the lip of the fountain.

I should be dashing into Dad's house to email Ruby, to ask her what to do about Eloise, and Jacques, and everything. Except Ruby is likely at the Fourth of July party, and not so available to advise me. Which makes me feel even more like crying.

The fountain burbles behind me. I sigh. I don't want to leave France, but I also want nothing more than the comforts of home. If only I could be in two places at once. If only I could split myself, like a croissant, into halves.

I tilt my head back to look at the starry sky, thinking of my front porch and Mom's theories about the universe. This sky, here in France, is the same sky we see in Hudsonville. The exact same sky! That seems as impossible as Mom's theories.

The night is getting cool, and I don't know what time it is. But I sit on the fountain's edge a while longer, staring up, as if searching the stars for answers.

PART TWO

Broken Homes

Monday, July 3, 9:43 p.m.

I answer the call.

I bring the phone to my ear and step to one side.

"Hello?" I venture. I can feel the boarding agent watching me.

There's no reply, only static.

My heart is still racing. *"Hello?"* I repeat, sort of regretting that I picked up.

"Summer?"

A man's voice cuts through the static. A familiar voice, but not one I expected to hear *here*, in the New York airport, seconds before my flight.

"Dad?" I cry, smiling. I move to stand next to one of the terminal's brown chairs, and adjust my tote bag so that it sits more securely on my shoulder. Is Dad calling to confirm when my plane lands? That seems too organized for him. "What is it?" I ask.

"Listen, my sweetheart"—Dad pauses, and there's more static—"I'm—not sure—good idea—come—right now." His voice goes in and out.

I press a finger to my other ear, feeling a beat of nervousness. "Dad, I can't hear you!" I practically yell. The boarding agent clears her throat. "What did you say?"

There's rustling on the line, and then the static lessens somewhat. "Is that better?" Dad asks. "I'm at my hotel in Berlin, and the reception here is terrible—"

"Berlin?" I repeat, confused.

"Miss? Excuse me? Miss?"

I turn around to see the boarding agent scowling at me.

"The plane has to push back now," she explains, her tone struggling between polite and annoyed. Annoyed is winning. "Are you still boarding?"

"Oh. Um," I reply, starting toward her. I suddenly notice that there are no other passengers at the gate. "Dad? Can you hang on a sec? I need to get on the plane."

Dad gives an anxious laugh. "Well, that's just it, honey. I don't think you should."

I stop walking. Ice settles in my stomach. "Don't think I should what?"

"Right now, miss," the boarding agent snaps.

I hear Dad sigh. "I don't think you should come, Summer." He's silent, and so am I, and then he begins speaking very rapidly. "I know it's quite literally at the last minute, and I truly apologize, sweetheart, but I've thought about this a lot and it's not really the best time for a visit, I mean, with me being in Berlin for work and all, and there are some other things that might come up, so, maybe next summer . . ."

Next summer? Not the best time? Dad's words don't make sense. My head feels like it's being squeezed in a vise, tighter and tighter, pain blooming behind my eyelids.

"I shouldn't come?" I whisper, my throat thick. "I shouldn't get on the plane?"

"I'm so sorry, sweetheart," Dad says softly. "It's simply not the right ti—"

He's interrupted by a mournful spiraling noise, and then silence. I pull my phone back from my ear and stare, dumbfounded, at the blank screen. Right. The battery died. I kind of feel like making that same noise and going blank myself.

"If you're not boarding, miss," I hear the agent say to me, "I have to close the door. Sorry." Her tone has moved beyond annoyed and into furious.

I look up at her, tears blurring my vision. "My dad just told me not to come," I tell her, as if she'll understand, as if she cares.

But I guess she takes that as a go-ahead. I watch disbelieving as she walks on her high heels over to the door that leads to the plane. *Click.* She shuts the door with a finality that makes me shudder.

My head is really hurting, and my legs are shaky, so I let myself fall into the brown chair behind me. I hug my tote bag to my chest, holding back a sob. *I don't think you should come,* Dad had said. His voice reverberates in my ears. Why would he do this, reverse everything, ruin everything? Couldn't he have told me sooner? All my planning and packing and excitement—gone in one phone call. Done. Poof. Magic.

And then Mom's voice starts ringing in my ears, like my parents have joined forces to form a discordant chorus. *I'm worried you'll be let down. You know how* he *is.* I shake my heavy head. I do know, now. I *have* been let down—well, more like dropped. Quickly, and from a great height.

Out the long windows, I see it: the sleek white plane, backing up slowly, moving away from the gate.

No! I want to scream. I want to jump up and knock over the boarding agent and tear open the door like I'm in an action movie. But I won't, of course. I can't. There'd be no point, even, in trying. The sob I'd been biting back escapes my lips.

The boarding agent speaks up, her tone kinder now. "There is another flight to Provence at the same time tomorrow," she tells me.

I glance over at her, blinking my watery eyes. "It doesn't matter," I say flatly. "I'm not going at all."

I feel a weariness wash over me. How depressing, how embarrassing, to now have to retrace my steps. To call Mom, who—my stomach tightens—will no doubt gloat on some level. To text Ruby that guess what, I'm back, I never left, and all the talk of gorgeous French boyfriends seems really stupid now. I sigh.

I should ask my new best friend, this boarding agent, if I can borrow her phone. I should figure out the logistics of leaving the airport, and getting home to Hudsonville.

But, for now, I do nothing. I remain frozen in the chair, as if staying here in the airport will keep me in limbo, away from reality. I stare blankly at the runway. The storm has stopped.

The night is serene: no thunder, no lightning, the sky a crystal-clear black.

I watch as the plane starts zooming, picking up speed, and I hold my breath as it lifts off the ground, its nose pointing skyward.

There it goes. There *I* go, or should have gone. I bite my lip. The plane climbs higher, taking with it my suitcase, and my hopes, and my dreams. And I am left behind, to face what will likely be my worst summer ever.

Tuesday, July 4, 2:22 p.m.

"The best!" I hear my mom exclaim from the kitchen. "You're the best, Lydia. I mean it. You saved us from a blueberry shortage!"

Huh? I think, opening my eyes. I am lying in my bed, canyoned between all my soft pillows. The shades in my room are drawn tight. My head aches and my cheeks have that taut, stiff quality they get after I've been crying for a while. Why is my mom shouting to my aunt about blueberries? Why am I here at home, and not in France?

As I sit up, the memories come rushing back to me. Answering Dad's call at the gate. Borrowing the boarding agent's cell phone to call Mom, who arrived almost immediately at the airport, all in a huff about Dad, but also looking kind of relieved. Mom driving me home while I sat beside her, tense, trying hard not to cry. Then running straight into my room, where I stayed up all night, alternately fuming and sobbing.

Yawning, I stand and stretch. When I glance at the mirror on the wall, I'm not surprised to see my hair puffing out in all directions, or my rumpled pajamas. What does surprise me is the large crack running the length of the mirror.

Oh, right. Another memory surfaces. Last night, I'd unpacked my tote bag ferociously, flinging items everywhere. I'd been about to fling my new camera from Aunt Lydia, but thankfully I'd caught myself. Instead, I'd yanked out my South of France guidebook and chucked it hard across my room. The book's spine had hit the mirror, fracturing the glass.

I'd winced, superstitious as ever. *Seven years of bad luck!* Then I'd reminded myself that I already had bad luck anyway. Bring on the broken mirrors.

Now I pad over to my window shades and snap them up, squinting against the bright afternoon sun. The light washes over my walls, landing on my favorite Renoir poster: two sisters, one in a white dress, the other in pink, singing at a piano. Today, something about the painting seems trite. Babyish.

My phone, on my messy desk, lets out a buzz. I grab my cell, thinking it might be Dad. But no, it's a text from Ruby, one of many that have come in since this morning.

Sheepishly, I remember the frantic volley of texts I'd sent my best friend last night, once my phone had charged. Texts like *Emergency!!!* and *Stuck in Hudsonville!* and *My dad=the enemy.* Ruby had clearly been sleeping, like a sane person, but her silence had only stoked my rage. My final text to her, sent around dawn, was something along the lines of *YOU SUCK*, and then I'd finally stumbled into bed and fallen into a dreamless sleep.

I'm relieved, as I scroll through Ruby's responses, that she's not mad at me for texting like a lunatic. Instead, she seems as despondent and concerned as I am regarding the state of my summer. *Have you called your dad back yet???* the most recent message reads. *Do it now!!! Convince him that you HAVE to go to France, no matter what!*

I nod down at the phone. *You're right as usual, O Wise BFF,* I text back. I should call Dad, to finish our conversation, to get more answers. And maybe—I feel a tiny spark of hope—I *can* convince him to let me come.

Sifting through the detritus on my desk, I find the printout of Dad's email with his phone numbers on it. Nervously, I dial his cell, only to get a hopeless beeping response. It seems my cell phone can receive international calls, but can't make them.

I open my door and creep out into the carpeted hallway. Our house is one level; from down the hall, I can hear Mom and Aunt Lydia talking in the kitchen. Mom says something that sounds like "Don't tell." Aunt Lydia murmurs a response, and then I distinctly hear my aunt say, "Why not give it a chance? It's been long enough!"

Why not give *what* a chance? What are they discussing? I strain to hear more but the water in the sink starts running. Oh, well. I'm just glad Mom is otherwise occupied. I turn and tiptoe into her sunny bedroom, where our landline phone sits on her nightstand.

My orange tabby cat, Ro, is curled up on Mom's bed, and he mewls at me. I ignore him. Ro is technically my pet—a sympathy gift from Mom when she and Dad split up—but he seems to prefer Mom. She even named him; his full name is Schrödinger, after a famous physicist who I guess had some theory involving a cat. I'd wanted to name him Crookshanks, after the cat in Harry Potter, but Ro had hissed at me whenever I called him that, so I'd stopped.

I sit on the edge of Mom's bed, a safe distance from Ro, and pick up the phone with sweaty palms. I dial Dad's cell number again, and this time, the call goes straight to voice mail. The recording is Dad saying something unintelligible in French, which intimidates me, so I hang up. Then, with a shrug, I figure I'll try his house. It could be he's back from Berlin, and ready for me to come after all.

The house line rings once. Twice.

"*Allô?*"

A girl has answered, her voice light and melodic.

I clear my throat, nervous, trying to recall some scrap of French. "Um, *bonjour. Parlez-vous,* um, *anglais?*" I ask haltingly.

"Yes, I speak English," the girl replies, with hardly any accent. She sounds a little out of breath, like she's been rushing. "Who is calling?" she asks.

"Um, Summer," I reply. "Summer Everett. Ned Everett's daughter?" I bite my lip. "I was wondering if I could speak to my dad. I think this is his house?"

There's silence on the other end, and I worry I've lost the connection.

"He is in Berlin," the girl then says, her tone clipped.

"Oh. Still, huh?" I let out a sad laugh. The girl doesn't respond. "Are you, like, his assistant?" I add. "I was supposed to be his sort-of assistant this summer, but . . ."

"I am not," the girl replies shortly. "I have to go; I am late to meet friends."

I look at Mom's clock, calculating the hour in France. Almost nine at night. I wonder who this girl is. One of those artist friends Dad mentioned? She sounds my age.

I start to ask her if I can leave a message when I hear the dial tone. She's hung up.

Well, that was helpful. I roll my eyes and plunk the phone down. I gaze forlornly at the familiar framed poster on Mom's wall, a typed quote on a plain white background: *You cannot step into the same river twice. —Heraclitus*. I know it means something philosophical, but I don't quite know what.

Ro, perhaps sensing my glumness, pads across the bed toward me. I start to stroke his head but he arches his back, meows, and nips at my fingers. Rejected, again.

I get up and crumple Dad's email in my hand. I almost toss it into Mom's wastebasket but then decide not to. I pop back into my room and drop the useless piece of paper onto my desk. Then I shuffle along the hall into the kitchen.

Mom and Aunt Lydia are standing at the counter, their backs to me, still chattering away. Mom is slicing bananas and Aunt Lydia is pouring ice into our blender.

"What are you guys doing?" I demand, sounding even surlier than I'd intended.

Two identical faces turn in my direction. Actually, Mom and Aunt Lydia look very different to me: Mom wears glasses, Aunt Lydia doesn't. Mom's straight brown hair comes neatly to her chin, while Aunt Lydia's is up in a crazy twist anchored by chopsticks. Mom has on a pink collared blouse, Aunt Lydia a vintage Bob Dylan T-shirt.

I've always thought it would be amazing to have a twin—a built-in best friend/sister/clone. Mom and Lydia even work together, at Hudsonville College. It's funny to think of them there on campus, Mom teaching philosophy, Aunt Lydia photography. The two matching Professor Shapiros.

And they *are* pretty close. I remember how, after the divorce, Aunt Lydia came over almost every day, bringing bags of chips and her homemade guacamole ("healing food," she called it) and staying up late with Mom, the two of them whispering in the living room while I tried to sleep down the hall. Lately, though, she and Mom do more of their own things: Mom's idea of a good time is listening to classical music and reading a book on Plato, while Aunt Lydia takes impromptu road trips to see Arcade Fire and goes on dates with guys who have tattooed arms and hipster glasses. As a result, I don't really see my aunt as much as I'd like.

Now she and Mom both smile at me.

"Morning, sleepyhead!" Mom singsongs, her brown eyes bright. "We're making red, white, and blueberry smoothies, of course. I ran out of blueberries, so your aunt brought some over! Crisis averted."

Oh. It's the Fourth of July. I feel something—not happiness, but some form of non-sadness—stir in my chest. I love this holiday, the one that marks two weeks until my birthday, that tastes of Mom's strawberry, banana, and blueberry smoothies, that smells like chargrilled hamburgers, that feels festive and hot and carefree. Maybe I should thank Dad for allowing me to spend Independence Day in America this summer.

"Yep, I'm a hero," Aunt Lydia says, smirking at Mom and then at me.

I smirk back at my aunt. Mom gives a mock sniff and turns back to her bananas.

"So, kiddo," Aunt Lydia adds, her tone light as she eyes me thoughtfully from across the kitchen. "I heard you had a change of summer plans."

My heart squeezes. "You could say that," I mutter. I glance at Mom. I consider telling her about my thwarted phone calls to Dad just now. But she would only get agitated, and she seems more cheerful than she has in months. Even our fight from yesterday appears to have been forgotten, forgiven. Maybe because, in a way, Mom won.

"Oh, I spoke to the airline!" Mom pipes up, all chipper, looking at me over her shoulder. "They said your suitcase should arrive here within three to five business days."

"Great," I reply, trudging over to the pantry. I grab a box of Cheerios and scoop out a handful to eat. Mom hates it when I don't pour cereal into a bowl with milk like a civilized person (her words), but she doesn't chide me today. "My suitcase has seen more of the world than I have," I mumble, my mouth full.

I slump down at the linoleum table and stare out the window at the flat streets of our neighborhood: the other one-story houses with their squares of lawn and stuttering sprinklers. Later, I know, Ruby and I will go to Pine Park to see the fireworks. But what will I do the day after? I think of a line from the Shakespeare play we read in English class this year: *Tomorrow, and tomorrow, and tomorrow, creeps in this petty pace—*

"So, niece of mine," Aunt Lydia speaks up, rinsing a container of strawberries in the sink, "I have a proposition for you."

"Lydia," Mom says, shaking her head.

"Lucy, stop," Lydia tells Mom. "We discussed this."

I sit up straighter, intrigue poking through my fog of self-pity. I recall the snippets of their mysterious conversation that I overheard before.

"What?" I ask.

Aunt Lydia turns around, wiping her hands on a dish towel. "Did you know I'm teaching a photography course on campus this summer?" she asks me.

I nod. "Yeah, like Mom."

"Well," Aunt Lydia says, adjusting a chopstick in her hair, "your mother's hoity-toity philosophy course is only for college students. But *anyone* can take my class." She waggles her eyebrows at me.

I look back at her, not getting it.

Aunt Lydia laughs and throws her hands in the air. "Come on, Summer! Do you want to take my class or not?"

"Wait. *Me?*" I blink at her, startled. She nods and laughs again while Mom noisily opens the refrigerator. "But—I don't even know anything about photography," I protest.

"That's why it's a *class*," Aunt Lydia points out. "You *learn*. Besides," she adds, her brown eyes sparkling, "don't think I haven't noticed that, your whole life, you've been taking pictures. You might know more than you realize."

I feel my cheeks warm up and I shrug. "I take pictures like everyone else. Nothing artsy." But it's true that I was the first among my friends to join Instagram, and I've been known to spend whole days following Ro around with my phone to get shots of him napping. And I *had* been excited to use my new professional-y camera in France . . .

"You already have the camera for it," Aunt Lydia adds, as if she's read my mind. She plucks a perfectly ripe red strawberry from the container and holds it up to the light. "I lend those kinds of Nikons to my students, you know."

"Really?" I say. I glance over at Mom, who's rummaging around in the fridge. My intrigue is growing. Last summer, my friend Alice went to Vermont for a History of Music course, and it had sounded really cool.

"The class meets every day, in the morning," Aunt Lydia continues, nibbling on the strawberry, "and three times a week, in the afternoon, there are labs—that's where we do darkroom stuff, or Photoshop. We'll probably also take a field trip or two."

I watch as Mom starts silently spooning yogurt into the blender. "Mom, you'd let me do this?" I ask in surprise. Maybe it's like my uncivilized cereal eating, I think; Mom will bend her rules this time, because she feels sorry for me.

Mom sighs and turns around, spoon in hand. "Look, if you really want to. But I'd prefer that you get a summer job—"

"*Lucy*," Aunt Lydia cuts in, rolling her eyes. "I told you I'd waive the class fee."

"It's not about the money," Mom snaps. "It's about being responsible and . . ."

As the two of them bicker, I drum my fingers on the table. I'm torn. Part of me agrees with Mom—a summer job is the responsible thing to do. It's what I always do. I could even ask Ruby if there are openings at the coffee shop; it would be fun to work side by side, like we did two summers ago at the movie theater.

But a bigger part of me can't shake the feeling that taking Aunt Lydia's class would be refreshing and different. Something new.

And the biggest part of me still hopes—wishes—that maybe France isn't totally out of the question.

Mom and Aunt Lydia continue to argue and I stand up abruptly, pushing the chair back. "I'm going to Ruby's," I announce. Ruby's is my refuge, the place I want to be whenever I'm wrestling with a decision, which is almost always.

Mom glances away from Aunt Lydia and nods at me. "Okay," she says mildly. "Have fun at Pine Park. I'll put a leftover smoothie in the fridge for you."

I realize that, for Mom, everything has gone happily back to status quo. It's summer, I'm home, I'll be hanging out with Ruby.

Ideally getting a job. It's as if the promise of visiting Dad was all a dream.

"Hey, kiddo, think about my offer," Aunt Lydia tells me before I leave the kitchen. "But think fast. The first day of class is Monday."

● ● ●

I ride my bike to Ruby's, sweat making my T-shirt stick to my back. Although it's humid, like yesterday, the sky is blue, shot through with wispy clouds. *Did last night's thunderstorm even happen?* I wonder as I pedal up the incline of Deer Hill.

I know this route so well I could take it blindfolded. I pass by my high school, which looks as abandoned as a haunted house. The elementary school, on the next block, is equally, eerily empty, its playground swings creaking in the hot breeze. Ruby and I met on that playground when we were six.

As I reach the crest of the hill, I catch a glimpse of the Hudson River down below. Along the banks of the river sits our town: a strip consisting of one bank, one bookstore, one coffee shop, one restaurant, one pharmacy . . . For any real shopping, any real "excitement," there's the mall: Exit 2 off the highway.

I round the corner onto Ruby's street, Briar Lane, and park in front of her small apartment building. I gather my hair off my sweaty neck and up into a ponytail, and I prop my sunglasses on top of my head. Then I walk up to the entrance, buzz Ruby's apartment, and shout "Me!" into the intercom when Ruby's mom asks who it is.

Ruby's parents got divorced when she was nine, so when my parents followed suit two years later, Ruby was like my guide through Divorced Kid Land. In some ways, she had it worse than me, because she, her mother, and little brother had to move out of their big house into a cramped apartment. In other ways, she had it better, because her dad is only in Connecticut, instead of an ocean away, and he's always giving her and her brother expensive electronics and taking them on vacations to the Caribbean.

"We both come from broken homes, Summer," Ruby once told me during a sleepover at my house, her eyes wide and dramatic. "That's why we're so close."

Though I'd liked the idea of Ruby and I being bonded by life's difficulties, I didn't like the notion of a "broken home." Yes, Dad had left, but that didn't mean my house was crumbling or cracked.

"'A house divided cannot stand,'" I had quoted back to Ruby in the darkness; we'd just been studying Abraham Lincoln in school. She'd burst out laughing and thrown a pillow at my head, calling me a dork.

When I get off the elevator, Ruby's mom is standing in the doorway to their apartment, taking me in with her big, Ruby-identical eyes.

"Precious!" Mrs. Singh exclaims in her lilting Indian accent, giving me a peck on the cheek. "Why are you here? Didn't you leave yesterday?"

I feel a sting. I should prepare myself for people asking me this question this summer. Still, I imagined that Ruby would have looped in her mom by now.

"Ruby didn't tell you?" I ask.

Mrs. Singh flaps a dismissive hand, her glass bangles clanking. "Ruby doesn't tell me anything. She's been holed up in her room with Alice all day, getting ready."

I feel a funny twinge in my stomach. "Getting ready for what?" I blurt. And why would Ruby have Alice over without inviting me, too? Alice is our friend, but she and Ruby aren't really close enough to warrant one-on-one time. Usually, when we hang out with Alice, it's as a foursome: me, Ruby, Alice, and Alice's best friend, Inez Herrara, who is away in California at dance camp this summer.

"Forgive me, dear, but I was on my way out," Mrs. Singh is saying, stepping around me. She's wearing her scrubs and sneakers, and holding her purse. Ruby's mom is a nurse at the hospital, and is constantly working. "It's bound to be a busy day of firecracker injuries." She sighs, heading onto the elevator. "See you later?"

I wave distractedly and enter the apartment, kicking off my flip-flops in the foyer, per Singh house rules. I pass through the living room, where Ruby's brother, Raj, is watching *Oklahoma!* on TV. Most eleven-year-old boys are addicted to their video games, but Raj is always glued to some musical. He's kind of awesome.

I'm oddly nervous as I knock on Ruby's bedroom door. Ordinarily, I'd just barge in, but something doesn't feel ordinary at the moment.

"I thought you were leaving, Mom," Ruby grumbles, tearing the door open. Then she blinks at me. "Summer!"

I blink back at her. She's wearing a cute new striped tank dress, winged eyeliner, and her gold *R* pendant necklace. Over her shoulder, I see that her usually pin-neat room is a mess: Lipsticks, mascara tubes, earrings, and bracelets are scattered across her dresser, and clothes are puddled on her purple rug. Alice is dancing on the rug, eyes closed, a Taylor Swift song floating out of the speakers on Ruby's desk. A sense of anticipation hovers in the air, along with the scent of Ruby's flowery perfume.

"Hi," I say, giving Ruby a quick hug. "What's going on?" Why is this *weird*?

"Have you talked to your dad yet?" Ruby asks, hugging me back.

"*Summer?*" Alice cries, her eyes popping open. She stops dancing and flits over to me. Alice reminds me of a wood sprite, tiny and delicate. She always wears her white-blond hair up, with little braids encircling the crown of her head. Today she has on a long-sleeved floral minidress, and her pale lashes are darkened with mascara. "Aren't you supposed to be in France?" she breathes.

There's that sting again. "Long story," I reply. I glance at Ruby in confusion. "I guess you didn't exactly broadcast my news, bestie?"

Ruby gives a short laugh, her cheeks looking pink. Or maybe she's just wearing blush. "I *assumed* you'd already talked to your dad and fixed everything," she explains, her tone a little defensive. "Have you?" she adds, raising her eyebrows.

I shake my head. "I tried. I couldn't reach him. I spoke to some rude French girl who's staying at the house. I don't—I don't know how great my chances are," I admit. Saying this out loud, especially to Ruby, makes my throat tighten. She frowns at me.

"Well, you're here now!" Alice bubbles, taking my wrist and tugging me into the room. "Which means you can come with us!"

"Come with you *where*?" I demand, looking at Ruby. A sensation like suspicion crawls up my spine.

Ruby walks over to her dresser and begins sorting through her jewelry. "So, I didn't tell you because I knew you wouldn't want to go, and you were headed to France, which is obviously more exciting . . ." She's talking fast, kind of like Dad did on the phone last night. My stomach turns cold. "But Skye is hosting this barbecue at her house; it starts pretty soon, and she has a great view from her yard to see the fireworks—"

"Hold on," I interrupt, disbelief making me dizzy. "Skye? Skye *Oliveira*? The girl you once said was the essence of evil distilled into human form?"

"I said that?" Ruby half laughs, sliding on a tall stack of woven bracelets. My own bracelets feel snug on my wrists. "I mean, yeah, she can be brusque sometimes . . ."

"I think she wasn't hugged enough as a child," Alice announces, folding herself into a lotus position on Ruby's bed.

"I wish she'd been hugged by a boa constrictor," I mutter.

My head swimming, I plop down beside Alice on Ruby's paisley bedspread. I don't get it. Skye has been our Enemy Number One ever since she arrived in Hudsonville two years ago, all super-long hair, sports prowess, and snide comments. She'd quickly amassed an army of clones to prey on the weak and defenseless. Ruby, Alice, Inez, and I were never direct targets, but we were still treated with casual scorn. "*Ewww, Sum-mer!*" Skye and her cronies would chorus when I inevitably failed to serve the volleyball over the net in gym class. Freshman year, just for kicks, Skye stuck out a foot and tripped Ruby in the hall, sending Ruby's textbook flying. Ruby, cool as ever, had simply retrieved the book and laughed, "Your soccer skills are kinda weak, Skye."

And now Ruby wants to go to her *party*?

"I thought it might be fun," Ruby explains. She meets my gaze in the mirror above her dresser. "We always do the same thing, year after year—"

"Pine Park!" I interrupt, my throat tightening even more. "We love Pine Park. Don't you love Pine Park?" I ask Alice, trying for an ally.

"I love being in nature," Alice replies dreamily, unfolding her legs from her yoga pose and slipping off the bed. She drifts over to stand next to Ruby at the dresser, idly picking up a lipstick. "But the party will be in Skye's backyard, so . . ."

I struggle not to roll my eyes. "How did you guys even get invited?"

Ruby fiddles with her necklace, zipping the *R* pendant up and down its chain. "Skye stopped in at the coffee shop the other day and mentioned it," she explains lightly.

"Since when do you and Skye have little chitchats?" I ask, hearing the accusation in my tone. What I really want to ask is: *Since when do you and I not tell each other everything?*

"Ooh," Ruby says, not answering me. She grabs her cell phone off her dresser. "Let's take pictures before we go!"

"You too, Summer!" Alice calls, waving me over. She poses next to Ruby, holding the lipstick to her mouth, the two of them grinning up into Ruby's phone.

I feel like I'm moving through molasses as I drag myself off Ruby's bed and go join them. I stand on Ruby's other side, smiling in a way that I know looks hollow. Ruby snaps shot after shot, her cheek pressed against Alice's, and I can't help thinking that I don't belong in this picture. It's like I've been cut and pasted in—a bad Photoshop job.

Satisfied, Ruby lowers her phone and begins posting to Instagram, and Alice returns to the mirror to check her lipstick. I turn away and swallow the tears that threaten. How annoying. I thought I'd gotten all my crying done last night. I study the colorful tapestries that hang on the walls; Ruby bought them on a trip to India years ago. Her room has always had an international, sort of glamorous vibe, which was why coming here always felt like an escape. It was—is—my second home.

"Hey, babe." Ruby touches my arm and I stiffen. "You okay?" she asks softly.

"Tired," I lie, swiping at my eyes. "I don't think I'm up for any parties," I add in a rush, which *is* true. I cannot *begin* to imagine traipsing over to Skye's house now, carrying with me the weight of the canceled trip, and this sudden tension—is it tension?— with Ruby. Nodding and smiling at all the kids from school I don't like, feeling even more awkward than usual. *No thanks.*

"Are you sure?" Ruby asks, but she sounds distracted, looking down at her phone to see if the new photo has gotten any "likes" yet.

"I'm not even dressed for it," I say, which is also true. I'm wearing my ratty YMCA Day Camp T-shirt and old denim shorts. Everything nice I own is in my suitcase, supposedly winging its way back to me within three to five business days.

"Borrow something from Ruby!" Alice protests. But I'm already shaking my head, telling them that they should text me all the details, even though I don't really want to know anything. I hug Alice good-bye, then turn to Ruby.

"Love you times two," we say at the same time, and we both start laughing. Ruby orders me to keep her posted on Operation Convince Dad, and I promise I will. For a second, things seem totally normal, like I was imagining the strangeness earlier.

Then I leave the room, listening to Ruby and Alice talk as they continue to primp for the party—*Skye Oliveira's* party. And I realize that things couldn't get stranger.

Outside, the afternoon sun makes me squint, and I pull my sunglasses down over my eyes. I'm tempted to go back home and curl up in my room. Hide. Mom teases me for believing in astrology, but my sign is Cancer, and I *can* be crablike; I retreat into my shell when the world gets overwhelming.

But, as I climb on my bike, I feel sort of restless. Antsy. So I coast down Deer Hill. The delicious, mesquite-y scent of barbecue drifts out from backyards. A group of little kids waving red, white, and blue sparklers dart across the street. I have to brake abruptly and I yell at them to be careful, like some old lady. They ignore me.

I pedal onward, passing houses and sidewalks that I know by heart. I pass the hospital where Ruby's mom works, where I was born. Where, at age eight, I went to get stitches when I fell off my bike. Dad had squeezed my hand while the ER doctor sewed up my knee. It's weird to think of Dad being around back then. Though he wasn't around *that* much. He was already traveling to Europe a bunch, entering art shows, trying to get his paintings sold. Maybe things between my parents were starting to break well before the divorce, the way the ground has a fault in it before there's an actual earthquake.

Reaching the bottom of the hill, I turn onto Greene Street, our main street. It's an ill-suited name, I think, because the prevailing color of the town is gray. Gray pavement, gray streetlamps, gray-trunked elm trees. Even the Hudson River, which runs alongside the street, is always a choppy gray, regardless of any blue-sky weather.

Today the town is dead, of course—well, deader than usual. No one is out walking, and I only have to contend with a couple of snail-paced cars. Everything is closed: Get Well Pharmacy,

Hudsonville Bank, Orologio's Fine Italian Dining, Miss Cheryl's Antiques, PJ's Pub, Szechuan Kitchen. In the distance, I hear the lonely whistle of the Metro-North train.

I pedal past Between the Lines, the bookstore where I worked last summer. It seems the owner, Mr. Fitzsimmons, has let his hoarding tendencies get the best of him: The books are stacked so high that I can't see through the window. Next to the bookstore is Better Latte Than Never, the coffee shop where Ruby works. I realize I forgot to ask her about job openings there. But do I still want to work with Ruby? I pluck at the woven bracelets on my wrist. Maybe I *should* take Aunt Lydia's class instead.

I feel a tingle in my stomach that could be excitement. Or is it hunger? I haven't eaten anything besides that handful of Cheerios. And I know where I can get some good food now.

There's a stubbornness stirring in me as I pedal to the end of Greene Street, make two sharp lefts, and arrive at my destination: Pine Park. Who cares what Ruby said? *This* is the place to be today. I defiantly lean my bike against the fence, tuck my sunglasses into my back pocket, and walk onto the wide expanse of grass.

Families are spreading their blankets on the lawn, securing spots for the fireworks display later. I breathe in the crisp scent of pine that mingles with the fried-food, carnival-y aromas drifting over from the vendors who circle the perimeter.

I see Mr. Fitzsimmons, my white-haired old bookstore boss, settling himself into a lawn chair with a big can of bug spray. I also spot Raj, Ruby's brother, tossing around a Frisbee with some friends; it's funny to think I just saw him at Ruby's—when? How long ago was that? I veer to avoid him; I don't want Ruby knowing I was here.

On the band-shell stage at the front of the park, the mayor of Hudsonville is adjusting the microphone stand. Mayor Rosen-Tyson is an elegant blond woman who wears fashionable tailored suits, and who also happens to be Hugh Tyson's mother. The tall, handsome African American man standing next to her is Hugh's father, and also her chief of staff. Most years, Hugh is here, too—either onstage with his parents, or sitting off to the side in the grass, writing in his Moleskine notebook. I've never interacted with Hugh at the Pine Park fireworks, of course; I'll always just death-grip Ruby's arm and observe him from a safe distance.

This year, I know Hugh isn't here; last night, in between texting Ruby, I'd scrolled through Instagram. Hugh had posted a photo of the Empire State Building, and his caption said that he was in New York City visiting his cousin. Social media is a very handy tool for gathering intel on your crush without ever having to speak to the person.

I head over to the vendors, bypassing the guys selling glow sticks and miniature American flags, all the trinkets Ruby and I would buy and then discard by night's end. I stop at one of the food stalls and order a hot dog with the works—mustard, ketchup, relish, and fried onions, piled high. I also get a large Coke and then, going for broke, a vanilla-chocolate-twist ice-cream cone. When I pay, I notice the euros in my wallet and feel a pang. What a waste.

Balancing everything in my hands, I carry my feast over to a bench. I scarf down the hot dog first, enjoying the familiar salty taste. I remember how one year Ruby and I had two hot dogs each, plus corn on the cob, ice cream, and cotton candy, and were still surprised when our stomachs ached all night. I smile and sip my Coke, full of nostalgia. I'm starting on my ice cream when I see them—two little blond girls, maybe sisters, turning barefoot cartwheels between the pine trees.

I watch as the girls flash their grass-stained soles, and then land on their butts, laughing. One of them pops up and races toward the vendors, shouting something about corn dogs, and the other girl follows in her wake, still laughing.

I try to swallow the lump in my throat with a gulp of Coke, but it doesn't work. Ruby and I were those girls. *Were.* Past tense. Time has passed, but I'm still stuck in Pine Park. Suddenly, I feel sort of gross and sad, an almost-sixteen-year-old, my hands sticky with melting ice cream, my mouth stained with ketchup, like a child. No one else at the park is my age. It's all kids like Raj, or old folks like Mr. Fitzsimmons. Ruby understood it before I did: We don't belong here anymore.

"Happy Fourth of July, Hudsonville!" Mayor Rosen-Tyson is announcing from the stage as I stand up. "My husband and I are so happy to welcome you . . ."

I throw what's left of my cone into a garbage can, along with my Coke. Then I maneuver past the crowds streaming into the park, and get back on my bike, wondering where I *do* belong.

A dark kind of curiosity drives me forward, and I find myself pedaling over to Argyle Road. Argyle is known as the "fancy" street in town because all the big, stately, multistory homes are here. This evening, the houses look like white elephants, sleeping under a sky that's turning a faint orange.

It's easy to spot Skye Oliveira's elephant; silver balloons are tied to her mailbox, and loud music pours from the backyard. I recognize a couple of kids from school walking up the pebbly driveway.

Hugh Tyson's house is across from Skye's. In Hudsonville, everyone pretty much knows where everyone else lives. (I also *may* have dabbled in some light stalking by casually bicycling past Hugh's house on weekends.) Even if Hugh weren't in New York City now, he wouldn't be at Skye's party; he's not remotely cool enough. Then again, Ruby and Alice are going, so anything's possible in this topsy-turvy world.

I slowly get off my bike. What exactly is my plan here? I'm hot and sweaty, my legs are sore from biking around all day, and I can feel curls escaping my ponytail. I must look dazzling. There's no way I can simply stroll into the backyard—no way that I want to. I'm not that courageous, or stupid. Still, I want— *something.*

I guess I want to look. To see. Maybe, to understand.

I try to noiselessly push my bike along the pebbly driveway. I walk on my tiptoes, feeling like a burglar, like I'm about to be caught at any minute. I make it around the house and stand hidden in the shadow of two large hedges. Holding my breath, I peer into the backyard.

I needn't have worried; no one looks my way. Everyone is too absorbed in this fabulous-seeming party to consider that there might be a random girl lurking on the outskirts, watching.

A live band is playing, and a professional-looking chef is grilling steaks and shrimp. Girls in shiny, tight dresses step carefully across the manicured lawn in their high-heeled sandals, clutching the arms of boys with gelled hair. A long table boasts a red, white, and blue cupcake tower; a red, white, and blue macaron tower; and a bowl of chips, which I guess would be hard to put into a tower shape.

For a moment, I *do* understand why Ruby and Alice wanted to come here. Why anyone would want to come. It's like peeking into a wonderland, an alternate version of life where everyone is pretty and polished and dines on steak instead of hot dogs.

I notice Skye Oliveira posing for a picture with a couple of her clones. The girls all stand identically: hand on one hip; head tilted to one side; long, wavy hair spilling over one shoulder; body angled slightly; smile not too big. Creepy. I almost want to take out my phone and snap a picture of that picture. I think of Aunt Lydia's photography class again, and I half smile to myself.

The photo shoot breaks up, and Skye turns to flirt with a handsome dark-haired boy I recognize as Genji Tanaka, who will be a senior next year. I glance away from them, disinterested, and my gaze lands on Alice. She is watching the band, swaying to the music, and eating a blue cupcake. Alice is so mellow that she can adjust anywhere; she looks perfectly at ease. My stomach twists. She really did it: She came—which means that Ruby did, too. Right?

I begin to search the crowd, my heart in my throat. And then I see her—striped tank dress, gold *R* necklace. My best friend is standing at the far end of the yard, by the drinks table. The tall guy next to her—gelled blond hair, blue button-down shirt—is ladling punch out of a bowl and into two cups, one of which he hands to Ruby. The guy is our classmate, Austin Wheeler, he of the basketball stardom and vacant eyes. I'd thought Austin was dating one of Skye's clones, but I'm not really caught up on the love lives of those in the upper social echelons.

I watch as Ruby laughs at something Austin says, her eyes sparkling. Austin laughs, too. I feel my chest constrict. I know that Ruby has long thought that Austin is cute—everyone thinks that; his cuteness is an objective fact. But does she *like* him? She leans closer to him, putting a hand on his arm. I remember how she told me she wanted this to be the summer she fell in love. Was she thinking of Austin already? Why did she keep that from me? What else is she keeping from me?

I'm suddenly chilled in the hot evening air. I'm used to seeing Ruby flirt with boys, and I'm used to feeling envious of her ability to do so. That's not what has me rattled now. It's that Ruby—and Alice—seem so at home at this exclusive party, among these exclusive people. And what is wrong with *me*, that I don't want this—this popularity and privilege?

It hits me then, like it did in Pine Park: I don't belong here, either.

The sensation that I'm going to cry—*again*—sweeps over me. I hurriedly back away, clutching the bike handlebars, my flip-flops crunching over the pebbles. I bump into some arriving guests—more gelled-hair boys, more tight-dress girls—but I don't apologize, I just jump on my bike and start pedaling as hard as I can.

A couple of tears slip down my cheeks and I make a blurry turn onto College Avenue—not the direction I'd planned to go, but close to home, at least. My mind is jumbled, my thoughts leaping from Ruby to Austin to Pine Park to Hugh Tyson to Dad to, of all things, that cold French girl on the phone.

The gray stone gate of Hudsonville College looms to my left, and I pause in the middle of the street. I am all alone: Everyone is at a barbecue, on a porch, on a rooftop, waiting for the fireworks to start. The sun hasn't set yet, but the sky is darkening. I squint through the gate at the quiet campus. Maybe it's a sign that I happened to bike this way, at this moment. Maybe it means I should try something new after all.

I've stopped crying by the time I reach Rip Van Winkle Road—my street. I toss my bike down on our tiny lawn and run up to my house, out of breath. Mom and Aunt Lydia are sitting on our porch, sipping their smoothies from plastic cups.

"Summer! Why aren't you at the park?" Mom cries.

I shake my head, not in the mood to explain, and I collapse next to her on the cushioned bench. This is where we sit on those nights when we study the stars and talk about crazy theories like parallel worlds.

Aunt Lydia, on Mom's other side, leans over and hands me her cup. "The view's better here than in Pine Park," she scoffs, and I smile at her gratefully.

I take a long sip of the cold, thick drink, and then I say, "Aunt Lydia?"

"Yeah, kiddo?" she asks, her face tilted up, even though nothing is happening yet. The sky is a calm navy blue. Funny to think it will soon be lit up, transformed.

"I think—if I still can—I'd like to take your photography class," I say.

"Really?" Mom asks, glancing at me, surprised. I'm a little surprised myself.

"Of course you can," Aunt Lydia says. She shoots me a grin. "Monday morning, nine o'clock, Whitman Hall. Don't be late." Then she looks back up at the sky. I do, too, and after a moment, so does Mom.

The three of us sit there in silence, gazing up, holding our breaths. Waiting for the sky to explode with colors, for everything to change.

Monday, July 10, 8:48 a.m.

I'm early.

I walk under the arched gate of Hudsonville College, realizing that I underestimated how quickly I could walk from my house to the campus. Now, I have extra time to fill before class.

I slow my pace and wave to Max, the sweet security guard who sits in the booth behind the gate. I've known Max Siegal since I was a kid. Everyone knows Max. He's a campus fixture—always in his blue uniform with his paper cup of coffee, his shaved head and trim brown beard unchanged over the years.

"Good morning, Summer!" Max calls, his brown eyes twinkling. "You're here for your aunt's photography class?"

I nod, tugging on the straps of my bookbag. I feel the weight of my Nikon camera and my notebook inside. "How'd you know?" I ask, wondering if I'm giving off a collegiate-type vibe. I'm wearing jeans and flip-flops and the gray Hudsonville Hawks hoodie Mom bought me from the campus store last year.

Max shrugs, sipping his coffee. "Lucy—your mom—told me. It sounds pretty great." Something flickers across his face—an expression that seems to suggest that he wants to say more, but he doesn't. Suddenly, I wonder if he knows about France; he and Mom are friendly, so maybe she confided in him. I bristle a little.

A car is pulling in behind me, beeping its horn, so I nod to Max and stroll forward onto the campus.

I head for Whitman Hall, flip-flopping along the flagstone path. The morning is cool and crisp, like July is flirting with September. The rolling green grounds and redbrick buildings of the campus look bright and scrubbed clean.

I pass through the quad, where a few early-riser students are sprawled out in the grass, reading and texting. Others are stepping out of the dorms and yawning, tennis rackets in hand. The college remains pretty active over the summer, with courses and sports programs.

I pause in front of Sagan Hall, which houses Mom's office. Mom won't be coming onto campus until later this afternoon. But I remember visiting her at her office when I was little. I used to daydream about attending Hudsonville College myself. Now the campus feels small and predictable to me; I want to go someplace far away—like the Sorbonne, in Paris, so I can see Dad more often.

Although maybe it's time to rethink that plan.

My phone buzzes in the pocket of my hoodie. I take it out to see that the minutes have zipped by—it's now almost nine o'clock—and that I have a new text from Ruby.

Good luck in class! she's written. *Headed to Better Latte now.*

Austin is meeting me here for my lunch break!!!! Eeep! PS Any progress on Operation Convince Dad??

I frown and keep walking. I've felt unsettled about my best friend ever since the Fourth of July. But we've both been acting as if nothing is out of whack. Ruby texted me the morning after Skye's party, saying it had been amazing—there'd been a band, and a chef, and she'd talked to Austin Wheeler all night. I'd played along, writing *Wow!* as if I hadn't witnessed all that with my own two eyeballs. Then, when Ruby and I went to the movies with Alice on Thursday night, none of us spoke of the party at all.

My fingers hover over my phone as I climb the stone steps of Whitman Hall. I want to write back and ask Ruby: *What is happening? Are you really going to date Austin Wheeler? Are you popular now?* But I don't. Instead, I write, *Good luck to you, too!* Then I add, *No Dad progress*, which at least is true.

Dad had emailed me the night of the Fourth. He'd apologized profusely for canceling on me "like that," but said he was still very busy in Berlin, and intended to speak to me very soon, sweetheart. I'd deleted the message.

I pull open Whitman's heavy wooden door and hurry down the hallway. When I reach classroom 122, I draw in a deep breath.

I don't feel ready to meet a whole class of new students. I didn't interact with another human being all weekend, except for Mom. Ruby had been off visiting her dad in Connecticut, so I'd retreated to my room, reading the South of France guidebook.

The second best thing to being there! the book's subtitle promised. But the glossy photos of sunflower fields and cobblestones, and the descriptions of quaint cafés, seemed like the number one worst thing for me to see in my state.

Trying to quell thoughts of France, as well as my anxiety, I walk into the classroom. It smells, not unpleasantly, like musty old books. The desks and floors are all dark wood, and big windows face the campus. It feels so different from the fluorescent-lit, carpeted classrooms of my high school. I hope I'm not in over my head.

Aunt Lydia isn't here yet. Some students are still trickling in behind me, while others are taking their seats. There are a bunch of college kids, a few people around Mom's age, and I recognize a couple of elderly women who frequented the bookstore last summer.

And then—I do a double take. There, in the last row, is an even more familiar face: pale complexion, short scarlet hair, slash of black lipstick. It's Wren D'Amico, who is in my grade. I hadn't expected to see anyone from my school here.

I give Wren a feeble wave, and she studies me warily from beneath her thick bangs. Wren is flagrantly, aggressively weird. She'll scrawl song lyrics on her arm with a Sharpie, and blurt out non sequiturs about time travel in the middle of math class. Wren herself seems like she was beamed in from another time (except for the hair dye); she wears floor-length skirts and dresses, is always reading some nineteenth-century novel, and she doesn't have a single social media account or, rumor has it, a cell phone.

Skye and her clones *love* making fun of Wren. When she got the flu last spring, they dubbed her "Typhoid Wrenny," and created a fake "Typhoid Wrenny" Instagram account, which I'm sure Wren was never aware of. If she had been aware of it, she probably would have been flattered.

I consider texting Ruby: *Typhoid Wrenny is in my photography class!* Ruby and I never overtly pick on people, not the way Skye and her clones do, but the two of us might occasionally laugh at someone in private, feeling secure in our own, Switzerland-y social status. But now something seems different, as if the known borders have shifted. I put my phone back in my pocket.

There are two empty seats beside Wren. I'm tempted to take the one farthest from her, on the aisle, though that would be too obvious an avoidance. I sit down next to her, but *she* shifts her desk away from me. I hope Aunt Lydia won't be big on partners.

"Welcome, welcome, burgeoning photographers!" Aunt Lydia exclaims, entering the classroom with a giant box in her arms. Everyone sits up straighter in their seats. "I'm Professor Lydia Shapiro," she goes on, setting the box down on the desk at the front of the room, "but if you don't call me Lydia, I will feel as ancient as a daguerreotype. If you don't know what that is, you will learn about it this summer, I promise."

She smiles and surveys the rows of students. When she spots me, her smile grows the tiniest bit wider, and I tense up. I don't want anyone to know I'm her niece, to assume I'll be the teacher's pet. Especially since I have *no* idea what a daguerreotype is.

"Fourteen of you signed up for this class," my aunt goes on, checking a sheet of paper on top of the box, "and yet only thirteen of you are here now. Maybe someone chickened out."

The class titters, but I think, *Bad omen.*

"In here," Aunt Lydia adds, patting the box, "are the cameras you'll be using for the summer. I'll hand those out at the end of class." She reaches up to adjust the chopsticks holding her bun in place. I'd imagined that my aunt would dress more formally for class, but she's wearing a Rolling Stones T-shirt and jeans, like she would if she were hanging out in our kitchen. "First, I have a . . ." She trails off when the door to the classroom swings open.

Aunt Lydia glances at the person in the doorway. "Hello, latecomer!" she says. "You must be our fourteenth."

The person steps inside, and my heart stops.

I mean it actually *stops*, as in ceases pumping blood to the rest of my body.

Because the latecomer, the fourteenth student, is Hugh Tyson.

He stands there, impossibly, his hands in his pockets, his bookbag on his back. He looks like he always does, with his close-cropped dark hair and light-gray-green eyes behind black-framed glasses. Hugh is *here.* How? Why? Shouldn't he still be in New York City? Or helping out his mom in the mayor's office, like he does every summer (thank you, Instagram!)?

"I'm sorry," Hugh tells Aunt Lydia in his low, slightly scratchy voice. He rubs the back of his neck. "I wish I had a better excuse, but the truth is, I lost track of time."

A couple of the students chuckle, and Aunt Lydia shakes her head. "Well, you get points for honesty," she tells him. "There's an empty seat back there."

And she motions toward the desk next to me.

My heart starts working again, sending *all* the blood straight to my face. I watch in disbelief as Hugh starts down the aisle.

I've known Hugh Tyson since elementary school, but I've only had this debilitating crush on him for the past two years. Growing up, he was just another boy—albeit shy and bookish, not rowdy like many of the others. I knew that his mother was Hudsonville's deputy mayor, and then the mayor-mayor. Hugh himself lacked any sort of politician-charm. He had a few similarly smart guy friends—one of them recently invented a studying app (no joke)—but he mostly kept to himself, reading or writing alone in the cafeteria. I never paid him any mind.

Then, one day in freshman year English class, we were presenting our poetry projects, and Hugh stood up to give his report on Robert Frost's "The Road Not Taken." I'd been daydreaming, looking up at the fluorescent lights. Then I heard Hugh say something so insightful—about regret, and second chances—that I'd glanced over at him. And I *saw* him, as if for the first time.

He's cute, I'd realized, taking in his bright eyes and broad shoulders as he read from his piece of paper. *Really cute*. My face had warmed up. How had no one else seen it? I felt like I'd discovered a planet or something.

As soon as I made my discovery, I became incapable of talking to Hugh—not that we'd chatted a lot before, but asking him to borrow a pencil hadn't required a second thought. Suddenly, I clammed up in his presence, and took it one step further, regarding him with a coldness that I hoped would hide my true feelings. Ruby had termed it my "Hugh face"—the studied, almost-cruel, I-don't-care-about-you expression that I put on whenever I passed him in the hallway.

Hugh reaches the desk beside me and sits down. I stare straight ahead, acutely aware of his nearness as he slides off his backpack and takes out a notebook and pen.

"You're late," Wren D'Amico whispers teasingly, leaning across me.

"I got that," Hugh whispers back to her, and I hear a smile in his voice.

I stiffen. Are Wren and Hugh *friends*? I don't think I've seen them together at school. I guess they both like to read. Oh God. Are they *more* than friends?

"Okay!" Aunt Lydia calls, clapping her hands. I blink, coming back to earth. "As I was about to say, I have a question. Who here has taken a photography class before?"

Three students raise their hands—one of them is Wren, who looks proud of herself. I glare at her.

"Great," Aunt Lydia says, pacing back and forth. "Maybe you guys already know some of the basics. And we'll get into all those nuts and bolts. Over the next four weeks, you'll learn about shutter speed, aperture, lens settings. We'll manipulate digital images, and develop old-school prints in the darkroom." She pauses, and I feel overwhelmed. "However, today, there's something more important to discuss."

I've never seen my aunt in professor mode until now. I've watched my mom give lectures, and she's always very solemn and exacting. Aunt Lydia is more animated and passionate. She makes you want to lean forward and listen closely. I'm almost forgetting about the fact that Hugh is sitting right next to me. *Almost.*

"Do you realize," Aunt Lydia goes on, perching on the edge of her desk, "that all we do, all day long, is take pictures?" No one responds, and I'm mystified. "Not literally," Aunt Lydia says, grinning. She taps the corner of her eye. "But we are all viewing the world through our own private lenses, taking quick mental snapshots of every person we meet, every landscape we see, *everything.* Right?"

"Right," the class choruses, and I nod, too. I've never thought of things in that way before. I dare a glance over at Hugh, my pulse pounding, and I'm relieved to see that he's focused attentively on Aunt Lydia. Maybe he doesn't even know I'm here.

"Summer?" Aunt Lydia calls out, and I jump in my seat. *Oh no.* "Do me a favor?" my aunt continues, smiling at me. I can only hope it's not a smile that screams *That's my baby niece!* to the rest of the class. "What color is your hoodie?"

I know that my *face* is the color of a beet with a bad sunburn. In my peripheral vision, I can see that Hugh is looking at me.

Everyone is. I want to kill my aunt. I glance down at my hoodie, then back up.

"Gray?" I mumble.

"Thank you," Aunt Lydia says, going over to the whiteboard and writing *Perspective* in big letters. "The hoodie could be described as gray, yes. It could also be described as a pale charcoal. Or maybe slate-colored. Everyone who sees that gray hoodie will see the gray in a different way. It's totally a matter of perspective!" She turns around, her eyes sparkling. "And that's what photography is. Photographs allow us to share our perspectives with others. And since everyone experiences the world in a unique way, every photograph is like its own unique world."

Even though I'm still mad at my aunt for calling me out in front of Hugh and the entire class, I have to admit that what she's saying is kind of cool.

Aunt Lydia laughs, shaking her head. "Sorry," she says. "My sister"—her gaze darts over to me and I shift uncomfortably in my chair—"is a philosophy professor, so I'm influenced by her. You guys will have to stop me if I'm ever rambling, okay?" The class laughs and I sigh. "Now," Aunt Lydia says, capping the whiteboard marker, "I want you to partner up with the person sitting next to you, and write down—don't draw—a brief description of what they look like to you."

The class is murmuring excitedly but all I can think, dread seeping through me, is: *Partners?* I peek over at Wren, then at Hugh. Hugh is looking at Wren, clearly about to ask her to partner up, and I'm sure she'll agree, and then I'll be stuck between them, wanting to die. But then the elderly woman sitting in front of Wren turns around, saying, "We've both taken a photography class before, dear. Shall we?"

Wren nods, and the woman swivels her desk so that they're face-to-face, and in that terrifying moment, I realize that everyone in the class is partnering up, and fourteen students means there are even sets of two, so the only person left to be my partner is—

"So," Hugh says to me, his tone flat, "I guess it's us?"

Agh.

My adrenaline spikes. For a second, I consider springing up from my seat and running out of the classroom forever. How would I explain *that* to Aunt Lydia?

"I guess," I reply coolly. I turn in my chair, putting on my best "Hugh face." My mask of indifference. My defense mechanism.

Hugh looks similarly reluctant: frowns slightly and drums his fingers on the desk, as if he'd also rather be anywhere but here. My heart hammers in my ears. *I will have to stare right at Hugh Tyson while he stares back at me.* In retrospect, having him gaze lovingly at Wren while I sat in between them would have been heaven.

All around us, people are studying their respective partners, and then scribbling in their notebooks. There are a few nervous laughs.

Hugh's gaze sweeps over my face—I'm frozen like an ice cube—and then he lowers his head and begins writing in his notebook.

What?! I wonder wildly. *Frizzy hair? Eyes of different sizes? Off-center nose??*

I half want to peek but Hugh is protecting his notebook with his hand.

"I thought," he says a little gruffly, still writing, "that you were in France."

I'm so startled by his words that I forget to feel the sting they normally elicit. *Hugh knew about my trip?* I suppose I did discuss France a lot in school, probably loudly and excitedly, with Ruby and Alice and Inez, and he might have overheard me. I cringe.

"I—" My voice comes out croak-like. I try to compose myself, and I sit up straighter. "Yeah. No," I say curtly. "That's not happening." I swallow hard.

"Too bad," Hugh tells his notebook. Probably because if I *were* in France, he wouldn't have to endure this awkwardness with me.

Almost without thinking, I lean over my notebook, my hair curtaining around me. I grip my pen in my fist.

I wish I could tell you more, Hugh Tyson, I write, letting my thoughts spill onto the page. *I wish I could tell you about my dad's phone call, which is how I ended up stuck in Hudsonville, which is why I'm taking this class. I wish I could tell you that I like you, which is why I act like I hate you. I wish I didn't have to do this assignment, because I already know your face: I know your long lashes and full lips and the small birthmark next to your right ear. I wish I could talk to you, to boys in general. I wish*

"All right, time's up!" Aunt Lydia calls.

I stop writing, horrified. What if Aunt Lydia is going to make us give our notes to our partners? I put my hand on my page, ready to rip it out and tear it up if need be.

"You don't need to do anything with your description at the moment. Save it for later," Aunt Lydia adds as people begin turning their desks back around. I let out a huge breath of relief. "But," Aunt Lydia adds, and I listen in growing terror, "the person you paired up with will be your partner for the summer."

Excuse me?

"I'll be giving you individual assignments every day," she continues, setting up a laptop and a projector on her desk, "as well as biweekly projects that you'll do with your partner. The final assignment for the class will involve the exercise you just did. Now, let's look at this slide show I've put together of famous photographs . . ."

I can't pay attention. I refuse to even rotate my head in Hugh's direction. I hear him cough, and I'm sure he's equally unhappy. We're going to have to *work* together every week? No. Not possible. I'll have to tell my aunt that I need a new partner.

That's the only way I'll be able to get through this summer.

• • •

The rest of the class passes in a blur, and before I know it, Aunt Lydia is telling the class to come up and get their cameras. Since I already have mine, I dawdle at my desk. I watch as Hugh and Wren walk up together to the front of the room, pick up their cameras, and leave together. How sweet. I roll my eyes, then finally stand up and head over to my aunt.

"So, kiddo," Aunt Lydia says with a smile, scooping up her big laptop bag, "what did you think of the class? Want to go get some coffee?"

"Uh, sure," I lie. I'd prefer to be alone right now to process seeing Hugh, but I can't be rude to my aunt. "The class was . . ." I pause, searching for the best word. "Inspiring." That, at least, is true (well, it's true of the parts I was able to focus on). Already, my fingers are itching to start today's assignment: taking a picture of food or drink from an interesting angle. Of course, nothing I eat or drink here in Hudsonville would prove too interesting. I wonder what I'd be dining on if I were in France . . .

"Inspiration is the goal," Aunt Lydia replies, beaming. She turns and leads me out of the classroom. We walk down the hall and step outside. The day has warmed up considerably, and I unzip my hoodie.

One small thing, I imagine saying to my aunt as we climb into her car in the Whitman parking lot, *I have a crush on the guy I partnered with today, you know, the cute latecomer in the white T-shirt and black-framed glasses? Like, a can't-even-talk-to-him crush. So I'm wondering if maybe you can un-partner us? That way, I can pay better attention and complete the weekly assignments like a normal person. It's a win-win!*

No. Even unspoken, the words sound silly. I shake my head as Aunt Lydia turns up her music. It's a pretty melody. A woman is singing, "Truth is just like time/It catches up and just keeps going."

We drive through the campus gate. "See you later, Max," Aunt Lydia calls, rolling down her window to wave to the security guard.

Max waves back, grinning. "See you, ladies. Aren't you lucky, Summer, getting a lift from your professor?"

I smile but my stomach tightens. Exactly. I shouldn't be asking my aunt for *more* favors. Having her switch around partners for my benefit would kind of fall under the "nepotism" umbrella. And I definitely want to keep the fact that we're related a secret, at least from my classmates.

Maybe, I think as Aunt Lydia turns onto Greene Street, I can somehow soldier on with Hugh as my partner. After all, he and I have classes together in school (*Though you've never been partners in school!* I remind myself). Ruby would certainly think it a dream opportunity to be partners with my crush. But maybe Hugh will find me so off-putting that *he* will ask Aunt Lydia for a new partner. That would be ideal.

I'm so deep in my thoughts that I give a start when I see that Aunt Lydia has parked in front of Better Latte Than Never.

"Is this okay?" she asks, unbuckling her seat belt. "I'd drive us to Starbucks at the mall, but I'm meeting a former student for lunch on campus . . ."

"It's perfect!" I exclaim, feeling a burst of joy. "Ruby works here." Despite any lingering weirdness with my best friend, I desperately need to catch up with her now. I jump out of the car and charge into the coffee shop, Aunt Lydia following behind.

The air conditioner is on full blast, and the narrow space smells of coffee beans and vanilla. People are getting their drinks to go, or sitting in the wooden booths against the walls. The chalkboard above the counter lists the regular offerings, as well as the daily special: a "July Black Eye"—a large iced coffee with a double shot of espresso.

"I think I need that level of caffeine," Aunt Lydia says, pointing to the special as we get in line. "What would you like, kiddo?"

"Iced mocha with whip," I reply—this is one decision I never agonize over. I stand on my toes and scan the brown-aproned baristas behind the counter. Ruby is not there. I deflate, but then I hear her laugh—I think it's her laugh; it sounds more high-pitched than usual. I look to my right and see Ruby in her brown apron and platform sandals, standing by one of the booths and chatting with the seated customers.

"Do you mind?" I ask my aunt, inching out of line.

Aunt Lydia chuckles. "Please. I'll get our drinks and grab us a booth."

I thank my aunt and sprint toward Ruby, my bookbag bouncing. The second I reach my best friend, I squeeze her arm.

"OMG!" I whisper-shout. "You don't understand. *Hugh Tyson* is in my photography class. And we're *partners*! I actually almost died. And Wren D'Amico is there, too, and I can't tell if she and Hu—"

The words stick in my throat the instant I notice the customers in the booth. Ruby had been blocking them from sight before. They are Austin Wheeler and Skye Oliveira.

I am seized by horror. *Did they hear me?*

Blessedly, Austin's head is bent over his phone, and he's scrolling through what look like sports stats. Skye's colorless eyes, though, are trained on me.

Behind her masterfully applied makeup, Skye Oliveira is plain. And I envy her plainness. She has a straight nose, thin lips, wavy hair that's neither blond nor brown but somewhere in between. Her features are even: nothing strange or Picasso-ish. Therefore, she is beautiful. She was voted Prettiest Sophomore in our yearbook. Today, she's wearing a pink tank top and a khaki miniskirt, her hair up in a high ponytail. She also has on several gold bangles and one of those blue "Stand Up to Bullying" rubber wristbands, which I think may be the textbook definition of *irony*.

I anxiously twist one of my own bracelets. Sure, Ruby had mentioned that Austin was coming to Better Latte, but it's not time for her lunch break yet, is it? And I never imagined that *Skye* would be part of the equation.

"Summer!" Ruby cries, her voice strained. She pries her arm out of my grasp. "You're done with class?"

I nod. "I'm here with Aunt Lydia," I explain, my heart thudding. I glance over my shoulder to see my aunt carrying an iced mocha and a July Black Eye to a booth.

"What I don't understand," Skye speaks up, as if she's continuing an ongoing conversation, "is why some people would choose to go to *school* in the summer."

I look back at Skye, my face growing warm. So she did hear me. Ruby shifts from one foot to the other, and Austin stays absorbed in his phone.

Skye lazily stirs a straw in her milky iced coffee. "I mean," she goes on, her tone as casual as her drink stirring, "I guess Hugh Tyson would jump at any chance to read more." She grins at me slowly. "He's kind of hot, isn't he, like in a nerdy way?"

I clench my teeth. There's nothing worse than someone you don't like liking what *you* like. What you *discovered*. I discovered Planet Hugh! Not Skye Oliveira.

Besides, she has a rotating cast of gelled-hair boyfriends, à la Genji Tanaka. Hugh isn't in her orbit. She's clearly messing with me. I stay silent.

"Typhoid Wrenny," Skye continues, stirring faster, "is no surprise. What else does she have going on? If I were as much of a freak, I'd hide out in classrooms twenty-four-seven, too."

I feel something like an explosion inside my chest. I think of fireworks.

"Wren is not a freak," I hear myself spitting out. "Just because she doesn't conform to the societal norms of, like, taking selfies every second doesn't mean she should be ridiculed."

Oh my God. What did I say? I'm shaking. Why did I furiously defend Wren? I don't even *like* her. Why would I snap at *Skye Oliveira*?

Skye's straw stills, and this time, Ruby squeezes *my* arm. Hard.

"Come on, Summer," Ruby says, forcing out a laugh. "You need to rest. I know you're still stressed about France—"

"No," I protest, even though maybe France was part of it, part of the frustration and anger that came bubbling up out of me.

"Oh, *you're* going to France this summer?" Skye demands, regarding me with what could be hatred, or shock, or grudging respect. "I'd heard someone in our school was, but I didn't know who . . ."

"Well, I'm *not* going—" I start to explain, but Ruby is dragging me away, making apologetic noises toward Skye and Austin, like a mother hustling her tantruming baby off the playground.

Austin glances up from his phone, his eyelids at half-mast, wearing a dazed smile. "Later, Ruby," he says. "Lunch in half an hour, right?"

Ruby manages to nod and smile in his direction as she continues to pull me toward the counter. We pass by Aunt Lydia, who looks up from her coffee and knits her brows at us. I don't know what to say. To my aunt, or to my best friend.

When we reach the counter, Ruby ducks under and stands facing me, the slab of wood between us. All her fellow baristas are busy taking orders, except for a bearded guy who is opening bags of coffee and possibly eavesdropping on us.

"What *was* that?" Ruby hisses, narrowing her eyes at me. "Since when do you care so much about Wren D'Amico?"

"I—I don't know!" I sputter, slumping against the counter. Customers step around me, huffing, and I'm reminded of being at the airport, hesitating with my buzzing phone while the other passengers got annoyed. I wonder what would have happened if I *hadn't* answered my phone. If I had just boarded the plane and gone on blithely to France, unaware that Dad didn't want me—

"Hey, Ruby!" another barista calls from down the counter. "I need a small latte with extra foam and skim milk!"

Ruby nods and jams the coffee filter holder into the espresso machine. "It was embarrassing," she mutters to me. "Did you have to, like, go on a crusade for justice?"

"I'm sorry," I whisper. My stomach forms a pretzel knot. The bearded barista glances over, as if waiting to hear the rest of my response. "I was super flustered from Hugh being in my class," I explain. "Which we totally need to discuss, by the way. And then"—I draw in a shaky breath—"seeing you talking to Austin and Sk—"

Ruby rolls her eyes and grabs a carton of skim milk, her woven bracelets slipping down her wrists. "I know you won't understand this, Summer, based on how immature you're being about Hugh, but I *talk* to the guys I like, okay?"

Her remark about Hugh burns, even though she has a point. "What about Skye, though?" I whisper. I peek behind me; thankfully, Skye and Austin are busy taking selfies with Austin's phone. I look back at Ruby and make myself ask the question that's been gnawing at me. "Are you guys . . . friends or something?" My voice breaks on the last word, which kills me.

Ruby shrugs, setting down the milk carton and avoiding my gaze. "Well, she's good friends with Austin . . . so . . ." She glances up again and her eyes are dancing. "I think he likes me!" she whispers excitedly. "We're having lunch today, and then he asked me to go to the movies tonight! This might be *it*, Summer."

It. The summer she falls in love. My stomach-pretzel twists even more. I want to be happy for Ruby. Of course I do. But she didn't say she *wasn't* friends with Skye. And the Ruby I know wouldn't fall for Austin. The other boys Ruby's dated have been more interesting. Smarter. Like the boy she met in India, who sent her old-fashioned love letters for a year. Austin is a . . . cliché. The Popular Boy.

"This doesn't make sense," I blurt. "Do you *really* want to hang out with people like Austin and Skye? I thought we didn't care about that stuff—"

"Would you be quiet?" Ruby snaps, even though I've been whispering. I jerk back, startled. Ruby is bossy, yes, but she never barks at me. We never fight. The bearded barista raises his eyebrows, as if he's surprised, too.

Ruby and I are silent, staring at each other. The air feels thick. I remember her dropping me off at the airport, when everything felt normal.

I pluck at one of my bracelets. "What is going on?" I whisper. "Are you mad at me?"

Ruby shakes her head, her dark-brown eyes full of regret. "It's just—you never want things to change, Summer." She rakes a hand through her hair, looking exasperated. "You weren't even supposed to—" She stops and looks down at the milk carton.

My limbs get cold. "I wasn't supposed to what?" I ask quietly. What was Ruby going to say? Do I want to know what she was going to say? I feel a tingle of dread work its way down my back.

"*Ruby!*" the barista hollers from down the counter, sounding peeved. "That skim latte, please? What are you doing?"

"Sorry—coming right up!" Ruby calls back, her face turning red. She glances at me, and I know we can both tell that something between us has splintered, ever so slightly. A small crack. I think of my broken mirror. "We'll talk later?" Ruby says to me, busying herself with the espresso machine. Her mouth is tight.

"Yeah." I step back from the counter, reaching down to twist my two bracelets; they feel flimsy. "Love you times two," I say tonelessly.

Ruby echoes the words, and they hang between us, random syllables strung together like a banner. Then I turn away and start toward Aunt Lydia's booth, my bookbag heavy on my shoulders. I slide into the empty seat, take off my bag, and cup my chin in my hands.

"Do you want to talk about it?" Aunt Lydia asks softly, pushing my iced mocha toward me.

I'm glad that she didn't ask if something was wrong; that much is obvious. But I shake my head, in no mood to share.

I stare down at my drink. I've probably had hundreds of iced mochas at Better Latte over the years. This one looks like all the others: a perfect whorl of whipped cream floating atop the creamy-brown drink. Except—no. This one is different. It's the mocha I will drink after having had that conversation with Ruby. It's the mocha I will drink while feeling different myself.

I think of our homework assignment, and feel a tug of inspiration. I reach into my bookbag, remove my camera, and bring it to my eye. At first, I only see darkness—the cap is still on the lens. I unscrew the cap, and the iced mocha comes into focus. I don't quite know how to work the camera yet. But I still manage to snap the picture: a close-up of this different drink.

"Nice work, young student," Aunt Lydia tells me, and I bring down the camera. I'd been concentrating so hard on shooting the iced mocha that I'd almost forgotten she was there. She smiles at me, and I semi-smile in return.

Out of the corner of my eye, I notice that Skye is getting up from the booth. She blows Austin a showy kiss—ugh—and trots outside onto Greene Street, her ponytail swinging. Austin remains seated, spellbound by his phone, waiting for Ruby.

I glance back at Aunt Lydia, meeting her open, sympathetic gaze. She'd asked me if I wanted to talk. My aunt seems like she'd be easier to confide in than, say, my mom. Or even than Ruby right now. Aunt Lydia has never been married, but she's been in many relationships. She might know something about boys, and heartbreak. I wish I could tell her about Hugh, and Wren. About Ruby, and Austin, and Skye. I wish—

"I wish I were in France."

The words leave my mouth before I even realize I mean them. Before I realize that they are at the root of my sadness, right below what just happened with Ruby. If I were in France, nothing *would* have happened with Ruby. Right?

Aunt Lydia nods at me. "I'm sure you do," she says quietly. She takes a sip of her July Black Eye. "It's really unfair, how the rug got pulled out from under you."

Unfair. Exactly. A word no one has used yet, not Mom, not Ruby, not Dad. I feel a flare of fury, like someone's lit a match in me. I nod back at my aunt.

"My dad called me *at the gate*," I tell her, my face hot. "A second, or a minute, or whatever, before I was supposed to get on the plane." I wrap my hands around my iced mocha, gripping the plastic so hard I worry I'll crush it. "Like, 'FYI, darling daughter, stay put, okay?'" For the first time in six days, I don't feel like crying; in fact, I let out a short laugh, struck by the absurdity of it all.

Aunt Lydia gives me a small, wry smile. "I know," she murmurs. "Your mother told me. I'm sorry, Summer." She gazes down at the ice cubes in her cup, a look of annoyance flitting across her face. "I have to say, your father is pretty good at coming out of nowhere with shocking surprises—"

Then she pauses and brings a hand to her lips, as if she's trying to hold the rest of her words in.

I lean forward, curiosity and fear churning in me. Why are people suddenly unwilling to finish their thoughts in front of me?

"What do you mean?" I ask. "Dad did something like this before?"

My dad is the king of canceling plans; even before the divorce, he was always bailing on school plays and parent-teacher conferences because he had to stay in France one extra day, something had come up, so sorry, sweetheart. What he's done now *isn't* really a surprise. I have the creeping sense that Aunt Lydia is referring to something else.

My aunt stares at me for a second before shaking her head.

"Well, you know, he's never been exactly reliable," she says quickly. She gets to her feet, gathering up stray napkins and her empty cup. "Look at the time!" she adds, which I never thought was a thing people really said in real life. Also, as usual, I don't know the time. Almost noon?

"I should be back on campus," my aunt goes on, her cheeks splotchy. "You're okay getting home, kiddo?"

"Yeah," I reply, even though I still feel uneasy. "I'll catch the bus on Deer Hill."

I follow Aunt Lydia to the door, blindly passing Austin in his booth. I forget to look back at Ruby at the counter. My thoughts are acrobats, tumbling and flipping. *Shocking surprises*, I think. Why did Aunt Lydia use those words? What else was she going to say?

As I step outside, Aunt Lydia is already getting in her car, waving to me and saying she'll see me in class tomorrow. Then she speeds away, leaving me alone on Greene Street, with only my iced mocha and my questions.

I take a sip of my drink. Asking Mom what Aunt Lydia might have meant would be a dead end. If only I could ask Dad himself. I stare across the street at the gray Hudson River, as if it might contain the answers.

But all the river does is remind me that I am here, in Hudsonville, and Dad is in Berlin or France or someplace. Someplace that feels impossible—as impossible as time travel, or Hugh Tyson being my class partner, or Mom's theories about parallel worlds.

I sigh and turn to walk toward Deer Hill. There are no answers, for now.

PART THREE

A Field of Poppies

Wednesday, July 12, 10:49 a.m.

"*Bonjour*, Summer!"

Bernice, the silver-haired, flour-dusted woman behind the counter, greets me with a smile as I step inside the bakery. The bell over the door chimes.

"*Bonjour*, Bernice," I reply, breathing in the sweet smell of rising dough.

Without having to ask, Bernice promptly reaches into the glass display case and takes out a fresh golden-brown *pain au chocolat* for me.

Why does this kindly French bakery lady know my name, and my order? Because for the past week, I have followed an unshakable morning routine:

Wake up stiff-necked after a night of restless sleep (I haven't yet adjusted to the time difference, or the narrow twin bed). Steal downstairs, praying not to bump into Eloise (who is usually still sleeping). Pass through the kitchen, where I exchange *bonjour*s with Vivienne (who is usually getting ready to go paint in the barn). Then, cross the street to the bakery, where I purchase what has become my favorite new breakfast.

Now Bernice hands over the *pain au chocolat* in its white paper sleeve.

"*Ça va?*" she asks me brightly as I fish in my shorts pocket for euros.

Though I haven't exactly mastered the language, I have, thanks in part to Bernice, learned a few useful French phrases. I know that "*Ça va?*" means "How's it going?" and that the appropriate answer, funnily enough, is "*Ça va,*" which means "All is well."

"*Ça va,*" I echo, giving Bernice a weak smile, along with the euros. There's no need for her to know that, in fact, not all is well.

It's been a long, lonely stretch of days since I've arrived in Les Deux Chemins. Dad is still in Berlin, and I feel like I've been holding my breath, waiting for his return. His house, while charming, has a coldness, almost a creepiness, to it. Maybe because of the people who are staying there.

Eloise, when she's not sleeping, crying in the shower (I've heard her doing that twice now), or dashing off to her art class and dinners with friends, continues to be the worst. She stalks around in her stylish sundresses, slamming doors, huffing, and eyeing me with the disgust usually reserved for rodents. Sometimes, if I'm, say, eating in the kitchen and she'll walk by, I'll catch her staring at me—in an intense, scrutinizing way that's unnerving. If I meet her gaze, she'll look away.

Vivienne is worlds nicer than her daughter (granted, that's a pretty low bar). She seems sympathetic to my sorry situation, and asks me every morning how I'm doing: am I sleeping well? (no); am I eating well? (yes). It's Vivienne, I know, who keeps the fridge and pantry well-stocked: I'm always able to find tasty cheeses and little jars of yogurt, cans of sardines, and fresh sliced fruit. Last night, I came upon a small glass tub of something called "tapenade" that turned out to be a delicious paste made of crushed olives. I'd spread it onto a hunk of bread and called that dinner.

I'd been hoping that Vivienne and I might have a meal together—or at least another hot-cocoa chat. But, for all Vivienne's politeness, I sense an aloofness from her. She's forever going out to eat, or dashing off to paint in the barn, or whispering on the phone in the living room. So I'll eat my lunch and dinner quickly, and alone, at the old oak table. Which has made me feel pretty invisible. Almost like a ghost.

I've taken to holing up in my medieval chamber, wishing my phone worked and reading my South of France guidebook, underlining the places I want to visit. Like the Riviera: a string of glamorous beaches not far from here. And most of all, Galerie de Provence, the gallery outside of town where Dad's portrait of me hangs. But I don't actually *go* anywhere, except for the barn studio and, occasionally, Boulevard du Temps. And, of course, the bakery.

"*Merci,*" I tell Bernice, opening the door with my *pain au chocolat* in hand. The bell chimes again. "*Au revoir!*"

"*Au revoir,* Summer!" she calls back, and I can tell she gets a kick out of the novelty of my name.

I think of Cute Waiter Jacques—how he, too, found my name amusing—and my heartbeat quickens as I step out into the sunshine. Jacques's note is still buried in my tote bag; I haven't dared call the number he left me. On my rare trips to Boulevard du Temps, I *have* dared to stroll past Café des Roses, my pulse pounding while I tried hard to look nonchalant. But I never once spotted Jacques there, waiting tables. Maybe his parents banished him to dishwashing for good. Or maybe I dreamed him up completely.

Crossing Rue du Pain, I pluck the *pain au chocolat* from its paper sleeve and take a bite. Buttery flakes of pastry and hunks of dark chocolate fill my mouth. *Mmmm.* If I were in Hudsonville, I'd be having dry Cheerios right now.

Well, no—not *now*, I remind myself. It's six hours earlier in Hudsonville. I imagine the peach pre-dawn sky stretching over the hushed houses and the gray river. I picture Ruby in her room, sleeping beneath her colorful tapestries. Then I feel a pang of disquiet, thinking of Ruby's email from last night.

I push the thought aside and push open the gate that leads into Dad's garden. The lemon trees cast shade over the stone benches, and the rows of lilacs emit their fragrant scent. The overgrown grass tickles my calves as I walk past the pool.

My second day here, I eagerly put on my bathing suit and hurried into the garden, only to have my hopes crash. The pool's shiny blue surface is a trick—its bottom tiles are all scummy. Mom would roll her eyes and say that was just like Dad, to have a pool for status but never keep it clean enough to swim in.

Not that I've told Mom about the pool. Or, you know, about Dad's absence. A surge of anxiety tightens my throat, and I half choke on a piece of *pain au chocolat*. Mom has been emailing me every day, asking if I'm okay and also if Dad would please call her already. She must sense that something is up. I've written back to assure her that all is well (*"Ça va!"*) and that Dad and I are busy. But the lying is starting to make me feel sick and knotted-up inside. I'm not sure how much longer I can go without breaking.

"Non!"

The annoyed shout comes from inside the house. I stop in the middle of the garden and peer up at the green shutters. I can't see anything, but I do hear another raised, female voice, speaking in French. *Eloise and Vivienne*, I realize. They're fighting. They must be in Vivienne's room, which is at the end of the second floor, and, like mine, faces the garden. Vivienne always keeps her door shut, and her curtains are drawn now, too.

I stand still, listening, wondering what the fight is about. After a moment, though, the voices die down, so I resume walking.

I pass the rosebushes, and the sunflowers, and finally arrive at the red barn. I swallow the last of my *pain au chocolat* and wipe the crumbs off my mouth before opening the creaky door.

Dad's studio is spacious and airy, with rough-hewn wood floors and sunbeams slanting in through the skylight. It smells strongly of paint and turpentine, which is how Dad's clothes always smelled. I smile at the memory, as I do every time I come in here.

There are easels set up around the room, and stacks of sketch pads, and containers full of paintbrushes and charcoals.

It feels like an artist's haven, and I guess it is; in addition to Vivienne, various paint-stained women and men pop in regularly, claiming an easel and wordlessly working. Today, though, only Monsieur Pascal is here, wielding his paintbrush and studying his canvas.

Monsieur Pascal is approximately ninety-nine years old, and very cranky. Vivienne explained to me that he's a famous artist who lives in Les Deux Chemins, though she didn't introduce us, which I didn't mind. I did, however, realize that Monsieur Pascal is the elderly man standing with the rosebushes in Dad's painting, the one that hangs in the living room here. I recognized his gray beard and straw hat.

I keep quiet as I walk past Monsieur Pascal toward the far corner of the barn, where there is a small desk alongside several big cardboard boxes. This is where *I* work, although I'm not doing any painting or drawing, of course. I am fulfilling my duties as Dad's "summer assistant."

Over the weekend, Dad emailed me from Berlin to apologize (for the millionth time) and to say that, since I was asking, and if I *really* wanted to, I could start organizing his papers and sketches in his studio. So, for the past few days, I have been doing just that. It's no easy task—Dad's desk was strewn with receipts, email printouts, old tubes of paint, notes scribbled on index cards. And his sketches are all stuffed haphazardly into the boxes. I guess I inherited my messy tendencies from Dad.

But to my surprise, I have found it satisfying to turn his chaos into order. I cleared off his desk, wiped the dust with a rag, made labels for the file folders inside the desk drawers, filed the loose papers.

Who am I? I think now as I survey the spotless desk. It's like another Summer has taken over.

I sit cross-legged on the cool wood floor and turn my attention to one of the big boxes of sketches. Dad told me that he had all his old sketches shipped here from Paris for the summer, to use as inspiration.

As Monsieur Pascal's paintbrush makes soothing swish-swish sounds, I lean forward and flip through the large sheaves of drawing paper. Some sketches are only smudged charcoal silhouettes; they remind me of a photograph that comes out blurry on the first try. Others, like a woman standing in the distance on a beach, are a bit more detailed.

Then I come upon a sketch that looks familiar: a mailman pushing his cart down a tree-lined city street. It takes me a minute to realize that the colorful, painted version of this sketch hangs in the Whitney Museum in New York City. Ruby and I went there over winter break, and I'd felt immensely proud, seeing Dad's painting on the wall and the official placard beside it: THE DELIVERER, BY NED EVERETT, OIL ON CANVAS.

It looks like there's something written on the back of the sketch, so I turn the paper over. *Afternoon Mailman, 53rd Street, Manhattan,* Dad has scrawled there, along with the date: seven years ago, when I was nine. Pre-divorce. I picture Dad back then, taking the train down to New York City and sketching various passersby. I guess he eventually decided *The Deliverer* sounded more artsy than *Afternoon Mailman*.

I continue flipping through the sketches, and find one that makes me smile. It's a charcoal rendering of an old man in a straw hat standing between two rosebushes: the sketch version of the Monsieur Pascal painting. On the back, Dad wrote: *Claude Pascal, Les Deux Chemins.* The date is from last summer.

I realize that the rosebushes are from the garden here. I glance across the studio at the real Claude Pascal, and then back down at Dad's handwriting. It's so cool to get a glimpse of how my father works, to learn that he draws a sketch first, and then creates his painting based off that. It feels, in some modest way, like I'm growing closer to him, even though he is still far away.

Creeaaak.

The noise startles me, and I look up to see the barn door opening. Vivienne storms inside, her face flushed, clutching her paintbrush. She's wearing a silky white blouse with paint-spattered cuffs, and her reddish hair is in its usual low ponytail. She doesn't acknowledge Monsieur Pascal, or me. She probably doesn't even see me; I am sitting obscured by the boxes.

A second later, someone else storms through the door—Eloise. It's clear that she's followed her mother in here, and that neither of them is very happy. In fact, Eloise is crying—tears glisten on her cheeks and her mouth quivers. It's super irritating that she looks pretty even now. From behind the boxes, I watch as she and Vivienne stand facing each other. I remember how I heard their raised voices earlier.

"*Maman!*" Eloise spits out in a rage, her hands making fists at her sides. "*Ne marche pas—loin de—moi.*" She's sobbing, trying to catch a breath between her words. "*J'en peux plus! Elle—*"

"*Arrête!*" Vivienne snaps. She shuts her eyes and rests her fingertips against her forehead. "*Il n'y a rien que je peux faire,*" she adds, sounding drained and exhausted.

I try to remain motionless in my hiding spot. Even with my newly acquired French skills, I have no idea what Vivienne and Eloise are saying. But it's fairly obvious that they're having a major argument. Again, I recall fighting with Mom before I left home. I wonder if we looked the same—frustrated mother, daughter in tears.

Eloise lets out another sob and starts to say something else, when Monsieur Pascal turns away from his easel. He scowls at Eloise and Vivienne, as if they should know better than to disturb the master at work.

Looking embarrassed, Vivienne walks over to him and says "*Pardon!*" plus more French words that must be apologies. Meanwhile, Eloise stands still, sniffling and wiping her wet cheeks with the heels of her hands.

What were they fighting about? I'm so curious, and I don't even know why I'm so curious. I guess I don't have a lot going on in my own life right now, so it's interesting to peek in on someone else's.

As Vivienne talks to Monsieur Pascal by his easel, Eloise gazes forlornly around the studio. I feel a reluctant twinge of sympathy toward her, and then—

She looks right at me, her eyes widening.

I freeze.

She can see me? I thought I was hidden by the boxes! Not for the first time, I have the sense that Eloise is sort of otherworldly. Spooky.

She glares at me, her face chalk-white and her lips in a line. I watch in horror as she starts marching toward me. The sunlight shines on her golden curls and her lace-edged white dress, making her look deceptively angelic. I hug my knees to my chest and try to shrink into myself. Disappear.

"What are you doing here?" Eloise demands, towering over me. In spite of my fear, I notice how seamlessly she is able to switch from French to perfect English. I'm a little jealous. "Were you listening?" she presses, her eyes bugging out of her head. "Were you *spying* on us?"

Okay, I guess I was sort of spying, but not intentionally. And, I realize as I peer up into Eloise's frantic face, I have every right to be here. I feel a flash of righteous anger. This is my father's house! I may be adrift and disoriented, my only friend in this country may be Bernice the bakery lady, but that doesn't mean some random bully can steamroll over me. Right?

I lift my chin, twisting the woven bracelets on my wrist, thinking of Ruby. Then I think of Skye Oliveira, and that gives me enough fuel to get to my feet and rise up to my full height, which is a couple inches taller than Eloise.

"I was here first," I tell her, surprised by the strength in my own voice. I gesture down to the boxes. "Going through my dad's sketches. *You* came in from nowhere with all the drama about who knows what." My hands are trembling, so I clasp them together.

Eloise's cheeks turn scarlet, and she jerks her head down to look at the boxes. Then she glances up at me, and for no discernible reason, her eyes fill with tears again. I wonder if she's one of those cruel people who are incongruously thin-skinned: the very definition of being able to dish it out but not take it.

"You're wrong," she snaps at me. "You have it backward."

I frown at her, confused. I can feel that my own face is flushed, and that my throat is tight. But I'm more annoyed than hurt. It's all frothing up inside me: the burden of lying to Mom, the recent weirdness with Ruby, the loneliness of the past week . . .

"I don't know what you're talking about," I blurt. "And I don't know what you have against me." Eloise blinks, and I'm shocked myself. I'm not used to speaking so plainly to anyone. But I keep going, wondering if this is a new Summer, like the one who cleaned Dad's desk. "From the day I arrived," I hear myself saying, "you have been nothing but rude to me, and I never did anything to you."

I clasp my hands together even tighter. Eloise's mouth opens slightly, and now I can't read her expression—is she surprised? Angry? Regretful? Maybe some combination of all three? The notion of her apologizing seems impossible.

Before Eloise can speak, though, Vivienne is hurrying over to us, flapping her hands like she wants to wipe away any negativity.

"*Pardon*—I am sorry, Summer," she says, looking worriedly from me to Eloise and back again. "I did not realize that you were in the studio. What—what are you two talking about?" Her voice is tight and she is gripping her paintbrush hard.

"Actually, I was just leaving," I say, which isn't true, but I'm trembling again and I want to get away from Eloise before I crack and lose any of the composure I'd magically gained moments before. "Excuse me," I mutter, stepping around the boxes. I head for the barn door with my heart in my throat. Monsieur Pascal has gone back to painting, as if nothing happened.

I rush out into the garden and exhale once more. My hair is getting into my eyes, and I brush it back carelessly. I can hear Vivienne and Eloise inside the barn, speaking to each other, their voices hushed and strained. I hope they're not planning to stay at Dad's much longer this summer. Even though the house would be eerie empty, I'd prefer that to the specter of their mysterious issues.

Sighing, I cross through the garden and open the gate. I've stopped shaking, but my head is still spinning from my rare moment of bravery. I wipe my sweaty palms against my purple tank top—another Ruby hand-me-down.

I pause next to Dad's front door, and consider going inside to email Ruby. I could fill her in on what just happened in the barn. But that would also mean responding to her message from last night, and I don't quite know how to do that. I frown and kick at a pebble beneath my flip-flop.

Ruby's latest email was an explosion of exclamation marks and all caps, letting me know that she and AUSTIN WHEELER were now DATING.

We went to the movies on Monday and when the spaceship was landing on Earth 2.0, he leaned over the popcorn bag and totally KISSED ME!!!! she'd written in one breathless stream. *This is IT—SUMMER OF FALLING IN LOVE, baby!!!*

I'd stared at the screen, feeling hollow. I knew I was supposed to write back with exclamation marks of my own, and expressions of excitement and joy. I couldn't. I'd been the one to leave Hudsonville and yet here was Ruby, leaving me behind again. Falling in love. This was supposed to be my "best summer ever"— the summer I turned sixteen. Once, I'd heard the phrase *Sweet sixteen and never been kissed* and it had stuck in my head like a drumbeat. Not only had I never been kissed, I'd never had a boy like me. I couldn't even *talk* to Hugh Tyson.

As I'd reread Ruby's email, it struck me that time didn't care whether or not you were a late bloomer—it continued along at its regular pace, aging you, while you went on unkissed. And others, like your best friend, hurried ahead, right on schedule with their rites of passage.

I turn away from Dad's house, my chest heavy. The fact that Ruby's summer love is Austin Wheeler makes the whole situation even worse. Austin is bland and blond—another cog in the popularity machine. He's buddies with Skye Oliveira, and I can't help but fear that Ruby is headed in that same direction.

Although Ruby hasn't mentioned Skye in any of her emails, I've seen upsetting evidence on Instagram.

Like the photograph Skye posted from her Fourth of July party, of herself and some of her clones posing in her fancy backyard. And there, in the background, wearing a striped dress and chatting with Austin, was a beaming Ruby. It had felt like a stomach punch, seeing that picture.

A few days later, Austin posted a photo of himself, Skye, and Ruby all squished into a booth in Better Latte Than Never—Ruby in her barista's apron and Skye and Austin drinking iced coffees, everyone grinning like BFFs. Stomach punch number two.

Meanwhile, Ruby and I have been trading benign emails. I'll tell her about life in Les Deux Chemins, and she'll tell me about visiting her dad in Connecticut. In typical Ruby fashion, she'll urge me to not only call up Cute Waiter Jacques (*Do it!*) but to take photos of him to send to her (*Pics or it didn't happen!*). We still sign every email with *Love you times two.* But something feels different.

I trudge down Rue du Pain, my hands in the back pockets of my shorts. I hate feeling distanced from Ruby. From home. I'm certain that if I were in Hudsonville, everything would be normal. Ruby and I would be honest with each other, like we've always been. I'd know all the secrets, have all the answers.

Here, I've had to rely on Instagram for answers. It's not just Ruby, Skye, and Austin I stalk on there. Alice has been posting pictures of her trip to California to visit Inez; they've looked relaxed and happy on the beach, as two best friends should. Hugh Tyson—who is not very active on Instagram, but when he does post, it still makes my heart jump a little—posted a photograph of a Nikon DSLR camera, similar to the one Aunt Lydia gave me. His caption read: *Summer photography course for the win!* I wonder if he's taking that course in New York City.

I've been using my Nikon every day, taking photographs of the lemon trees in Dad's garden, of the breads and pastries fresh out of the oven at the bakery, of the cupid fountain on the corner. Now, as I turn onto Boulevard du Temps, passing by the fountain, I'm a little sad that I didn't bring my camera along.

I could have taken a picture of the white stone cathedral, framed against the vivid blue sky. Or the two elderly women sitting on the cathedral steps, sharing a baguette while pigeons peck around their feet. The red sign of the *tabac.* Café Cézanne, its outdoor tables crowded with people eating lunch in the sun. The clothing boutique, with its display of sherbet-colored ballet flats in the window . . .

I hesitate in front of the boutique, and something compels me to step inside. I haven't been shopping since I went to the mall with Ruby in May, to get new flip-flops for my trip. This boutique has polka-dot wallpaper, vintage bags on shelves, perfume bottles on trays, and stylish little dresses hanging on hooks. It would seem out of place at the mall back home, but it feels right for Les Deux Chemins. It also feels right for me to select a filmy, short-sleeved blouse printed with small red flowers—they look kind of like poppies. I take the blouse into a fitting room, where I shed Ruby's purple tank top.

"*Très jolie,*" the saleswoman tells me when I emerge to study myself in the full-length mirror.

I understand that she's saying the top is "very pretty," and I know it's her job to say those things. But as I look in the mirror, and pile my untamable hair on top of my head, I have to admit the blouse . . . is nice. The color brings out the pink in my cheeks, and I like the loose, flowy shape paired with my denim shorts. It's not something Ruby would wear—she prefers more fitted tops—but maybe that's okay. Maybe that's good.

I feel a kind of recklessness, similar to what I felt back in the barn when I stood up to Eloise. In a stammering mix of French and English, I tell the saleswoman I will buy the blouse—I have enough euros in my pocket—and ask her to cut off the tags. A few minutes later, I am outside, wearing the very pretty new blouse and holding Ruby's tank top balled up in my hand.

The warm afternoon breeze makes the back of the blouse billow. I smile, feeling weightless, floating along the cobblestones. The boulevard is bustling, and as I'm passing Café des Jumelles, I bump against a passerby's shoulder.

"*Excusez-moi,*" I say, proud that I went automatically to French.

The passerby is a teenage boy, a couple heads shorter than me, with a mop of curly brown hair and brown eyes. I'm confused when he stops and smiles slowly.

"*Bonjour, mademoiselle,*" he says to me, an invitation in his voice. "*Ça va?*"

Wait. My face flames. Can it be that this guy—is he, like, *hitting* on me?

I think again of the mall back home, how random guys would sometimes say hi to Ruby, grinning at her, as she and I walked between stores. If the guy was cute, Ruby would say hi back, and occasionally they'd exchange numbers. I always stayed silent, the unseen sidekick. No one ever grinned at me or spoke to me, and I was accustomed to that.

I am not accustomed to *this*.

The brown-eyed boy seems to be waiting for a response. But I'm far too flustered to say "*Ça va*"—or anything—back to him. So I spin away and continue down the boulevard, my pulse quickening. I do sneak a glance over my shoulder and the boy is still watching me, still smiling. Then he shrugs gamely and walks on.

My heart thuds beneath my new blouse. *I don't get it.* Was it the blouse itself that cast some sort of spell, causing a boy to notice me? Maybe it's something about France, or French boys. After all, there was that interaction I had with Jacques at the café, even if it seems unreal now, and never to be repeated.

Distracted, I find myself turning into the sunlit plaza that hosts the daily farmers' market. Stalls overflow with cheeses and vegetables, fruits and flowers. Whole fish lie glistening on beds of ice, and bottles of lavender oil and packets of herbs are arrayed on tables. I pause to touch bundles of thyme tied with twigs, wondering if these would be good souvenirs to bring home in August. Not that Mom would necessarily want a reminder of France, and Dad. Not that Ruby would have much use for thyme. I glance down at her tank top in my hand.

I wander through the crowds. Men and women stand haggling with the different sellers, and there's a pleasant buzz of business all around. I stop at a vegetable stall, admiring a mound of ripe red tomatoes. Maybe I'll buy one for lunch, along with a wedge of Brie from the cheese stall. I'm reaching into my pocket to see if I have any euros left when I hear a familiar voice behind me.

A boy's voice.

My heartbeat accelerates again and I turn around.

There, standing by the barrels of olives, talking with the man selling them, is Cute Waiter Jacques. I feel my breath catch as I take in his profile: his high cheekbones and strong nose, his shock of black hair. He's *here*. It's like I conjured him with my thoughts.

I hesitate beside the tomatoes, my heart and mind racing in tandem. I could surrender to my standard shyness and scurry away. Or . . .

I think of the boy saying *Ça va?* to me on the street. I remember Ruby's email about falling in love. I picture Hugh Tyson, off on his photography course, living his life. My new shirt is soft against my skin, and I can smell the herbs and the flowers in the air. Everything conspires in me, and that feeling of recklessness from earlier returns. And before I can continue my inner dance of indecision, I walk right up to Jacques.

"*Ça va?*" I venture, which seems appropriate.

Jacques glances away from the olives and his dark-blue eyes widen at the sight of me. Butterflies form a colony in my stomach. *What am I doing?* I ask myself, but it's too late, I'm already doing it, it's already happening right now.

"Summer!" Jacques exclaims, his wolfish smile spreading across his face.

He remembers me? He remembers me!

He leans forward, so close to me that I can smell the cologne on his neck, and he kisses me quickly on each cheek. I feel myself blush a deeper red than the flowers on my shirt, than the tomatoes behind me. Suddenly, this cheek-kiss custom doesn't seem so bad. I stand still in the middle of the busy market, the butterflies frantic in my belly.

Jacques draws back. "One moment, *s'il te plaît?*" he asks me, and I nod. Now that I've taken this initial step, I can wait a moment, an hour, a day, all summer . . .

I watch as Jacques turns to the olive seller and begins speaking in fast French, gesturing with his hands. I try to breathe normally. The seller scoops a bunch of glossy green olives into a big container and hands it to Jacques.

When the transaction is done, Jacques flashes me a grin. "My parents, they were missing some ingredients at the café," he explains, "so they sent me here, you see."

I notice that he is wearing his waiter uniform, but his white shirt is untucked and rumpled, and his black necktie hangs undone around his collar. Somehow, this makes him look even handsomer than the last time we met.

"I see," I manage to say.

Jacques chuckles. *"Alors*, Summer," he says as we walk away from the olive stall, side by side. Our arms brush, and I feel a zap of electricity. "You did not ever call me for French lessons." His tone is teasing, and his eyes sparkle. "Where have you been?"

My pulse flutters at my throat. "I—" I'm reluctant to explain that I've never actually called a boy before. "I don't have my own phone," I finally offer, lamely. I explain how my cell doesn't work here, and Jacques tells me that I can purchase a temporary mobile and a phone card at the *tabac*. I thank him for the tip, even though, in some ways, it's been sort of refreshing to be without my phone (once I got past the initial withdrawal).

"Where have *you* been?" I volley back as we stroll past a stall selling sunflowers. Then I bite my lip, hoping this question hasn't revealed the fact that I've been taking occasional strolls past Café des Roses, on the lookout for him.

Jacques laughs, pushing a hand through his tousled black hair. "Ah. My family and I, we were out of town for a few days," he replies. "We went to Antibes, on the Côte d'Azur—the Riviera. You know this place?"

"I do!" I exclaim, recalling my South of France guidebook. "I mean, um, I don't *know*-know it," I amend, blushing again.

Jacques looks amused. "I've never been. But I've read about the Riviera. I'd like to go there someday."

"*Oui?*" Jacques raises one eyebrow. I'm seized by the terror that he thinks I'm suggesting *he* take me there. The idea of being on a beach with Jacques, in my swimsuit, makes me want to crawl under the stall of eggplants we are passing now.

"I'd like to go to lots of places," I babble on, picturing the underlined passages in my guidebook. "There's Avignon, which has the Palace of the Popes. And the Camargue, where you can see wild horses . . ." I'm starting to sound like a guidebook myself. "Oh, and most of all, Galerie de Provence, which is pretty close to here, right?"

"Yes, it is not far," Jacques says as we maneuver around a family of four who are sampling slices of salami at the meat stall. Jacques glances at me, a smile playing on his lips. "*Pourquoi?* Why 'most of all'?" he inquires.

I wonder if I should simply say that I like art, and that it seems a shame to come to France and not visit a museum. Which is all technically true. But the deeper, realer truth, about my portrait and Dad—would that sound like I was boasting?

I settle on something in between. "There's a painting there I really want to see," I explain, my eyes on my flip-flops. "By, um, my father. He's a painter," I explain.

Jacques looks impressed. "*Vraiment*, a painter? That is cool," he says, his accent making the *o*'s extend in a very cute way. "He is French, your father?"

I shake my head, passing by a stall that's selling herbed goat cheese. "He's American, but he lives in Paris, and spends the summers in Les Deux Chemins." It occurs to me then that maybe Jacques has heard of Dad, or knows him from the town. "His name is Ned Everett?" I venture.

Jacques smiles, giving me an amiable shrug. "I am afraid I am not familiar with any painters of today. But there are always artists living here in Provence. I think perhaps it is because of the beautiful light." He holds aloft his container of olives; the mellow sunlight turns them golden.

I nod, wishing again that I had my camera. "Like Paul Cézanne, and Vincent van Gogh," I say. I'm no longer as nervous as I was a few minutes ago. Especially because I'm on familiar ground now; I know artists.

Jacques nods back at me, his dark-blue eyes sparkling as he takes me in. "So you are here, then, visiting your father, Summer?"

His gaze makes my nervousness return. "Sort of," I reply, hoping to avoid the whole Berlin issue. "I'm staying at his house, on Rue du Pain." *Agh.* I cringe, wanting to disappear. What if Jacques thinks I'm *inviting* him to Dad's house? Just when I was starting to relax and not feel like a complete freak in front of a boy . . .

"My parents' café is closed this Friday," Jacques says, stopping to survey a pile of peaches. I guess he's changing the subject, which is a relief. "For *le quatorze juillet*—sorry, July fourteenth. Bastille Day. You know, France's Independence Day? It is like your Fourth of July."

"I know about Bastille Day," I say with a smile. *Thanks to my trusty guidebook.*

"But Galerie de Provence, I believe it will be open then," Jacques goes on, picking up a peach and examining it in the sunlight. "Perhaps we could—"

Oh my God, I think, the butterflies doubling in number, and then a girl calls out, "Jacques!"

I look around, my brain foggy. A tall, model-esque girl with dark skin and brown hair in a short, fashionable pouf, is coming our way, holding hands with a sandy-haired boy in a Phoenix band T-shirt. The boy has a bookbag on his shoulder, and the girl is carrying a large sketch pad under one arm.

I recognize them, but from where? Then it hits me: They're the couple I saw kissing in front of the cupid fountain my first day here, and the couple I saw with Eloise at Café des Jumelles that first night. They are Eloise's friends. And they know *Jacques*?

Tensing up, I whip around and pretend to be deeply absorbed in the peaches. I let my hair fall into my face, hoping it disguises me sufficiently.

I listen to Jacques greeting the couple—he cheek-kisses the girl, and slaps the guy on the back. He calls the girl "Colette"— *that's right; Colette!*—and the guy "Tomas." As the three of them exchange more pleasantries in French, I stare at the peaches, silently imploring Jacques not to introduce me. Thankfully, he doesn't, and Colette and Tomas don't linger long. I hear Tomas call *"À bientôt!"* which I know means "See you later." Then, carefully, I turn around, gripping a peach in my free fist.

"Those are cool people I have met this summer," Jacques explains cheerfully; over his shoulder, I see Colette and Tomas trotting away. "They have been coming to the café often, with some other friends from their art class."

I know, I think, and something solidifies in my mind, something I hadn't put together before. If Eloise and her art class besties, Colette and Tomas, always go to Café des Roses (when they're not avoiding me), then Eloise and Jacques know each other.

My stomach falls. If Jacques knows Eloise, he's surely noticed her beauty. And, as far as I can tell, Eloise, unlike Colette, doesn't have a boyfriend. I squeeze the peach in my hand. This feeling of possessiveness is foolish; I have no claim on Jacques.

Then Jacques reaches out and gently takes the peach from my grasp. Our fingers touch. I feel my heart give a kick, and all thoughts of Eloise flee.

"*Merci*, Summer—thank you for choosing this one," Jacques says, holding up the peach. "It is ripe enough for the dessert my father will make." He pauses, and then adds, "So, I will pick you up on Friday, and we can go to the gallery on my moped?"

Hold on. What? I stare at Jacques, my blood thrumming in my ears.

"Galerie de Provence?" he prompts, grinning at me. "Shall we go?"

The full implication of his words makes my skin go hot with shock.

Is this a date? A date with a BOY?

Excitement and disbelief swell up in me. I don't remember how to speak—my tongue is stuck to the roof of my mouth—but I muster up a nod.

I hear Jacques asking for my address, and his voice sounds fuzzy and far off. As I stand there in the middle of the farmers' market, I realize that today has been full of impossibilities. It's like I'm in an alternate world, where the regular rules don't apply.

And, maybe I'm getting way ahead of myself, but I think I now have a response to Ruby's email.

Hey, BFF, remember how you predicted a French boyfriend for me? Well, let's just say you might not be the only one with a summer love story . . .

Friday, July 14, 10:56 a.m.

I am running late. Literally, running.

I dash out of the bakery, ducking under the blue, white, and red French flag that hangs in the doorway; it's Bastille Day. Bernice greeted me with a hearty *"Bonjour!"* before handing me my *pain au chocolat*, which I now clutch as I race across the street. I narrowly miss being hit by a car that's bumping over the cobblestones of Rue du Pain. My stomach is a ball of nerves, and sweat trickles down my neck.

Jacques is supposed to pick me up in four minutes.

Please don't let him be punctual, I pray as I burst into Dad's house. I pause in the empty kitchen, planning to scarf down my breakfast. But I'm too anxious to ingest anything. I was silly to go to the bakery—I'd thought I had time to carry out my regular morning routine. Then I'd seen the clock on the wall behind Bernice, and panicked.

I toss the uneaten *pain au chocolat* onto the kitchen table and thunder up the stairs. I'm relieved that I showered already; I hear the water running in the bathroom. It must be Eloise in there, because I saw Vivienne heading to the barn studio from my bedroom window when I woke up.

I'd slept much later than I'd intended. I'd been up all night, tossing and turning, seesawing between glee and fear, until I finally drifted off around dawn.

On the one hand, I felt ridiculous for even thinking the words *boyfriend* and *love* back at the farmers' market on Wednesday. I *had* emailed Ruby later that day, but I'd downplayed the news. *It might not even be a real date*, I'd written, wrapping myself in the familiar blanket of doubt.

On the other hand, the anticipation building in me has been undeniable. Now I feel it surge as I barrel into my medieval chamber and shake my brand-new sundress out of its plastic bag.

Yesterday, I went back to the chic boutique on Boulevard du Temps, where I bought this dress—it's a brilliant sky-blue color, with a scalloped hem and straps that crisscross in the back—as well as a pair of cream-colored sandals that lace up my ankles.

I quickly change out of my shorts and T-shirt and into my new clothes. Then I face the broken mirror. Even through the fragmented glass, I can tell that the dress is lovely, the nicest thing I have ever owned. I do notice, however, that the orange-and-green colors of my woven bracelets clash with the blue of the dress.

Ever since Ruby made those bracelets for me freshman year, I've worn them steadfastly, no matter the outfit or occasion.

But I've never had an occasion like this. I wonder if Ruby would even be bothered by their absence.

Things still feel distant between me and my best friend. Although she did respond enthusiastically to my email about Jacques. *OF COURSE it's a real date!!!* she'd written. *Didn't I call this?? Am I EVER wrong? No I am not!!! Hugh who??*

I'd smiled at the screen. I couldn't deny that my thoughts of Hugh were starting to fade and curl, like an old photograph. But I'd wondered why it was so important to Ruby, always being right. Maybe because it gave her all the power.

I sigh and wriggle the bracelets off my wrist. I place them gently on the top of the dresser. Then I reach for my brush, hoping to untangle my long, shower-damp hair.

Knock, knock. Knock, knock.

Someone is downstairs.

He is *punctual,* I think, frustrated, as I hastily run the brush through my hair and dig up some lip gloss from my toiletries bag. I swipe the gloss across my mouth and grab my tote bag. I start to leave the room when I remember my camera. It's sitting on the windowsill; I'd been taking pictures of the garden last night. I grab the camera, stuff it into my bag, and, at last, dart out.

I sprint down the stairs and into the kitchen before I come to an abrupt stop.

The front door is open and Jacques leans against the frame, his arms crossed over his chest. And facing him, one hand on the doorknob, wearing her white bathrobe and a towel turban, and—maybe worst of all—holding my *pain au chocolat,* is Eloise.

I feel a rush of irritation. She must have gotten out of the shower, heard the knock, and flown downstairs on her ghost feet to answer the door (and snag my breakfast).

"Ah. Summer!" Jacques says when he sees me. He smiles, but his face is etched with confusion. Eloise turns to me, wearing a similar expression. Only she is not smiling.

"How do you know Jacques?" she asks without preamble, her voice sharp.

Right. In all the excitement of the morning, I'd momentarily forgotten about the potential Eloise-Jacques connection. From the way Eloise is standing, her body angled as if to shield him from me, it's clear she not only knows Jacques, but possibly *likes* him.

And does *he* like *her?* My stomach constricts as I peer at Jacques. Thankfully, he doesn't seem to be swooning over Eloise. Instead, he's glancing from her to me, his brow furrowed, looking for all the world like he's trying to solve a puzzle.

"I—um—" I clear my throat. Out of nervous habit, I reach for my wrist but it's bare; there are no bracelets to twist. "We—we met at Café des Roses," I finally reply. I straighten my shoulders, refusing to buckle under Eloise's stony gaze.

The thing is, since our face-off in the barn, Eloise has been . . . different toward me. It's incredibly subtle. We still don't speak when we pass each other in the house. But she no longer looks at me with her lip curled, she no longer huffs, and she no longer slams doors. It's as if she's grudgingly accepted that I'm, at the very least, human.

Now, though, she's regarding me with pure venom. Just like the old days.

"*Je ne comprends pas,*" Jacques speaks up, frowning. "I do not understand." His dark-blue eyes ping-pong between Eloise and me. "Summer, *you* know Eloise? You are both living here? Are you—"

"Eloise is just staying here," I cut in. I want to establish that *she* is the interloper, while this house, for all intents and purposes, is mine. "With her mom, who's one of my dad's artist friends."

Jacques nods, still looking a bit bewildered. Eloise gives a sharp bark of a laugh.

"Staying here," she echoes bitterly, her mouth twisting. It occurs to me then that maybe Eloise resents spending the summer in this house. Maybe that's what her "stress" is all about. If that's the case, I guess Eloise and I do have something in common: We both want Eloise gone. "By the way," she adds, turning to me and holding up my *pain au chocolat.* "It's cool if I eat this, right, Summer?" A taunting smile spreads across her face. "I found it on the table, so . . ." Without waiting for my reply, she takes a huge bite.

My blood boils. I fight down the urge to wrest the pastry from her, to shout "That's mine!" like we're two little kids squabbling over a piece of candy. But I won't lose it in front of Jacques. I ball my hands into fists while Eloise chews smugly.

Jacques bites his lip to keep from smiling, as if he finds our hostility entertaining. "This is a funny coincidence, *non*?" he asks us.

"Hilarious," I mutter. Eloise, her mouth full, doesn't answer.

"So," Jacques says into the tense silence. He uncrosses his arms and puts his hands in his jeans pockets. It's the first time I've seen him out of his waiter's uniform, and I take a moment to absorb how cute he looks in his faded red T-shirt and black Adidas. My heart skitters. He raises his eyebrows at me. "You are ready, Summer?"

"*Oui*," I say instantly, stepping forward and brushing past Eloise to join Jacques on the threshold. As nervous as I am about our—outing (a less scary word than *date*), I am more nervous about the prospect of remaining in this awkwardness with Eloise.

"Well, have *fun*, you guys," she snaps, taking another bite of my *pain au chocolat*. I stiffen, and hope she won't ask us where we're going. Visiting the gallery feels personal, almost private. Then I notice that her cheeks are splotchy, and I can tell she's actually struggling *not* to ask, to act as if she doesn't care.

I feel a twinge of satisfaction: Is Eloise ... jealous of *me*? There *is* reluctant approval in her eyes as she takes in my new dress, my sandals, my lip gloss. Bundled up in her robe, her princess hair hidden under a towel, she's suddenly the less glamorous one. We've switched roles.

"Thanks," I reply, trying for nonchalance, and Jacques adds a friendly "*Au revoir!*" before leaning over to kiss Eloise on both cheeks. Now it's my turn to be swept by a wave of intense jealousy.

Eloise smiles at Jacques—I feel myself glaring—and speaks to him in rapid French; I catch mentions of "*Colette et Tomas*" and "*le café.*" There's nothing flirtatious about their exchange, but I can't help feeling a pang of paranoia. I wonder if there was ever *something* between the two of them.

I'm still wondering when Eloise gives me a smirk and, popping the last of my *pain au chocolat* into her mouth, slams the door. Her specialty.

Slowly, I turn to face Jacques as we stand together on the doorstep. I'm not sure if I should apologize, or explain—although what would I even say? I don't understand Eloise myself.

"That was . . . weird," I mumble at last, tucking an errant curl behind my ear. The day is growing hot and sultry, and I can feel my hair drying against my neck. I'm grateful for the light material of my new dress.

Jacques shrugs. "*Un peu bizarre,*" he admits, letting out a chuckle. He ducks his head. "So, how do you—I mean, I thought—" He pauses and I wait, terrified that he's going to confess that he and Eloise dated. After a second, though, he looks back up and flashes me his charming grin. "Forget it," he says.

And, like magic, I do. My spirits lift, and I return his smile. In that instant, it seems, we've reached a mutual agreement: There's no need to discuss Eloise any further.

I follow Jacques away from the house and over to the moped—shiny white and sleek, with two white helmets perched on the seat—that's parked in the street. When Jacques hands me one of the helmets, I hesitate. I ride my bike around Hudsonville all the time, but a moped seems very different—faster, wilder, scarier.

"Come on, you will love it," Jacques assures me, his eyes glinting with mischief.

I'm doubtful, but since I've been brave enough to make it this far—out of my room, out of my shell, on an "outing" with a boy—I take a breath and slip the helmet on my head. It fits snugly, muffling the birdsong of Rue du Pain.

Jacques dons his helmet as well, managing to look handsome even as he adjusts his chin strap. Then he jumps gracefully onto the moped. I climb on behind him, clumsy and careful, moving my tote bag into my lap and trying to sit without my dress bunching up. I'm glad he's not facing me.

"But there is one thing you should know before we go," Jacques says, revving the engine and glancing back at me.

"Yes?" I ask over the motor, my stomach clenching.

His dimple appears when he grins. "You look very beautiful today."

Wait. What?

My heart swoops up and into my mouth, rendering me speechless. I can't have heard him right. The helmet, the motor, the heat of the day—I'm hallucinating. Ear-hallucinating. Is that a thing? It has to be, because I'm me. Summer Everett. She of the Picasso-like face, she who is invisible to boys. Not beautiful.

Although . . . what if? What if I *did* hear him right? My pulse pounds. Before I can ask Jacques to repeat himself, he's faced forward again, and we're zooming off.

The speed of the moped matches my heartbeat. And the dizzying, tilting feeling I get when we careen down Rue du Pain mimics what's happening in my head.

I struggle to keep my feet planted on the footrests and then, without thinking, I reach forward and wrap my arms around Jacques's waist.

Oh my God.

I'm shocked by my own boldness. At the same time, anything seems possible now. I can feel the warmth of Jacques's back through his T-shirt, and I smile to myself as we zip along Boulevard du Temps.

All the storefronts and cafés are draped in French flags and blue, white, and red bunting for the holiday. The streets are nearly empty, the way they are back home on the Fourth of July. I remember what I read about Bastille Day, how it kick-started the French Revolution. What is it about July, about the heat of summer, that inspires people to rebel?

Leaving Boulevard du Temps in our wake, we shoot out onto the open road. The wind whistles inside my helmet and whips against my bare arms and knees. The sensation is frightening, and freeing.

We're surrounded by nothing but azure sky, dark-green cypress trees, and the occasional passing car or fellow moped. In the distance, there are the mountains. The same, sloping, green-brown mountains I saw on my taxi ride from the airport. I was a different Summer then, one who would have never imagined

I'd be on the back of a boy's moped, holding him. If only that Summer could see me now.

Jacques expertly steers the moped to the right and we begin climbing, threading up the side of a reddish cliff. I forget to be terrified, because the view is so gorgeous—other rust-colored cliffs all around and down below, a ribbon of turquoise water and fields of lavender. Their sweet scent is everywhere.

We reach a plateau and round a corner onto a tree-shaded path. Up ahead, there it is—a small white building with columns. A banner hanging from the façade reads GALERIE DE PROVENCE.

I feel a prickle of regret. I should have come here with Dad. It would feel so meaningful, going inside with him to look at my painting—his painting—together.

But I'm also impatient; I don't want to wait around for Dad to return from Berlin, whenever that will be. In his latest email, he promised he would "try" to be back by my birthday, which is this Tuesday. I figure if he doesn't return by then, I'll have to tell Mom the truth. I swallow at the thought as Jacques parks in front of the gallery.

Reluctantly, I drop my arms from around his waist. With equal reluctance, I remove my helmet, knowing that my hair must be a staticky mess. But when Jacques takes off his helmet—his hair, of course, looking as appealingly disheveled as always—he turns around and grins at me, and I remember his words from before: *very beautiful*. I can't help but grin back, a blush stealing across my face.

As I turn to dismount from the moped, Jacques gives me his hand to help me hop off. And then he doesn't let go.

My head spins. I imagine texting Ruby: *Am holding hands! With a real live boy!* But now that I've put my arms around Jacques, the act of holding his hand doesn't feel quite so foreign and impossible.

As Jacques and I head toward the gallery, our hands still linked, I feel a thrill race through me that has nothing to do with our hand holding.

I'm about to see my painting.

We walk up the steps and enter the cool marble lobby. There's an information desk, and a sign on the wall reads *Photographies interdites*, beside a drawing of a camera with a red slash through it. I guess I won't be able to take pictures. Off the lobby, I can see spacious rooms with framed paintings on the white walls. Other than me and Jacques, the woman behind the information desk, and a sleepy-looking security guard, the gallery seems empty. Probably because of the holiday.

"Have you been here before?" I ask Jacques, hoping he can't feel that my palms are getting clammy with nerves.

"Not for a long time," Jacques replies as we approach the information desk. "I came on a trip with my class my first year of *l'école*—high school. Some of my classmates, they would like to become painters, so they have returned more often, after." He releases my hand—I'm both disappointed and relieved—and steps forward to speak to the woman behind the desk. She waves us onward; entry to the gallery is free.

"You don't want to be a painter?" I ask Jacques as we enter the first room, our footsteps echoing on the marble floor. I start scanning the walls, my heart pounding.

"*Non*," Jacques laughs. "Me, I want to become a chef. A cook. Like my father. And you?" he asks me. "Do you want to be a painter, like *your* father?"

I shake my head. I'm about to tell Jacques that I have zero artistic talent when I spot a painting that looks familiar: a wristwatch floating on the surface of the ocean. It's very spare and modern, and reminds me of something by René Magritte or Salvador Dalí. I read the artist's name on the placard: VIVIENNE LACOUR.

"Oh!" I say, pointing. "I know her. That's—that's Eloise's mom." I hate that Eloise has to come up, here and now. Must her awfulness pervade everything?

But Vivienne isn't awful, I remind myself. I also realize that Vivienne must have painted the floating grandfather clock that hangs in my room; its style is nearly identical to the watch painting here. I bet there's artwork by Monsieur Pascal in this gallery, too. It's cool to really see how Dad belongs to this community of artists in Provence.

"Ah, I did not realize that Eloise's mother was a painter," Jacques says as we turn away from Vivienne's painting. I feel a beat of gladness that Jacques and Eloise are, at the very least, not close enough to have exchanged family details.

Then Jacques and I step into the second room, and I stop.

I gasp.

Because I see it.

Straight ahead, hanging on the center wall, inside a gold frame, is . . .

Well, me.

My heart vaults and I bolt forward, not caring if I look silly. I run up to the painting, standing as close as I can without actually touching it.

There I am: a solemn-faced little girl with long blond ringlets that won't turn frizzy and unmanageable for a couple more years. I wear a white dress with a round collar and I stand, skinny arms at my sides, in a field full of bright red poppies.

A shiver goes down my back. It's both strange and wonderful to see yourself—a past version of yourself—captured in paint and framed on a wall.

Faintly, I'm aware that Jacques has walked up beside me and is looking at the painting, too.

"Wow," he says softly. "Is that—"

"It's me," I whisper, half prideful, half embarrassed. Young Summer stares back at me, her eyes as wide as mine must be right now.

Jacques is silent. I take a second to glance away from my portrait and over at him. He's studying the painting, his forehead creased.

"Me when I was little, of course," I clarify with a nervous laugh. "This—this is the painting of my father's that I wanted to come here to see," I explain, my cheeks hot.

Jacques nods, a smile crossing his face. He looks at the square placard below the painting, and I do, too. Dad's name is typed on it, along with the date—the year I turned eleven—and the title: FILLE.

That is one French word whose meaning I have known for a long time, well before this trip. *Fille* means "girl." It also means "daughter."

Without warning, tears spring to my eyes. *Oh no.* I can't cry here, in front of Jacques, on my very first—outing. I didn't expect the sight of my portrait to make me so emotional, to churn up these muddled feelings of loss and joy. I press my lips together and try to swallow.

"It is incredible, Summer," Jacques murmurs, peering back up at the painting. I'm relieved he doesn't seem to notice my choked-up condition. "You have not seen it before?" he asks.

I take a breath, pulling myself together. "Only online," I manage to reply. I dab at my eyes and refocus on the painting, soaking in all the details: the swirls of Dad's paintbrush in the blue sky, the tiny crack in the lower right-hand corner of the canvas. The deep, saturated red of the poppies. "My dad painted this in France and sold it here."

I'm stung by a sudden memory: I was eleven and solemn-faced, with long blond ringlets, and I found Mom sniffling in front of our computer in the den. I saw that she was reading a website called Artforum, and right there on the page was a painting I'd never seen before—me, standing in a field of red flowers. I was surprised and embarrassed, and I came closer to read the caption: *Ned Everett's* Fille *heralds the arrival of a major new talent whose style evokes the Impressionists.*

I didn't understand any of that, so I asked Mom what it meant, and she jumped, startled to see me. Then she closed the website and took me into her lap—I was getting tall and gangly, and barely fit—and told me that Dad had sold a painting to a big-shot art dealer in France, and Dad might become rich and famous. I wondered why she didn't say that *we* would be rich and famous, too—why Dad was separate from us.

Two weeks later, Mom came home with an orange tabby kitten in a crate, and she took me in her lap again and told me that she and Dad had decided to get a divorce, but they both loved me so much, and she and I would stay in Hudsonville, together, and Dad would move to France. Dad was already in France at the time—he'd been there for a while, and I'd been overhearing Mom fighting on the phone with him. She would sometimes cry, and it made me scared. I knew about divorce, because of Ruby's parents, so part of me had anticipated and dreaded what was coming.

Afterward, after Dad had returned home to collect his things and kiss and hug me good-bye while Mom watched us, stone-faced, it occurred to me that maybe my painting had been the catalyst for what had happened with my parents. I'd always sensed that Dad was searching for his chance to live a fancy artist's life, and the sale of my painting had allowed him to do that. Soon, he would sell many more paintings, like *The Deliverer.*

I didn't resent my portrait, though; I was captivated by it. I'd sneak onto the Artforum website and gaze at myself, a little Narcissus, pleased with how Dad had rendered me. I'd read about how the painting was displayed in a French gallery in the Provençal countryside. I'd type the word *"fille"* into Google Translate and smile at the English definitions. But I kept my fascination a secret from Mom; any mention of Dad made her sigh or scowl.

"Do you remember posing for it?" Jacques asks me now.

I blink, ripped into the present. The gallery is cold, and I rub my arms.

"No," I say, looking from the painting to Jacques and back again. "My father must have painted this one from his imagination. Or from memory."

I rewind time once more, back to when I was eight, nine, ten. I do recall that occasionally, while I was, say, reading on our porch, Dad would sketch me. Then I'd peek at his sketch pad, giggling at the drawings of my face and curls. After the divorce, I never saw my father long enough for him to sketch me again. I also never got a chance to really talk to him about *Fille*—I brought it up once, on a Skype call, and he said he was glad I liked it, but had to run, sweetheart. So I don't really know about its genesis.

"I've definitely never been in a field of poppies," I add, studying the red flowers.

"No?" Jacques says, and I glance at him. He raises one eyebrow, giving me a mysterious smile. "When we leave here, I will show you something."

I'm intrigued, but I'm not ready to leave yet. Jacques seems to sense this; he strolls off to look at a Cézanne painting of green-brown mountains, allowing me some alone time with *Fille*.

It could be that an hour passes, or maybe only a few minutes, as I stand there, examining my painting, wishing I could somehow take it with me. Then I realize that I can. I reach into my tote bag and grab my camera, backing up a few paces to get a good shot. Within seconds, though, the no-longer-sleepy security guard appears at my side, barking at me in French and wagging a finger.

I'd forgotten. *Photographies interdites.* I frown, considering telling the guard that it's me in the painting. Shouldn't that give me special clearance? I feel an uncharacteristic rush of self-assurance; I am a part of this gallery after all. It's like a second home. I belong here.

Jacques, who was admiring a Matisse painting of bright shapes, lopes over and asks if everything is okay.

"Ça va," I say, while the guard continues to glower at me. "Maybe we should go, though. Get some food?" As much as I want to continue communing with *Fille*, I'm a little light-headed—from hunger, and the whole whirlwind of the morning. Anyway, I intend to return to the gallery very soon—ideally with Dad.

As Jacques and I walk toward the lobby, I keep glancing back at my painting. I crane my neck and squint my eyes at what is soon nothing more than a colorful dot.

When we step out into the heat, I feel a swell of sadness, missing *Fille* already.

"Okay," Jacques says, taking my hand—I'm too distracted to get flustered this time. "We will go have lunch. But first, like I said, there is something you should see."

I nod vaguely, barely paying attention as Jacques leads me down a path behind the gallery. We follow the gentle slope of a hill, and I glance around at the reddish cliffs and large, fairy-tale-ish olive trees that surround us.

"Where are we?" I ask. I'm disoriented, my mind still back at the gallery.

"This is all Les Deux Chemins," Jacques explains. "The rural part of it. Where the farmers who come to the market live and work, you see."

I nod again, my stiff new sandals rubbing against my ankles. The scenery is stunning, but I'm not quite sure why we're taking this little detour.

Then we reach the bottom of the hill.

"*Voilà*," Jacques says, gesturing ahead of us. "Look, Summer."

I look. And my mouth drops open.

We are facing a field full of bright red poppies. The flowers go on and on, a vibrant carpet that stretches toward the green mountains in the distance.

It is identical to the field in my painting. It *is* the field in my painting.

"How—oh my God," I stammer, feeling my face break into a huge smile. I turn to Jacques in wonder. "How did you even—know about this?"

Jacques beams, clearly proud of himself. "Well, I am from here," he reminds me, a teasing note in his voice. "When I saw your father's painting, I thought right away of this field. Of course, there are other poppy fields in Provence, but I bet this is the one . . ."

"The one that inspired my dad," I finish, my heart lifting. I imagine my father, seeing this very field and then linking it with the drawings he had of me in his sketchbook. Like he was bringing me here, to France. Again, I think I might cry.

I let go of Jacques's hand and step forward. I'm still holding my camera in my other hand, so I snap a few pictures of the field, trying to get the full, panoramic sweep. I feel my own flash of inspiration.

"Would you mind taking my picture?" I ask Jacques, giving him my camera. Before I can second-guess myself, I bend down and unlace my sandals, and run barefoot into the field, the soil cool and loamy beneath my toes. I stop and spin around, arms at my sides, mimicking my pose in *Fille*.

"Ah, I get it!" Jacques calls, bringing my camera to his eye. "Very cool."

As he starts photographing me, I expect to feel self-conscious; I generally hate how I come out in pictures. And I prefer to be the one behind the camera. But now, standing with the sun warming my hair and the poppies swaying all around me, I feel brave and carefree and maybe even . . . beautiful.

The beginnings of a blush climb up my face. Across the field, Jacques lowers my camera and studies me in an intent way that makes me blush even more. Can he tell what I'm thinking? Does he remember what he said to me on his moped?

"Remember?" Jacques suddenly calls, walking forward, shielding his eyes from the sun. My stomach jumps. "Remember when we first met," he adds, stopping in front of me, "and I caught this camera?"

"Oh—yeah." I let out a laugh, brushing my hair away from my forehead.

"I am glad I did," he says, his eyes sparkling. "You seem to like it."

I like you, I think. But this crush feels different from my crush on Hugh Tyson, or any crushes past. With Jacques, it seems as if something could *happen*, as if I could *make* something happen. Like I'm no longer a passive passenger, watching life go by outside the car window.

"I am glad you did, too," I hear myself say, over the loud pounding of my heart. "I am glad we met."

Jacques grins at me, biting his bottom lip. "For you," he says, extending my camera toward me. When I accept it from him, he takes hold of my hand and pulls me in toward him. I can smell the clean, spicy scent of his cologne and feel the softness of his red T-shirt and, up close, his eyes are an even darker blue than I'd thought, and I'm catching my breath, and time seems to speed up and slow down all at once—

"For you," he says again. And then he tilts his head and he kisses me.

Jacques kisses me.

My heart leaps. His lips are warm against mine, and the sensation is at once unfamiliar and natural.

My first kiss.

And I am kissing him back. At least, I think I am. I seem to know exactly what to do, without ever having been taught. It's miraculous. It's as if all those years of yearning and hoping and imagining have led in a straight line to this moment. *Sweet sixteen and never been kissed,* I think as Jacques wraps his arms around my waist and I melt into his chest. I have been spared that fate. I made it just under the wire.

We kiss and kiss, in the middle of this field of poppies, surrounded by mountains and sky, here in Provence. My life has been divided: Before the Kiss, and After the Kiss. Nothing will ever be the same.

• • •

Four days After the Kiss, on my sixteenth birthday, I wake up smiling.

I stretch in my narrow bed, feeling well-rested, my jet lag finally conquered. The light coming in through the window is gloomy and gray. Jacques did tell me that it rains approximately two times each summer in Provence. Maybe today is one of those rare days. Today, my birthday.

I sit up and swing my sun-browned legs off the side of the bed. I wonder what time it is; I got in late last night, after taking a moonlit stroll with Jacques along Boulevard du Temps. I know

I officially turn sixteen at two minutes past noon. Maybe the change has happened already.

I study myself in the broken mirror, trying to discern if I look any different. And I do. My curls have been lightened by the sun, and my face has a rosy flush to it, also from time spent outdoors. I notice that, even in my pajama bottoms and baggy T-shirt, I appear to have gotten actual *curves*. Thanks, I'm sure, to all the delicious food here, like my *pains au chocolat* from Bernice, or the Nutella crepes sprinkled with powdered sugar that Jacques and I devoured last night on our walk. I smile again.

Then I bring my fingers to my mouth, thinking about how I am different in other, invisible ways. I have been kissed. I know what it's like to run my hands through a boy's thick dark hair. I know what it's like to stand with that boy in front of the cupid fountain—the same spot where I saw Colette and Tomas kissing all those days ago, feeling like they were on a different planet—and touch my lips to his. It's like I've learned a new language, though I'm not fluent yet.

My heart fluttering, I turn away from my reflection and leave the room. Eloise's door is closed, so I tread softly. No need to wake the monster.

Because I've been out of the house so much lately, I haven't seen Eloise at all since the evening of Bastille Day. Jacques and I had gone to watch the fireworks display, joining the crush of convivial onlookers on Boulevard du Temps. I'd been lit up like a firework myself after everything that had happened that day.

We'd been joined by Jacques's friends from school—mellow, shaggy-haired guys in jeans and slip-on sneakers who could've been members of a French emo band. They'd greeted me with easy smiles and cheek kisses, taking the presence of the new American girl in stride.

When the fireworks started, I'd glanced around, thinking that the awed faces of the crowd would make a great picture. I'd brought my camera up to my eye and then, through the lens, I saw her: Eloise. She was standing a few feet away with Colette and Tomas and some other kids who were probably art class friends, taking pictures on her phone. I'd stiffened, hoping and dreading in equal measure that she'd glance over and see me and Jacques together.

But she'd kept her gaze skyward, and in that unguarded moment, she'd looked relaxed and joyful, almost childlike. Another Eloise. I'd felt a pang of confusion—and something else, too. Was it *fondness*? Recognition? That wouldn't make sense. Still, wanting to capture the surprising moment, I stealthily took her picture.

Now I head into the bathroom to shower, hoping I can continue my Eloise-less streak today. I'm meeting Jacques at Café des Roses for lunch; he promised to prepare the meal for me himself. I've requested *bouillabaisse* and birthday cake.

My routine has been disrupted: Over the past few days, I've stopped visiting the bakery and spending hours in Dad's studio, or curling up, like a crab, in my room with my guidebook. Instead, I have been exploring—going to the places I'd read about.

Jacques begged his parents for some time off work, so on Saturday, we rode his moped to Avignon. We visited the grand Palace of the Popes, and I got to see the famous stone bridge of Avignon, the one there's a children's song about. Dad used to sing it to me when I was little: *"Sur le pont d'Avignon/On y danse."* I sang it for Jacques, feeling only a little shy, and he laughed and told me I was *"très adorable."* And then he kissed me. Which was worth any slight embarrassment.

Outside of Saint-Rémy-de-Provence, we picnicked on bread and cheese and fruit, lolling in a field of sunflowers. Then we went to Arles, the sun-washed town where Van Gogh had lived and painted. We had coffee—I got hot chocolate—at a pretty yellow café named for the artist, and Jacques good-naturedly rolled his eyes at how it was "all for tourists," but I didn't care. I was too busy snapping pictures of everything.

On Sunday, we took the train to Cannes, a town on the Riviera. It was all fancy hotels, elegant people, and beaches with creamy sand and the bluest ocean water I'd ever seen. I didn't even get *too* uncomfortable wearing my bathing suit in front of Jacques. He, of course, looked tanned and gorgeous in his dark-blue swim trunks, which matched his eyes. When he caught me staring, he smiled at me in his wolfish way, and then he raced me into the surf. I beat him, splashing into the warm Mediterranean, feeling free.

After the beach, we ate fresh fish and salads on the boardwalk, and then we rode the train back to Les Deux Chemins, sandy and sunburnt and pleasantly tired. Jacques had said that next weekend, maybe we would take another train, this one up to Paris.

I could live here, I think now. After all, I have almost mastered the slippery shower nozzle that I'm holding now. And my French is improving—just yesterday, I learned that *"joyeux anniversaire"* means "happy birthday" (Jacques murmured it to me when we were kissing in front of the cupid fountain). I may still be a late bloomer, but here I *am* blooming, unlike in Hudsonville, where I was starting to wilt.

I mean, I wouldn't leave Hudsonville for good; I'd be like those celebrities who say that they "divide their time" between two cities. It would be like my parents had joint custody, instead of Mom getting me all to herself.

At the thought of Mom, my stomach tightens. I step out of the shower and wrap myself in a thin towel. Today is my self-imposed deadline; Dad is not yet back from Berlin. So I have to do it. I have to tell Mom.

Yesterday, she'd called the house—her first time doing so since my first day—and I happened to answer the phone; I'd been expecting Jacques's call. Mom had sounded extremely anxious as she peppered me with questions about Dad, and I'd felt awful as I fudged my answers. I'd asked what was new with her, and she'd replied strangely, with a nervous chuckle and a vague "We'll catch up when you're home." I didn't mention Jacques; that would be another minefield to cross. But at least it wasn't a *total* lie when I told Mom I had to go because I was waiting for a call from a—friend.

I blush as I return to my medieval chamber. I pull on the sky-blue dress I wore the day I first saw my portrait, and got my first kiss. A lucky dress. I toss a glance at Ruby's woven bracelets, which are still sitting out on my dresser, but I leave my wrist bare again. Then I lace on my now-comfortable sandals and go downstairs.

The house smells tantalizingly of roasting chicken. I hear Vivienne moving around in the kitchen. I wonder why she's cooking. She and Eloise rarely eat in.

I think back to last night, how I saw Vivienne's light click off in her room when I came upstairs. Had she been waiting up for me? I know she's felt some chaperone-like responsibility for me, given that my father has been MIA.

In the living room, I go to the computer to check the time. By now, I've learned that, in Europe, the hours are counted differently: Noon doesn't split the day down the middle like it does at home. Here, one p.m. is thirteen hours, two p.m. is fourteen, and so on, until midnight, when the clock resets. It's confusing, and also totally clear, which is how time itself is, I guess.

The numbers in the upper right-hand corner of the screen tell me it's *13:05*—five minutes past one p.m. So I have officially turned sixteen. Well, at least in France I have. In Hudsonville, six hours in the past, I am still fifteen. The bizarreness of this fact makes me laugh.

I sit down and log in to my email. I told Jacques that I'd be at Café des Roses at one-thirty, so I don't think I need to rush.

There are three new emails waiting for me, all from earlier

this morning. One is from Mom, one is from Dad, and one is from Aunt Lydia. I feel my stress spike, and then decide to open my aunt's—the least stressful one—first.

Happy sweet sixteen, kiddo! it reads. *I'm up before dawn like a crazy person to photograph the sunrise. Anyway, you've been on my mind a lot this summer. A couple of high school kids are taking my photography class, and I think you would've really enjoyed being in it, too. Have you been getting some good use out of the Nikon? I can't wait to see your pictures when you're back. I hope you're surviving in France. You know you can talk to me about anything that happens, right? Love, Aunt L.*

I frown, unsettled by her last two lines. What does she mean by "anything that happens"? It's almost as if she knows that Dad is in Berlin. But how?

Also, what she's said about a photography course—and high school kids taking it—rings a faint bell in my mind, though I can't quite make the connection I'm seeking.

Shaking off the weirdness, I close my aunt's email, and open Dad's:

My sweet Summer, his reads. *Joyeux anniversaire! Perhaps you now know what this French phrase means. And I have some good birthday news for you: I am returning today! My flight from Berlin lands early in the afternoon. I cannot wait to see you!*

I stare at the screen, feeling a huge grin take over my face. Dad is coming back! I won't have to confess to Mom! I do a little dance in my chair, and keep reading:

And before I forget, sweetheart: I hope you can do me one quick favor? I've misplaced a sketch of mine that I urgently need to mail to my agent. Would you mind searching for it in my studio? It's of an elderly lady taking bread out of an oven, and on the back it should say: Bernice, Les Deux Chemins. *I'm sure it's stuffed somewhere in my messy sketch boxes. I am sorry to ask you to do work on your birthday, sweetheart, but it would be a big help. Merci beaucoup, and see you soon.* —Dad

I don't care that Dad has asked me to do work on my birthday. Nothing can bother me at this moment. In fact, I love that Dad drew a sketch of Bernice the bakery lady. Maybe I can even show it to her before I mail it off.

Still grinning, I open Mom's email, which is a brief message saying happy birthday, and telling me that she's awake early, so I should call her. I will, once Dad is back, and I can put him on the phone with her. Then there will be no more secrets, no more lies. I feel light and balloon-like. Untethered.

I log out of my email, realizing with a pang that Ruby hasn't sent me a birthday message yet. I'm sure she's sleeping now. But I haven't heard from her in three days, a new record. My fingers stray to my bare wrist. If I were in Hudsonville, Mom would be taking me and Ruby (and Alice and Inez, if they were around) to Orologio's, the nice Italian restaurant on Greene Street, for my birthday.

Since I'm a "summer baby," as Mom likes to say, I'm used to having small birthday gatherings rather than big parties (unlike the Sweet Sixteen blow-out Ruby's dad threw for her this past

April). People tend to be away in the summers, at camp or on trips. And I prefer low-key birthdays, anyway: Orologio's always felt just special enough. The waiters would bring me a cake and sing to me, loudly, and I'd bury my face in my hands while Ruby chortled.

As I get to my feet, I think of the photo I saw when I checked Instagram after getting in late last night. Ruby had posted a picture of herself, Austin, Skye, and Genji Tanaka at Orologio's—our place—beaming over plates of pasta. *Celebrating!* Ruby's caption had read. *#dinnerout #doubledate*

I'd wondered what they'd been celebrating. I'd wondered if Ruby had been thinking of me, and my birthday, at all. Mostly, though, I'd felt a wave of sadness. There it was, the reality that my other half, my stand-in sister, was drifting farther and farther from me. But the sadness hadn't pulled me under. Because I was drifting away from her, too. She didn't know about my adventures with Jacques. I hadn't even told her that I'd been kissed—an omission that, weeks ago, would have been a crime. Now I no longer feel the need to update Ruby on every detail of my existence; there is something liberating about keeping certain things to myself.

Still, there's a small lump in my throat as I walk from the living room into the kitchen. I'm not willing to admit that Ruby and I are irreparably broken.

Vivienne is busy chopping vegetables at the counter, and she doesn't even notice me pass by. The roast chicken is done, sizzling in its pan on the stovetop. I'm tempted to ask her for some, but I resist. I should save my appetite for Jacques's lunch. As I open the front door, I realize that, as usual, I have no sense of what time it is now—whether I will be late to the café or not. Regardless, I want to take care of Dad's errand first.

The sky is a low, foreboding gray, and the cool air makes me shiver. I hug myself as I hurry through the garden. The surface of the pool is murky, finally matching its guts, and the roses stand out starkly against the fog, red as blood.

The barn door is half open, creaking and groaning in the wind. I figure Monsieur Pascal is inside, but when I enter, the studio is empty. The smell of turpentine is stronger than I remember—I haven't been in here since last Thursday—and the skylight only lets in more gloom. Someone's unfinished canvas—a close-up of a face—stares at me from one of the easels. I shiver again, unsure as to why I feel creeped out.

Moving quickly, I kneel in front of Dad's sketch boxes and start flipping through the sheaves of paper. A woman's hand picking tulips, schoolchildren lined up at a bus stop, a man in a beret on a bicycle . . . no Bernice taking bread from an oven. Frustration flares up in me; why *can't* Dad keep better track of his sketches? In a way, he's messy and careless about everything, isn't he?

I realize then, sitting there on the cold studio floor, that I'm still angry with my father—angry about Berlin, about him leaving me here on my own. Maybe even angry at him for leaving me in Hudsonville years ago, after he sold *Fille*. I take a deep breath, coming to the end of one box. I wonder if my anger will dissipate when I finally see Dad. I'll probably be so relieved that I'll just hug him and forgive him.

I pull forward another box, one that was hidden behind the others. I cough at the dust that rises from the sketches. I flip and flip and then, I see it—a folded-up piece of paper, crammed down low between two other sketches. It has to be the missing Bernice sketch. I feel a sense of satisfaction, of having solved a mystery, as I unfold the paper.

My brain takes a minute to catch up to my eyes. The drawing on the paper is not of Bernice. No. It is of a curly-haired, big-eyed little girl in a white dress, standing in a field of poppies. The poppies are not red, because the sketch is done in black charcoal. But I know that the poppies are bright red in the final painting, which hangs in the Galerie de Provence. I am looking at the sketch of *Fille*.

I let out a startled laugh, which echoes through the studio. I didn't know there was a sketch of my painting. I flip the paper over, to see what Dad has written on the back.

There's the date—five years ago.

And the words *Eloise, Les Deux Chemins*.

Wait.

I don't understand.

I feel my brow furrow as I reread Dad's scrawl. Then I laugh again, because it's so absurd, the idea that it would say *Eloise* on the back of my sketch. But the laugh sounds strange and distorted to my ears, louder than normal.

Eloise?

The Eloise I know, the Eloise sleeping upstairs in Dad's house? Or another one?

It should say *Summer* on there. *Summer. Summer. Summer.*

Eloise doesn't make any sense. Right?

Something is taking shape in my head, a dark, slithery, and terrible thought. I am thinking of how Eloise has blond curls and big eyes. And how, five years ago, she could have easily been here, in Les Deux Chemins. She could have stood in that field of poppies for real. But why would Dad have sketched her?

My mind slams shut like a door. I stand up, gripping the sketch. The walls of the studio feel very close. I have to get out of here. The turpentine smells toxic.

I back up a few paces, staring in confusion at the boxes of sketches, realizing dimly that I didn't find the Bernice sketch, and that I need to leave soon to meet Jacques. Except Jacques, and everything else that seemed so important a few seconds ago, no longer seems to exist.

I turn and run out into the garden, where it's starting to rain. Hard. Cold drops land on my arms and legs, on my nose and cheeks. It must look like I'm crying. The surface of the pool is all ripples, and rain slides down the leaves of the lemon trees, drowns the lavender. I keep running, holding on to the sketch, aware that it's getting wet. I don't care. I almost want to see the charcoal bleed, to see the evidence destroyed.

I'm out of breath when I reach the house. What am I going to do now? Take the sketch upstairs, crawl back into bed? Pretend that this day hasn't happened yet?

I open the door and step into the foyer, my muddy sandals making sucking noises on the floor. I almost trip over a plush-looking leather suitcase that's sitting there. A suitcase. Someone has arrived.

A man's voice is coming from the kitchen. A very familiar voice. Speaking in French. A woman answers him, also in French.

I walk into the kitchen. Vivienne is standing at the table, carving the roast chicken, and my dad is sitting down, a plate in front of him, ready to eat. The chicken was for him.

"Hi, Dad," I say. My voice is small and strangled.

He looks up, his eyes widening. Vivienne looks up at me, too, and stops carving.

"Summer! Sweetheart!" Dad springs up from the chair, beaming. "Happy birthday! Oh my—you've grown into such a beautiful young lady."

He strides toward me, his arms outstretched. I stare at him. He looks the same as I remember: his blond-gray hair combed back off his forehead in waves, his face tanned, with only a few new wrinkles around his green eyes. He wears dark-blue jeans and a white button-down shirt under a thin brown leather jacket. His thumb is stained with paint. When he wraps his arms around me, he smells just as I remember, too: shaving cream and mint gum mixed with paint and turpentine. I'm going to suffocate.

"Sweetheart?" Dad asks, still hugging me, but less tightly now. "Are you all right? You're trembling." He lets go of me and takes a step back, frowning.

I realize then that I'm soaking wet, my hair plastered to my cheeks, my lucky dress hanging soggily, my hands pressing the damp sketch to my chest. And I realize how pale I must be, how lifeless and cold my skin feels.

"What's the matter?" Dad says, putting a hand to my forehead. "Why were you out in the rain?" I don't answer, and his frown deepens, his wrinkles standing out more. "Are you upset with me, because of Berlin?" he asks dolefully. "I am so sorry, sweetheart. But I am back now, and there is so much to catch up on—"

"Why is Eloise's name on my sketch?" I ask.

Dad's tanned face turns white. "What?" he murmurs.

I hold the sketch out toward him, the paper so brittle and wet between my fingers.

Behind Dad, there's a loud clatter. I look past him, and I see that Vivienne has dropped the carving knife. It lies on the kitchen floor, a discarded murder weapon.

Behind me, I hear footsteps—light, almost noiseless. Ghost steps. Eloise appears in the kitchen, just like she did my first day here, in her lacy white nightgown, her golden ringlets spilling over her shoulders.

"What's going on?" she asks. At first, because she is speaking English, I assume she is talking to me. But no. She is looking at my father. She is speaking to him.

And she sounds sort of frightened.

It's then that I feel my own fear, slicing through my belly like a knife. *Happy birthday to me*, I think, incongruously. I keep holding the sketch forward. I am shaking.

Dad's gaze travels from the sketch up to my face, and then over to Eloise. Then he glances back at Vivienne. The four of us stand motionless in the kitchen, the only sound the raindrops hammering the windows.

Finally, Dad faces me again. He clears his throat, and reaches out to take the sketch from my hands.

"Summer," he says softly. "There is something I have to tell you."

PART FOUR

Don't Tell

Friday, July 14, 9:13 a.m.

"All aboard! This is the nine-fifteen express to New York City!"

The overhead announcement makes me smile as I slide into my window seat and settle my bookbag in my lap. I wonder if boarding the flight to France might have felt something like this—the strong blast of air-conditioning, the smell of coffee, the murmured conversations all around, the beat of anticipation in my chest.

Of course, I am not on a plane but a train—the steaming silver Metro-North that's about to depart the Hudsonville station—and the destination isn't quite so foreign or thrilling. Still, I haven't been down to New York since my trip with Ruby in December, and I'm excited and nervous to go back, especially under these different circumstances.

"Okay, class!" Aunt Lydia calls from where she stands in the middle of the aisle. "Everyone ready for our big field trip? I'm going to hand out your tickets soon."

Her brown eyes dart from seat to seat, and I can tell she's taking a mental tally of who's here. I did the same when I boarded the train, flushed and relieved to be on time, and I noticed that neither

Hugh nor Wren had arrived yet. Now I glance out the window, bracing myself for the sight of them running together, maybe hand in hand, down the steps onto the gray platform.

The past three days in Aunt Lydia's class have been full of amazing discoveries: I now know that a daguerreotype is a black-and-white, very early kind of photograph, invented by a French artist in the nineteenth century. I've learned how to load slippery film into an old-school camera, and how to use the more advanced settings on my new Nikon. I've learned that, way back in ancient times, a box with a hole in it, called a camera obscura (which means "dark chamber" in Latin) was the start of photography. And apparently the word *photography* itself means "drawing with light" in Greek. When Aunt Lydia told us that, I got a small shiver down my back. *Drawing with light.*

But I have yet to discover what, if anything, is going on between Hugh and Wren. And I certainly haven't learned how to speak to Hugh at all.

I've even moved to sit in the front row of the class, teacher's pet–like, to distance myself from the two of them—and, you know, to better focus on Aunt Lydia's awesome lectures. Still, my ears prick up every time I hear Hugh murmur something to Wren, or vice versa, in the back row.

Yesterday, when Aunt Lydia brought us to the college darkroom, showing us the print tongs and developing trays, I'd kept my eyes trained on Hugh and Wren, trying to discern if they were standing *too* close to each other in the dim, small space. At one point, Hugh had glanced my way and I'd turned around so fast that I'd knocked over a (thankfully, capped) bottle of toner.

Smooth.

Now I feel a bolt of surprise as I see Wren—alone—fly onto the platform, a scarlet-haired blur in a long dark dress. A second later, I hear her thunder onto the train car, breathing hard. There's a sharp whistle and then the train begins to move. My stomach plummets in disbelief as I watch the platform recede. *Hugh isn't coming?*

"You made it!" Aunt Lydia says cheerily when Wren appears in the aisle.

"Barely," Wren replies, sounding pleasanter than I would have expected.

And then she plops into the seat beside me.

Oh no.

I feel my whole self tense up. I also can't help facing Wren, a question hovering on my lips.

"Where's Hugh?" I ask her.

Wren is fiddling with the zipper on her fringed bag, and she glances up at me. She might raise an eyebrow, but it's impossible to tell because of her bangs. They're like an impenetrable curtain. I notice for the first time that her eyes are a startling violet color.

"Alien abduction," she answers drily, the corner of her mouth twitching. "A UFO sucked up the mayor's mansion last night. You haven't heard?"

I stare back at her, at a loss for words. The train rocks us both from side to side.

"Nah," Wren says after a moment, a smile crossing her face. "He's already down in NYC. He went last night to stay with his cousin, so he'll meet us at the museum." She unzips her bag and starts riffling through it. "Man. Your expression was priceless."

"I—" I shake my head, and, in spite of myself, I laugh. "I didn't *believe* you."

"Really?" Wren asks, and this time I'm positive she is arching her eyebrow behind her bangs.

"Here you go, ladies," Aunt Lydia says, appearing next to Wren's aisle seat and giving each of us our round-trip tickets. She shoots me the quickest of smiles before turning and walking to her seat near the front of the car. In this fallow time after rush hour, the sunlit train is quiet; our class fills most of the seats.

"Your aunt is a great professor," Wren says, still digging in her bag.

"What?" I glance at her, startled.

"She's great," Wren repeats, nodding toward the front of the car. "I took a photography course at the YMCA last year and I didn't learn half as much."

"How—how do you know she's my aunt?" I stammer. I inch closer to the window, feeling defensive. I thought I'd been doing a thorough, careful job of keeping my secret. In fact, it hasn't been hard; ever since our strange interaction at Better Latte Than Never, my aunt has seemed a bit distant. There've been no more invitations to coffee, no more special call-outs in class. I'm at once grateful and unsettled.

Wren shrugs, taking from her bag a thick, tattered paperback: a collection of poems by Emily Dickinson. "It's pretty obvious," she tells me.

"How?" I press as the conductor comes over to punch our tickets. "We don't even look alike." Mom and Aunt Lydia are brunettes, while I inherited Dad's coloring—the blond hair and light eyes. Not that I really bear a strong resemblance to anyone in my family.

Wren tips her head to one side, thinking. "You kind of do," she says, accepting her ticket back from the conductor. "Something in your expressions. Anyway, it was more that Lydia knew your name on the first day of class, before she learned who the rest of us were. Also, she said that her sister was a philosophy professor. I remembered on Career Day in fourth grade, how your mom came in and told us about her job and I'd thought it sounded so cool."

"Oh," I manage to say, shocked that Wren was able to deduce the truth. And that she remembers Career Day. Although I do, too. I'd wanted Dad to come speak to my class—in my nine-year-old opinion, *painter* sounded much cooler than *philosopher*—but he'd been in France for work. Wren's parents had come, I recall; they were both lawyers, which had seemed oddly ordinary for the already-weird Wren. "I just didn't—I didn't want anyone to find out," I add haltingly.

The train curves, screeching, around a bend in the track. I hold tight on to the armrests. *Does Hugh know, too?* I wonder, my cheeks burning.

Wren shrugs again, opening her book. "It's nothing to be embarrassed about," she replies. "And why should you care what people think?"

I watch Wren as she reads. The sun flashes through the train windows and alights on her bright hair. Her long dark dress is shapeless and looks like a Victorian nightgown. Her nails are bitten down, and she has a clunky old leather watch on her wrist. Wren is like nobody else. It hits me then that *she* doesn't care what anyone thinks of her. Some people say they don't care, but in Wren's case, I can tell it's true.

I care, I realize, plucking at my woven bracelets. Ruby *really* cares. I've learned that about my best friend recently. I glance down at what I'm wearing—a white linen sundress that Ruby gave me when she cleaned out her closet last year. I'd packed the dress to take to France, and the airline finally returned my wandering suitcase to me. But now I almost wish I'd put on something else this morning.

Reaching into my bookbag, I move aside my Nikon camera, and my notebook, and the cardigan Mom suggested I bring right when we were leaving the house, even though it's already eighty-six degrees outside. I grab my phone from where it's slipped down to the bottom of the bag and check the screen. No texts from Ruby.

I sigh. What was I expecting? My best friend is now officially dating Austin Wheeler. She broke the news to me on Tuesday, when I'd stopped by Better Latte after my Photoshop lab. "It's my summer of falling in love!" she'd squealed, hugging me, our tension from the day before apparently forgotten.

That was the last time we'd spoken this week. Normally, in the summers, I'd see Ruby constantly. On weekends, we'd spread a blanket in Pine Park and spend a whole afternoon there. Or we'd sneak into the YMCA pool and swim until our fingers pruned and the chlorine had thoroughly soaked into our hair. We'd ride our bikes side by side, licking Popsicles that melted and ran and got our woven bracelets sticky. We'd movie-hop at the multiplex, feeling like we were allowed to because we'd worked there before. Ruby would sleep over at my house, and we'd turn up the air-conditioning in my room so high that our toes would become icicles.

Last night, when we should have been doing any one of those things, I'd been home alone. Mom had gone out to dinner with a friend from work, and Alice was in California visiting Inez. I didn't feel like reading, there was nothing appealing on Netflix, and I was avoiding Instagram, so as not to witness the Ruby-Austin "summer of love" story no doubt unfolding on there.

So I'd sat cross-legged on the porch bench, eating cold leftover lo mein from Szechuan Kitchen. Ro, curled up beside me, had sent occasional hisses in my direction, to remind me that he was not a fan. The stars had winked overhead, and I'd wondered if this was it—the sum total of my summer here in Hudsonville. I'd felt a flash of anger toward Dad, whom I haven't heard from once since the Fourth of July.

Now I gaze sadly out the window. The train is winding southward along the Hudson River. Here, a good distance from Hudsonville, the wide river does look blue under the sun. I knew it; I knew my town is cursed with grayness.

Beside me, Wren turns a page in her book. I glance at her again.

"Is that good?" I ask, wanting to get my mind off Dad and Ruby and the ache in my chest. The train pulls to a stop in a station with a sign that reads TARRYTOWN.

Wren nods. "I love Emily Dickinson. Like, look at this." She flips the book around to face me.

I read the typed words on the page, the beginning of a poem: *I felt a Cleaving in my Mind— As if my Brain had split—*

"Um, yeah," I say, even though I don't really understand. Poetry mystifies me most of the time. That's partly why I'd been so impressed by Hugh's brilliant Robert Frost presentation that fateful day freshman year. My assigned poet had been Walt Whitman, and I'd had trouble parsing his strange poems about leaves of grass and astronomers. I'd fumbled through my own presentation, and I'd gotten a B-minus.

"Did you know," Wren says, turning the book back toward her, "that Emily Dickinson was a recluse? She never left her house. Or her hometown of Amherst, Massachusetts. She was considered a weirdo in her day." Wren pauses, flipping another page. "It's kind of amazing, isn't it? That she understood the world so deeply without having ever really seen it?"

"I guess," I say. I look at the cover of the book—a daguerreotype (I know this now!) of the poet, a pale, solemn-eyed young woman in a dark dress, her hair pulled back in a bun. I wonder if Wren relates to Emily Dickinson, the "weirdo." But I see now that Wren isn't actually that weird. Or, rather, she's weird in a good way. And super smart.

Is that why Hugh likes her? I find myself thinking. I frown. Does he like her? They do seem like they'd be an intellectual match. I fight down a pang of jealousy.

"My boyfriend lives in Amherst," Wren goes on, idly turning another page, "so when I visited him over spring break, I got to see her house. I also went to her grave, which is maybe sort of morbid, but it was really cool."

Nothing else Wren said has registered except for the words *my boyfriend*.

"You have a boyfriend?" I blurt. I realize that sounds cruel, à la Skye Oliveira: *Typhoid Wrenny has a boyfriend?!* But that's not what I meant. "I thought you were, like, dating Hugh or something," I add. My face flames. That's even worse. *Shut up, Summer!*

Wren's mouth curves into that smirk I'm beginning to recognize. "I'm not dating Hugh," she answers, her violet eyes regarding me thoughtfully. I feel my stomach jump. "Why would you think that?"

"I—um, you guys are always talking, and leaving class together, and stuff," I say in a rush. *Oh God.* If Wren has Sherlocked out the fact that Lydia is my aunt, then she will surely be able to tell from this little exchange that I like Hugh. We're pulling into another station—YONKERS—and I give some serious thought to getting up and casually strolling off the train, maybe starting over with a whole new life in this Yonkers place.

Wren chuckles, closing her book. "We're friends," she tells me, as if I've overlooked the most obvious thing in the world. "I got to know him this past year because my mom started working as a lawyer for the mayor's office, and Hugh and I were always winding up at boring events together." She stuffs the book back into her fringed bag and begins rooting around in there again. "Hugh's awesome, but he's not my type. And besides, he's into another girl."

Another girl? My pulse is pounding. *Who?* I'm debating whether or not I want to preserve any dignity, or just ask, when Wren pulls a phone out of her bag.

"This is Will," she explains, her voice softened with affection. She's showing me the picture on her screen, of a grinning guy with green hair that's shaved on one side and floppy on the other. He's holding his hands forward in a heart shape, and he has words scrawled on his arm—they look like song lyrics—just as Wren often does. Maybe that's, like, some sweet, couple-y thing they do. Who would've guessed? "Isn't he cute?" Wren asks me.

"Very," I lie. Mostly I'm relieved to know that Hugh *isn't* Wren's type.

"We met at a Walk the Moon concert last summer," Wren explains, smiling down at the photo, "and even though we're long distance, it works. We Skype all the time."

I nod at her, floored. The fact that Wren has a cell phone—and Skype—feels more noteworthy than the boyfriend revelation. I'd assumed she shunned all technology. But that was only because of cruel comments made by Skye and her clones over the years. It's turning out that I knew nothing about Wren D'Amico. What was the phrase Aunt Lydia used in regard to Dad? *Shocking surprises.* Wren, it seems, is full of shocking surprises herself.

"Are you on Instagram?" I ask her, curious as to what else I might not know.

Wren rolls her violet eyes. "Nah. It can be so fake. People just post things that make them look good. You never get the whole story."

I look at my phone in my hand. *Pics or it didn't happen!* Ruby likes to say. I think of that picture I posed for with Ruby and Alice before Skye's party. Even though a photograph might exist, it *isn't* always evidence of what really happened.

"I guess it depends what kinds of pictures you post," I say. I haven't put anything up on Instagram all summer. Maybe I'm waiting to post something real.

"Hey, photographers?" Aunt Lydia calls, turning around in her seat to face the class. "Next stop is Grand Central Station. That's us."

Dazed, I peer out the window. The trees and rocks and water have given way to the bridges and buildings of the city. The train ride flew by. I glance down at my phone again, and imagine texting Ruby: *Wren D'Amico is really fun to talk to.* I imagine how Ruby, especially this new Ruby, would respond.

"What about you?" Wren asks me as the train dips below-ground into a tunnel.

"Yeah, I'm on Instagram," I say distractedly, returning my phone to my bag.

Wren laughs. "That's not what I meant. Do *you* have a boy-friend?" she asks matter-of-factly as she zips up her bag.

"Oh." I shake my head, and I can't help but laugh myself. "Not on this planet."

The train judders to a stop inside Grand Central and we all stand up, gathering our things.

"Huh," Wren says as we follow Aunt Lydia, our classmates, and the other commuters off the train onto the platform. "I would've pegged you for someone who has, like, a secret, sophis-ticated boyfriend somewhere in Europe."

"Me?" I'm so astonished that I almost crash into a passerby. "That is insane," I tell Wren as we walk up the platform toward the main hall. It occurs to me then that perhaps Wren also saw me in a certain way. And we were both off base about each other. I want to laugh again, at the notion that I seem like someone with a European boyfriend.

But what if . . .

I let my mind wander. What if I *had* gone to France, and Ruby's prediction had magically come true? What if I'd met a gorgeous French boy—

No. Don't be ridiculous.

We've arrived in the station's main hall, and I tip my head back to admire the beautiful vaulted ceiling. It's a deep blue-green, decorated with drawings of the constellations. There's Orion, and Pegasus, and Aquarius. And Cancer the crab—me. I reach into my bookbag for my Nikon and take a picture of the indoor sky.

"Everyone, please put down your cameras," Aunt Lydia says, sounding amused.

I notice that all my classmates are also standing still in the mad whirling rush of the station, their cameras pointed up. I smile, feeling an unfamiliar flash of belonging. Aunt Lydia motions for us to follow her to the famous bronze clock, the one with four identical faces. We stand in a clump as she starts speaking.

"Here's the game plan," she tells us, adjusting the chopsticks in her messy bun. "We're going to walk up to the Museum of Modern Art, and I want you all to observe the sights and sounds and shapes of the city. Feel free to take pictures, obviously—just don't get so distracted you get lost." She grins, and I feel a twinge of nervousness. "Then, at the exhibit," she adds, gesturing enthusiastically, "you can compare your visions to those of the masters. After that, we'll get lunch. Any questions?"

One of the college kids asks a question about the museum. I bite my lip, gazing over at the clock. When Aunt Lydia told us on Tuesday that we'd be taking a field trip to see a photography exhibit at the Museum of Modern Art, I'd thought instantly of Dad. His painting of a mailman, *The Deliverer*, hangs in the Whitney Museum: a quick cab ride downtown from here. I'd wondered if I'd have a chance to break away from my class and go see the painting, even though I'd recently visited it with Ruby, in December.

Now, as Aunt Lydia leads us to the exit, I realize that I don't want to interrupt this day for my father. He decided I shouldn't be a part of his summer, so why should he be a part of mine? A stew of hurt and regret swirls in me as I step out onto the street.

Horns honk and sirens wail. The air is thick and sticky—the temperature feels hotter than it did back in Hudsonville, and not just because it's later in the morning. Heat seems to rise up from the sidewalk in waves. People swarm everywhere, shouting at one another and staring at their phones, juggling sweating cups of iced coffee, hailing yellow taxicabs.

I remember how scared I'd been when I'd stood in this same spot with Ruby. This time, though, I don't have the urge to hide. In fact, I feel a swell of excitement, breathing in the scent of pretzels and mustard coming from a cart on the corner. The city crackles with energy, and I'm energized, too, holding the solid heft of my Nikon in my hand.

As the class starts walking west, I point my camera up, taking dizzying shots of the skyscrapers, their spires glinting in the sun. Someone bumps into me and I stumble. Wren grabs my arm, steadying me, and I thank her. It's tricky to maneuver around the constant stream of passersby and cars. But there is so much to look at, and capture.

There is the huge library on Fifth Avenue, with its two stone lions out front. There are the revolving doors of department stores, which suck in and spit out people at once. There are elegant women in tall heels and pencil skirts and big sunglasses, and children eating dripping ice-cream bars in their strollers. We pass a perspiring man selling handbags on the sidewalk, and carts hawking hot dogs and sodas. I recall the vendors at Pine Park; that seems like another world. Strange to think it's only two hours away.

We walk past Rockefeller Center, with its colorful flowers and flags, and the statue of the Greek god, Atlas, holding the earth on his shoulders. We are turning onto 53rd Street when I spot a mailman pushing his blue cart. I stop and stare, recalling Dad's painting. Could this be the same city mailman Dad saw all those years ago? It seems impossible. Still, I snap the mailman's photo—he scowls at me—and then I hurry to catch up with my class.

I see that they've already gone inside the museum, a glass building with a banner reading MOMA—Museum of Modern Art—out front. As I enter the cool, airy lobby, I wonder what it would have been like to visit that gallery in the South of France this summer. To finally see my portrait, *Fille*, hanging on the wall. I swallow down my bitterness, and join Wren and the others by the ticket counter.

"Sorry," I say to Wren, stashing my Nikon inside my bag, "I was taking a picture of—" I pause, my heart leaping, when I notice who's standing next to her.

Hugh.

"Oh. Hi," I mutter, blushing while also attempting to put on my "Hugh face." I'd forgotten that he would be meeting us here.

I feel the weight of my notebook in my bag—the notebook with the embarrassing letter I wrote to Hugh on the first day of class.

"Hi," Hugh replies shortly, his hands in his jeans pockets. He looks really handsome in a green-checked button-down shirt with the sleeves half rolled up. He has his Nikon on a strap, slung over one shoulder, and this gives him the appearance of a rugged photographer about to go shoot wildlife or something.

I suddenly have the funniest desire—to walk right up to Hugh and twine my arms around his neck. My stomach flips. What am I *thinking*? I wouldn't even know how to do that. And Hugh would surely stagger away in confusion and disgust.

I feel Wren watching me with her knowing violet eyes. I glance down at my beat-up Converse sneakers and brush my hair off my flushed face.

"How's your cousin?" I hear myself ask.

Wait.

A wave of shock rolls over me. *I just spoke to Hugh Tyson!* Voluntarily!

I mean, technically, I was addressing my sneakers. But I did ask Hugh a question, and my voice sounded like a normal human voice. I think.

Where did my bravery come from? Maybe from knowing, for sure, that Hugh and Wren are not together. Or maybe from Wren telling me I seemed like a person who could have a European boyfriend. Regardless, this progress feels promising; Hugh and I are supposed to work together on our class assignment this weekend. I'd been dreading it, but perhaps I won't be a complete disaster around him after all.

I glance up. Hugh looks surprised, too. His gray-green eyes are wide behind his glasses, and his lips part slightly.

"He's well," he replies after a moment. I think about the fact that only Hugh Tyson would use *well* instead of *good*. This kind of makes me want to embrace him even more. "It's his birthday," Hugh adds, adjusting his camera strap on his shoulder. "That's why I came in last night. We went to a baseball game."

"My birthday's on Tuesday," I blurt. *Agh! What? Why did I say that?* There were a million other things I could have said in response. Like: *Who was playing?* Or the ever-reliable: *Oh, cool.* But noooo. I had to share unnecessary information about my birthday. I *am* a disaster.

Mercifully, Aunt Lydia chooses this moment to announce to the group that we can head into the exhibit. I let out a huge breath, and stride ahead, away from Hugh and Wren, hoping to spare myself further mortification. I also hope that, over the course of the day, Wren won't reveal anything to Hugh about what I said on the train.

"Stick together," Aunt Lydia says as she leads the fourteen of us out of the lobby. We climb a staircase to the exhibit hall, weaving around the other visitors who are milling about, holding maps and brochures. "Pretend you're in elementary school."

Some of the students laugh. The last time I was in this museum, I *was* in elementary school; I'd come with my parents.

Pre-divorce. We'd seen the permanent collection: the incredible paintings by Chagall and Matisse, Picasso and Van Gogh. I'm almost surprised that a photography exhibit is on display here now—I've always thought of photographs as somehow separate from paintings, from "real art."

But the exhibit, which is called *Manhattan in Pictures*, is as incredible as any collection of paintings. There are countless photographs, some in black and white, some in color, some old, some current. They all show different pieces of New York City— the skyscrapers, the crowds, the subways, the taxis. I think of the pictures I took earlier, and I'm eager to improve on them.

"Look closely," Aunt Lydia instructs us, motioning to the framed pictures on the walls. "See how the photographers paid attention to angles and lines, shadows and light. To strange and interesting people. This is the work of Robert Frank and Richard Avedon, Alfred Eisenstaedt and Cindy Sherman. Learn these names. Learn from them. They had sharp eyes. You can make your eyes sharp, too."

I listen to my aunt, and examine everything. I take notes on my phone. If only I were half as devoted a student in regular school! I'd probably have Hugh Tyson–level grades.

At one point, I find myself standing next to Aunt Lydia; we are both studying an old photograph of construction workers eating their lunches high above the city.

"Hey," I say to her, feeling a rush of gratitude. "This trip is so great." I mean it, I realize. I also realize that I miss talking to my aunt. And after my conversation with Wren on the train, I no longer feel such a desperate need to hide my niece-hood.

"I'm glad to hear it, kiddo," Aunt Lydia replies.

Our eyes meet, and I remember what Wren said, about our expressions being similar. For a second, I think my aunt is going to say something else. Then she turns away, walking toward a photo of the Brooklyn Bridge across the room.

I watch her go, feeling a strange pit in my stomach. Maybe I'm being paranoid, but it almost seems like my aunt is avoiding me. Why?

• • •

On the train ride back to Hudsonville, I sit next to my aunt, wanting to test out my theory. And I fear I'm right: Immediately, she tells me she has to do some research and she spends the whole trip with her earbuds in, working on her iPad.

Wren and her elderly class partner, Maude, are sitting right behind us. I can hear the two of them discussing the merits of some vintage store near the mall, where Wren buys her clothes and Maude sells hers. I'm envious of their conversation.

Hugh stayed in the city to spend another night at his cousin's. When he'd said good-bye to the class at Grand Central, he'd glanced at me and added a quick, "I'll text you on Sunday." He hadn't sounded very excited about it. At lunch, Aunt Lydia had given us handouts listing everyone's cell phone numbers so we could get in touch with our partners over the weekend. So now

I have Hugh Tyson's phone number burning a hole inside my bookbag.

The sun is a low red ball in the sky by the time we pull into the Hudsonville train station. It's also gotten chillier out. When I step onto the platform, I reach into my bag for the cardigan, now grateful that Mom told me to bring one.

"Is your mom picking you up?" Aunt Lydia asks me—the first full sentence she's spoken to me since we left Manhattan. We walk side by side up the station steps and toward the parking lot.

"Yeah, there she is," I say, pointing to my mother's waiting car. Mom blinks her headlights at me. I wonder if Aunt Lydia was going to offer to drive me home. I also wonder if she might stop by Mom's car to say hello to her twin.

But Aunt Lydia just squeezes my arm and says, "See you Monday, kiddo." Then she speed-walks over to her own car, parked a few feet away.

I frown as I climb into Mom's car and shut the passenger side door. Out the window, I see Wren getting into her parents' Volvo; as if she can sense me watching, she glances over her shoulder, smirks, and waves. I wave back, marveling anew at our unexpected . . . is it a friendship? I'm not sure I'd call it that yet.

"So let me guess," Mom says brightly, checking the rearview mirror and pulling out of the parking lot. If she's at all offended that Aunt Lydia didn't come over to greet her, she doesn't show it. "New York was noisy, overcrowded, and didn't smell great. But you survived it okay?"

I smile, setting my bookbag down between my feet. "Actually I . . . liked it," I tell her. "A lot." I realize then that I'm no longer afraid of the city the way I used to be.

"Well," Mom says, sounding surprised, her eyes on the highway. She reaches up to adjust her glasses. "How about that."

I study Mom; she hadn't been too happy when I'd gone to Manhattan with Ruby over winter break. And she'd protested this field trip, too, asking me twice if I was *sure* Aunt Lydia would be chaperoning at all times. I wonder if Mom herself, with her poor sense of direction, finds the city a bit daunting. Or maybe she only wants to protect me from whatever dangers she thinks it harbors. Was that how she'd felt about France, too?

"You must be tired, though," Mom says as we drive past the Shell gas station. "And hungry. I prepared meat loaf, so you don't need to eat any more leftover takeout tonight. You'll find it in the fridge, and you can warm it up in the microwave."

I hold my belly. "I am still so full from lunch," I reply, laughing. "After the museum, we took the subway down to Lombardi's, which I guess is the oldest pizzeria in the country? Anyway, Aunt Lydia ordered all these delicious pies . . ." I trail off as I digest the rest of Mom's words. "Hang on," I add. "You're going out again tonight?" Disappointment rises in me.

Mom nods and tightens her grip on the steering wheel. Also, it's the strangest thing—she appears to be *blushing*. I don't think I've ever seen this phenomenon before, but there it is: an undeniable pinkness creeping across her fair cheeks. I also notice then that she's wearing a pretty black dress, heels, and lipstick.

"Where are you going?" I ask, uneasiness mingling with my disappointment.

We exit the highway, approaching College Avenue. Mom lets out a cough and slows at a stoplight, even though it's distinctly yellow.

"I figure now is as good a time as any to tell you," she begins.

My heartbeat speeds up. *Don't tell me*, I want to say. I am increasingly certain that whatever Mom will say will change things.

"I've . . . well, I've started seeing someone," Mom says, her cheeks becoming pinker. "It's very early days, nothing too serious," she goes on in a rush. "I wasn't even planning to see him again this evening, but he got us tickets to the philharmonic in Albany, so . . ." Mom looks over at me. I'm silent. "I thought you should know. I didn't want it to be a—secret." She clears her throat.

The light changes from red to green but Mom doesn't move. All the pizza seems to be churning in my stomach.

"You—you have a *boyfriend*?" I stutter in disbelief. It's the second time today I've posed this question. Randomly, I think of Will, grinning and green-haired on Wren's phone. "Is that who you had dinner with last night?" I ask, searching my mind for clues. When Mom came home, she'd been wearing lipstick then, too. "I thought you were with a friend from work!" I add, my tone accusatory.

Someone behind us honks and Mom finally accelerates. "Well, it's funny," she says, glancing over at me. Then she gives the kind of forced chuckle that never precedes anything *truly* funny. "I sort of was. You know Max?"

Max? I can't summon up anyone named Max. I stare out the window. We are driving down College Avenue, past the campus. Something clicks in my mind.

"Max the security guard?" I burst out. *"He's your boyfriend?"*

"Now, now," Mom says calmly as she turns onto Rip Van Winkle Road. "I wouldn't call him a 'boyfriend' yet, per se. But yes, I've known Max for many years, as have you, and he's just a lovely guy."

I'm speechless. I think of Max sitting in the security booth behind the gate, wearing his light-blue uniform and sipping his coffee.

"How long has this been going on?" I demand, feeling a sense of betrayal. I wrap my cardigan tighter around myself.

"I told you—it's recent," Mom says as our house comes into view. "He asked me out about a month ago. I was reluctant at first. And then . . ."

"What changed your mind?" I ask numbly.

"Well." Mom clears her throat and pulls into our driveway. "Actually . . . it was your France trip."

"It *was*?" I ask, whipping my head toward her in surprise. "How? I thought you didn't even want me to go!"

Mom shrugs, putting the car in park. "It just made me realize that . . . you know, you won't stay at home forever. Someday you'll be going off to college." Her voice has a note of sadness. She reaches for my hand, but I shift away from her, closer to the car door. "I thought it couldn't hurt to . . . try something different for myself." Mom gives me a tentative smile. "As your aunt likes to remind me, I've been divorced for a while now."

I stare ahead at our dark house. So Mom *wouldn't* have been lonely with me in France. That should make me feel glad for her, but . . . it doesn't.

"Max is divorced, too," Mom goes on. "We have a lot in common—he loves to read, we both enjoy classical music. We sort of . . . discovered each other."

"*Ew*, Mom," I groan. I bend forward, covering my face with my hands. "Please stop." It's true that Max isn't bad-looking for, like, a parent-age person. But still. *Ew*.

"Summer." Mom sighs. "You're overreacting."

"What if you wind up getting married?" I cry, looking over at Mom, my imagination whirring. "What if you end up having a *kid*? Then I'll have a half sibling, which would be so weird—"

Mom's face tightens. "Enough with the 'what ifs,'" she tells me, her voice growing sharper. "We'll discuss this at greater length another time. Why don't you head inside and relax? I don't think I'll be home too late."

My stomach falls. "I didn't realize you were going to Albany *now*," I say sourly. I look back at the house. I can see Ro curled up in the front window, his eyes little slits, no doubt in a sour mood, too. Faintly, I hear Mom explaining that she's going to drive to Max's house first and leave her car there, and then *he'll* drive them to Albany . . .

"Can you drop me off at Better Latte?" I interrupt. I know Ruby is still working at this hour. And suddenly she is the only person I want to see, regardless of how strained things have felt between us. I can only hope that Austin—or Skye—won't be there.

Mom seems like she's about to argue, but then, thankfully, she presses her lips together and takes the car out of park. We don't speak as she makes a U-turn. She zooms up our street and down Deer Hill, driving faster than she normally would.

To my knowledge, Mom hasn't dated anyone since she and Dad got divorced. And selfishly, I liked it that way: It kept things safe and steady; it kept Mom always around. I assumed that Dad wasn't dating anyone, either. So maybe, on some tiny, childish level, I hoped that he and Mom would one day get back together. Or, at least, with both of them single on either side of the Atlantic, things felt . . . even.

"Listen, Summer," Mom says when we reach Better Latte. I have my hand on the car door handle, and I glance back at her. "There's still a lot you don't—understand." She coughs again. "Not about Max—just, you know."

"No, Mom, I *don't* know," I snap, opening the car door. I feel a wave of déjà vu, reminded of our fight before I left for the airport. It's like my mother and I are repeating the same dance, over and over. I grab my bookbag and spring out of the car.

"Summer!" Mom calls out after me, but I'm already storming up onto the curb and into the coffee shop.

"Summer!" Ruby says, like an echo of Mom. She looks up from where she stands behind the counter, texting on her phone.

Aside from Ruby and one other barista, Better Latte is empty. It's almost twilight, on the cusp of dinnertime, so people are either heading to PJ's Pub or Szechuan Kitchen, or, if they're feeling fancy, Orologio's. Or they're preparing meat loaf at home for their kids. No one is getting coffee. The cheerful scents of vanilla and coffee beans linger in the air, but there's also a hollow, melancholy feeling. Or maybe that's just me.

"What's wrong?" Ruby asks as I trudge over to her. I drop my bookbag on the floor with a thunk and lean my elbows on the counter.

"Got an hour?" I sigh.

"Is half an hour okay?" Ruby asks. She tucks her phone into the pocket of her brown apron. "Austin is coming to pick me up because—how sweet is this? He wants to plan out our two-week anniversary celebration ahead of time." She grins at me.

I might have grinned back, if not for the ridiculous phrase *two-week anniversary*.

"So . . ." Ruby nods toward the espresso machine. "Want anything? Iced mocha?"

I shake my head.

"Bastille Day Special?" she offers, gesturing up to the chalkboard.

"What is that?" I ask, momentarily distracted from my gloom. I read the words written in blue, white, and red chalk:

Bastille Day Special! Iced French vanilla coffee topped with whipped cream and a blueberry/raspberry crisscross drizzle. Ooh là là!

"July fourteenth is France's Independence Day," Ruby explains by rote, clearly having made this speech to many a customer today. Then she notices my stricken expression. "Oh God, Summer." She slaps her forehead, her woven bracelets sliding up her arm. "I'm so sorry. You probably don't want anything French right now."

"You know what?" I shrug. A kind of recklessness is rising in me. "I'll have one. It sounds gross, but I already feel sick, so why not pile it on?"

"Uh, okay," Ruby says, looking at me worriedly. She picks up a plastic cup.

"Hey, Ruby," the other barista calls from the opposite end of the counter. It's the bearded guy who eavesdropped on our conversation on Monday. "I got this. You go chill with your friend. Seriously. I'm all out of lives on Candy Crush, so I need something to do." He waves his phone sadly and comes over to take the cup from Ruby's hand.

"Really? Thank you, Brian!" Ruby gushes, widening her dark-brown eyes winningly. I know Ruby doesn't have a crush on this Brian, but I also know she can't help herself: Flirting with guys comes as naturally to her as breathing.

As Brian graciously starts on my drink, Ruby ducks out from under the counter and the two of us sit down in a booth.

"Tell me," Ruby orders. She reaches across the table and squeezes my hand.

It's been so long since we've talked one-on-one (I mean, if we ignore Brian the barista), and my best friend's presence feels so familiar and comforting, that tears immediately well up in my eyes. Trying not to full-on sob, I fill her in on Mom and Max.

"Apparently I'm the only person *not* having a summer of love," I finish, oh-so-attractively wiping my nose on the sleeve of my cardigan.

Brian comes over and deposits my Bastille Day drink down in front of me. It's a monstrosity, a trembling tower of cream and syrups. Brian must notice my sniffling because he beats a hasty retreat back to the counter.

"I can't believe it," Ruby murmurs. "Your mom is dating?" She picks up the unopened straw Brian put next to my drink and twirls it. "Good for her," she adds.

For a moment, I'm so stunned I don't know how to respond.

Ugh, poor you, I'd hoped to hear. Or *That's bad and crazy!* Or *Come spend the weekend at my house so you can avoid your mother for forty-eight hours.*

Not *Good for her.*

"Excuse me?" I finally spit out, staring across the table.

"I said, good for her," Ruby repeats, lifting her chin. "I wish my mom would date. All she does is work and worry about me and Raj. Meanwhile, my dad has been remarried for a year!"

"Yeah, except—" I reach across the table to snatch the straw from my best friend. I rip off the paper and shove the straw into my drink. "That's *your* family. Mine is different. Our homes aren't broken in the same way, Ruby."

"Fine," Ruby says, holding up her hands like I was attacking her. "Look, I get that you and your mom are close. Like, *Gilmore Girls*-close—"

"I wouldn't say *that*," I protest, even though I'm a little pleased.

"Oh, come on," Ruby scoffs, running a hand through her shiny black hair. "With your stargazing and snacking and deep talks about outer space and stuff?" She pauses, and I wonder, for the first time, if she's ever felt jealous of Mom and me. "But," she continues, looking right at me, "sometimes you need to let people go a little."

I feel my whole face get hot. Ruby isn't simply referring to the Mom situation anymore, is she?

To avoid Ruby's gaze, I glance down at my drink. It would make an interesting photograph—a kind of companion to the iced mocha picture. I reflect on how much Ruby doesn't know about me now. She doesn't know I was at a photography exhibit in New York City today, with Hugh and with Wren. I remember being here, in Better Latte, on Monday, when I'd defended Wren to Skye. That was before I even knew Wren at all.

I trace a circle on the wooden table with my finger. I have the sudden, ugly urge to taunt Ruby—to hurt her, maybe. "I should probably confide in someone else," I say quietly. "Like Wren D'Amico. She'd be more understanding." *She probably would be*, I think.

Ruby frowns. "What does Wren D'Amico have to do with anything?"

"Well," I say, the recklessness surging in me again, "I'm sure your idol, Skye, wouldn't approve, but Wren is cool, okay?" My voice is rising and Brian the barista can probably hear me, but I don't care. I want to say it all, everything that has been building silently between me and Ruby for the last ten days. "I doubt Wren would *dump* her best friend," I go on, gathering steam. "You know, ignore all her texts and not want to ever hang out, so she could cozy up to the populars—"

"Is that what you think of me?" Ruby cuts in. Her face is turning so red it's nearly as purple as the pretty sundress she has on beneath her apron. "I'm not dumping you!" she says, her voice breaking. "Yes, I'm spending a lot of time with Austin . . ."

"Stop pretending," I make myself say. "There's more to it than that."

Ruby's jaw drops. My limbs are trembling. I realize, then, why she and I have never fought before: because I always acquiesced to her. She was right; I was wrong. Any conflict was ignored. Buried. Until now.

The corners of Ruby's mouth turn down, and she's silent for a moment. "I just wanted . . . a change," she murmurs. "You weren't even supposed to—"

She catches herself, like last time. The exact same words as last time. *You weren't even supposed to.* A chill goes down my back.

"Say it," I tell Ruby. I stare right at her, hugging myself. "Finish it."

"You weren't even supposed to be here this summer," she breathes through clenched teeth. She looks down at the table and rests her forehead in one hand. "You were supposed to be in France."

I sit back in the booth, exhaling, all the energy leaking out of me. It's almost a relief, to hear it, to know.

"I thought it would be . . . healthy," Ruby continues, still looking down, her words coming out in a tumble. "For us to be apart for a while. We were always together, in our little world." She glances up at me, her eyes teary. "I wanted to see what it was like, to branch out. And I *knew* you wouldn't approve," she says, tapping her palm against the table for emphasis. "I knew you'd roll your eyes if I told you I liked Austin and wanted to date him. I knew you'd get all huffy if I told you Skye wasn't so bad—"

"She's the worst," I mutter.

"See?" Ruby cries. She shakes her head. "That's why I invited Alice to Skye's party with me, because I knew she'd be more easygoing about everything."

I nod slowly, my throat tightening. It makes sense now— how eager Ruby was for me to go to France, how upset she was when Dad canceled on me. It wasn't about my summer; it was about hers.

"I get it," I say. My blurred vision turns Ruby fuzzy across the table. "If I went to France, that would have been your big opportunity. To be free of me."

Ruby dabs at her eyes. "You make it sound so awful, Summer—"

"Don't worry," I interrupt her. My own tone is cold, unfamiliar to me. "I won't hold you back anymore."

Ruby's phone buzzes inside her apron pocket. She takes it out and checks the screen. Her bottom lip quivering, she looks up at me.

"It's Austin," she tells me tightly. "He's outside. I should go."

"Go," I say. *Go,* Ruby had said to me before I got out of her car at the airport.

I watch, shivering in my cardigan and Ruby's old white dress, as Ruby stands up and unties her apron. She ducks under the counter, and Brian the barista makes a concerted effort to appear immersed in his phone.

I peer out the coffee shop window at the darkening street. Austin is there, waiting in his blue convertible. He's not alone; Skye and her boyfriend, Genji Tanaka, are in the backseat, their arms in the air, dancing to the song coming from Austin's radio. They look like the picture of summer.

"Have fun with your new friends," I say snidely as Ruby emerges from behind the counter with her purse. I feel small and petty, but powerful, like I'm two people at once.

"And have fun with yours," Ruby replies, equally snidely, even though her cheeks are wet with tears. Mine are, too; I can feel them coursing down to my chin.

Then she turns and walks out the door. It's the first time in ten years that Ruby and I have parted ways without saying *Love you times two.* The absence of those words buzzes in my ear like a mosquito.

I sit still in the vacant café, the air conditioner blowing at my back. I hear the tinny music of Brian's game coming from his phone. My Bastille Day Special is in front of me, untouched, the whipped cream dripping a little. I lean forward and take a sip. It's terrible. It's too sweet and too bitter. It's like my sorrow distilled into liquid form. I push the drink away. Some Bastille Day.

I reach up to wipe my cheeks with the heel of my hand, and the rough rope of my bracelets—Ruby's bracelets—scratches my face. Mournfully, I remove both bracelets and stare down at the exposed, pale strip of my skin. I wonder if this is what it feels like to break up with someone. Or get a divorce. This sense of loss mingled with freedom.

The summer stretches ahead of me, without Ruby in it. I'm terrified and also, strangely, exhilarated. The worst has happened. So, now, in a way, anything can.

Sunday, July 16, 3:03 p.m.

Hi, Summer. Would you be available to meet today at 3 p.m. outside Between the Lines? Let me know if that works for you. —Hugh Tyson

For the umpteenth time, I reread the text message Hugh sent me this morning. The formality of his tone—the fact that he signed his full name—makes me laugh. But mainly the sight of the text causes butterflies to storm my stomach. Because it means that our meeting is really happening.

I check the clock on my phone.

Oh God. It's happening *now*.

I'm totally late.

My heart flips over and I finish lacing up my new sandals. I spring out of the kitchen chair and turn to grab my bookbag off the table. Unfortunately, Ro has draped himself over the bag and isn't budging.

"Tell me, Summer," Mom says, strolling into the kitchen with her eyes on her phone. "How many people should I make the reservation for?"

"What reservation?" I ask, trying to scoop up Ro without incurring his wrath. I have been on the receiving end of his

218

scratches before, and the last thing I need is showing up to meet Hugh with gashes across my face and arms.

Mom peers up at me, her forehead furrowed. "Your birthday dinner? At Orologio's? I assume we're going there Tuesday night?"

Right. I release Ro, who meows in triumph. I'd briefly forgotten—or maybe pushed aside—the looming specter of my sixteenth birthday. *Sweet sixteen and never been kissed,* I think, like a singsong rhythm in my head.

"I know you mentioned that Alice and Inez are both out of town," Mom continues. She nudges Ro's side, and the cat complies, easing himself off my bag with no complaints. Of course. "So it'll be you, me, Ruby, and Aunt Lydia," Mom continues, stroking Ro's head. Then she glances at me, and that pink stain is coloring her cheeks again. "Also . . ." She clears her throat. "If you wouldn't mind, I was hoping to invite Max as well . . ."

"No Ruby," I say flatly. My insides twist.

Mom raises her eyebrows in surprise. "What?" she asks. "Why not?"

I reach down to feel the empty spot on my wrist where the woven bracelets used to be; they're now up in a jewelry box in my room. I try to tamp down my rising sadness.

"I can't get into it now," I reply, brushing cat hair off my bookbag and sticking my arms through the straps. "I have to go do that photography assignment."

Mom knows that my class partner is Hugh—"Oh yes, the mayor's son, that smart boy!" she'd said merrily when I'd told her—but of course she doesn't know about my crush. Nor does she know what happened between me and Ruby at Better Latte on Friday evening. I've done a deft job of avoiding Mom this weekend.

"Well . . . is it okay if Max comes, then?" Mom calls after me, sounding incredulous, as I open the door and head outside.

"Sure, whatever," I shout over my shoulder, jumping on my bike.

If I had my druthers, I think, pedaling up Rip Van Winkle Road, I wouldn't have a birthday dinner at all this year. I was meant to be celebrating in France, anyway.

The warm wind teasingly lifts the hem of my dress. *Oh no.* I struggle to hold the material in place with one hand as I coast down Deer Hill. Maybe jeans would have been a wiser choice for this outing. But I'd been eager to wear my new purchases.

Yesterday, dying for a distraction, I'd texted Wren to ask her about that vintage store I'd heard her mention. Wren had been working on her class assignment with Maude, but she'd gamely given me directions. I took the bus to the mall and, one block behind it, found a small shop called Second Time Around. I'd had no clue it was there all these years. It was filled with racks of gorgeous retro clothes, and shelves of shoes, purses, and accessories like Wren's old watch. I'd taken pictures and browsed, and then stumbled upon a black-and-white polka-dot sundress that was different from anything I owned. I'd bought it, along with the never-worn Grecian sandals I also have on now.

I reach Greene Street, and it feels like the butterflies in my stomach are starting a tango. Taking a big breath, I park my bike in front of the bank and hurry down the street toward the bookstore. In another life, I'd be popping into Better Latte to beg Ruby for some boy wisdom. My fingers stray to my bare wrist. I haven't had any contact with Ruby since Friday. It's crazy to think that she has no idea that I'm about to see Hugh.

My brain is so focused on Ruby that I almost *don't* see Hugh. He's waiting outside Between the Lines, leaning against his bike and writing in his Moleskine notebook. He's wearing the same green-checked shirt he wore to the museum, board shorts, and flip-flops. I stop just short of walking right into him.

"Sorry I'm late," I say, trying to appear calm and unruffled even though I'm definitely sweaty and messy-haired. *"Hugh face"*! I remind myself, and tighten my features.

Hugh glances up and quickly closes his notebook. "Oh. Hey," he says, straightening his glasses in an adorable way. "You're not late. I thought I was early."

"Um." I start reaching around for my phone in my bookbag. "Isn't it after three?"

Hugh shrugs, looking sheepish. "Probably. I'm sorry. I'm sort of bad with time."

His words are as surprising as the laugh that bubbles up out of me. *"You* are?" I can't help but say. "No. *I* am." I'd assumed that perfect-student Hugh was forever punctual. But now I'm recalling how he's often been late to photography class. Come to think of it, he'd sometimes arrive to school late, too; I'd never paid attention because I was too busy stressing about my own lateness.

A small smile tugs at Hugh's full lips. "Then we have something in common."

I nod, a blush burning my face. The afternoon sun beats down on my head, and I'm faintly aware of people strolling past us into the bookstore.

"So," Hugh says. He glances down at his feet and rubs the back of his neck. "Should we start with your location?"

I bite my lip. For our assignment today, each partner was supposed to pick one spot to photograph. As Aunt Lydia explained it, both partners were to take pictures of both spots, and then compare their different visions. The problem is, I haven't yet selected my place to photograph. My indecisiveness took over, and I spent much of yesterday and this morning waffling between Pine Park and the train station and even the bookstore Hugh and I are standing in front of now. Nothing has felt right, though.

"I—let's start with yours," I fudge, smoothing down the skirt of my dress. Maybe I'll settle on something as the afternoon goes on. Or I'll make a last-minute decision out of desperation.

"Okay." Hugh nods, looking a little uncertain himself. He runs a hand over his close-cropped dark hair. If I didn't know better, I'd think he was nervous. But that's not possible, is it? "Mine isn't too close by," he warns. "Do you have your bike?" He turns to his own bike and takes his bookbag off the handlebars.

"I do." I point to where I parked my bike at the bank. I wonder what location Hugh chose; I'd figured it was somewhere on Greene Street.

"Ideally, we'd drive there," Hugh says, tucking his notebook into his bookbag, "but I don't have my license yet."

"Me neither," I say. *Something else we have in common*, I think, but thankfully, don't add. I turn and walk toward my bike, proud of my relatively normal behavior. If I make it through the assignment without humiliating myself, I will consider it a success.

I climb onto my bike, and Hugh pedals up alongside me. For a second, he seems like any other Hudsonville boy on his bicycle, someone I'd pass on Deer Hill, say. He's not some mysterious and intimidating figure that I've built up in my head. I can talk to him. I can laugh with him.

Then, just as quickly, the perspective shift passes. Hugh becomes Hugh Tyson: Terrifying Crush again. The butterflies resume their dance routine in my belly.

"It's this way," Hugh says, raising his soft, slightly scratchy voice above the wind. He pedals ahead of me, and I follow. He turns onto Deer Hill, but instead of following the familiar incline, he turns again, onto a side street called River Alley.

I've passed by River Alley countless times, and always thought it was a dead end; it's flanked only by the backs of houses and skinny trees. Now I see that the alley goes on for a while, maybe a mile, with flashes of the river visible through the gaps in the trees. It's too narrow for two bikes to fit side by side, which is fine by me; I can pedal behind Hugh, admiring the way his shoulders fill out his shirt, without having to make stilted conversation. I also don't have to worry about my skirt occasionally fluttering up. My heart thumps and my feet work the pedals and it feels good, to be biking this distance, like I'm putting space between myself and Greene Street, and Ruby, and Mom.

Eventually, River Alley tapers off, turning into a dirt path lined with majestic oak trees; it's like the twiggy ones that we passed earlier decided to grow up. My wheels bump over the ruts in the path, and I hear the sound of water lapping against rocks. I'm about to ask Hugh where we are exactly when the path opens up and we emerge onto a thin strip of grass. Hugh stops his bike, and I stop mine.

I have to catch my breath—not just from the long ride, but from the beauty of this small, enchanted-looking place. Pine trees and boulders ring a shimmering circle of blue-green water. A waterfall burbles down a steep slide of boulders, and a bird caws in the treetops. It feels hidden away, entirely separate from Hudsonville. From the world.

"What—what *is* this?" I sputter, before I can remember to sound composed in front of Hugh. I climb off my bike and shed my bookbag, taking out my camera and looking around in amazement.

"You've never been to the swimming hole?" Hugh asks with a smile in his voice as he props his bike against an oak tree.

"Never," I echo. *How is that possible?* I wonder as I wander across the patchy grass toward the water. I've lived in this town my whole life, and there was still a place unknown to me? Then

I recall the vintage store I went to yesterday: That, also, was new. It's true that I—well, Ruby and I, together—always stuck to a circumscribed path: our school, our homes, Greene Street, Pine Park, the mall. Maybe we made our small universe even smaller than it needed to be. I reach the water's edge and swallow hard. I remember what Ruby said to me on Friday, about wanting to stretch beyond the bounds of our friendship. Maybe, on some level, I want that, too.

"I've been coming here since I was a kid," Hugh says, walking up beside me with his camera and notebook in hand. "It's kind of—my escape," he adds, a little shyly.

I lift my camera to take a picture of the waterfall. "I can see why," I say. "Do you swim here?" Instantly my cheeks flame at the very nice thought of Hugh in swim trunks, in the water. At the same time, I am amazed that, blushing and all, I am standing here and simply conversing with Hugh. Like I'm another Summer.

"I'll swim," Hugh affirms, setting his camera and notebook and pen down on the grass. "But mostly I'll sit and write—short stories and poems and stuff—and enjoy my parents not bothering me."

I want to ask Hugh more about what he writes; I'd love to *see* what he writes, although I know that would be the longest of long shots. So I address the other point that's piqued my curiosity.

"Your parents bother you?" I ask. Mayor Rosen-Tyson and Mr. Tyson and Hugh seem to be a perfect united front, a symbol of Hudsonville wholesomeness. There's nothing broken there.

"Of course," Hugh says with a low laugh. He peers out at the pine trees across the water. "They think I should go into politics, like them. They definitely don't think I should be a writer. Even though I've always written. Sometimes I'll stay up all night writing. But they say anything artistic isn't practical." He nods down toward his camera. "I had to fight with them to take this class! Actually, I'm going to miss class the next three days. They're dragging me along to some conference in Washington, D.C."

"Oh. Sorry," I say. Selfishly, I feel a pang of sadness at the thought that Hugh won't be in class.

Hugh shrugs. "I'm pretty sure it would be easier if I had a sibling. Then I wouldn't be the repository for all my parents' hopes and dreams."

There's a lightening, a lifting, in my chest. "I'm an only child, too," I say. *Another thing we have in common.*

I look at Hugh, familiar Hugh: his light-brown skin and gray-green eyes, his long lashes and strong jaw, the small birthmark next to his right ear. Even though I'd been focused on him for two years, I never really *knew* him. I didn't know he wanted to write or didn't have his license. And I guess I never gave him a chance to know me.

"My dad's a painter," I go on. "But luckily, since I have zero artistic talent, there've been no expectations put on me." I smile to myself.

Hugh laughs again. He looks at me and I feel my pulse quicken. "Is that why you were going to France this summer?" he asks. "To visit your father?" Then he glances down, and I could swear he's blushing. "I—I overheard you saying something about that in school," he adds in a rush.

I'm blushing, too. I had for so long assumed that Hugh didn't pay any attention to me. That no boys did. But maybe Hugh had paid a little attention? My heart races.

"Yeah," I say, turning my camera over in my hands. It occurs to me that if I *had* gone to France this summer, if Dad hadn't canceled, then I wouldn't be here now—talking to Hugh, at this magical swimming hole. I would have missed out on this.

Hugh kneels down to pick up his camera, and he takes a picture of the water from that position. Again, I think he looks kind of like a wildlife photographer, and I have the crazy image of the two of us traveling together, someplace exotic, like a safari, taking photographs, Hugh writing stories—

I shake my head to clear it of these insane thoughts. Hugh, meanwhile, is sitting down on one of the large, flat boulders. He leans back on his elbows and kicks off his flip-flops, stretching out his long legs and letting his feet dangle in the water. I can see the comfort and ease he feels at the place. He's no longer the formal Hugh I know.

I hesitate for a moment—*Should I? Shouldn't I? What if I look silly?*—before following his lead. I set down my camera and unlace my sandals—my fingers are trembling a bit—and then I sit on the sun-warmed boulder. Carefully, I dip my toes into the water; its coolness is a shock, but a pleasant one.

There's silence between me and Hugh, but for once it doesn't feel awkward. Birds chatter overhead. I take pictures of the pine trees and the water, and so does Hugh. It's a glorious summer day, the kind Hudsonville hasn't seen in some time, with a pure blue sky and no humidity in the air. The surface of the water sparkles. I close my eyes, tilting my face skyward and feeling the heat of the sun.

"I know," Hugh speaks up, sounding thoughtful, "that you don't really like me."

My eyes fly open and I'm so stunned that I think I will slip off the rock into the water. "What?" I ask.

Hugh stares ahead, a muscle in his jaw jumping. He is definitely blushing now. "I can tell. You sort of avoid me in school. You kind of get this look on your face like I bother you." He frowns and casts a glance at me. "And I know you weren't too happy to be my partner this summer."

I open my mouth. But only a strangled sound—half cough, half laugh—emerges. How can I reply? *You're wrong, Hugh. I the-opposite-of-don't-like you.* My head spins as I stare at him. I guess my "Hugh face" *did* work—too well.

"I thought *you* weren't happy to be *my* partner," I finally squeak out. My blood is roaring in my ears. *Oh God.* So much for not humiliating myself today.

But Hugh shakes his head, and he smiles at me. It's the first time I think he's full-on smiled in my direction, and the effect is as brilliant as the sun. "You're a good partner," he tells me. "I mean, today hasn't been half bad, has it?"

I shake my head back at him. I smile, too, and it's so freeing, to finally drop the fake indifference of the "Hugh face." I can feel it: that same recklessness I felt at Better Latte on Friday night, only this one is fiercer. Wilder.

"It's been wonderful," I admit. "Impossible and wonderful."

I'm not making sense. And I'm blushing even more now—a blush that is spreading across my neck and arms and legs. I want to cool off. I want to hide. There's only one thing I can think to do. I put down my camera, scoot forward on the rock, and plunge feetfirst into the water.

I submerge completely. It feels deliciously cold, and my new-old polka-dot dress balloons up around me. My hair floats in all directions and I let my feet paddle lightly.

"Summer!" I hear Hugh calling from above. "What are you doing?"

A second later, there's a splash and he's underwater beside me. I feel his hand on my arm and we swim up together, breaking the surface and treading water.

"Are you okay?" Hugh asks me. He must have removed his glasses before he dove in. His eyes are so bright, his dark lashes are wet, and his face is spattered with droplets of water. He's still holding on to my arm, and his fingers feel warm on my skin.

I realize he was worried about me. "I am," I assure him, laughing. My hair is streaming down my back, my soaking dress is sticking to my skin, and I feel sort of . . . beautiful. And brave. Not brave like Ruby, but like me. "I don't need saving," I add.

Hugh grins at me, bobbing up and down in the water. "I figured you don't," he says. "That's not really why I jumped in."

So why did you? I want to ask, but my bravery wavers. Our faces are close together and our knees bump underwater. My heart does the stop-start thing it did on the first day of photography class, when Hugh walked in. *What is happening?* I think, because something *is* happening, here, now, in this hidden spot in Hudsonville, surrounded by pine trees and a waterfall.

I remember what Wren said on the train ride, about Hugh liking a girl.

What if? I ask myself, paddling in the water, looking at Hugh. No. It can't be.

But seriously, Summer. What if?

The notion I'm flirting with is too impossible—too wonderful. I feel like my heart might burst. So I turn and paddle back to the shore. Our cameras and Hugh's glasses and notebook and pen sit there, waiting, mute witnesses.

I pull myself up out of the water and sit, dripping, on the rock. Hugh does the same, and we don't say anything. Then we glance at each other, both of us soaking wet in our clothes with only the sun to dry us, and we both start laughing.

We laugh and laugh, and the charged moment from when we were in the water seems to dissolve. Maybe I'd imagined it.

Hugh picks up his glasses, still laughing. "I'm glad I had the foresight to take these off," he says, examining the lenses. "Get it? *Foresight?*"

I snort. "You shouldn't be a writer," I say, wringing out the ends of my soggy hair. "You're clearly a comedian."

"I know. My humor is a rare gift." Hugh slides on his glasses as I chuckle. Then he squints at me. "I think I need a new prescription," he says. "You don't wear glasses or contacts, do you?"

I shake my head. "Twenty-twenty vision. For now."

I think about vision. I look down at my camera, and over at Hugh. He is no longer Hugh Tyson: Terrifying Crush. And this time, my perspective shift is staying. He is the Hugh who laughed with me. The Hugh who jumped into the water after me. He will always be that Hugh, from now on, I realize. Everything has changed.

The sound of a car pulling up behind us, on River Alley, makes me jump. I turn to see a bunch of little kids tumbling out of a station wagon, shrieking and armed with towels and water wings. I'm envious of their towels. The kids tear past me and Hugh, and cannonball into the swimming hole.

Wordlessly, Hugh and I exchange a glance; our peace has been disrupted. So we stand, still damp and dripping, and gather our belongings and head over to our bikes.

"So," Hugh says, brushing his hands down his wet board shorts, "it's pretty cool to now be able to say you swam in the Hudson."

I'm lacing up my squishy sandals. "Hang on," I say, confused. I look toward the swimming hole, now dotted with hollering children and a haggard-looking father. "That's the *Hudson*? I thought it was, like, a creek or something."

"Nope." Hugh smiles his brilliant smile, putting on his bookbag. "It's part of our mighty river. Funny, right?"

I stare out at the blue water. It *is* funny, how the river here seems totally different from the gray one that runs along Greene Street. I remember the poster that hangs in Mom's bedroom, with the quote from Heraclitus: *You cannot step into the same river twice.* Maybe that's because rivers, like people, are constantly changing.

Hugh and I get on our bikes, and pedal back onto River Alley. I lead the way this time, going fast, my wet hair flying behind me. Dappled sunlight filters through the leaves of the skinny trees. I don't know the time, but we must have been at the swimming hole for a while; the air has a subtle, almost-evening chill to it. The breeze tickles my neck and lifts the hem of my dress again. I don't mind as much now.

Without thinking twice, I go straight to Deer Hill and pedal up and up until I reach Rip Van Winkle Road. Home.

"Oh God," I say, realizing. I stop the bike in front of my house, and look back at Hugh. My face flushes. "I'm sorry. I just came here automatically. This is—this is where I live." Did I ever think Hugh Tyson would be on my street? No. But did I ever think anything that happened today could have happened?

Hugh rests his elbows on his handlebars and grins at me. "I thought you brought us here to shoot this street for the assignment," he says. He cranes his neck to read the street sign on the corner. "Rip Van Winkle Road." He looks back at me, his eyes sparkling. "Like the story?"

I nod, dredging up my memory of the story Mom and Dad used to tell me when I was little. The legend of Rip Van Winkle, a man who fell asleep and woke up twenty years in the future, to find the whole world changed.

"I've never been here before," Hugh adds, glancing around. I follow his gaze, taking in the familiar squat houses and the squares of green lawn. So different from the grandeur of Hugh's street, Argyle Road, with its sleeping-elephant mansions. Rip Van Winkle Road is as new to him as the swimming hole was to me.

And I realize that my street *should* be my spot for the assignment. The decision I'd been wrestling with for days suddenly seems easy.

I tell this to Hugh, and we take out our cameras and prop our bikes against my porch. My house looks dark—Mom must be out, probably with Max, I think a little bitterly. I can see Ro at his perch in the window. His narrow eyes are watching me with intrigue, as if I am now worthy of attention because of the boy beside me. I smirk.

Hugh and I take pictures of my street—of the pale-blue sky above the rooftops, of the identical houses standing in a row like soldiers, of the slight bend in the road up ahead. Then we sit down on my porch steps to scroll through our cameras' digital feeds and review our work from the day.

The evening breeze has almost dried us off, and I can feel my hair curling against my back. I can also feel the warmth of Hugh's arm near mine as we sit close together.

Hugh is intently studying both our camera screens. "Check it out," he says, showing me his photograph of the waterfall alongside mine; the colors and angles are very different. "We didn't see the same spot in the same way. Lydia is right."

I smile, grateful to my aunt for inadvertently putting me together with Hugh. "But," I argue as I lean over to take his camera from him—our hands brush and my skin tingles—"it could be that we took those photos a few seconds or minutes apart, so the sunlight changed. Maybe it's about time."

"Maybe." Hugh nods, his eyes on my camera. "By the way," he says, in an offhand manner that's not really offhand, "what you said before wasn't true."

I freeze. "What do you mean?" I ask. Is he going to wade back into the question of whether or not I dislike him?

Hugh holds up an older picture on my camera screen—the iced mocha from Monday. It seems like eons ago now. "When you were talking about your dad," Hugh says, keeping his earnest gaze on me, "you said you had zero artistic talent. That's not true. You're an amazing photographer, Summer. You—you *see* things. You really see them." He glances down quickly.

My heart jumps. The sound of him saying my name—and the weight of what else he's saying—makes my cheeks flush. "Thanks," I say, shaking my head, "but a lot of people can take pictures. It doesn't make me an artist. You're good, too," I point out, holding up his camera.

"Come on." Hugh nudges me, and my face flushes hotter. "I'm not even as close to as good as you are. You don't just take pictures—you, what is it? You 'draw with light.'" He grins, but his eyes are still serious. "Of course you're an artist."

I can't deny that his words send small shivers of pleasure down my back. I think of the exhibit at the museum, and let myself wonder—fleetingly—if my photographs could ever be displayed someday. *Like Dad*, I think. Am I more like Dad than I thought?

I brush off the notion for now, and give Hugh's camera back to him. Since he's going to be in Washington, D.C., for the next few days, he says he'll email me his photos tonight. That way I can put together our portfolio and present it to Aunt Lydia tomorrow.

We get to our feet. There's emptiness in my stomach at the thought that our day is over. I can't believe that mere hours ago I was so scared and stiff around Hugh—we were both stiff around each other. I feel like Rip Van Winkle, like I've woken up to find that the world is new and different.

I expect Hugh to say good-bye and head toward his bike, but instead he walks me up the porch steps to my front door. I can feel Ro watching us from the window.

I adjust my bookbag strap on my shoulder, feeling the old nervousness rise up in me. Hugh glances down and rubs the back of his neck, a movement that I now recognize as him feeling nervous. I try to breathe evenly.

"Thank you for a fun day," Hugh says, in his formal way. "I'll see you when I'm back from D.C.?"

I nod, knowing that I'll see him in class—but does he mean I'll see him in another context, too?

"And before I forget," Hugh adds, his face reddening, taking a step closer to me, "happy birthday."

He remembered? I think in shock. *He remembered my rambling at the museum on Friday?* I'm trying to process this fact when Hugh gently brushes a curl off the side of my face. He does this like he thinks my hair is pretty, not too messy or frizzy. Then, even more impossibly, he leans in so close I can smell his soapy-clean scent. And he kisses me on the cheek.

Hugh Tyson kissed me? Hugh Tyson kissed me!

It wasn't a real kiss, of course. But from the way his lips lingered on my skin, from the way his hand tilted my chin up, it felt like a kiss with . . . potential. A *what-if?* kiss.

I feel myself melting, so I lean against the door. Hugh takes a step back, biting his full bottom lip. I think—I hope—I wish—that I no longer need to tell Hugh that I don't dislike him. And I think—I hope—I wish—that I no longer need to ask Wren who Hugh likes.

I watch as Hugh walks down the porch steps and gets on his bike, waving to me as he pedals off into the dusk. I wave back, my heart dancing, and then I turn to unlock my front door. Ro, in the window, eyes me, impressed. I grin and float into my house. Suddenly, I am looking forward to my birthday.

• • •

Two evenings later, on my sixteenth birthday, I am still floating. Even as I head into Orologio's with Mom for the dinner I don't want to have, I can't keep myself from smiling. The day with

Hugh—the *what-if?* kiss—has been playing on a loop in my head, making me smile at random moments. And I'm sure Aunt Lydia had no idea why I was blushing like crazy when I presented photos of the swimming hole and Rip Van Winkle Road to the class on Monday.

"The birthday girl is glowing!" exclaims Jerry, the maître d' who has worked at Orologio's forever. He welcomes me and Mom inside with a sweep of his arms.

I glance at the mirrored wall next to the restaurant's entrance. My skin is flushed and my lips are pink from the gloss I swiped on in the car. I look . . . nice, even with my Picasso-ish features and messy tumble of hair. I'm wearing the polka-dot dress, which, after the day with Hugh, I've started thinking of as my "lucky dress" (I laundered it after my dip in the Hudson). I also have on the Grecian sandals and hoop earrings, and I'm carrying a black purse Mom lent me for the occasion. My wrist seems naked without Ruby's woven bracelets; I still haven't gotten used to their absence.

"Your friend Ruby was in here yesterday," Jerry adds, as if he's read my mind. He picks up two menus and motions for me and Mom to follow him. "With Austin, and another couple. Some kind of anniversary double date, they said."

"Oh," I say, my smile wilting. *Right. The stupid two-week anniversary.* And I'm sure the other couple was Skye and Genji. Ugh.

I feel Mom shoot me a sidelong glance as we walk into the dining room. I'm annoyed at Jerry for knowing everyone in town, and for blaring peoples' business to the world like he's a human

Instagram. I've made it to today without telling Mom about my fight with Ruby, and I'd really prefer not to get into it now, in the middle of Orologio's.

The dining room is spacious and bustling, with its candle-lit, white-cloth-draped tables, and cheerful red-painted walls. The homey aromas of olive oil, tomato sauce, and cheese drift from the plates the waiters are whisking around. Jerry leads us toward the round table in the back that Mom always reserves; I see that Aunt Lydia is already there, sipping a glass of red wine.

I wonder where Ruby and her crew sat last night. Had Ruby thought about me, and all my birthday dinners here? Had she felt any remorse or regret? I guess the fact that she hasn't so much as texted me *Happy Birthday* today tells me all I need to know.

"Happy birthday!" Aunt Lydia calls, rising from her seat. Tonight, for once, she and Mom look identical. They're both wearing black dresses and high heels, and Aunt Lydia's hair is down. Behind her glasses, Mom even has on the same kind of eyeliner as Aunt Lydia. It's eerie. "You look so grown-up, kiddo," Aunt Lydia adds, giving me a hug as Jerry sets our menus on the table and walks away.

I thank my aunt and hug her back. It's funny to think that I saw her only a few hours ago, at our Photoshop lab. I'd been relieved that she hadn't made some announcement about my birthday to the class, or, worse, led them in song.

So it had been a surprise when, after the lab, Wren had presented me with a gluten-free cupcake she'd baked herself—it tasted awful, but I'd pretended to enjoy it—and a gift certificate to Second Time Around.

"Hugh told me it was your birthday," she said, her violet eyes dancing.

I wasn't sure what else Hugh had told her—or if he'd told her *anything* about our day together. I'd been tempted to fill Wren in, but then I'd opted not to.

I'd been similarly tempted, over the past two days, to break down and text Ruby all the details. I'd resisted, of course. It feels surreal, that no one knows what happened between me and Hugh, except for me and Hugh. At the same time, I sort of like keeping it as a secret. Something to turn over in my mind and smile about.

I realize I'm smiling again as I slide into the seat next to my aunt and put down my purse. Mom sits on the other side of me and begins scanning the room.

"Mom, you don't have to make a big thing out of whispering to the waiter to bring me cake," I tell her, taking a sip of my water. "It's not a surprise anymore. I know it's coming." I glance at my aunt. "She does the same thing every year."

Aunt Lydia laughs, passing me and Mom the breadbasket. "Yeah, Lucy. You need to drop it. Summer's sixteen now."

My aunt wasn't at my birthday dinner last year—she'd gone to some music festival in Canada—but I remember her being at Orologio's with us the year before that, when I'd turned fourteen. I hadn't paid attention to her then, though; I'd been too busy giggling with Ruby. Now it's nice to have Aunt Lydia here, especially because Ruby *isn't*. And because I've still had the niggling feeling that my aunt has been avoiding me.

"I'm not looking for a waiter, you two." Mom sighs, tearing off a piece of bread. "I want to be sure Max finds us when he gets here."

Max. The bread I've been chewing seems to go stale in my mouth. Mom hadn't mentioned anything about him on the drive to the restaurant, so I'd been fervently hoping that he'd bailed, or even better, that he and Mom had broken up.

"I'm really glad you gave Max a chance," Aunt Lydia says, lifting her wine glass in a toast to Mom. I glower at my aunt, and Mom gives her a surprised smile. "He's a terrific guy," Aunt Lydia continues in her impassioned, genuine way, "and you deserve a terrific guy, sister of mine, after the last prize you had."

"Lydia!" Mom snaps. She scowls, and her eyes dart quickly over to me.

"You mean Dad?" I glance from my mom to my aunt. I almost want to laugh, even as I feel a stab of hurt, and a rush of loyalty toward my father.

I'd finally heard from him last night—he'd sent me a gushy email wishing me a happy sweet sixteen and sending love and saying that he'd be back in France soon and wanted us to speak on Skype. *I have something important to tell you*, he'd written at the end. Those words had troubled me a little, but mostly I'd been pleased that he hadn't forgotten my birthday. After the France debacle, the bar for Dad was set pretty low.

"I'm sorry, Summer," Aunt Lydia says, dipping her bread into the saucer of olive oil on the table. Her jaw is set, and her brown eyes are filled with a kind of steeliness. "But you should know I'm not a big fan of your father."

I nod, remembering what my aunt had said—or rather, didn't say—to me at Better Latte last week. I almost want to bring up that incident now, but there seems to be a sudden air of tension at the table.

"Well . . . neither is Mom," I point out. I turn to my mother, whose jaw is also set. "You say worse stuff about Dad," I tell her.

"That may be," Mom replies in a taut tone, unfolding and refolding the white napkin in her lap. "But this isn't the appropriate time to discuss such matters."

"When is the appropriate time, then?" Aunt Lydia asks, looking at Mom.

"Good evening, folks! Are you ready to order?"

A waiter wearing a burgundy vest, bow tie, and a toothy smile is standing eagerly at our table. I almost want to jump up and hug him for interrupting the awkward moment.

"Yes, give me one second," Aunt Lydia says, skimming her menu. I already know what I want: the spaghetti Bolognese, my favorite. My stomach growls.

"Actually, we're still waiting on someone," Mom tells the waiter. "We should hold off until he—"

Just then Max appears, slightly out of breath. He's wearing a nice suit and tie, and holding a paper bag from Between the Lines.

"Sorry, everyone, sorry," Max says. I watch in horror as he leans down and gives Mom a super-quick kiss. Then he sits in the chair beside her and opens his menu. "You guys start ordering, and I'll catch up," he adds.

"I'll have the spaghetti Bolognese," I say flatly. My appetite has vanished.

Aunt Lydia orders the ravioli, and Mom, rubbing her forehead, asks for the lasagna and a glass of wine. Max gets the lasagna, too—*ugh*—and the waiter leaves.

Silence blankets the table. I take a big gulp from my water glass and crunch the ice between my teeth. Maybe, despite our fight, I should have invited Ruby to this dinner. Or Wren. Or Hugh, if he wasn't in Washington, D.C. And if I'd had the guts.

"Happy birthday, Summer!" Max finally pipes up, his tone cheery. As if it's not totally weird that he's here. As if I didn't pass by him on campus several times today. "Here's a little something," he says now, handing me the Between the Lines bag.

"Max, you shouldn't have!" Mom cries, which is super annoying.

"I thought we were doing presents after dinner?" Aunt Lydia asks, and I feel a little pulse of anticipation. I guess being sixteen doesn't stop you from wanting presents.

"Summer can open this one now," Mom says, smiling at Max. Then she smiles up at the waiter, who's come over with her glass of wine.

Hesitantly, I reach into the bag and take out a big, shiny book called *Famous Photographs through the Ages*, with a black-and-white picture of twin girls on the front. My mouth drops open and I look up at Max, feeling a swell of happy surprise.

"Oh, good, you like it," Max says, and grins with relief. "I know you've been taking that photography class, of course." He nods toward Aunt Lydia, who's busy admiring my book over my shoulder. "And your mother tells me you're very talented."

"Really?" I blurt, glancing at Mom. I haven't shown her any of the pictures I've taken this summer.

Mom smiles, her brown eyes sparkling. "According to your aunt, you're her best student."

My heart soars. I glance questioningly at Aunt Lydia. I remember what Hugh said about my photography on Sunday.

Aunt Lydia gives me a wry smile. "I'm not really supposed to admit such things. But I guess I can make an exception this time." She peers at my book again, murmuring, "You better let me borrow that one day, kiddo."

Our food arrives then, and my hunger returns. Steam rises from my bowl of spaghetti, and my head buzzes from the compliments. We all dig in, and I'm grateful to be squished comfortably between my mom and my aunt. Even Max's presence at the table doesn't bother me as much as I would have expected. The book he gave me sits on my lap, and I know I will stay up late tonight leafing through it.

All around us, there's the pleasant din of forks and knives and conversation. I realize that there's no place I'd rather be on my birthday but Orologio's.

When the waiter comes over to clear our plates, Mom signals

to him and whispers something in his ear. Aunt Lydia and I exchange knowing smiles. But I don't really mind that Mom kept up the act of secrecy. It feels like a tradition.

"Okay, present time!" Mom sings once the waiter is gone. Her cheeks are red, maybe from the wine, and I grin at her, feeling full from the meal and excited and kind of like a little kid again. "I mean, it'll be hard to top Max's gift," Mom adds, reaching into her purse. Max chuckles, and Mom hands me a small black box trimmed with gold.

I hold my breath as I open the box's lid. There, on a bed of cotton, is a pair of tiny diamond earrings, glinting and catching the light from the restaurant's chandelier. I've never been one for fancy jewelry, but these earrings are special.

"Oh, Mom," I whisper, giving her a hug. "They look like stars."

"That's what I thought," Mom whispers, hugging me back. Her glasses bump against my cheek. I hurriedly remove my hoops, replacing them with the diamond studs. Mom watches me with a proud smile. Our arguing, our frustration with each other that has lingered all summer, seems so far away now that I can barely remember it.

"Remember, Lydia?" Mom is saying to my aunt. The tension between them seems to have lifted, too. "Our parents gave us diamond studs when we turned sixteen?"

"Of course I remember," Aunt Lydia laughs, picking up her tote bag. "I promptly turned one of mine into a nose ring, and Mom just about killed me."

I laugh, too, feeling that familiar twinge of I-wish-I-had-a-twin envy.

Aunt Lydia reaches into her bag and takes out a flat, square package that's wrapped in brown paper and tied with twine. "So, I know I gave you a camera back in June," she says, handing me the package, "but this is something . . . from *my* camera."

I smile at my aunt and accept the package, intrigued. Everyone at the table watches expectantly as I untie the twine and tear off the wrapping. Then I hear myself gasp.

Aunt Lydia's gift is a framed photograph of me. I can tell she must have taken it from the window of her classroom in Whitman Hall. I am standing beneath the pink magnolia tree that's right outside of Whitman, with the green campus spread out behind me. I am in the process of raising my Nikon to take a picture of something in the distance. My eyes are wide and my hair is unkempt, yet somehow I don't mind how I look. I look sort of . . . like an artist.

"Thank you, Aunt Lydia," I say, getting choked up and giddy all at once, turning in my seat to hug her. "It's—beautiful. Does that sound conceited?" Mom and Max laugh while Aunt Lydia grins and shakes her head. "It's just that no one's ever done my portrait before," I explain. *Oh. Except for Dad*, I think.

"Well, you're a beautiful subject, niece of mine," Aunt Lydia says, patting my arm. "I saw you taking pictures before class one morning and I got inspired!" She pauses and leans forward, lowering her voice. "This is top secret information, of course, but our final class assignment is actually going to be portraits. You'll each take portraits of your respective partners, and then compare the pictures to how you described their faces in your notebooks on the first day of class! After that, you'll each do a self-portrait."

"Wow," I say. The thought of photographing Hugh, and Hugh photographing me, makes my stomach leap. I look back at my photograph, and then around the table. My face hurts from smiling so much. Even at Max.

"You know," I continue, feeling magnanimous. "I'm aware that I've kind of been a baby about the whole France thing. And it's funny, because maybe it's better that I ended up staying here." I tap Aunt Lydia's photo admiringly. "I mean, this almost makes up for me not getting to see Dad's painting of me in the gallery."

As soon as the words are out of my mouth, I feel bad. I shouldn't have said *almost*. I hope I didn't hurt Aunt Lydia's feelings. I really do love her photograph.

But Aunt Lydia doesn't look hurt, only confused. "Which painting of you?" she asks me.

"The one that's in France," I reply. I let out a little laugh—why do I suddenly feel nervous?—as I trace my finger along the photograph's frame. "With the poppies?"

Aunt Lydia frowns, lifting her wine glass. "But that painting isn't of—"

Then she stops. Her eyes widen and her cheeks turn splotchy as she presses her lips together. Once again, I'm reminded of that moment at Better Latte, when Aunt Lydia started to say something about Dad, but caught herself.

"What?" I ask my aunt. I feel a slight coldness start to spread through my gut. "That painting isn't of—what?"

"*Lydia,*" Mom says, her voice a knife-sharp warning.

I glance over at my mother. Her cheeks are red, too, and she is staring at Aunt Lydia so hard I think her eyes can shoot fire. Max appears to be as bewildered as I am; he is studying Mom with concern.

"Mom?" I press. The coldness in my belly spreads up and out, into my limbs. "What's going on?"

"Nothing," Mom says, gripping the stem of her wine glass.

But it doesn't feel like nothing. It feels, well . . . like everything.

"I'm sorry," Aunt Lydia interjects, sounding aggravated. My head swivels from my mom to my aunt and back again. They look so much alike right now—their faces twisted in distress—that it's scary. "It was an accident," Aunt Lydia goes on, gesturing in her impassioned way, almost knocking over her wine glass. "It's getting harder and harder to keep tiptoeing around—"

"Lydia, stop it." Mom slaps one hand on the table, startling me. "Don't do this. Not tonight."

"What are you guys even *talking* about?" I burst out, frustration rising in me. "You know, in case you've forgotten, I'm officially sixteen." I glance down at my presents. "So can you please stop being all weird and cagey with me?"

Silence answers me. Max gives an uncomfortable cough. The rest of the restaurant continues to chatter and hum.

Finally, Aunt Lydia turns to me. "Summer—" she begins softly, and something in her tone makes me freeze all over. My throat tightens. I'm going to cry, right in the middle of Orologio's, at my birthday dinner.

"Lydia, don't," Mom snaps, and I realize she sounds frightened. "Don't tell."

Don't tell. I'd heard Mom say those same words to my aunt in our kitchen, the morning of July fourth. *I have something important to tell you,* Dad had written in his email. But nobody has told me anything. Rebellion surges in me. I refuse to be in the dark any longer.

"No," I say, my voice thick. "Tell." I stare at my aunt. "Tell me. Whatever it is, I want to know."

Hesitation flits across my aunt's face. "I—" Her eyes dart over to Mom. "Lucy?" she says softly, as if she's asking for permission. "She has every right to know. Don't you think it's time she learned the truth about her father?"

The truth about my father. I take a deep breath. I worry I'm going to throw up all of my spaghetti Bolognese.

For a long moment, no one speaks or moves. Then, all the fight seems to leave Mom's body. She lets out a heavy sigh and bows her head, staring down at the napkin in her lap. Her whole pose suggests defeat.

"I never intended for this to come out tonight," she says at last, her voice quiet. She keeps her eyes on her napkin. "But your aunt is right, Summer. You're both right. I suppose it is . . . time that you learned the truth." She looks up at me, her chin quivering. "And I should be the one to tell you."

"Happy birthday to you, happy birthday to you . . ."

I blink and turn my head, my eyes full of unshed tears. Our waiter is at our table, holding a big chocolate cake that is aflame with seventeen flickering candles—sixteen, plus one for good luck. He is surrounded by the rest of the waitstaff, and Jerry, and everyone is singing. They are singing "Happy Birthday" to me. The whole restaurant is singing, people turned around at their tables and pointing at me with big smiles.

No one at my table joins in the song.

Our waiter sets the cake down in front of me. I remember how Mom used to tell me about the day I was born, how it was so hot outside she wanted to wear a bathing suit to the hospital. And how Dad was so nervous he practically passed out in the delivery room. When I was born, Mom said, I looked like an alien, all big eyes and tiny body.

I feel like an alien now, staring blankly down at the candles on the cake, not knowing what to do with them. What is this strange earthly custom?

"Make a wish!"

Faintly, I hear Jerry call out this command.

Aha. That triggers my memory, my human instincts. I close my eyes, the restaurant disappearing, aware only of Mom beside me. At another time, I would have wished to go to France, to kiss a boy, to be as brave as Ruby. *I wish for light instead of darkness*, I think now. Then I blow out the candles, which seems ironic.

Everyone claps, except for everyone at my table, and the waiter takes the cake away to cut it. The silence is a relief. I dab at my eyes with my napkin.

"Summer and I are going to step outside," Mom announces. "Will you be okay here?" she asks Max and Aunt Lydia. They nod mutely. Aunt Lydia's eyes are teary.

Mom picks up her purse and stands, and I do the same; I wonder if we'll even be coming back here. My heart is pounding as I follow Mom out of the restaurant and onto the street. But I don't feel as scared as I did before I made my wish.

The night is hot and stifling, with no breeze. Earlier today, around noon, it had rained, hard. The gray pavement is still slick with puddles and the sky is black and heavy with clouds. It's hard to see any stars. Most of the shops along Greene Street, like Better Latte than Never, are closed.

Mom looks up at the starless sky, hugging herself. I wonder if she, like me, is cold, in spite of the heat. I hug myself, too, and wait for Mom to speak.

"Do you remember," she begins, after a moment, "how often your father used to travel to France? I mean, before he and I got divorced?"

I nod. I hear the whisper of the river across the street, and the whistle of the train in the distance.

"Well," Mom says. "That's because he had—he has—another family there."

The ground seems to tilt beneath me, and shake, like there's an earthquake.

I turn to face my mother. I can't make out her eyes behind her glasses.

"I don't—another family?" I repeat. The words are gibberish on my tongue.

"Yes," Mom says. She finally looks away from the sky, and at me. Her eyes are watery but her voice is even. "There was—there is—another woman," she explains. "A painter. Your father met her in Paris. And they had a daughter. They *have* a daughter."

A lone car drives down the street, its wheels splashing in a puddle.

"Dad . . . has a daughter?" I say numbly. It seems all I can do is echo Mom's words back to her as a question. Nothing she's saying seems possible.

Mom nods, and she draws in a deep breath. Her expression is full of pain and dread, but also—somehow—relief. "Her name is Eloise. She must be fifteen now."

"Eloise?" I parrot. "Fifteen?" Randomly, I think of the book I loved as a kid, about the blond girl named Eloise who lived in New York City. "Fifteen," I say again. I'm shivering, my teeth chattering, like it's wintertime. "So—I was—" I sputter and stop, the easy math suddenly very difficult. "I was *one* when she was born?"

Mom nods again. She seems calm and untroubled, ready to answer all my questions. "I know it's a lot to take in," she tells me softly.

I tip my head back and peer up at the dark sky. If only there were some stars, some pinpricks of light to guide me. But there's nothing.

I start pacing, up and down the street, as if being in motion will help. My head throbs. I remember the line of poetry I saw in Wren's Emily Dickinson book: *I felt a Cleaving in my Mind— As if my Brain had split*—I understand it now. Completely. My brain has come apart, unable to hold all of this new knowledge.

"So, Dad—when I was growing up—while you were married— he—" I catch my breath. It's like trying to put together the world's most twisted puzzle. "All along, had these *other people*"—I can't say the word *family* again—"living in France?"

"Yes," Mom says patiently. She reaches out her hand to me, but I jerk away, still pacing. "I didn't know about it, either," she murmurs. "He finally broke down and told me, when you were eleven. I'd suspected something was going on. I'd suspected for years. But denial is a powerful thing. We see what we want to see."

I stop pacing and stare at Mom. A mosquito buzzes in my ear, and I don't care if it will bite me, if it will suck out all my blood.

"I knew then that our family couldn't hold itself together anymore," Mom goes on. Her arm hangs outstretched between us, like a pale, ghostly thing. "Not after that revelation. I told your father to go. And he went. To France. To . . . them."

Them. What are *they* like? How do *they* look? I turn and stare out at the black river. I usually have a vivid imagination, but I can't picture anything now.

"Do they know about us?" I finally ask, my voice hoarse. I glance back at Mom.

"They do," Mom says. She coughs. "That's why your father wanted you to come to France this summer." She drops her arm to her side. "He wanted to tell you the truth. He wanted you to meet . . . them."

"Oh my God," I whisper. I feel chilled to the bone. *Meet them?* The prospect is horrifying. What would have happened?

"And that's why I didn't want you to go," Mom says, speaking faster. "I didn't think you were ready to know yet. I was—afraid." Her voice breaks, and my heart seizes. Parents aren't supposed to be afraid. "I wanted to protect you," Mom adds quietly.

This time when she reaches out to me, I let her. She takes my hand, and squeezes. Her fingers are as icy as mine.

"I didn't want you to get hurt," Mom goes on, tears welling in her eyes. "I'm *still* not sure you're ready. I'm sorry it had to happen this way."

Behind us, the restaurant door opens and people spill out, chattering happily. It's absurd to think that Aunt Lydia and Max are back in there, with slices of birthday cake on the table, while Mom and I are out here, having this conversation.

Aunt Lydia knew, I realize. Of course she'd known, all along. And she'd almost let something slip that afternoon at Better Latte. That's why she'd sort of been avoiding me since then. She was afraid she'd say more. She must have *wanted* to say more. She'd believed that I should know.

"My painting," I say to Mom, hearing how raw my voice is. I draw my hand out of her grasp. "What was Aunt Lydia going to say about my painting?"

Mom's face crumples. "Oh," she whispers.

My stomach squeezes. I brace myself, even though part of me feels like I can handle anything now. Can't I?

"The . . . painting," Mom says haltingly, looking down at the wet pavement. "It's of . . . Eloise. When she was a young girl." Then she looks back up at me. "Do you understand?" she whispers.

I shake my head, even though I do understand. It's shocking, actually, how swiftly I have understood, and how swiftly the pain of understanding has followed.

"My" painting is *not* mine anymore. I am not *Fille*. I never was.

It was always . . . *her*.

I bend at the waist and press my hands into my abdomen, trying to hold myself together. I open my mouth to cry but nothing comes out.

"When you—when you first saw the painting online," Mom goes on, tears sliding down her cheeks, "and you thought it was your portrait . . . I never had the heart to tell you otherwise." She catches her breath. "I'm sorry."

I manage to straighten up, but the pain still shoots through me. Wave after wave of fresh hurt, like a Band-Aid that keeps getting ripped off. Even after everything I've learned tonight, this one revelation cuts the deepest. Or maybe it's just the exclamation mark, the final point at the end of a very long and messy sentence.

"Do you understand?" Mom asks me again, and I realize I haven't been speaking.

I nod, even though I have questions. So many questions. Like where Dad had painted *Fille*. And if Aunt Lydia was mad at Mom, for keeping all these secrets from me. My questions will never stop.

But I am also tired. So tired. My mouth is dry and my eyes are burning and my head aches. I don't think I can bear any more questions—or answers—tonight.

Mom seems to sense what I'm feeling. She kisses the top of my head, and I lean into her, comforted, even though part of me simmers with fury toward her. Toward Dad. Toward everyone.

"Let me go inside and settle up the check," Mom says, reaching up under her glasses to wipe her eyes. Pulling herself together. "Then we can go home."

Home. What is home? I think vaguely, like I'm an alien again. Home is now a place where everything was hidden. And false.

"I'll be back in a second." Mom hurries into the restaurant, her heels clattering.

My phone buzzes in my purse, and I take it out to see a text message from Ruby.

Happy birthday, it says. *I hope we can talk soon.*

If the message had arrived ten minutes earlier, I would have surely felt something—relief, joy, annoyance, satisfaction. Now I only feel empty. Hollowed out.

I lift my gaze to the sky again. A handful of stars have finally appeared, tiny and bright. But their arrival reminds me of Ruby's text: too little, too late.

PART FIVE

Daughter

Tuesday, July 18, 2:04 p.m.

I tear out of Dad's house, my flip-flops slapping the cobble-stones, my chest heaving with sobs. It's stopped raining, but puddles splash up the back of my legs and stain the bottom of my blue dress. I don't care. I just want to get away.

I run down Rue du Pain. The bakery and the pastel houses all blur in my vision. My instinct about bad omens on my first day here was right. Street of Pain, indeed.

If I had known—if I had known that Dad was going to lead me out of the kitchen, leaving Eloise and Vivienne to stare after us, and sit me down in the living room and gently tell me all those impossible things—I wouldn't have gotten out of the cab that day. I wouldn't have gotten on the plane in New York.

I called you, Dad had said, in the living room, after I'd started crying. *You must have been at the airport, or on the plane. I chickened out. I wanted to tell you not to come. I thought maybe your mother was right, that you weren't ready to know yet. And I was in Berlin, anyway. It made sense to postpone. But you didn't answer the phone.*

I didn't answer the phone.

I whip past the cupid fountain, the memory of my ringing phone haunting me, chasing me. I didn't answer my phone at the airport, and Dad had been on the other end, trying to stop me from coming to France. If I had answered my phone, I would be okay. I wouldn't know what I know now.

I'm stumbling and running up Boulevard du Temps, aware that the passersby can see that I'm in tears, that I'm unwell. I'm beyond shame or embarrassment, though. Dad's words—his other words, the ones he spoke before I started crying, the ones he said quickly, like a slash to the chest—are replaying in my head, loud and ugly.

You see, Eloise is my daughter.

YOU SEE, ELOISE IS MY DAUGHTER.

YOU SEE, ELOISE IS MY—

I keep running, tripping over someone's leash that's attached to a poodle. The poodle's owner snaps at me in French. I ignore them. The faster I run, the sooner I will get to Jacques. And the sooner I get to Jacques, the sooner I can say those words to someone else. I can vomit them out of my mouth so they stop blaring in my ears.

There's a burning stitch in my side, and no breath left in my lungs, when I finally reach Café des Roses. The outdoor tables are wet and empty; everyone hustled indoors when the rain came down.

I go inside the café, where it's not nearly as pretty or as charming. It's small and cramped, and the windows don't let in enough light. Framed, faded paintings of roses adorn the beige walls. The customers seated at the tables eye me warily as I brush past them, starting for the swinging doors that lead to the kitchen—

"Summer!"

Jacques emerges from the kitchen, holding a cake in his hands. It's round and frosted white, and red squiggles spell out the words *Joyeux anniversaire!*

"Where were you?" he asks me, frowning a little. "I was becoming worried."

I stare dumbly at my birthday cake. *Oh.* I'm late for my lunch. My sweet sixteen.

I look up at Jacques, and then he notices—the tears streaking my cheeks, the no-doubt-splotchy color of my face, the fact that my breath is coming out in wheeze-sobs. His dark-blue eyes widen in alarm. I remember something Ruby said once, that crying girls tend to freak boys out. That's fine. Jacques can go ahead and freak out all he wants. He'll never be more freaked out than I am at this moment. We can even have a contest.

"*Qu'est-ce qui se passe?*" he murmurs, stepping closer to me. "What is wrong? Come," he adds before I can unleash my answer. He balances the cake in one hand and reaches out with the other to take my arm. "First you must sit down, no?"

I shake my head but Jacques is already leading me to a small table by the window. Our table. There is a red rose in a vase, and two bowls of *bouillabaisse.* Picture-perfect.

Jacques sets my cake on the table, moving aside the vase to make room. I swipe at my wet cheeks with the heel of my hand

and sink into a chair. Jacques sits across from me, smoothing the front of his white waiter's shirt. He looks gorgeous, as always.

"The *bouillabaisse* probably got a bit cold," he tells me apologetically, as if food matters at all to me right now.

I gaze down at my fish stew. My stomach rolls over.

"Eloise is his daughter," I blurt out.

There. I exhale. I said it. But I feel no relief. The last word continues to pound in my brain. *DAUGHTER, DAUGHTER, DAUGHTER.*

Jacques frowns again. "*Quoi?*" he asks. "What did you say? I do not understand."

"Join the club," I reply, and then, in spite of everything, I begin to laugh. A real, full-on belly laugh, like what has happened to me is absurd and hilarious, not absurd and horrible. A few diners and waiters glance over at me, this insane person in their midst.

"Summer?" Jacques says, looking more alarmed than he did before. Actually, he looks overwhelmed—unsure of how to deal with the crazy American girl across from him. I bet he was not expecting any of this when we ate our crepes and strolled down the boulevard late last night, sticky fingers intertwined. I mean, neither did I.

I manage to stop laughing, and I press my palms against the tabletop. I breathe in, and out. Jacques watches me, waiting.

"Eloise," I begin, the name sour in my mouth. The syllables are so elongated and odd, I think. *El-oh-eeze.* Jacques nods. "She's my father's daughter," I say.

It's a statement that makes no sense. It's like one of those riddles I enjoyed stumping my parents with when I was a kid: *What comes down but never goes up? (Rain.) What has hands but cannot clap? (A clock.) How can Eloise be my father's daughter, when I am my father's daughter?* There is no answer.

Jacques himself doesn't answer; his eyes only grow wider. So I continue. I tell him everything—how my dad, while married to my mom, met Vivienne, a fellow painter, in Paris. How he and Vivienne had a baby girl, Eloise. How my dad kept Eloise, and Vivienne, a secret from me and my mother, for years and years and years. How he shuttled back and forth between France and Hudsonville, living two lives, until my mom found out, and they split up. And how I'd known nothing, until today.

As I'm talking, I feel detached, like I'm recounting a story that in no way pertains to me. All these players—Dad and Mom, Vivienne and Eloise—are characters from science fiction, not real people. At the same time, I am very present in the moment. I am aware of Jacques sitting across from me, silent, both of our bowls of *bouillabaisse* untouched. I hear the French being spoken around us in the café, the sound of coffee being poured and of spoons clinking against delicate cups.

I am also aware that anyone sitting near us who understands English can easily eavesdrop on me. I'm making no effort to whisper, to hide what I'm saying. *Let them listen,* I think, anger flaring up inside me. Let them know that Ned Everett, the great artist, is a liar and a fraud.

"You remember my father's painting?" I say to Jacques, my

throat tightening. "The one we saw in the gallery?" I've saved the most painful part for last.

Jacques nods. *"Fille,"* he says. The first word he's spoken since he said my name.

"Fille," I echo. I feel an ache in my chest, and tears sting my eyes. "That painting is of Eloise when she was little. Not me, like I'd always thought." My voice breaks. "I'm not *Fille*. She is."

When Dad had explained that to me, in the living room, holding the sketch of Eloise in his shaking hands, I'd felt like the floor had split open and swallowed me whole. Like I'd ceased to exist for a minute or so. Because if it wasn't me in that painting, then who was I?

"Oh là là," Jacques says, and I realize that I have been silent, staring into my lap and fighting back tears. I look up at him. He makes a tsk sound and shakes his head, his eyes still wide. *"C'est incroyable.* I am sorry you have gone through this, Summer. And on your birthday?" He leans forward to take my hand. *"Ma pauvre."*

I sniffle and squeeze his hand. I'm grateful for his sweetness and his sympathy. I do feel like a *pauvre*—a pitiful one. But I'm surprised that *he* doesn't seem more surprised, or outraged.

"I must admit something," he goes on, studying his *bouilla-baisse.* "I had assumed that you and Eloise were related."

"You—what?" I sputter, startled. I free my hand from his and collapse back against my chair. Outside, the wind shakes the leaves on a lemon tree and sends drops of water to the ground. A false rain.

Jacques lifts his gaze to me and shrugs one shoulder. "You two look very much alike," he tells me, as if this is obvious. "The evening I met you?" He nods out the window, at the spot where we'd first spoken. "I thought you were her, from the back."

I squint at Jacques like my vision is bad—like *his* vision is bad. "That can't be," I tell him. Then I realize that I'd made the exact same mistake, five years ago: I'd also thought that Eloise was me, in the painting. I feel a chill pass through me. "Why didn't you say something?" I ask.

He picks up the toasted baguette wedge from his bowl and takes a bite. "In the beginning," he explains, swallowing, "it seemed only to be a coincidence, that you resembled someone I knew. Then when I came to your father's house and saw you and Eloise together . . ." He trails off, shrugging again. "It did not seem to be a coincidence anymore. I thought perhaps you were cousins, but that you did not like each other very much."

"That second part is true," I mumble.

I remember how, earlier, I'd dashed sobbing out of the living room, and into the kitchen, where Eloise stood in her nightgown, staring at me. Vivienne had sat at the oak table, her head in her hands. Dad had made it clear, when he tossed his little hand grenade, that both Vivienne and Eloise knew everything; I was the only one on the outside. As I'd wrenched open the door, I'd heard Eloise say my name but I'd barreled ahead, wanting nothing to do with her. Especially not now.

"Only you are not cousins," Jacques points out, dipping his spoon into his cold *bouillabaisse* and taking a sip of the broth. "You are sisters, *non?*"

"*Non,*" I snap instantly. I shiver. *Sisters.* I refuse to go there. "Don't say that," I order him, knowing I sound much younger than sixteen. The frosting on my cake looks like it's wilting.

"Okay," Jacques says, holding up his hands in surrender. *"Je comprends. C'est une situation très difficile. Très compliquée."*

"*Oui,*" I reply, gritting my teeth.

The situation *is* very difficult and complicated. And yet Jacques seems to be taking it relatively in stride. He reclines in his seat, draping his arm across the back of his chair. A tentative smile tugs at his lips, and I can make out the dimple in his right cheek.

I scowl. It could be that there's a slight language barrier. Or a cultural barrier. Regardless, I feel a wave of frustration. I want to be able to rage and weep with someone.

"I am sorry," Jacques is saying. For a second, I think he's apologizing for his nonchalance. Then I see that he has taken his phone out of his pocket and is checking the time. *15:00.* Three o'clock. *"C'est dommage.* I only had one hour to take for lunch, so I am late for my shift. I prefer to never be late," he explains.

I feel a flash of panic. Although I'm upset with Jacques, I don't want him to go. I can't imagine sitting here, alone with my dark thoughts, amid the swirl of happy café chitchat. Nor can I imagine going back outside, into the unrelenting prettiness of

Les Deux Chemins. The sun has started peeking out, and a bumblebee drones by the window.

And most of all, I can't imagine returning to Dad's house, facing him and Vivienne and Eloise. The whole . . . *family*. I shudder at the word. What would I say to them? What would *they* say to *me*? What a nightmare.

I need to escape.

"Let's go somewhere," I burst out, desperation rising in me as I look at Jacques. "Let's go back to the Riviera. No—let's go to Paris! Right now. We said we would!"

"Now?" Jacques laughs. He glances down at his phone again. "Summer, I cannot. My mother would not allow—"

"Please?" I say, clasping my hands together. The promise of boarding a train, leaving Les Deux Chemins in my wake, is the only thing that appeals to me at the moment. I've always wanted to see Paris. And a big city is exactly what I need—to get lost in the anonymous crowds, to walk the ancient streets until my feet blister and bleed.

Jacques lets out a sigh. "All right." He smiles at me, and his dark-blue eyes sparkle with spontaneity. "It *would* be nice to drop everything and go." I feel a twinge of hope. He stands, lifting my uneaten birthday cake. "I will put the food in the kitchen and then ask my mother. Come with me? She is upstairs, in our apartment."

The day we'd gone to Cannes, I'd met Jacques outside the café that morning, and he'd briefly introduced me to his parents, Monsieur and Madame Cassel. His mother had been as imposing as I'd remembered her from my first night in Les Deux Chemins, and his father was a gentle, quiet, mustached man. Now I feel a small beat of nervousness at the prospect of seeing Jacques's home.

I pick up the two bowls of *bouillabaisse* and follow Jacques through the swinging doors into the kitchen.

"I'm sorry I didn't eat any of your food," I tell him sadly.

"We will save the cake for another time," he tells me, opening the industrial-size refrigerator and stashing the cake inside. "You can throw out the *bouillabaisse*," he adds, a little mournfully, and I feel guilty.

The kitchen is tiny and hot, overflowing with waiters yelling out orders and people in aprons washing dishes and slicing hunks of meat. I see Jacques's father in his chef's hat at the stove, and he waves to us when we pass by.

As Jacques leads me through a door in the back of the kitchen, I think of my own father. The mere notion of him fills me with pain and a sort of sizzling fury. I wonder what he did after I stormed out—if he cavalierly went to paint in his studio, or if he left to search for me. Maybe he sat down and had a bonding session with Vivienne and Eloise. Or maybe he called my mom.

Mom. Following Jacques up a narrow, winding staircase, I realize I am furious at Mom, too. She'd known the truth, all these years, and she'd kept me in the dark. *Honesty is a two-way street,* she'd always said, which, it turns out, is a total lie. I remember her inexplicable level of hostility toward Dad, how reluctant she'd been about me coming to France. At least that makes sense now. That's the only thing that makes sense.

Jacques unlocks a door with the same kind of old skeleton key Dad's house has, and we step into a cozy, cluttered apartment. The smells of food from the café permeate the place. There are overstuffed couches and framed family photos on the piano. I see shots of Jacques at different ages with a beautiful girl who resembles him; that must be his older sister, Hélène, whom he's mentioned. She's off at university in Normandy.

Jacques's mother is seated at the dining room table, going through a stack of bills and receipts.

"Maman?" Jacques begins hesitantly. She peers up at the two of us over the rims of her glasses. "You remember *mon amie*, Summer Everett," Jacques goes on. He puts a hand on my waist, which normally would make me blush, but there is nothing normal about today.

I force out a *"bonjour"* to Madame Cassel. I don't want to bother with any small talk. I want to get her okay for Paris, and go.

Jacques begins speaking in rapid French to his mother; I can make out something about the train to Paris, and work, and the café. Then I distinctly hear him say: *"Elle a beaucoup des problèmes avec sa famille."* I sigh, silently translating: *She has a lot of problems with her family.* Indeed.

It sounds like Jacques is making a good case but before he's even finished, his mom is shaking her head.

"I know," she says in accented English, for my benefit, "you think that because you are handsome, Jacques, that you can show your dimples and get away with anything. I understand that this works on many girls." Her eyes cut over to me and I stiffen. I wonder how many girls Jacques has introduced to his mother before. Whatever. That's literally the least of my worries right now. "But it does not work on me," his mother goes on sternly. She clucks her tongue. "No Paris today. Go downstairs and tend to your tables."

Her words make my heart drop. I turn to Jacques, feeling tears threaten again. "I'll go to Paris alone," I tell him, thinking out loud, full of desperation once more. "Just tell me how to get to the train station from here . . ." I bite my lip. Despite how brave I've been lately, could I really master a trip to Paris all by myself?

Madame Cassel clucks her tongue again, this time at me. "What are you saying, *jeune fille*?" she asks. "You will run off to Paris now? You will not arrive until the nighttime, and then where will you go? Where will you stay?" she demands, and I have the sinking realization that she's right. I glance down at my empty hands. I brought nothing with me when I fled Dad's house: no wallet, no change of clothes. No camera. I can't go to Paris without my camera.

"I can't go—" I hear my voice waver. "But I can't go back to my father's." I look up at Jacques, and I'm unable to stop my tears from spilling out. "I won't."

Jacques gets that overwhelmed expression on his face—the one that seems to say *I didn't sign up for this madness*. "Do not cry," he tells me in a harried way, which confirms Ruby's theory.

"Let her cry." Madame Cassel stands up and hands me a tissue that seems to have materialized from nowhere. She pats my shoulder as I blow my nose. "Jacques tells me you are having family troubles. Why don't you stay here? Make yourself comfortable," she tells me, pointing to one of the sofas.

"Really?" I manage to ask Madame Cassel through my tears. She nods. I feel a surge of gratitude so deep that I almost hug her, as if she were my own mother. Suddenly, it hits me that, however angry I am at Mom, however many secrets she has kept from me, I need her. Especially today, on my birthday, after everything that happened, I want to hear her familiar, soothing voice.

"I will be down in the café, then," Jacques is saying. He gives me a quick kiss on the cheek—his mother is eyeing him, hawk-like—and says he will see me when he's finished his shift. I expect to feel bereft when he leaves but I don't.

"Do you have a phone I could use?" I ask Madame Cassel, who has returned to reviewing her bills and receipts. "It's an international call, so I can pay you back . . ."

"*Bof.*" She waves a hand. "You can use the telephone in Hélène's room, if you would like some privacy." She points down the hall. I thank her profusely, and go.

On my way, I pass what I'm sure is Jacques's room; there are soccer posters hung everywhere, and cookbooks stacked on the shelves. I pause in the open doorway, feeling a faint flutter in my belly. I'd dreamed that one day this summer, I'd be able to see Jacques's room, his house. But definitely not under these circumstances. Life is strange.

Hélène's room is as small as my medieval chamber back at Dad's, but much more welcoming, with French movie posters on the walls and a bright-yellow bedspread. I gingerly sit down on the bed and pick up the cordless phone from the nightstand.

I dial the international code, which Mom made me memorize before I left for France, and the number of my house. I feel a stab of nervousness, wondering how Mom will react to what I say. If she will get defensive, or upset, or spiteful. But I am eager to be honest with her—for both of us to finally be honest with each other. No wonder Mom had sometimes acted so weird and so worried, no wonder she'd been so protective of me. What a burden, to carry that secret.

The line rings. My mind feels foggy as I try to calculate the time difference: It must be about nine in the morning in Hudsonville. Mom wouldn't be on campus yet.

"Hello?" she says, answering at last.

I take a big, ragged breath. "It's Summer," I say.

"Happy birthday!" Mom cries, sounding pleased and also apprehensive, as if she can tell something is up. "What have you been doing so far today—"

"Mom," I interrupt. I swallow. "I know. I know about Dad. He told me."

"Oh," she says softly, brokenly. But I could swear she also sounds relieved.

• • •

Later that night, after Mom and I have had our long talk, after we have both cried and raged, and apologized and explained, after Mom has offered to fly me home from France early, and I've told her, honestly, that I don't yet know what I want to do, I eat dinner with Jacques and his parents.

They eat after-hours, once the café has closed, at a table near the kitchen. Monsieur Cassel serves us a simple, cold salad of penne with fresh corn, tomatoes, hard-boiled eggs, and sliced cucumbers, drizzled with olive oil and salt, plus rustic bread and butter on the side. My appetite has finally returned; in fact, after not eating all day, I'm ravenous. I wolf down my food, thanking Monsieur Cassel between bites.

It's clear that by now Jacques has told *both* his parents that I have "family problems"; Monsieur and Madame Cassel are extra nice and attentive, offering me more sparkling water when my glass runs low and then, at meal's end, bringing my birthday cake out of the kitchen with much fanfare.

As Jacques and his parents sing me *"Joyeux anniversaire"* to the tune of "Happy Birthday," I think about how strange and surreal it is, to be celebrating not with Mom or Ruby, or even with Dad—who is here, in town—but with this foreign family, a family much more whole than mine ever was.

But all of today has been strange and surreal. So in a way, it's fitting.

I'm digging into a slice of Jacques's very tasty vanilla-cream cake, about to compliment him on his culinary skills, when he tells me, "I spoke to Eloise."

I choke, coughing a little, and Madame Cassel helpfully hits me on the back.

"When?" I demand, glaring at Jacques.

Jacques gives one of his matter-of-fact shrugs. "She came to the café this evening," he explains. "Not with Colette and Tomas. Alone. She said that her father—your father—" This time, it's Jacques who coughs, his cheeks reddening. Madame and Monsieur Cassel exchange a glance; I wonder how much they know. "He was very worried about where you had gone," Jacques finishes.

"Good," I mutter, staring at the piece of cake on the end of my fork. *Let Dad worry. Let him feel terrible.*

Jacques takes a sip of his water. "Eloise said that she thought you might be here, with me, and this is why she came." He looks straight at me. "She was also very upset."

"Good," I say again, even though I feel a small pang of remorse. I put down my fork. "What did you tell her?" I ask.

"The truth," Jacques says with another shrug. "That you were upstairs in my family's home and you did not want to see your father. So she left."

"Oh," I say, relieved that Jacques didn't send Eloise up to fetch me. "I still don't want to see him," I add, pushing my plate away. "Or any of them."

A weak window fan blows warm air at us; outside, in the night, I see people strolling along Boulevard du Temps, licking ice-cream cones and laughing, completely alien to me.

Madame Cassel clears her throat. She and her husband exchange a glance again. "If you are still feeling so troubled, *chérie*," she tells me, "you are welcome to spend the night. Hélène's room is empty, as you know."

I hadn't even considered this; I hadn't even thought beyond right now, sitting slumped in the wicker chair. I know I'm imposing on the Cassels like crazy. And the idea of sleeping over at Jacques's place turns my face hot. But Madame Cassel's offer also makes me weak with relief. The longer I can hide out somewhere, the better.

"You can't avoid Dad forever, you know," Mom had told me on the phone, when I'd explained where I was calling from (this meant I'd also had to briefly mention Jacques, but thankfully Mom didn't dwell on that point too much). "Even if you decide to fly back to Hudsonville tomorrow," she'd said, "you will still have to face him again."

But not tonight, I think. I agree to stay over, and tell the Cassels *"merci"* about a million times. As Jacques's parents clear away the plates and the cake remnants, I notice that Jacques looks a little uncomfortable. Does *he* not want me to stay? He has seemed distant, not quite himself. Maybe because our interactions, until today, had been so light and fun, all poppy fields and moped rides. And then I'd swept in with all this darkness, like a rain cloud in the middle of summer.

Monsieur Cassel sets about closing up the café while I go upstairs with Jacques and his mother. Jacques says he's exhausted—he does look drained, no doubt from all the drama. He kisses me quickly on the cheek before going into his bedroom to crash. Madame Cassel gives me a toothbrush, and I thank her again for her ridiculous hospitality and she says, *"Bof,"* and shoos me off.

In Hélène's room, I collapse on her yellow bed in my "lucky" blue dress. I'm too tired to look in the wardrobe for a nightgown or pajamas to borrow. I close my eyes and think of my empty room at Dad's house—the bare bed, Vivienne's surrealist painting on the wall, the moon glow coming through the window. What is happening in the rest of the house? Is Eloise still awake, after her visit to the café?

I roll over onto my stomach. Sleep will not come. I wonder if I should call Mom again, but I don't want to run up the Cassels' phone bill. I wish I could text Ruby. Even after everything—seeing her *#doubledate* on Instagram, the fact that we haven't spoken in so long—I miss her. I know now that I can get by on my own, without her. That I don't require her guidance—or, you know, her bossiness—at every step. But it would be nice to hear from her again.

I finally drift off, and I dream of Ruby, and home. I dream that Ruby and I are standing outside of Better Latte Than Never and across the street, the Hudson River sparkles in the sun. I dream that Hugh Tyson pedals past on his bicycle, and we smile at each other. I dream that I'm sitting with Mom on our front porch, the stars above us.

When I wake up, dawn is creeping through the window. And I have reached a decision—without excessive waffling, for once. I will go back to Hudsonville early. Maybe even today, if there's a flight. But not because I'm running away from Dad. In fact, I know I need to face him now, for real.

Rubbing my eyes, I get up and leave Hélène's room, padding through the silent, dim apartment. I brush my teeth and do my best to finger comb my hair. When I emerge from the bathroom, I almost crash into Jacques.

"*Salut*," he says, smiling sleepily. He looks adorable in boxer shorts and a thin gray T-shirt with a picture of a soccer ball on it.

"Good morning," I answer in English, smiling back. "Did I wake you?"

He shakes his head, his dark hair falling into his eyes. "*Non.* I always wake up at the same time every morning." He pauses, and I think about how different we are: how Jacques, despite his mellow attitude, is so punctual, and I am, well . . . me. "Are you feeling better?" he asks.

I make a so-so motion with my hand and repeat a French phrase he taught me. "*Comme ci comme ça.*" Jacques laughs. "But thank you," I add, looking at him seriously. "For getting me through yesterday."

Jacques shrugs. "I am happy I could help," he says, though I can tell it was all a bit too much for him. He still looks tired.

"And thank you for . . . everything else," I say. "For our adventures."

Jacques smiles, showing his dimples. We stand in the hallway of his apartment, gazing at each other. I know I'm bedraggled and sleep-deprived, my dress wrinkled and my hair a serious problem. Still, I feel a spark pass between us: the old spark, that was there before yesterday afternoon. Then, just as quickly as it came, the spark fizzles out, like a firework.

"Are you going home?" Jacques asks me, running a hand through his tousled hair.

I nod. I don't know if he means Dad's house or home-home, but I don't clarify. Either way, this feels like a good-bye.

In another world, if I'd stayed blissfully ignorant of Dad and his secret family, things might have gone differently with Jacques. I'd have remained in France, and we would have gone to Paris together. We would have kissed in front of the Eiffel Tower. Maybe I would have even called him my boyfriend—"*mon petit ami.*" My heart thumps at this *what-if?* but then I give Jacques a sad smile. Maybe none of that would have happened, anyway.

"*Au revoir,*" I say to Jacques, stepping close to him. I reach out and take his hand.

"*À bientôt,*" he tells me, which I know means "till later"—a less final kind of farewell. And it's true; who knows what the future will bring?

Jacques brings my hand up to his mouth and kisses it. Then he leans close and gives me a real kiss. I kiss him back and twine my arms around his neck. I try to memorize the feel of his lips, the texture of his hair under my hands. I don't think I will forget anything.

After the kiss, I rest my head against Jacques's warm chest for a minute. Then I start for the front door, telling Jacques to thank his parents for me.

"I hope your family will be okay," Jacques says, letting me out.

I hope so, too, I think, walking down the winding staircase. I leave through the café, where Monsieur Cassel is in the process of opening up shop. All the cafés along Boulevard du Temps, I see, are starting to open, the owners lifting the grates and hosing down the sidewalks with soapy water. The early morning light colors everything pink.

I walk on, feeling melancholy, missing Les Deux Chemins even though I'm still here. I pass the shuttered boutique with its pretty dresses on display, and the *tabac* with its unlit red sign. The church bells are tolling seven. I turn at the cupid fountain, and I hold out my hand to catch some of its spray, as if for luck.

Rue du Pain is sleepy, the only sound the chirping of birds. My stomach tightens with fear as I approach Dad's house. I see that the bakery is open—I can smell the rising dough—so I duck inside. I have no euros on me; I can't buy a *pain au chocolat*. I guess I just wanted to buy myself some time.

Bernice is busy at the oven, and I think about Dad's sketch of her, the one I never found. When she notices me, she smiles and says, *"Bonjour*, Summer!" like nothing has changed. And to her, it hasn't. No matter what may break or collapse out in the universe, Bernice will be here, taking fresh loaves from the oven. That's comforting.

Before Bernice can reach for a *pain au chocolat* for me, the bell over the door chimes. A flood of early-morning customers spill inside, gabbing in French about baguettes and croissants. I take the opportunity to slip through them, like a fish through water, and back outside. There, I square my shoulders, and cross the street to Dad's.

PART SIX

Double Lives

Wednesday, July 19, 7:59 a.m.

One, one thousand. Two, one thousand . . .

I lie flat on my bed, my covers kicked down, the air conditioner whirring. I am tense, counting the seconds until my alarm clock will blare from my nightstand. Until that happens, I tell myself, I can remain in this hazy, suspended state between sleep and waking. I can stave off thinking about what Mom told me last night. About Dad, and his—those—other people in France.

Twenty-four, one thousand. Twenty-five, one thousand . . .

I flip my pillow over to the cool side. I'd actually dreamed about France. I think it was France. I was walking in a garden, surrounded by rosebushes and lavender, eating a croissant. I spotted a shiny pool and leaned over to peer at my reflection, and I saw a girl with messy blond hair, but she wasn't exactly me: more like a distorted twin. As I stared at her, her eyes and mouth became gaping black holes—and then I'd jerked awake, my heart racing, a full minute before my alarm was set to go off.

Thirty-eight, one thousand. Thirty-nine, one thousand . . .

Rolling onto my side, I gaze around my dim room. At least *it* hasn't changed. There are my haphazard piles of books. The broken mirror. The Degas poster of ballerinas, and the Renoir poster of two sisters. If it weren't for the polka-dot dress—my "lucky" dress—tossed on the back of my desk chair, or the photography book from Max and the framed portrait from Aunt Lydia sitting out on my desk, then I could pretend that my birthday dinner—and everything that came after—never happened.

Fifty-eight, one thousand. Fifty-nine, one thousand—

I hear the faintest of clicks, and the radio blasts to life on my nightstand. Even though I was expecting it, I'm still startled.

"Waaake up, Hudsonville! You're listening to Bob and Bob in the Morning. It's shaping up to be a real scorcher today, with highs in the hundreds and the humidity going nuts. And no rain in sight to bring us any relief . . ."

I reach over and slap the button, silencing the talking. Despite my air conditioner dutifully pumping out its cold breath, I can feel the intense heat of the day seeping inside the house. Normally, this kind of late July heat—the word "scorcher" itself—would give me a little thrill of anticipation. The hotter it is, the more it really feels like summer. My season. I'd be eager to get up and slide on my flip-flops and run out into the sunshine.

But today, I am not eager to face the world. I sit up in bed, scratching at the giant mosquito bite on my elbow. I'd prefer to be like a crab, hidden by my shell, scuttling to safety beneath the sand.

There's a knock on my door, and then Mom pokes her head inside before I can say "Come in," which is a classic Mom move.

"How are you doing, honey?" Mom asks softly. "Did you get some sleep? I heard your alarm go off."

It's clear that Mom herself did not get any sleep. Her face is pale and drawn, and there are dark circles under her eyes. She's still in the black dress from last night, barefoot, with her Hudsonville College coffee mug in hand.

After we'd returned from Orologio's, I'd stumbled straight to my room and Mom had gone to the kitchen to brew coffee. It hadn't occurred to me that she wouldn't even attempt going to bed. Clearly, we were both haunted.

"I did sleep," I reply, shuddering a little as I remember my nightmare.

"You must have been very tired," Mom says, opening my door wider. I see that Ro, of course, is with her; he stands alert by her ankle, his tail held high. I scowl at him, resenting how much he favors Mom.

And resenting Mom, too. Still.

But then, to my surprise, Ro pads into my room and leaps up onto my bed. He promptly nestles against my side, curling into a ball and purring. I look down at his orange fur in shock. Did he sense, in some magical, catlike way, that I could use extra kindness this morning?

"Look at that," Mom says with a laugh, coming over. She sets her coffee mug on the floor and sits down on my bed, Ro between us. She looks at me with sympathy in her eyes, and I stiffen. I hope she's not hoping for some sort of heart-to-heart. My own heart feels too mixed-up and jumbled, too full of hurt and confusion.

But Mom doesn't bring up the topic that looms over us like a shadow. She asks, "Are you feeling up for class?"

Right. I have photography in an hour. That's why I'd set my alarm last night, acting on autopilot before I'd crawled bleary-eyed into bed.

I glance down at my floor where my bookbag lies, half unzipped, my Nikon camera peeking out. I love photography class, I realize then; I get excited about Photoshop cropping, and darkroom developing, and learning about the history of taking pictures. I feel a flutter of flattery as I recall what Aunt Lydia said about my being her best student. That makes me want to try even harder in class.

Except, I cannot imagine strolling onto campus today. Waving to Max, like he didn't witness the drama at Orologio's. Sitting down beside Wren, whom I don't feel ready to confide in about something so big. Looking at Hugh's empty desk, both wishing and not wishing that he were there, instead of in D.C. with his parents. And, of course, seeing my aunt, who first broke open the shell of Dad's secret and coaxed the truth out.

"No," I tell my mom, my voice a faint croak. "I think I need a day off."

I expect Mom to chide me on the importance of responsibility; she never lets me stay home from school, unless I'm truly sick. But now she nods in understanding.

"I'm considering canceling my afternoon class myself," she tells me, yawning. "So I can, you know, nap." She pats Ro's head and glances at me with a small smile. "Or would you want to do something? See a movie maybe?"

I shake my head. Does Mom truly believe things can go back to the way they were? How are we supposed to move forward now that I possess this knowledge? I feel suddenly antsy, like the itchiness of my mosquito bite is spreading to the rest of my body. I have the urge to jump off my bed and bolt. Escape. Where would I go, though? To New York City, to get lost in the anonymous crowds?

I know. I could go to France. I let out a short, slightly unhinged laugh.

Mom frowns at me. Before she can ask me why I am laughing at nothing, my cell phone rings on my messy desk.

"Who'd be calling now?" I mutter, scrambling off my bed. I let myself engage in the brief daydream of it being Hugh. More realistically, it's probably Aunt Lydia, checking up on me.

I grab my phone off my desk, and what I see on the screen makes my breath catch in my throat.

UNKNOWN CALLER.

Just like at the airport, weeks ago.

I know, without a doubt, that it is Dad calling again.

And I answer, again.

There's a crackle, the sound of lines being connected across oceans.

"Hello?" I say, pressing the phone to my ear. I can feel Mom and Ro watching me from where they sit on my bed.

"Summer?" Dad says, and his voice sounds rough and ragged, like he hasn't slept, either. "I'm glad I caught you."

Why? My heart thumps. Does he know that I know about—him, and them?

Or is he completely oblivious, and simply calling to wish me a happy belated birthday, sweetheart?

"Sweetheart," Dad goes on, and I can hear how anxious he is. There's a flick of a lighter and an exhale, and I realize he is smoking. I didn't even know he smoked. I suppose it's very French of him. "I understand that you have learned that—I—haven't been entirely truthful about certain things all these years."

Is *that* how he wants to put it? Anger flares in me. Dad is always an artist, isn't he? Covering up the facts, making prettiness out of nothing. I think of the term *con artist*. That suits him, more than any label given to the great Ned Everett.

"How—how did you hear?" I ask through gritted teeth. I'm already looking over at Mom, who is watching me sheepishly.

"Your mother called me, hours ago," Dad says. I briefly wonder what time it is in France, but I'm too upset to calculate. "And I've been working up the nerve to call *you*, sweetheart," he admits with a little chuckle, like this is all just a funny mishap.

"I'll let you have some privacy," Mom whispers to me, standing up with Ro in her arms. I glare at her, and I start to mouth to her that she should stay, but she's hurrying out of my room, and then I hear her own bedroom door close.

"I'm not a very brave man," Dad is saying on the other end. "That is why I told you not to come to France, you know." He takes a deep breath. "I mean, I really was in Berlin when I called you at the airport. I'm back in France now." He's rambling. "But the thing is, I got scared. I realized it was maybe too soon for you to find out. I panicked." He pauses. "I'm sorry."

My thoughts are whipping around. Is he apologizing for canceling on me so suddenly? Or for . . . everything? I can tell he is finally being honest and open. But is that enough? No. It's not. A *sorry* can't sweep away my thudding awareness of the dark truth. A *sorry* can't reverse the fact that *Fille* is not—and never was—me.

"I have to go," I burst out. I feel like I'm being strangled. My air conditioner has turned my room into an icebox. I could freeze to death in here, in the middle of summer. "I can't talk to you anymore," I tell my father.

"Summer, please," he begs. "Don't hang up on me. We need to communicate. We haven't until now. That's been the problem—"

"No," I snap. I'm trembling. I've never barked at my father before, but no rules seem to apply now. "The problem is that you lied and cheated."

Dad is silent, and I wonder if he's going to yell at me for disrespecting him, or if *he'll* hang up on *me*. I wish he would. Instead, he murmurs, "Maybe it would be better if we did this over Skype. That way, we could see each other. And you could even"—he clears his throat—"if you wanted, you could see Eloise. And Vivienne. Maybe that would make it seem more . . . real."

Nausea sweeps over me. *Vivienne.* So that's the name of the woman, the painter from Paris. And Eloise, of course, is . . . *her.* The person I have been blocking from my thoughts. I don't even want to know what she might look like. Snapshots of blond curly hair and blue eyes drift through my mind, a patchwork of images from the painting.

Stop.

I slam my mind shut again, like a window.

"I don't want it to be real," I tell Dad. And then, before I can weaken, before he can say anything else, I end the call.

I stand by my desk, trying to breathe. I look down at the phone in my shaking hands, regretting that I answered the call. What would have happened if I'd ignored Dad's call back at the airport? I guess I would have flown to France, and been confronted with everything I wish I could block out now.

But the truth has caught up to me, either way.

Distractedly, I scroll through my phone, and I see the birthday text message Ruby sent me last night. I read it again: *Happy birthday. I hope we can talk soon.*

In spite of everything, I realize what it is I want to do today.

I sit down on the edge of my bed, and I start to text.

• • •

It is easily a hundred degrees when I step outside around noon. I'm glad I stashed sunscreen in my bookbag, and that I included ice packs in with the sandwiches I made. My hair is up in a topknot, and I'm wearing my sunglasses, a blue tank top, shorts, and flip-flops. Also, after some deliberation, I put one of Ruby's woven bracelets back on my wrist. Just one. It felt like a compromise.

I climb on my bike, glancing back at my quiet house. Before I left, I'd peeked into Mom's room and saw her fast asleep in her bed. She'd looked so peaceful, with Ro curled up at her feet. I'd realized that, to some degree, it must have been a relief to her— releasing the long-held secret.

Sweat trickles down the back of my neck as I pedal up Rip Van Winkle Road, listening to the cicadas chirping. I make a right onto Deer Hill, and then a left onto Washington Irving Road, where Aunt Lydia lives. I pass by her rambling white house: the house where she and Mom grew up. It's funny to think that they were born and raised here in Hudsonville, and that they then returned here, as grown-ups, to work and live, while their parents moved down to Florida.

It was Aunt Lydia, actually, who'd introduced *my* parents to each other. Dad, a young, aspiring painter from Ohio, arrived as a visiting lecturer in the Visual Arts department at Hudsonville College. According to Mom, Aunt Lydia had promptly given him Mom's phone number because she knew the two of them would fall in love. And they had, I guess. Even though Mom was serious and proper, and Dad loose and carefree.

As I turn off Washington Irving Road onto Pine Street, I wonder if Aunt Lydia feels guilty for bringing Dad into Mom's life, given what transpired. If she hadn't done that, though—I wouldn't exist. That thought makes me shiver, despite the heat.

When I get to Pine Park, I lean my bike against the fence and walk onto the lawn, my bookbag on my shoulder. There are only a handful of people here—a few kids playing tag in the shade of the pine trees, and one ice-cream vendor. A couple dragonflies swoop around the empty band shell.

I shake my blanket out of my bookbag and spread it on the fresh-cut grass. Then I sit down and put some sunscreen on my bare arms and legs. I'm reaching into my bag for the sandwiches, when I hear a familiar voice.

"You're on time."

I look over to see Ruby approaching the blanket, shielding her eyes from the sun. She's wearing her platform sandals, a wide-brimmed floppy hat, and a lilac-colored tank top tucked into high-waisted shorts. She clearly left her brown apron back at Better Latte for the purposes of her lunch break.

"For once," I reply, and I can't help but give her a half smile.

Ruby half smiles back, gingerly sitting down beside me. The memory of our argument hovers between us in the hazy air.

"No fair! You pushed me!" one of the kids yells from down the lawn. The ice-cream vendor yawns and checks his phone.

"So," Ruby says after a moment, removing her hat and running a hand through her straight dark hair. "How does it feel to be sixteen?"

I hand her a cold bottle of water and a sandwich wrapped in tinfoil. "Different," I reply, which is very true. I do feel older. And not just because I've aged a year.

Ruby nods at me, slowly unwrapping her sandwich. She turned sixteen way back in April. She's a Taurus: the bull. Today, though, she seems much more hesitant than her usual bullish self.

I unwrap my own sandwich and take a big bite. I'd put together what I'd found in the fridge: turkey, avocado, and lettuce on whole wheat. It's good. Summers past, when Ruby and I used to regularly picnic in Pine Park, we'd take turns bringing the sandwiches. If there was a vendor at the park, we'd get ice cream for dessert, and then we'd strip down to the swimsuits we'd worn under our clothes. We'd slather on sunscreen and bake on the blanket.

Now we are back here, on the blanket, but aside from the sandwiches and the coconut-y smell of the sunscreen on my skin, everything has changed.

"I know," Ruby suddenly says, breaking the silence, "why you wanted to meet today." Her voice is soft and she puts her sandwich down on the blanket.

"You *do*?" I blink at her, midbite. There's an instant in which I believe that Ruby really *could* know about Dad. She is always-right, all-knowing Ruby.

She nods, examining her half-eaten sandwich. "You're still mad at me." She pauses to take a sip of water. "You think we should, like, break up."

"What?" I feel a jolt, and I take off my sunglasses, as if to see her better. "No," I say. Yes, the pain from our last conversation is still fresh. But it's also become duller, dimmer, in the wake of my family trauma. That Friday night at Better Latte, I'd thought the worst had happened; I'd had no idea what fate had in store for me. "Ruby—you're wrong," I continue. "There's . . . something else going on. That's why I wanted to meet."

"Oh," Ruby says. It's almost satisfying to see the surprise cross her face. On some level, she'd believed that my world began and ended with her. On some level, it used to.

"My father has a secret family in France," I say, all in one breath.

The phrase floats there, out in the open, sounding as nonsensical as it did in my head. The word *family* leaves a toxic taste on my tongue. I set down my sandwich.

"Hold on." Ruby gapes at me, her already-large eyes growing enormous. Her face turns ashen. "What are you *talking* about?" she whispers.

This was the kind of shocked reaction I'd been hoping for when I'd told Ruby that Mom was dating Max. Although, in retrospect, that hadn't really been shocking at all. I know what *shock* means now.

I take a deep breath. And there, among the pine trees and playing children, under the broiling noonday sun, I explain. I explain why Mom was so weird about me going to France, and why Dad had canceled on me at the eleventh hour. I explain about the other girl—I won't say her name—and "my" painting, and Aunt Lydia, and what I'd said to Dad this morning on the phone.

As I talk, and as Ruby listens, I know I'm also explaining—or trying to explain—things to myself. But it still seems like a story about someone else, another Summer.

When I finish, I chug from my bottle of water, my throat parched. So I'm caught off guard when Ruby tackles me, wrapping me in a huge hug and almost knocking me over onto the grass.

"Oh my God, Summer," she whispers, squeezing me. *"Oh my God."*

"I know," I say, hugging her back. We're both sticky with sweat, and I am—as Ruby mentioned earlier—still sort of mad at her. But it feels good to hold on to someone, to keep from drifting up and away into space.

"What happens now?" Ruby asks, pulling back, her tone tremulous. "With you, and your mom, and . . ." She trails off. Usually, she'd be telling me what to do. Now she appears as lost as I feel.

"I have no idea." I sigh. There is no future I can envision; I can only take things second by second. "It's a little bit like my life as I know it is . . . over, I guess." That's the kind of overdramatic thing Ruby would say, except, in my case, it feels pretty earned.

"I can't even imagine," Ruby murmurs, shaking her head. "The whole time—*the whole time*—when we were—growing up?" I nod, understanding her bewilderment. "But your—dad," she sputters. "He was always so nice."

I shrug, scratching at my mosquito bite. "Not everything is as it seems," I say, echoing what my mother once told me. But deep down, I feel a pinch of wanting to believe that my father *isn't* a bad person.

Ruby shakes her head again, looking dazed. "I wish you'd told me sooner," she murmurs. "You should've texted me right away! You could've come straight to my place from Orologio's!"

I remember how empty I'd felt last night, searching the sky

for stars. "I think I needed to be alone," I reply, digging my fingers into the plastic of my water bottle. "Besides . . ." My stomach tightens. "We haven't exactly been on great terms."

Ruby's face falls and she nods, fiddling with her woven bracelets. "That's true."

I pluck at my own, lone bracelet. "I know you went to Orologio's the other night, by the way," I tell her. "With Austin, and Skye, and Genji." I notice that I feel no venom now; mostly, I'm just relieved to get a reprieve from thinking about Dad.

Ruby glances at me, her eyebrows raised. "Instagram?"

I shake my head. "Jerry."

"Ah."

"So, two-week anniversary?" I ask, picking at my sandwich crust. "When were you guys counting from?" It's something I've been wondering, in the back of my mind.

Ruby resumes twisting her bracelets around on her wrist. "Skye's Fourth of July party." She pauses, and then begins speaking quickly. "The dinner was supposed to be on July eighteenth. But I told Austin we needed to do it the night before. I didn't even know if you'd be there on your birthday, but I knew it would feel wrong to be in Orologio's on that same night." She shoots me a tentative smile. "It's our place, you know?"

I feel a stirring in my throat like I might cry. But I don't know how I could; I must have used up my tear quotient for the year.

"This was our place, too," I say, gesturing around the park. The kids have moved on from playing tag to clambering up onto the band shell and dancing. "Remember?"

"Of course," Ruby murmurs. Tears are hovering on her bottom lashes. Her eyeliner is going to run. "Oh, Summer. I'm sorry."

"Don't be," I reply. "You didn't tell my dad to go have a secret family." I say this in a semi-joking way, like I can actually see through the awfulness to the absurdity of the situation. And maybe I do. Or maybe I will, one day.

Ruby smiles sadly, swiping at the black lines on her cheeks. "That's not what I mean. I feel bad because of—you know. Friday night. At Better Latte."

Of course I know. I tug on a blade of grass. "You were being honest," I murmur. I have a new appreciation for honesty now, hurtful as it can be.

"I think I was—frustrated." Ruby frowns. On the band shell, the kids are laughing about something. "I had, like, this set idea of how I wanted my summer to go."

"So did I," I remind her. My heart constricts. "We'd both assumed I'd be in France, and planned accordingly."

Ruby nods, sniffling, and a fly buzzes past us. I swat at it.

"But," I add, "you still got what you'd planned for." My tone is matter-of-fact, not spiteful. "Your summer of falling in love." Instantly, for no good reason, Hugh jumps into my mind. I feel my cheeks flush red. Ruby doesn't notice.

"My summer of love," she echoes, and she gives a short laugh. "Who knows if Austin and I will even make it to August?" She rolls her eyes.

"Really?" I ask. I struggle valiantly to *not* feel secretly pleased by this revelation. I pick up my sandwich again and take a bite. I see the kids leap off the band shell and run pell-mell toward the ice-cream vendor.

Ruby shrugs and picks up her sandwich, too. "He's sweet, but he can be sort of dense sometimes. I'm not totally sure if we're the best match. Maybe," she mumbles through a mouthful of turkey, "you were right."

I almost choke on a slice of avocado. "*I* was right?" I kind of cough-laugh. "Not you?" I ask. Ruby smiles sheepishly. I'm tempted to ask her about Skye—if I was right about her, too—but I don't want to push my luck.

"Could you guys form a line?" I hear the harassed-looking ice-cream vendor shout at the swarming kids.

I chew and swallow the rest of my sandwich, working up the nerve to say what I need to say next.

"You *were* right about something," I tell Ruby, and she looks at me. "It probably is . . . healthy for us. To not spend every waking minute together." It hurts to admit this. But I remember how freeing it had felt, to talk with Wren on the train. To venture to Second Time Around. To splash into the swimming hole. All without Ruby.

You weren't even supposed to be here, Ruby had told me. Suddenly, I wonder if she had it backward. Maybe I *was* supposed to be here. Maybe everything had happened for a reason. Maybe France wasn't my destiny; Hudsonville was.

Ruby nods, her bottom lip trembling. "I think we needed a breather," she says carefully. "I never wanted us to stop being friends, though."

I feel a pressure lift off my chest, and I peer up at the cloud-dusted blue sky. "Well," I say, thinking out loud, "I guess it's like conjoined twins, you know? They have those surgeries to separate them, but they're still twins."

Ruby sputters out a laugh and tosses her balled-up tinfoil at me. "You're saying we should have a surgery?"

I shrug, smiling fully for the first time since last night. "It's one idea."

"I have another idea," Ruby says, putting her floppy sunhat back on. She nods toward the ice-cream vendor, where the kids are still congregated. "Dessert?"

"Dessert," I affirm. We get to our feet and start across the lawn.

Some of the kids have already acquired their cones and are standing off to the side, rainbow sprinkles and vanilla soft-serve melting all over their mouths and hands. But two kids—two little blond, freckled girls—stand in front of the cart, solemnly reviewing the menu options printed on the vendor's striped umbrella.

I do a double take. These are the girls I saw here on the Fourth of July, turning cartwheels in the grass. The girls who made me think of me and Ruby.

I stare at them. Is their presence a sign that Ruby and I really *will* be okay? I don't know. I watch as they purchase their chocolate-and-vanilla-twist cones and scurry off together. Maybe their presence means something else.

"So . . ." Ruby says, interrupting my thoughts as she hands

me a twist cone of my own. She knows my favorite. "I was wondering. Aren't you kind of curious about her?"

I blink at Ruby. "Who?"

Ruby nervously takes a bite out of the top of her chocolate-almond cone. "The . . . other girl," she says, repeating the terminology I'd used earlier. She eyes me cautiously. "In France?" she adds. "She-Who-Must-Not-Be-Named?"

"Oh." I jerk my head back, startled. Somehow, I'd managed to shove *her*—and Dad—out of my mind. Now they're storming inside again. I grip my cone in my fist. *No*, I want to lie. *Curious? About* her? *Not at all.*

"I am," I confess, the truth spilling out of me. "She's my—she's . . ." I cannot say the word *sister*. Or *half sister*. I will not even think it. "She's a mystery," I finish. Which is also true.

"You're melting," Ruby tells me, and I look down to see ice cream dripping onto my fingers. I start licking the chocolate-vanilla swirl, and even through my fog of distraction, I'm aware that the cool sweetness tastes perfect—exactly like summer.

"Do you think you'll call your dad back, then?" Ruby adds gently, her tone very far from bossy. A hot breeze blows across the park, lifting the brim of her hat and loosing curls from my topknot. "Like he asked? Maybe . . . it *would* actually be helpful?"

An hour ago, I would have snapped at Ruby that she didn't understand, that there was no way I would ever acknowledge my father again. But now, standing with her in front of the ice-cream vendor, I feel that certainty being shaken. I am not sure what to do.

Should I call my father back?

A decision. I am terrible at making decisions.

The kids, including the two blond girls, dash past us and out of the park, treats in hand. They laugh with anticipation, the summer wide open ahead of them, the threat of August and school still light-years away. The younger you are, the slower time goes; the world seems bigger, and more possible. I watch as they scramble onto bikes and scooters and disappear into the hot blue day. I wonder if they're going to the swimming hole.

My phone buzzes once in the back pocket of my shorts, startling me. A text message. I ask Ruby to hold my cone and I take out my phone. My heart leaps.

Hey, Summer. I hope you had a great birthday and that the presentation went well in class. I'm sure you rocked it. I've been taking some cool pictures of D.C. Will have to show you when I'm back. See you tomorrow. —Hugh

I cannot prevent the smile that overtakes my face. It's so like Hugh, to still sign his name, as if I haven't had him saved in my phone since New York City. At the thought of New York, I smile wider. I wonder if Hugh and I might go there together someday. *See you tomorrow,* he'd written, meaning in photography class, of course. But the word *tomorrow* is in itself a hopeful one. A word with potential, like a kiss on the cheek.

"Okay, *what* is making you smile like that?" Ruby demands. She steps closer to me, holding our cones aloft in both her hands. "I'd grab your phone if I could."

Now I'm blushing in addition to smiling. "I got a text from Hugh," I say, taking my cone back from Ruby but keeping my phone tight in my grip.

Ruby's eyes bug out again. *"Hugh Tyson? Are you kidding me?"*

I shake my head, crunching into my cone. In the midst of all the drama, I'd forgotten that I'd never told Ruby about Hugh, and the swimming hole, and everything.

"How are you so calm? What is happening?" Ruby is asking, *her* ice cream now melting all over her hands as she stares at me in awe. "We're talking about the same Hugh Tyson, right? The mayor's son? Nerdy-cute? The boy you pretended to hate so he wouldn't know you were obsessed with him? Just like, casually, whatever, *texting* you?"

I laugh. "Yes, the same Hugh," I reply, my stomach giving a little flip as I think of his nerdy cuteness. "It's . . . a whole other story."

"Apparently," Ruby says, still wide-eyed. Before I can stop her, she is angling her head to look at my phone. But it's not to read Hugh's text—it's to check the time. "Ugh." She groans. "And of course I have to go back to Better Latte *now*. So unfair."

"I'll tell you later," I say, returning my phone to my shorts pocket.

Ruby looks at me, eyebrows raised anxiously. "Promise?" she asks.

"Promise."

She pops the rest of her cone into her mouth and then she leans forward to give me another big hug. I can smell her familiar flowery perfume. She steps back, saying that she will text me, and that Alice is coming home this weekend, so we should all get together. Then she waves, hurrying through the open fence. I wave back.

It's not until she's jumped onto her bike and pedaled off that I realize we didn't say *Love you times two*. But maybe that's okay. We might fracture, I see now, but we will also heal. I can let go of Ruby. It doesn't mean I will lose her.

I finish my cone and then I go back to my blanket to pack up. I stash everything into my bookbag and I leave Pine Park, knowing exactly where I want to go next. I pedal over to Deer Hill and turn onto River Alley, the skinny trees whipping past me.

The group of kids, I soon discover, did not come to the swimming hole after all. The secluded spot is as serene as when Hugh first showed it to me. I kick off my flip-flops and sit on the flat, smooth rocks, dipping my feet into the cold river—a balm in the heat. The waterfall burbles, and I take pictures, and I think.

Hours pass. The fierceness of the sun mellows a little, and the clouds stream across the sky. The water ripples around my ankles, growing cooler, growing warmer. Afternoon begins to bleed, ever so slightly, into early evening.

By the time I get back on my bike and pedal homeward, I have made my decision.

There are no more doubts or second guesses, I realize when I reach Rip Van Winkle Road. But, I think, hopping off my bike, uncertainty isn't always a bad thing. If not for uncertainty, people would never let go of grudges, or secrets, or fears.

I slip into my air-conditioned house. It's actually gotten too cold in here; I switch off the AC and push open the windows in the living room. Ro is napping on the sofa. While I was at the swimming hole, I'd gotten a text from Mom, telling me that she *was* going onto campus for her class, but that she wouldn't be home very late and, also, was I okay and where did I run off to? I'd texted back to say that I was okay, and that I didn't run anywhere too far.

I drop my bookbag off in my room, along with my sunglasses. Then I sort through the clutter on my desk, searching for the slightly crumpled piece of paper I left there weeks ago. When I find it, I take it with me into Mom's empty bedroom. I brush off my shorts before sitting on the edge of her bed and I draw in a big breath, lifting the phone from its cradle.

I dial Dad's cell but it goes straight to voice mail. I glance at Mom's clock; it's midnight in France. Maybe Dad is sleeping. I end the call, wondering if I should try him tomorrow instead. But no. I have gathered my courage, and I need to follow through. Besides, I think wryly, why not let Dad get yanked awake, abruptly, by the ringing phone? He upended things for me with a phone call; turnabout is fair play.

I try his landline next, and my heart thumps as the phone rings in my ear.

One ring, two rings—

"*Allô?*"

A girl has answered, like the last time I called. Her voice is still light and melodic, but now there's an undercurrent of worry. Of stress.

I feel a chill go through me.

It's *her*.

The other . . . girl.

It has to be.

Of course she answered the phone last time, and this time. She lives in France, in Dad's house. In *her* house.

"*Allô?*" she repeats, sounding annoyed.

The image that I've been trying to block out all day appears in my mind's eye again: long blond curls, blue eyes, white dress. A teenaged version of *Fille*. But the image is faint and wispy. Ghostlike. She *is* kind of a ghost, I realize. Her existence is sketchy, unreal. And she haunts me.

I sit silent on the bed, clutching the phone. I've lost my voice.

"*C'est qui?*" the ghost demands.

This phrase is familiar to me; I'd learned it online when I was studying French vocabulary before my trip. *C'est qui?* means "Who is this?"

Who am I?

I am Summer Everett. Ned Everett's daughter. All my life, I'd thought I was the one and only, and I was mistaken. But I am also more than a daughter. I am a good photographer. I am a good friend. I am sometimes late, sometimes early, sometimes on time. *I am large*, Walt Whitman had written in one of his poems. *I contain multitudes.*

When I open my mouth to speak, though, I don't say any of that. I don't even say my name. Instead, impossibly, I say hers.

"Eloise?" I ask.

I hear her sharp intake of breath. I'm surprised, too. As long as I didn't utter her name, she wouldn't become a person. Now I've crossed that threshold.

"Yes," the ghost—Eloise—says. All annoyance is gone from her tone; she sounds wary. Then she whispers: "Summer?"

Another chill races down my back.

That's right. She knows me.

Do they know about us? I'd asked Mom, standing shell-shocked outside Orologio's. *They do*, Mom had answered.

Which explains why, the last time I'd called and introduced myself, Eloise had been so cold to me. I was *her* ghost, a faceless mystery across the ocean.

"Yes," I answer.

Our *yes*es hang there, between us, like a rope we are both holding on to. A mutual confirmation. She knows that I know; I know that she knows. We are each aware of the other. There is no secret anymore.

"Do you want to speak to—him?" Eloise asks, her voice catching awkwardly on the *him*. I wonder what she calls my father—her father—*our* father. *Our father.* That will never not be weird.

"Is he awake?" I ask gruffly, looking at Mom's clock once more.

"He is," Eloise answers softly. "We all are."

We. My chest tightens. Eloise is not alone. She has my father, and her mother. She has an unbroken family. Unlike me. *Unfair,* Aunt Lydia had said. I swallow hard.

"He's upstairs," Eloise is saying. "Shall I go get him?"

I gaze out Mom's window at Rip Van Winkle Road. I try to picture the house in Les Deux Chemins, where I almost spent my summer. It must be two stories. Where is Eloise sitting, or standing, downstairs? I think of the pictures in my guidebook, of cobblestone streets and sunflower fields. Are there cobblestones outside her window? Is there a garden with sunflowers?

I remember my nightmare, with the garden and the ghostly face in the pool. But, like all dreams, it's faded, lost its power, now that the day has worn on.

"I—one minute," I say. My curiosity is bubbling to the surface. I'd called for Dad, but maybe I was meant to speak with Eloise all along. "Can I ask you something?" I add nervously. I press my feet into Mom's cream-colored rug to steady myself. "What has . . . he told you? About me?"

"Oh," Eloise says. She pauses, and in that instant, I can tell that she has a wealth of questions herself. "Not very much. I know you live in New York."

The impressed way in which she says *New York* makes me roll my eyes. "Not New York City," I tell her. "Although it's not too far away." How like Dad, to embellish that detail.

"Oh," Eloise says again. I hear a note of disappointment—of disapproval—in her tone. I wonder if she has a snobby streak. At the same time, there is something warm and familiar about her. Could that be because we're . . . related?

Oh God. We're related. My head spins.

"And I know that yesterday was your birthday," Eloise continues, and I try to focus back on what she's saying. "Happy birthday," she adds, a little stiffly.

"Thanks," I reply, equally stiffly, as if this is a perfectly normal, polite exchange. "When is your birthday?" I ask.

"June twelfth," she replies.

A summer baby, like me. Except she's a Gemini. The twins. Gemini are supposed to be two-faced, which sounds like a bad thing, but isn't, necessarily. Everyone has different faces that they show to different people. Everyone is a contradiction.

"Do you think you'll ever come to France?" Eloise asks me then, since I suppose it's her turn to do the questioning. She sounds tense. Concerned. As if she would dread my arrival, and also welcome it.

"I don't know," I answer honestly. I look around Mom's room, at the Heraclitus quote hanging on the wall. *You cannot step into the same river twice.* "Not this summer," I say with certainty. "Maybe another time." The prospect of meeting Eloise—and her mother—is daunting, though not as dreadful as it seemed last night.

Eloise is quiet. It's my turn now. There are a million questions on the tip of my tongue. I consider asking her if she'd ever visit America. Or if she visits *Fille* often, in its gallery. If she knows I'd assumed that painting was of me. If she hates Dad, or loves him, or both. If she hates *me*. If she likes to paint, or draw, or take photographs . . .

But before I can ask anything, I hear a man's voice in the background, saying something to Eloise. It's Dad.

"Hold on?" Eloise asks me, and then I hear her say to him, "Yes, it's Summer." I guess they speak to each other in English. No wonder she's so fluent. "Okay," Eloise tells him, sounding reluctant. Then, to me, she says, "He wants to talk with you."

I nod, as if she can see me. I sit up straighter.

"Would . . ." Eloise hesitates, clearly wrestling with something. Then, in a rush, she asks, "Would it be strange if I added you on Instagram?"

I feel my eyebrows go up; I wasn't expecting that question. Then again, I wasn't expecting *any* of this.

"It would be really strange," I reply. "But *everything* is really strange."

And I laugh; I can't help it. Eloise laughs, too. It seems the appropriate response to this surreal new world. I never would have thought that I'd be sitting here, on Mom's bed, talking on the phone with a girl in France who happens to be my—

My half sister.

Finally, I allow myself to think it. I let out a breath. I'm not sure I can *accept* it, but at least I can turn the words over in my mind. *Half sister.* That's what Eloise is to me after all. My half sister. My ghost sister. Only she isn't such a ghost anymore.

"Bye, Summer," Eloise says.

"*Au revoir,*" I say. I have a feeling that, in some ways, our conversation is just beginning. There are still so many questions to be asked.

I hear Eloise hand the phone over to Dad. A second later, he is on the line.

"Hi," he says, sounding relieved. And tired. "When I heard the phone ring downstairs, I hoped it was you." He pauses and asks, "Did you want to Skype?"

"No," I say. I was very deliberate about not contacting him on Skype.

"All right," Dad says quickly, although I can tell he's disappointed. "I'm glad you got to talk to Eloise a little."

"Yeah," I say. I draw a line in Mom's rug with my toe. For no real reason, tears prick at my eyes; I suppose I was wrong about being all done with crying for the year.

"I know that I hurt you," Dad says, his voice soft. "And your mother." This acknowledgment only makes my tears grow in strength and number. "And I know an apology only goes so far. There's a lot of work to be done. A lot of rebuilding. But I'd like for you to be able to trust me again." I hear him swallow and I wonder, with a prickle of fear, if he's crying, too.

Parents aren't supposed to cry. Or get scared. Or lie. Right? I thought I knew all the rules. But there are no rules.

"I can't imagine that right now," I tell my father, wiping my damp cheeks.

"I understand," he says with a sigh. "We'll take things one day at a time. The thing is . . ." I wait for him to continue, wondering if he has some other shocking surprise to reveal. *Shocking surprises*. Aunt Lydia put it well. "I was wondering how you'd feel about me coming to Hudsonville this summer. Maybe in early August?"

"You mean in, like, two weeks?" I ask. I glance out Mom's window again; the sky has the pink-orange glow that precedes sunset. What would it be like, to have Dad here again? "Why?"

"I think it would be good for us to see each other," Dad explains. "Face-to-face. That's why I wanted you to come to France in the first place," he goes on. "So I could finally tell you the truth, in person. I couldn't go on like I was, leading a double life."

Double life. That phrase sounds like it belongs in a spy movie. Like something criminal, and dark. It applies to Dad, and what he did. He tried to live two different lives, but in the end I suppose that's impossible. Eventually you have to choose, one path or another.

"Summer?" Dad says, and I realize I've been silent. "Would you be open to me visiting?" he asks. "I will tell you, I proposed that idea to your mother when we spoke earlier, and *she* seemed open to it . . ." He trails off, sounding hopeful.

"I'd be open," I finally say. That's the best I can do now—just be open. It doesn't mean I'll forgive Dad, or understand him. But I'd be willing to hear him out.

Dad lets out a big breath, and thanks me. He says that he'll call Mom tomorrow to work out all the details, and he'll book a flight.

"I love you, you know," he tells me. "Have a good night."

"Have a good night," I reply. I can't say *I love you, too.* Not yet.

I hang up and walk dazedly back into my room. I place the email printout with Dad's numbers back on my desk. Then I glance at the Renoir poster of the two sisters at the piano, and I feel a pang in my chest. I no longer find the painting babyish. But maybe it's time for a change, anyway. I peel the poster off my wall, leaving a blank space. I'll have to think about what to put up there next.

As I'm standing surveying my room, hands on my hips, I catch a glimpse of myself in my broken mirror. There I am—my falling-apart topknot and tear-stained cheeks, my Picasso-ish features, my blue tank top, my one woven bracelet. My fragmented reflection tells the story of my day. My conversation with Dad, and with Eloise, seems to appear right there in my eyes.

I remember what Aunt Lydia told me last night, about our class's final assignment: self-portraits. A surprising sense of inspiration rises up in my belly, and I reach down to unzip my bookbag. I take out my camera, focus the lens on myself in the mirror, and snap the picture. *Self-Portrait: Summer, in Pieces.* I smile. Perfect.

I guess I don't need Dad to have painted me after all. I don't even need Aunt Lydia to take my picture, as much as I like the photo she gave me. I can make my own portrait.

Darkness is starting to fall outside as I sit down at my desk with my camera and my phone. I attach my camera to my laptop and download all the photos. It feels like I'm seeing my summer unfold in reverse: there is the swimming hole, and the mailman in New York City, and the iced mocha. Of course, the summer isn't over. There will be more pictures to take.

I send some of the photos—including the self-portrait—to my phone, and then I post them on Instagram. This way, when Eloise does add me, she'll be able to see me.

I'm scrolling through my feed when I hear a huge crack of thunder outside. I put down my phone and stand up, peering through the window at the night. Abruptly, rain begins to pour down, in great, whooshing buckets. I thought no rain had been predicted for today?

I hurry out of my room to go close the living room windows. But they're all already shut. Mom must be home by now. It's no surprise that I hadn't heard her return; I'd been so wrapped up in my phone call and then in my photographs.

"Mom?" I call, wandering into the kitchen. Ro is lapping at his water bowl in the corner, but Mom is nowhere to be found. Is she in her room? Then I glance out the rain-lashed windows, squinting at our porch. Mom is sitting there, on the cushioned bench.

"Mom?" I repeat, a little worried about her as I open the door and step outside. I wonder if I should have taken an umbrella, but our porch is dry; it's set back far enough that it's protected from the elements. The rain comes down in sheets all around.

"Join me," Mom says, waving. She has stapled papers and sharpened pencils in her lap; she must have been grading papers out here, as she likes to do in the summer. "How cool is this?" she asks as I walk over. "We can watch the storm."

I sit down beside Mom. The air is cool and I rub my arms. The sky turns white with lightning—it looks like a giant camera flash. Then thunder booms again, so loud that our house seems to shake. It was storming like this the night I almost left for France—the same kind of power and wildness.

I think about telling Mom that I talked to Dad tonight. That I said it was okay if he came to Hudsonville. And that I met Eloise, over the phone.

But all that can wait until later, or tomorrow. Right now, it feels like a relief to simply sit in silence while the storm rages.

"I saw Lydia when I was on campus," Mom says after a while. She takes off her glasses and wipes the lenses with the shirttail of her pink blouse. "She asked after you. She said she didn't expect you to come to class today, but she was still concerned."

I feel grateful toward my aunt for understanding, for caring. I want to talk to her, really talk to her, someday soon. I want to hear her side of the Mom-and-Dad story. I want to get to know her even better in general. I hope I will.

"What did you tell her?" I ask Mom. I pull my bare feet up onto the bench and I hug my knees.

Mom glances at me and pats my arm. "I told her you're okay. That you will be."

I nod. A huge fork of lightning divides the sky. I imagine Aunt Lydia seeing that lightning from her house, maybe wanting to photograph it. Is Ruby seeing it, too? And Hugh, if he's back from D.C. tonight? Austin? Skye? Everyone in Hudsonville?

In a way, it seems like the storm is happening just for me and Mom. I think of that old expression: *Lightning never strikes twice in the same place.* I know that saying isn't about actual lightning, but more about things not repeating themselves.

"I was wondering," Mom goes on, raising her voice over the rain, "if you'd ever want to talk to someone . . . a professional." She glances at me again.

"Like, a therapist?" I ask, glancing back at her. When Ruby's parents got divorced, she and Raj were both promptly sent to sessions with therapists. I'd been almost envious then.

Mom nods, her brown eyes thoughtful. "I have found it helpful myself. It's just something for you to think about."

"I will," I promise. I reach over to take Mom's hand and I study her profile. I know I haven't fully forgiven her yet. But as Dad said, it will take one day at a time.

Earlier, on the phone with Eloise, I'd been upset that she had a complete family unit. I do, too, I realize now. I have Mom. And she has me. And we have Aunt Lydia, and Max, and other people who support us. All together, we make up a whole.

"Look," Mom tells me suddenly, her eyes widening. She points forward, and I turn my head, following her gaze.

The storm has stopped.

As quickly as it began, it's over. A few drops of rain plop from treetops onto the ground, and puddles reflect the moonlight. But the night is still and calm.

"How—how is that possible?" I ask Mom, glancing at her in bewilderment.

Mom shrugs. "Anything is possible," she tells me.

I stare out at my familiar street, beautiful and glistening after the storm. It looks different from what I'm used to. I think of Emily Dickinson, what Wren said about her, how she never left her hometown, but she still had a deep understanding of the world. I suppose it's not always about where you go, but what you see.

The best summer ever. That was what France was supposed to be. But if I'd had the opportunity to go back in time, to switch France for home, would I have? Now I'm not sure. If I'd gone to France, I wouldn't have discovered the swimming hole, and taken a photography class, and learned how not to be scared of Hugh Tyson.

I tilt my head back and peer up at the sky. The clouds have dispersed and the stars have emerged in their dazzling glory. There are so many of them, filling every inch of inky-black space.

"Tell me, Mom," I say, like I'm little again, and asking for fairy tales. "Tell me some theories. Like the one about parallel universes."

Mom laughs softly, also gazing up at the sky. "Well," she says. "Some philosophers, some physicists, believe . . ."

I listen to Mom, feeling delicious shivers down my back as I study the stars. There are so many secrets and mysteries out there—and down here, too. I'll never know them all, but maybe that's all right. In fact, maybe that's how it's meant to be.

PART SEVEN

Double Lives

Wednesday, July 19, 7:17 a.m.

The peach house with its green shutters looks vacant. I didn't bring a key with me when I ran away yesterday. My stomach clenches again, and I knock on the door.

Silence.

It could be my first day, me standing on this doorstep with my heart in my throat.

And then, just like on that first day, I see movement in a second-story window. A lace curtain flutters aside, and Eloise's pale face appears. She peers down at me, and I peer back up at her, holding my breath, wondering what she's thinking.

The curtain flutters closed, and the front door creaks open. And there is Vivienne, with her low red ponytail and bright-blue eyes, in her chic striped shirt and cropped black pants. I almost laugh. The world is on a loop, repeating itself.

Vivienne's eyes widen. "Summer," she says softly. *Some-air.*

She takes a step toward me, like maybe she's going to embrace me, or kiss my cheeks, but then she seems to think the better of it.

I stare at her. Here she is, the person who split my family down the middle. I should hate her. I should want to scream at her, or push her. Tell her not to talk to me or look at me. But there's a formality between us that somehow dilutes my anger. Vivienne is a stranger. It's like when Mom and I were driving to the mall last year, and some guy bumped our car from behind. Mom got out to exchange insurance information with him, and they were surprisingly polite toward each other. *Oh, you may have almost killed me, or destroyed my life as I know it, but it's nothing personal, so let's behave civilly!* I wonder if Mom would act that way toward Vivienne, too, if they were ever to meet.

"You did not see your father?" Vivienne is asking me now.

I frown. "What? Where?" I glance over my shoulder in confusion.

"He left here a minute ago," Vivienne says. She steps outside and squints down Rue du Pain. "You missed him?" She seems deeply perturbed by this mystery.

It's no mystery; I missed my father because I made the split-second choice to stop into the bakery. While I was in there, he was out here. But why?

"Where did he go?" I ask Vivienne. *Back to Berlin?* I wonder sourly. I wouldn't be surprised.

Vivienne wrings her hands. "To pick you up. From the Cassels' house. Jacques Cassel, he called Eloise last night to say you were staying there."

"Oh," I mutter. I feel a flicker of betrayal, picturing Jacques in his room on his phone, secretly updating Eloise on my whereabouts. I'm sure he thought he was doing the right thing, keeping my father from worrying about me. I roll my eyes.

"*Ton père*, your father, he was frantic," Vivienne tells me, as if she's followed my train of thought. As if I'm supposed to feel bad for Dad on any level. "I told him to at least wait for the morning to get you. He did not sleep all the night." She pauses, lifting her hands to rub her temples. "Nobody in this house did."

I look up at Eloise's window again. The curtain doesn't move.

"Please, come inside," Vivienne insists, stepping back into the house herself. "I will call your father's cell to tell him you are here."

Hesitantly, I step into the foyer. I wonder what Vivienne thought of me that first day—this other daughter, ignorant of the secret that breathed in the walls of the house like a phantom. Had she felt sorry for me? Curious about me? Had she been on edge, afraid she would accidentally say the wrong thing? No wonder I'd sensed a careful distance from her.

"Would you like—*euh*, something to eat?" Vivienne asks me now, nervously smoothing out a wrinkle in her striped top.

I shake my head and smile wryly, imagining us sitting down to some cheerful hot chocolate and croissants.

"I think I'll go upstairs," I say, wanting to escape the mounting awkwardness. Vivienne seems relieved, because she nods and murmurs something about going to the farmers' market. We stand still for a second, looking at each other, and I can see the worry and uncertainty in Vivienne's face. Finally, I turn around.

As I head for the stairs, I hear Vivienne murmur something else to me: *"Je suis désolée."*

I know that means *I'm sorry*. But what can I say? *It's okay, no worries, all is well, ça va?* So I say nothing. I keep on climbing the stairs, knowing that Vivienne is watching me go. As I reach the landing, I glance anxiously at Eloise's shut door. I don't exhale until I get inside my medieval chamber and close my own door.

Keep busy, I tell myself, grabbing my empty suitcase from the corner and unzipping it. I yank open one of the rickety drawers and pull out a handful of tank tops. As long as I'm in motion, the darkness can't swallow me. I can't fret too much about what will happen once Dad gets back to the house and we have to talk again.

I'm packing my tote bag—passport, wallet, creased magazines left over from the flight, chewing gum—when there's a knock on my door. I freeze.

"Dad?" I say, and then I mentally kick myself, wishing I'd called him *Ned*. That would get across how separate I feel from him.

The knob turns and the door opens. But it's not Ned Everett. It's Eloise.

"Hey," she says stiffly, like it's any other day. Except, on any other day, Eloise would not come by my room to say anything at all.

"Hey," I echo, just as stiffly, holding the pack of gum in my clammy palm.

She stands there, her arms dangling at her sides, the same way she posed in that poppy field five years ago. Her expression, too, is childlike: at once open and wary. Not her usual sneer. Also, her golden curls are matted and tangled, and there are bags under her eyes. Her white sundress is wrinkled, like she slept in it—or didn't sleep, according to Vivienne—and her pink nail polish is chipped.

It's undeniably satisfying, seeing her looking less than perfect.

But as I study her, I feel a pit form in my stomach. Because I see something else. I see the resemblance. What Jacques was talking about. It's subtle, but it's there, from the shape of her shoulders to the arch of her eyebrows to the way her hair—a lighter shade, more manageable in texture, but still, somehow, the same as mine—frames her face.

We look alike.

I take a step back, shaking. Eloise had always seemed sort of eerie to me. Maybe because I'd sensed, deep down, that if I looked at her too closely, I would see what I'm seeing now. Maybe the truth had been haunting me all along. But it had felt safer to bury my suspicions and wonderings, instead of exposing them to the light.

Eloise steps forward. Then she glances at my bed, where some of my belongings are spread out and my tote bag sits open.

"Where are you going?" she asks me, frowning. "Are you leaving?"

"What's it to you?" I snap, whipping around and dropping the pack of gum into my tote bag. I wish *she* would leave the room.

"Fine," she snaps back, her old huffiness returning. "Excuse me for caring. I wanted to see how you were doing, after—" She pauses, and I hear her breath hitch.

My heart feels tight, like a fist. "How do you think I'm doing?" I mutter.

Eloise sighs. I expect her to turn around and finally leave me be. Instead, she sits down on the corner of my bed, gingerly moving aside my South of France guidebook, which I guess I no longer really need.

I bristle. I consider telling Eloise to get up and get out. But then a resignation like fatigue washes over me. I sigh and sit down, too, although not right beside her. My camera forms a divider between us. We are both silent for a long while, as the birds chirp outside in the garden.

"When did *you* first find out?" I ask her, staring ahead at the cracked mirror.

Eloise picks at the chipped polish on her thumb. "I don't remember exactly," she says. "I always just . . . knew. Ever since I was very young. It was . . . in the open."

I glance at her, uncomprehending. "You always just knew," I echo in shock. I try to imagine a life in which I was blithely aware of my father's other family, across the ocean. "That he had . . . That there was . . ." I trail off, language failing me.

Eloise nods. "When I was little, he—" She shoots me a questioning look, checking to see if I am okay with her directly mentioning Dad. I don't protest, so she continues. "He was in America most of the time. I understood that he was with you and your mother then. I accepted it as normal."

"Until . . ." I fill in for her, sensing what's coming.

Eloise resumes picking at her polish, like it's a serious task she must complete.

"As I got older, I became uncomfortable with it," she explains in a rush. "I had never told any of my friends, and I realized why: It felt sort of shameful. But I also became curious. About you." She peers at me again, her cheeks red.

I redden, too. I picture a young Eloise—the girl from *Fille*—wondering about me, while I was doing my homework and having sleepovers with Ruby and bicycling up and down Greene Street, completely unaware of any girl in France.

"What did you know?" I ask. I glance down at our bare feet, side by side on the wooden floor. Our toes are the same, I notice; long and thin. Unbidden, the word *sister* springs into my head and I forcefully push it out.

Beside me, Eloise shrugs. "I knew your name, and that you lived somewhere in New York. That was all. I looked you up online, on social media and stuff, but everything was set to private. I tried asking him for more details, but he never said much. Only that it was a secret, and you didn't know about me. So I couldn't ever contact you."

She lets out a shaky breath, frowning. I wonder what's worse—a secret being kept from you, or you yourself being the secret.

"Then," she goes on, returning to her must-destroy-polish task, "one day this spring, he told us that you were coming. He said that you would be staying at our house in Provence for the summer, and he would tell you the truth."

I flinch. *Our house.* I peer outside at the blooming garden. This was never just Dad's house, but his house with Vivienne and Eloise.

"Suddenly," Eloise continues, the words pouring out of her, "you seemed real. Too real. I got scared." She looks up, her blue eyes very big. "There were all these rules put into place. My mother and I were not supposed to say anything to you. It had to come from . . . him. We had to pretend like we were visitors, in our own home. My whole life would be upended. I began to hate that you were coming. I began . . ."

She pauses, and I wonder if she's searching for the right words. I've noticed that her French accent has emerged more, the longer she's been speaking, though her English is still fluid. But of course it is. She has an American father.

"I began to hate *you*," she finishes.

She holds my gaze, and her expression is so raw and pained and real that I can't look away. I feel stung but I also understand. I would have hated me, too. I hate Eloise after all. Or do I?

At last, I break our staring contest and peek over at my dead phone on the bed. "I wasn't supposed to come, you know," I say. I run my finger down the phone's blank, innocent face. "He called to stop me but it was . . . too late."

"I know," Eloise says quietly. She studies her thumbnail. "When he was leaving for Berlin, he told us that he was going to postpone your visit. I was so relieved." She rips off the whole strip of polish, leaving her nail exposed. "It was like this emotional roller coaster. I'd been crying on and off, for weeks. And I usually don't cry very much—"

"Me neither," I cut in. "Except for this summer, I guess."

Eloise gives me a tiny smile, and I wonder if she's feeling choked up now, like I am. I remember her crying in the shower.

"So I arrived," I say, fitting the puzzle together, "and you weren't expecting me?"

She shakes her head vigorously, her hair getting in her eyes. "And I felt really . . . resentful. You were like some creature from a story I had heard growing up, and then you appeared in my house."

I snort. "A creature? What, like an ogre?"

Eloise smiles again, that tiny, hesitant smile. "Not at all," she says. "You were so pretty." I open my mouth in disbelief but she keeps talking, too quickly for me to interrupt. "And smart, and you came in acting like you owned the place. I remember when we were in the studio, when you said something about being there first. That made me so upset. Even though I guess you *are* the first—"

She pauses, and glances at me. *The firstborn*, I know we are both thinking, linked in the moment of discomfort. Then Eloise goes on.

"And my mother, she wanted me to be nice and welcoming to you, but I could not. It seemed like you were there to take what was mine." Eloise throws up her hands. "You even took Jacques!"

I blink at her. "Jacques—was yours?" I say.

She shrugs, her face flushing. "No. We did not date. But I liked him," she admits, her blush deepening. "Even though I'd been coming to Les Deux Chemins for many years, I only met Jacques this summer. I would go to Café des Roses with my friends after art class, and he always flirted with me. I thought . . ." She shrugs again.

I pick up my camera from where it sits between us and turn it over in my hands. "Jacques is not mine, either," I tell her, a little sadly. "At least, not anymore. Or maybe he never really was. I get the sense he likes to flirt with a lot of girls," I add, thinking out loud.

Eloise rolls her eyes. "A lot of French guys do," she says. "It is . . . how do you say it? A blessing, and a curse?"

In spite of everything, I laugh. Eloise laughs, too, a real laugh, not a snarky one. I remember how she looked on the night of the fireworks, relaxed and happy. I feel as if the curtain is peeling back, showing me the other Eloise, the one I haven't met yet.

There's a knock on my door. I realize I never shut it once Eloise came in, and I turn my head to see Dad standing in the threshold.

"Hi, girls," he says softly.

He looks exhausted, his eyes bloodshot and his face drawn, his chin dark with stubble. He's wearing the same clothes he had on yesterday, and his hair is sticking up in the back. But as he regards me and Eloise sitting on the bed, he smiles. I wonder if he ever imagined he would see the two of us together.

"I'm so glad you returned, Summer," he says. "Would you like something to eat?"

Now his fatherly instincts are kicking in. I shake my head, gripping my camera.

"Okay." He nods at me, clearly picking up on my simmering frustration. "If you want to talk, I will be in the studio." He nods at Eloise as well. "I'll see you girls later."

He leaves but his presence looms over the room. I let it sink in that Eloise and I share him. He is *our* father. He always will be.

"What do you call him?" I ask Eloise after we've been quiet for a moment.

"*Papa*," she replies. She fidgets, crossing and uncrossing her legs. "You?"

"Dad, I guess." I shrug. "Although I'm thinking of switching to 'Ned.'" I flip over my camera and press the button that allows me to see the most recent photograph I took. It's a nighttime shot of Boulevard du Temps, the stores lit up and sparkly.

"Can I see that?" Eloise asks. She shifts closer to me on the bed. I tense up, prepared to move away, but I don't. I angle the camera so that she can look at the screen.

"*C'est* cool," Eloise says, sounding a bit like Jacques. She tilts her head approvingly. "Do you have more?"

I begin scrolling backward. All the pictures I've taken in France appear, in reverse order, like a time machine: the azure ocean waves in Cannes; Jacques, leaning against his parked moped, grinning; the bridge in Avignon; cypress trees and sunflowers; the field of poppies . . .

I stop there. My breath catches. I glance at Eloise, wondering if either of us will address the epic awkwardness of those poppies, of the painting.

If Eloise is thinking about *Fille*, though, she doesn't show it. Instead, she glances up at me, her eyes wide. "Summer," she says. "These are incredible photographs."

I turn off the digital readout, feeling self-conscious. "Thanks," I say. "But they're not that special. It's kind of a fancy camera, and anyone can take pictures—"

"Not anyone," Eloise says firmly, shaking her head. "Trust me. My parents are painters. I mean—you knew that." She reddens, but then she moves on. "I've been taking art classes my whole life, basically. I'm not that good, though my mother wants me to be." She rolls her eyes. "Anyway, the point is, I know an artist when I see one."

"An artist?" I repeat. I give an incredulous laugh, and then I notice that Eloise is serious. "Oh," I say. "You're serious."

She nods. "You should display your photos somewhere," she tells me.

I laugh again. "Where? On Instagram?" But as I say it, I wonder if that's not a bad idea. Maybe my photos *are* better than I thought. I feel a small flash of pride. Maybe people would want to see them, see the story of my summer so far.

"I love Instagram," Eloise says. Then, casting a sidelong glance at me, she adds, a little tentatively, "Want to add me on there?"

"Okay," I reply, also tentative. "Is your last name Everett?" I ask, bracing for the answer.

Eloise shakes her head. "LaCour," she tells me, smiling. "My mother was very firm about that."

I smile back. *Eloise LaCour*, I think. *Nice to meet you.*

Eloise's smile fades and I wonder if she, like me, is realizing that this beginning of sorts is also an end. "So you're going back to New York?" she asks, looking down at my packed suitcase on the floor. "Are you sure?"

"I am sure," I reply, and it feels good and declarative to say that.

"Do you think you'll return to Les Deux Chemins?" Eloise asks, and I shrug. I truly don't know. "Or maybe you will come to Paris?" she offers.

Paris. Right. Where Dad lives when it's not summer. Where Eloise and Vivienne are, too. "Maybe," I say. I can't think about that yet. Any of it.

"I'm so sorry," Eloise says softly. She glances from my suitcase to me, and her eyes are teary. "For how I treated you this summer. That's not actually—me."

"I think I see that now," I say. I bite my lip to keep my own eyes from welling. My heart seems to open, a hand unclenching. I remember when I thought that Eloise was like Skye Oliveira; it's not such an easy comparison to make now. Unless Skye herself is more complicated than she appears. That could very well be the case.

Eloise hurriedly gets to her feet, dabbing at her eyes. "I'll let you finish packing," she tells me. Clumsily, she bends down and gives me a one-armed hug, one I'm too startled to return in time. Then she starts for the door.

"Wait," I say after her. "I meant to say—before. I'm not that pretty. *You* are."

Eloise smiles at me, tilting her head to one side. "Well, we are half sisters, *non*?"

Sisters. This time, I let the word stay in my head. *Half sisters.* Such a funny expression, like something in two pieces. But it's what Eloise and I are.

She walks out, and I hear her go back into her room. I stand up and, for a minute, study myself in the fractured mirror. I feel a rush of inspiration and I bring my camera to my eye. I take a picture of my broken reflection.

Then I have an idea. I sort through the stuff on my bed, finding the cord I need to attach my camera to a computer. I tap on Eloise's door and ask her if I can borrow her phone, promising to give it back right away. She looks only a little hesitant as she hands her cell over. I thank her profusely and bring her phone, my camera, and the cord downstairs to the living room.

I sit at the desk and attach the camera to the computer. Outside, the sky is a brilliant blue over Rue du Pain. I email all the photos to myself, and, with a few swipes and clicks, use Eloise's phone to upload the pictures to Instagram: my first post since leaving Hudsonville.

As each photo appears onscreen—the shots I took from the cab; my cool, broken-up self-portrait—I feel a sense of satisfaction, like I've completed something that I was meant to complete.

I'm writing captions when I notice that one of my pictures— the self-portrait—has already received a "like" and a comment.

From Hugh Tyson.

My heart skips a beat.

Amazing picture, Summer, he has written. *I'm taking a photography course for the first time. We should compare notes one day.*

I feel my face warm up. What does that mean? Does *he* think I'm taking a photography course, because of all my pictures?

Does he want to hang out?

I click over to Hugh's profile, as if that will give me some clues. His most recent picture, uploaded minutes ago, is of what looks like a hotel room window, facing the white dome of the Capitol Building. *Wide awake in the middle of the night, writing bad poetry in our nation's capital,* the caption reads. *Just as the Founding Fathers intended.*

I smile. I'm not sure I realized before that Hugh was funny. I never really got to know him at all. I wonder why he's in Washington, D.C., now.

And then I feel a surge of bravery. I "like" his picture, and type under it: *So. Are you about to meet the president or something?*

I sit back in the chair, a little proud of myself, a little disbe-lieving. But I know that the next time I see Hugh, I won't be so shy or skittish around him anymore.

A second later, a response pops up beneath my comment. My belly flips. Hugh wrote back! I guess he's online right now, across the ocean.

Haha, not quite, he's written. *Boring parent stuff. Looks like your summer is more interesting . . . ?*

I realize I'm grinning. Somehow, impossibly, I'm talking to Hugh Tyson. And I'm doing okay at it! I could respond to *his* response, and keep the conversation going. But I decide I'll let it be for now. Hope swells in me. Maybe Hugh and I can continue the conversation in Hudsonville. In person. Maybe that would be even better.

I'm still grinning as I log out of Instagram and, out of habit, log in to my email. There's one new message, sent yesterday. From Ruby.

Happy birthday, babe, it reads. *I hope you're having a magical time in France. I'm sorry I haven't been great about staying in touch this sum-mer. I guess part of me thinks maybe it's been good for us, to get a little distance. I don't know. I do miss you. We'll have a lot to catch up on when you get back. Love you, Ruby*

I let out a breath. Just yesterday I'd had the thought that it felt sort of freeing, to be apart from Ruby. Clearly, she'd been feel-ing the same, which explains all the Skye-Austin-Genji action—her new life—I'd seen on Instagram. But I don't feel the old hurt rise up in me, not even when I realize that Ruby didn't sign off with *Love you times two*. Only *Love you*. And maybe that's okay. What did *times two* mean, anyway? It must have made sense when we were little kids, but not all traditions hold up over time.

I close her email. I can't respond yet; I'll need to process what she's said. My head is full. I will call her when I get home, when my phone is charged. Then I can tell her about Dad, and Eloise. I can tell her I got my first kiss, and that Hugh Tyson and I were in touch on Instagram. We can talk about everything.

My thoughts tumble from Ruby to Hugh to Jacques, from Eloise to Dad, as I walk through the silent house and outside. I pad on bare feet through the damp grass of the garden and I push open the creaky barn door. Was it really only yesterday that I was in here, making my discovery? It seems like a lifetime ago. I feel old.

Dad is sitting at his desk, which is tidy now, thanks to me, looking at old papers. A lit cigarette rests between his fingers, which is surely a serious fire hazard. Fine. Maybe he'll burn this whole barn to the ground.

"Hello, Ned," I say coolly, walking over to him. This new name feels wrong in my mouth. He's *Dad*.

But it has its intended effect. He snaps his head up, blinking. "Oh. Summer," he says, a frown creasing his face. He seems to have aged in a day, too.

"I just wanted to tell you," I say, shifting from one foot to the other on the cold barn floor, "that I'm going back to Hudsonville. I mean, first I need to call Mom back and look up the flight times, but then . . ."

"Sweetheart," Dad says. He stamps out his cigarette in the ashtray on the desk. Then he extends his arm, as if to take my hand, but I step back.

"Please don't call me 'sweetheart,'" I say. I glare at him. It hadn't struck me until now how sick I was of that nickname, how empty and meaningless it always felt.

Dad raises his eyebrows, as if he doesn't recognize me. "I—okay," he stammers. "I wish you wouldn't call me *Ned*, but . . . what can I do?"

"What can you do?" I repeat, trembling. I'm letting it all out, finally—all my pain and rage. "You can be honest. You can not lie and cheat." I promised myself I wouldn't cry but, annoyingly, I feel tears building.

"Swee—" He catches himself, and shakes his head. "Summer. Listen. I am sorry. I know." He gets up from the desk, holding a folded piece of paper in his hand. I see his Adam's apple bobbing up and down in his throat. "I made a terrible mess of things, with you and your mother. The last thing I wanted was to hurt you. Either of you."

"It's kind of too late for apologies, Dad," I say. I hug myself. The barn feels cool and drafty. I'm glad no other painters are in here, although even if they were, I would have been forthright with Dad like this anyway. I'm tired of hiding things.

My father presses one hand to his lips. "You're right," he says softly. "But that's why I wanted you to come to France this summer," he explains. "To make up for lost time. To act quickly. So I could finally join together my—my double lives."

I stare at Dad, surprised that he admitted it so plainly. The fact that he carried on two separate lives.

"Well, I don't want to be a part of your other life," I tell him, even though that's not entirely true. I think of my conversation with Eloise. I think of Paris. I won't be able to ever un-know that I have a half sister, here in France. Still, I can't stand looking at my father anymore, especially not here, in this studio that smells of paint and turpentine, where I read Eloise's name on the back of my sketch and my world cracked open.

I turn to go, but Dad catches me, gently taking my arm and rotating me so that I have to face him again. I look down.

"I want to show you something," Dad says. He thrusts the folded-up paper out to me. "I was looking through my old sketchbooks, and I found this."

I'm a little fearful—can you blame me?—as I accept the paper from Dad. I unfold it with trembling fingers. My brain takes a minute to catch up to my eyes. Then I understand that I am looking at a sketch I have never seen before. A curly-haired, big-eyed girl, stretched out on a porch bench, a book in her hands. Barefoot, in shorts and a T-shirt, clearly enjoying the freedom of summer.

It's me.

"Do you remember this?" my dad asks me gently. "Back in Hudsonville?"

I do. I remember the mugginess of that July day, the mosquito bite behind my knee, the smell of pine in the air, and the book I was reading (*Harry Potter and the Half-Blood Prince*). I remember Dad kneeling across from me, telling me to hold still so he could sketch me. I remember it all.

I nod, but I don't want to soften. I refuse to soften. Just because Dad drew me as well as Eloise doesn't set things right. Things will never be right.

"I have to call Mom and book my flight," I say. I hand him back his sketch.

Dad takes my arm again, before I can turn to go. "Summer, I wish you wouldn't fly off like this," he tells me. "Why don't you stay in France a little longer? We can talk more." He sighs, studying my hardened expression. "I love you," he tells me. "You're my daughter. Nothing will change that."

I don't answer. My throat is sore with tears.

"All right?" Dad says, looking at me pleadingly.

"All right," I mutter, only to get away from him. I wrest my arm out of Dad's grip and storm toward the barn door. There's a piece of me that wishes he would follow me one more time, but he doesn't.

• • •

That evening, I arrive at Marseille Provence Airport right on time.

It's a new sensation for me, not being rushed or flushed or harried. Nor do I have to find ways to fill the extra, empty hours. I can simply sit in the boarding area with my tote bag in my lap, knowing my flight will be called shortly. Mom was able to book me on the earliest one leaving that day. I glance at the clock on the wall, and then out the window at the runway, drenched in the rosy glow of the Provence sunshine.

After I'd left Dad in his studio, I'd moved swiftly, calling Mom, returning Eloise's phone to her upstairs, and finishing the rest of my packing. Dad had come into the house to find me bumping my suitcase behind me down the staircase.

Despite my protestations that I could take a cab—"I already did it once," I'd reminded him pointedly—Dad had driven me to the airport. We'd been silent during the ride, but when we got to my gate, Dad had told me that he hoped I'd forgive him, that there was so much more he had to say. Whatever that was, though, would have to remain a mystery; I'd said a terse good-bye and jumped out of the car.

I will never forgive him, I think now, feeling a steeliness rise in me.

There's a crackle overhead, and the boarding agent announces that my flight—Delta 202—will begin boarding. I stand up, slinging my heavy tote bag on my shoulder. Then I notice them—the mother and daughter who had flown over here with me. Only with them now is the father.

My heart gives a kick and I stare at the small family as they gather up their bags and get in line. *Is it a sign?* I wonder. But if so, what does it mean? That maybe, one day, in time, I *will* be able to forgive Dad? That there will be some wholeness back in my own family, now that we all know the truth? I can't say.

I give the boarding agent my pass and flip-flop down the long corridor that leads onto the plane. As I step into the cabin, I fiddle with the single woven bracelet on my wrist; when I was packing, I'd come upon the bracelets and I'd thought about Ruby's email. So I'd slipped on one of them, leaving the other in my toiletry bag. Because that is still how I feel about Ruby: a little bit split.

This time, thankfully, I have a window seat, so I can ball my hoodie up into a makeshift pillow and relax against the wall. The petite, chic, elderly French woman who sits down beside me won't be any trouble, I can tell. I notice that the small French family are seated a few rows ahead of me.

The plane begins to taxi and I remember how it felt leaving Hudsonville, full of apprehension and excitement, certain that I was on my way to have my best summer ever.

And was it? I wonder as the plane gains speed, zooming forward at full throttle, the engines roaring. In a sense, it was the worst—the pain I'd felt yesterday, upon learning the truth, is still sharp in my chest. But then I think of Jacques, and eating *pain au chocolat* as I walked through Dad's garden, and taking pictures of the farmers' market, and hearing Eloise say that my photographs were incredible.

Would I have done things differently—not gone to France at all—if given the opportunity? Would I have traded this summer in for another, different one? As we lift off the ground, I realize that I'm not sure.

It's something I ponder throughout the long, bumpy flight, as I doze in and out of sleep over the Atlantic Ocean. Every time I open my heavy eyes, I'm disoriented by the pink sunlight streaming into the cabin; I keep thinking that night should have fallen by now. But because of the time zones, we fly straight from evening into evening.

When we start descending, though, the sky clouds over, darkens. And when our wheels hit the tarmac—and I let out a breath of relief; it's nice to be back on earth—it begins to storm. Veins of lightning split the sky and rain rattles the tiny plane windows. Everyone on board begins murmuring about the sudden weather and I feel a little chill, remembering the storm I took off in. This one is so similar, it's spooky.

I disembark from the plane, achy and cotton-mouthed. I wind up behind the small French family again, and I trail them to the baggage claim. I'm trying to keep my eye on them in the crowds of travelers when I spot a much more familiar face.

Mom.

I run to her, my tote bag swinging, and we hug, tight. Her tortoiseshell-framed glasses bump my cheek and I pull back to look at her, my mom with her pretty brown eyes and thoughtful smile. Something about her seems lighter than usual—her face is bright and relaxed. Maybe it's because there is no longer that huge secret between us.

"You look so grown-up!" Mom says, and I flush, thinking that I have grown in these weeks, beyond just turning sixteen.

"You look so happy," I reply, which is true.

Mom's smile widens. "We have a lot to catch up on," she tells me, and I wonder what she means exactly.

Before I can ask, Mom loops her arm through mine, and we

head to the baggage carousel. The suitcases go round and round, repeating themselves.

"Summer?" Mom adds, her voice careful. "I know I always said that honesty was a two-way street, and I'm sorry. I wasn't very honest with you, as it turns out."

I glance at her, my throat tight. "You weren't," I say.

Mom nods. "And in the spirit of being more honest, I should tell you something."

I stiffen, not sure I can take any more surprises.

"Your father called," Mom says, which is not what I expected.

"What did he want?" I ask sourly. I see my bag, and I step forward to grab it.

"Well." Mom clears her throat. "He'd like to come to Hudsonville. Sometime in early August."

"*This* August?" I say, spinning around to face Mom with my suitcase in hand.

Mom nods. "He said he wants to spend more time with you, because you left France so abruptly. And I can't say I blame you for that," she says, giving me an understanding look. "But the thing is, I actually believe your father. I think he might come through for once."

"Really?" I ask doubtfully. "Since when do you have faith in Dad?"

Mom shrugs, giving me a half smile. "He occasionally has good qualities, you know. What's that saying? 'Even a broken clock is right twice a day.'"

I laugh and shrug, too. Right now, none of it feels real—the prospect of Dad coming here, the memory of my trip to France.

In my tote bag, nestled alongside my camera and passport and guidebook, are bottles of lavender oil and packets of fragrant-smelling herbs. I ended up buying them at the farmers' market, when I went there on Monday. I'd been hesitant to bring the souvenirs home with me, but now I'm glad I did. They will serve as reminders that Les Deux Chemins wasn't all a dream. My head is heavy. I yawn, thinking of my bed.

"Come on," Mom says, taking my suitcase from me. "I'm sorry," she adds, as we head for the exit doors, "that I don't have an umbrella. The storm came out of nowhere."

I see the rain splashing down. We have no real protection. But I'm not scared. I know that, together, Mom and I can make it to the car safe and sound.

As we step outside, though, the rain stops, like someone has flipped a switch. The night is calm and peaceful, and puddles glint in the moonlight. Mom and I glance at each other, our eyebrows raised.

"Is it a sign?" I ask her.

"A sign of what?" Mom laughs as we continue on toward her car. "The weather being crazy and unpredictable?"

No, I think. When I left New York for France, the storm had stopped suddenly, just like this one has. It can't be a coincidence, can it?

Maybe it *is* a sign, about things coming full circle. I open the car door, thinking that I will soon be in Hudsonville once more. I will wake up in my familiar bedroom and I will pedal along Greene Street in the warm wind, almost like France didn't happen. Except it did, and it's forever changed me, even though I am back where I started from.

Let your soul stand cool and composed before a million universes.

Walt Whitman

The only reason for time is so that everything doesn't happen at once.

Albert Einstein

Epilogue

Friday, August 11, 7:37 p.m.

I pedal along Greene Street, the warm wind in my hair. Although it's a typically hot August evening, there's *something* in the air—a subtle cooling, a smell of freshness, like after a rainstorm—that hints at the September to come. It happens every summer: the first curled leaf you see lying on the sidewalk, the first night you don't need to sleep with your air conditioner on. I always feel a tug of sadness at these signs; I never want the summer to end. I resent the passage of time.

But now, as I park my bike outside the bank, that usual sense of despair doesn't rise up in me. It's been a tumultuous summer, a summer of surprise and change. An amazing summer, yes—but difficult. So, a part of me welcomes the calm coolness of the approaching fall, the shift in seasons. There are things to look forward to.

I smile to myself as I cross the street toward the river, my camera in hand. My loose hair swings down my back, feeling pleasantly wild and messy, and my flip-flops thwack against the sidewalk. My "lucky" dress swishes against my legs; I still think of the dress as new, even though I got it back in July.

July. I stop at the riverside, reeling. Was it really only last month, on my birthday, that I found out the truth about Dad— that my life fractured? In some ways, it feels much closer—like it all occurred yesterday. But in other ways, that moment of discovery seems to belong to another life.

It's almost sunset; the sky above the Hudson River is a pale, pearly pink. The water, streaming past, looks gray, as always. When I bring my camera to my eye, though, and look through the lens, I can catch shades of peach and blue and green, a whole host of colors, shimmering in the waves.

"I'd forgotten how lovely the Hudson is," Dad had said when he was here, earlier this week, standing beside me in this same spot. "It's easy to get caught up in the romance of Provence, but there's plenty of beauty here, too."

I'd nodded, thinking of sunflower fields and cobblestone streets. Provence and Hudsonville seemed to represent two different kinds of beauty. One wasn't necessarily better than the other; they were just different.

As I take pictures of the river, I recall Dad's visit. He'd come for four days, and stayed in the Marriot near the mall, renting a car so he could drive back and forth to the house to see me. Unlike his visits past, there were no fleeting lunches and calls of "Bye, sweetheart!" as he dashed off. No. Instead, we'd sat and talked for hours over burgers at PJ's Pub. We'd taken long walks up and down Greene Street, and wandered through the campus. We'd meandered around the mall, and went for drives.

On Tuesday night, Mom had even invited Dad to the house for dinner, shocking me. But Mom had become more open, once she saw Dad was making an effort. Also, she was now officially dating Max, which seemed to raise her spirits in general. And *I* was very slowly getting used to that new reality.

I'd been anxious about Dad coming over for dinner, but there wasn't as much hostility between my parents as I'd feared. They were both mellower, eating Mom's meat loaf and catching up while Ro meowed at the three of us from beneath the table. We'd felt, somewhat, like a family—dysfunctional, yes, but still, a family. I'd hoped that things would be easier, now that the secret was out in the open. Although Dad did not speak of Vivienne, or Eloise, in front of Mom, and I was grateful for that.

When he and I were alone, he did try to answer most of my questions—and I'd had a ton. About Eloise, about Vivienne, about Dad and Mom, and the painting, *Fille*. It wasn't like every answer he gave me was satisfactory; often, it hurt to hear the truth and sometimes, he dodged certain topics, saying things like, "You'll understand when you're older," which made me groan.

And it wasn't like, when we said good-bye on Wednesday afternoon, before he drove off to the airport, I felt we had perfectly healed what was broken. We hadn't. I wasn't sure we ever would. How can you recover from a shock like that?

But, standing in the fading golden sunlight now, I can feel some of the scars of the summer scabbing over. I can feel the promise of a new beginning. I take another picture.

"Hey, Summer."

My heart flips over and I spin around, careful not to drop my camera.

Hugh Tyson is standing behind me, hands in his pockets, his gray-green eyes bright behind his glasses. He nods once toward my camera, and then again at the river.

"I bet those are some good pictures," he tells me in his slightly raspy voice, giving me a small smile.

I wish my cheeks wouldn't flush, but they do. "Thanks," I reply, nervously shifting from one foot to the other. I wonder if there will ever come a time when I'm *not* somewhat nervous around Hugh Tyson. But then I think about how far I've come; after everything that has happened this summer, I'm so much braver than I used to be. "Hey, that photo you posted on Instagram yesterday was great," I add, glancing up.

I still use Instagram to spy on Hugh a little. But mostly, ever since I uploaded my pictures on there the day after my birthday, I've used the app as a way to study photography. I'll try out different filters on my photos, and I follow other photographers' accounts. Some photographers have followed me back, and I've gotten lots of comments on my pictures—especially on my self-portrait in the broken mirror. It's made me feel proud.

The other thing about Instagram is that I'm friends with Eloise on there. *Friends* is a strong word for what Eloise and I are right now, of course. But I feel as if I'm getting to know her, bit by bit. She doesn't post too often; she's put up some pretty pictures of Dad's garden—the rosebushes, the red barn, the pool. Yesterday, she posted a shot of a train—she was returning to Paris. They all were, I guess. I'm curious to get a glimpse of her life there; I still want to see Paris one day.

"The photo of Central Park?" Hugh is asking me. "Oh, thanks—I saw that you 'liked' it." His cheeks redden a little, too, which makes my pulse quicken. "It's good to be back from New York City, though," he adds, rubbing the back of his neck. "I mean, I enjoy going there for a few days to see my cousin, but I always end up missing Hudsonville."

His gaze strays to me, and I bite my lip, trying not to fidget too much, *or* to read too much into what he's saying. He said he missed *Hudsonville*. Not *me*. Right?

"Where are you headed now?" I ask him, before I can let my *what-if?* imagination carry me too far off.

Hugh gestures across the street. "Between the Lines, before it closes. I wanted to pick up some books for school."

"Oh," I say, thinking of school. The start of junior year is close, less than three weeks away. Again, I expect to feel my standard wave of dread, but it doesn't come. Instead, I feel a little tingle of excitement. "I'll go with you," I add impulsively. I haven't been inside Between the Lines in ages, not since I bought my guidebook for the South of France. That guidebook now sits in my room, on a shelf, having served its purpose.

"Cool," Hugh says, biting his lower lip as he smiles at me.

I step forward, my camera in hand, and cross the street with

Hugh. Our elbows brush together, and my stomach jumps. We walk past Better Latte Than Never, and I peer inside, seeing Ruby at the counter in her brown apron, busy at the espresso machine. I could stop in after I'm done at the bookstore to say hello, but there's no real need. We're supposed to picnic in Pine Park with Alice and Inez this weekend, anyway.

Automatically, I reach down and twist my woven bracelet around my wrist; I've been wearing one, instead of two, ever since the day after my birthday. And it's felt comfortable, and natural, like a solid decision does, I guess.

Hugh and I stop outside of Between the Lines. Right in front of us, hovering in midair, a firefly has lit itself up.

"Wow, look!" I say, pointing at the sudden spark, feeling like a little kid.

Hugh's eyes are also widening with childlike wonder. "Yeah, a lightning bug!" he says.

"Lightning bug?" I echo, cupping my hands to try to catch the firefly. Ruby and I used to chase after them with Mason jars when we were younger, but they always managed to escape. "I don't think I've ever heard it called that before."

"It's kind of a poetic name, isn't it?" Hugh asks, and I nod, watching as the firefly dims and then brightens again. It is like a little piece of lightning, a little piece of magic, brought down to earth.

Finally I manage to catch the lightning bug between my cupped palms and it hovers there. Then I open my hands and release it, watching as it drifts away, to freedom, switching itself on and off again—dark, light, dark, light.

I wonder briefly if the lightning bug was a sign. But of what? I'm not sure if everything always needs to be a sign. Sometimes things can just be.

I let out a contented sigh. Hugh reaches for the door handle, but before I turn to go in, I glance back at the river. The sun is starting to sink down, into the horizon. The breeze blows my hair across my forehead, and I feel a kind of electricity in the air.

"Hang on?" I say to Hugh, holding up my camera. "I want to take one last picture."

"Sure," Hugh says, releasing the door handle and coming to stand beside me. He grins. "I wouldn't want to interrupt the master at work."

I laugh and roll my eyes as I prepare to take the photo. But something about Hugh's teasing compliment, and the nearness of him, and the dazzling quality of the sunset, makes me fumble with the camera in my hand. It slips from my grasp, and I gasp—

"Whew," Hugh says, reaching his hand out just in time to catch the Nikon before it hits the ground. "Careful, there."

"Careful," I echo, a little dazed. I'm aware that, while Hugh was in the process of saving my camera, he reached out his other hand and put it on my arm.

We are suddenly close to each other, so close that I can see the birthmark next to his right ear, and I can study the shape of his full lips. So close that I can almost imagine feeling his heartbeat against mine.

Hugh is looking at me in an intent way, and I'm not sure if it's the electric August night, or the sunset, or the firefly. Or the fact that I had the summer I did. But suddenly anything seems possible. Something surges in me, a newfound courage, and I find myself tilting my face up, and—

I kiss him.

I kiss Hugh Tyson.

His lips are soft and warm, at once familiar and new. He kisses me back, in earnest, one hand moving up from my arm and along my neck and into my wild hair. I close my eyes and let myself take in how wonderful this feels.

Then we both pull apart, and we are both blushing, and I'm relieved that we are equally flustered and surprised and giddy. My heart is thudding in my ears.

"That was, um, to thank you," I improvise. "For, you know— the camera thing."

I reach out to take my Nikon back from Hugh, and he gently closes his hand around mine.

"Thank you for that thank you," he teases me, smiling.

We stand there, grinning, holding hands on the sidewalk. I don't want to let go of this moment. I wonder if I should take a picture. But no. I will remember.

Slowly, I turn and start to open the door to Between the Lines, still holding Hugh's hand behind me. I don't know what will happen between the two of us. How can I? I don't know how things will turn out with Ruby, either. Or with Dad, or Mom, or Eloise. I don't even know what will happen tomorrow. If I've learned anything this summer, it's that nothing can be predicted, or planned.

I smile, and my heart lifts as I step into the bookstore.

The possibilities are endless.

Acknowledgments

The writing of this novel took me a while, and I am indebted to so many people who were instrumental in so many ways. My apologies if, in my post-deadline haze, I forgot to include everyone that I'd wanted to here!

All the thanks in the world go to my editor, Abby McAden, for her patience, humor, and pep talks over fried chicken lunches, and my agent, Faye Bender, for *her* patience (I require a lot), sage advice, and unwavering faith in me. Without these two amazing women, this book would not exist as it does.

I am very fortunate to publish at Scholastic, which has also been my home as an editor lo these many years. My boundless thanks to the dream team that helped this book come together, especially David Levithan, Ellie Berger, Lori Benton, Alan Smagler, Elizabeth Whiting, Alexis Lunsford, Annette Hughes, Jacquelyn Rubin, Nikki Mutch, Sue Flynn, Betsy Politi, Terribeth Smith, everyone in Sales, Dave Ascher, Tracy van Straaten, Sheila Marie Everett, Caitlin Friedman, Bess Braswell, Lauren Festa, Lizette Serrano, Leslie Garych, Karyn Browne, JoAnne Mojica, Emily Rader, Elizabeth Parisi, Ellen Duda (thank you for the gorgeousness!), Sarah Evans, Jennifer Ung, Jazan Higgins, Anna Swenson, Charisse Meloto, Rachel Coun, Mark Seidenfeld, Yaffa

Jaskoll, Paul Gagne, Samantha Smith, Caite Panzer, Janelle DeLuise, Jacqueline Hornberger, Kelly Ashton, Beka Wallin, Siobhan McGowan, Jacquie Bloese for the French expertise, and so many other gifted colleagues and friends, for your contributions, dedication, and passion. Special thanks to Lisa Ann Sandell, as well as Liel Leibovitz, for their hospitality, warmth, and wisdom.

To the Falcitelli family, who hosted me in Aix-en-Provence all those summers ago: *merci beaucoup!* To Jennifer Clark, Jon Gemma, Robert Flax, Liz Hardenburgh, Martha Kelehan, Adah Nuchi, Jaynie Saunders Tiller, Emily Smith (and the Richmond/ Smith family), Nicole Weitzner, and other fantastic friends—thank you for understanding when I disappeared into the writing cave, and for sending me "you can do it!" texts throughout. Daniel Treiman's brilliant insights, kindness, and support helped and inspired me beyond measure.

My parents put up with me gracefully, and lovingly kept me fed and watered during my sojourns at their house. Extra thanks to my keen-eyed mom, for the lifesaving second reads. I am so grateful to my sister (my other half) and my brother-in-law for always welcoming me with open arms and giving such great guidance, and to my niece and nephew—my two summers—for bringing me sunshine and joy.

Aimee Friedman is the *New York Times* bestselling author of *Sea Change* and many other novels for young adults. She has also written middle-grade novels under the name Ruth Ames. She graduated Phi Beta Kappa from Vassar College, and has been a children's book editor ever since. Aimee lives, works, and writes in New York City, where she spends most of the year wishing it were summer. Visit her website www.aimeefriedmanbooks.com and follow her on Instagram at @aimeefriedmanbooks.